***

Honeysuckle Lane

By Squid McFinnigan

Chapter 1

Frank's palms slipped on the steering wheel. He was in a full panic attack now. Was the car following or not? His eyes flicked constantly to the rearview mirror. Hunched up over the wheel, his body hummed with tension.

"Jesus, Jesus, Jesus," he said, giving voice to his worry. He had to hit the brakes hard when a red Micra pulled out of nowhere. He had been so absorbed in the mirror, he'd failed to notice it coming from the slip road. The car behind him blasted its horn. Surely, that was good. If they were tailing him, why would they draw attention to themselves? Frank's exit was coming up; then he would know for sure. Leaving it to the last minute, he swerved into the turnoff, not even indicating. When he looked in the mirror, the black car was still there, taunting him, its grill smiling. It kept well back, but it was there. The windows were tinted, a man's car, an angry man's car, a violent car. Whoever it was, he was following him for sure, and Frank had a damn good idea who was behind the wheel. He had no choice now. He had to get home and quick.

Before long, Frank was weaving through the rabbit warren of houses, which made up the Dublin's commuter belt. The grid pattern of seventies estate design was being replaced with graceful swirls and twists of developments. Each revealed a small cluster of houses while cleverly hiding the massive number of identical clusters, a miracle of modern living. Down along Ivy Terrace, the black car stayed behind him. It was still there around Elder Close, then turning onto Elm Road. Wait, it didn't turn. The car was gone. Frank waited for the car to reappear, but it never did. Five minutes later, Frank pulled into Honeysuckle Lane, and his own driveway. He sat there, breathing hard, willing his heart to slow a little. He looked behind him, and the road was deserted. He must have been letting his imagination run away with him. He had to get a grip on things.

Nine identical, detached houses stood in a crescent, facing a small tree-planted green. Front gardens with no dividing walls, window boxes, and hanging baskets abounded; except for the last house, which was a bit of a mess. Despite it being early evening, not a person was to be seen. People didn't work or socialise here. They merely slept. That's commuter living. All kinds of people housed in identical boxes, those that couldn't afford city prices but still lived the city life. Frank stepped out of his car and took his bag from the backseat. He walked toward his door and behind him, his car beeped. Knowing the key had left, the car automatically locked. When he first got the car, he'd thought it was cute, like the car was saying good-bye. Now it just depressed him. Locking the car was yet another task modern technology wouldn't trust to a stupid human. Were we becoming obsolete, only useful for consuming and breaking things?

Frank strode quickly up the drive to the house. The feeling of being followed lingered like a bitter aftertaste in his mind. Once inside, he locked the door behind him. At last, he felt safe, in his own place. He rested his head against the timber, taking long, calming breaths. Sweat stuck the shirt to his back. Upstairs, a floorboard creaked, and Frank held his breath.

"Is that you, Frank?" Barbara shouted.

"Hi, Bar," he called back, with just the hint of exasperation.

Who did she think it was? Frank yearned for the woman Barbara used to be. The woman who'd playfully call, "Bill, you know you shouldn't be here. Frank will be home soon!" A woman who'd chase him upstairs for a quickie before the kids came home. Where did that Barbara go? Instead, he was left with the new Barbara, the one who was a member of the tennis club and the church committee, a woman preoccupied with what people thought about her. A Barbara who was obsessed with keeping up appearances. Frank hated it all for the pretentious shit it was, and to his dismay, he was starting to hate her as well.

When they'd met in college, she had been vibrant. He remembered it like it was yesterday, the first time he'd seen her dancing at a gig in the student union, moshing with abandon. Wild twists threw the hem of her skirt high into the air, flashing her knickers to the world. The wicked twinkle in her eye said she knew the effect she was having on all the men in the room, Frank included. When she caught his gaze climbing the long ladder of her bare legs, she didn't blush. If anything, she twisted faster, causing her skirt to expose more delicious young flesh. She smiled at him, and Frank couldn't believe it. He drank her in with his eyes, becoming drunk with lust. He couldn't help himself; he had to have her. He walked across that dance floor and set about sweeping her off those dainty feet, and swept she was.

In the months that followed, they spent hours spiralled across couches and single beds in a myriad of student flats, exploring each other's bodies with lazy hands. He missed the feel of her taut flesh beneath his fingers. He missed her wicked laugh and wanton habits, but back then, he wasn't a balding, forty-three-year-old estate agent. That bit of reality was harder to face. He knew he wasn't a Greek god by any means, but he was still a man, and a good man, he thought. He treated her well, gave her a good life, a nice house, and not once did he ever consider straying. Even now, when his mind wandered, it was to his wife's face, body, and spirit. It was her he visualised when they made love, just a younger, brighter, version.

Frank dropped his bag on the hall floor. He walked to the kitchen, flicking the switch on the kettle to boil some water. Upstairs, he heard the hoover roar into life, furniture scraped over the polished timber floor. Frank missed carpet, but Barbara wouldn't have it in the house.

"Carpet gathers dust," she'd told him, when she'd refitted the house from top to bottom with laminate flooring. Now the house echoed like a cathedral; every careful footfall sounded like the thunder of buffalo. There may be no dust, but there was no rest in here, either. It exhausted him. The only carpet to be found was in his shed, at the bottom of the garden. He loved his shed; it was his sanctuary. Inside, Frank had placed an old leather chair, formed to the exact contours of his back. The desk and files were dressing; he never did any work here. The shed was his playground; he went online, played games, or just sat in peace. It was the only place in the world he could be himself.

Sadly, this bastion of sanity was now tainted by dread. The computer that sat on the desk, hitherto a source of endless possibilities, was nothing more than the provider of limitless temptations. Everything is online these days: Facebook, news, YouTube, porn, gambling. All held dangers, but gambling proved to be Frank's weakness. One day, while flicking through his e-mail, a pop-up for a free poker site appeared. He clicked it. After all, what was the harm? It was free, no money, nothing to lose. He selected, "join game," and within a few hands, he had the hang of it. He started with two hundred virtual dollars, but within the hour, he had transformed that pitiful amount into a Herculean thirty-six thousand dollars, albeit virtual.

That night, he went to bed over the moon. He lay there long into the night, imagining if all that money were real, a year's wages in an hour. Flipping hell, it was like money for nothing. He played again over the coming days, walking away thousands in the black, his virtual bank busting with credits. Could it really be this easy to make money gambling? You never got to see who was on the other side of the keyboard. Frank imagined dozens of bored housewives or students sitting half-tanked in their underwear, flittering away money they didn't really need. It was nearly a sin not to take advantage of them. The thing was, this was only pretend money, the computer equivalent of playing for buttons.

Okay, people are stupid with fake money, but what if they were playing for real? Frank couldn't resist the urge to try. What's the worst that could happen? he reasoned. He might lose fifty, or even a hundred euro. Frank whipped out his credit card and punched in the numbers. The green oval table appeared, and Frank took his place. He felt his pulse quicken as the cards flipped in front of him. That could have been the moment he was taught a lesson. It could have been his wake-up call, but disastrously, he won.

His account grew to over a thousand euro in real money, even though he only played occasionally. Frank felt great. He enjoyed the games, and even more, he enjoyed winning. With a big stake behind him, Frank moved up into the bigger games, one-hundred and two-hundred-stake tables. The players here got better, and the wagers rose higher. He won some, lost some, but the thrill of the chase outweighed the gamble at all times. Slowly, his money dribbled away. Not quickly enough to alert him he was playing with fire. Frank dipped into his pocket for his credit card more often. It wasn't real money, after all, just a click of a button. When his next bank statement landed on his shiny hall floor, he owed nearly three thousand on his card, most of it to Emerald Eyes, Inc.

That was two years ago. Frank fought back, broke even, time and again. Each occasion, he promised himself never to play again, but each time, the call of the shed, the thrill of the win, crushed his resolve. Six months ago, he had a string of games that should have gone his way but didn't. It cost him a lot. He was on his third credit card; his first two were already maxed out. He owed seventeen thousand euro, an amount he could handle. It was the 21 percent interest that was killing him. He should have told Barbara everything then, cut up his cards, and paid off his debts. He should have manned up and taken his licks. He should have done it, could have done it, and now, he wished he had.

"Fool," he quietly berated himself. In his hollow-sounding kitchen, the kettle whistled, and the switch flicked up with an authoritative clank. Frank fixed himself a mug of tea. No matter what happened now, he was in too deep to simply stop. Frank sat on one of the high stools that bordered the breakfast bar, looking into his milky brew, wishing it were whiskey.

"Frank, don't forget you're picking up Enda in half an hour!" Barbara shouted over the sound of the vacuum.

"I remember, and where's Kirsty?" he shouted back.

"Still at work. She said she was going to be late. They are doing a stock take," Barbara said.

"Stock take, my arse," Frank huffed.

Kirsty was sixteen years old and had a part-time job in a newsagent's shop about a mile away. They did a stock take every second day, it seemed to Frank. It had to be a boy. He knew the signs. Her makeup got thicker by the day, and her skirts got smaller. Lately, it seemed the blouses she wore were opened so low, they were only joined by a single button. What the hell did he expect? She was hardly going to stay Daddy's little girl all her life, but Frank wasn't ready for her to turn into Madonna just yet.

"Check the chicken, will you?" Barbara asked as the hoover came thumping down the stairs. Frank looked through the glass door of the oven at the golden chicken, bubbling in a lava of its own fat.

"It's still in the oven."

He was amazed he could joke after the day he'd had. The hoover died, and in bustled a vexed Barbara. She was short and slim, with a neat blonde bob. She wore dark, pleated pants and white blouse. Her makeup was done. She wore a set of pearls on her tanned neck, a tad overdressed for housework, but what a fantastic-looking woman. She just didn't shimmer like she once did. Where was the dancing dervish that had ravished him till he thought he may die? How had she been ousted by the need to be accepted, the need to keep up with the neighbours and climb the social ladder? Perhaps that wasn't the complete reason

Barbara's spirit seemed broken. Perhaps it was being married to him, being the mother of his children that had silenced her desire?

"Men, I swear, are useless," she grumbled, opening the oven. She poked the poor bird with a knitting needle. Being dead and roasted wasn't enough torture, apparently.

"Give it five minutes, and then take it out," she said, as she went back to hoovering. Frank sipped his tea. As he waited, his mind reeled back to the moment his life went from bad to irreparable. Four Fridays ago, at five-thirty in the evening exactly, in the back room of the Black Swan Pub. Back to a poker game he'd not been even invited to join. If he hadn't stopped for a pint on his way home, everything would have been different now.

"Have you room for one more?" he'd asked, seeing the guy setting up the chips.

"Sure, but it's a cash game."

"Aren't they all?" joked Frank, walking over to the table. "What's the buy in?"

"We're in for three hundred each, but whatever you want to start with is fine. Rules are, half the pot, five euro, all in. Greg, behind the bar, holds the money. You can chip in with him."

Frank walked over to the bar and handed over three hundred euro, getting a fistful of chips in return. The men said little about themselves while they played cards, but even so, you can't sit at a table for two hours without learning a few things. Sean, the man wearing a well-tailored suit, owned a café in the middle of town. Then there was Martin Sikes, a big man with hairy hands, a builder who looked like he'd walked straight off the site. Ben Wiseman had a string of clothes shops spread all across the country that he had inherited from his wife's family. He was all right, in a looking-down-his-nose kind of way, but a bad card player. Next man at the table was a young lad called Chris McCarthy, who wore brash clothes, like some kind of LA rapper. Frank didn't like him much. He seemed like a cocky thug, too thick to ever have a real job. Frank did his best to keep his distance from him, as there was something not right about the boy. Chris was the son of the last player, Harry McCarthy. Harry wore a black leather jacket and black shirt. He was edging toward his sixties, but he looked solid, like a man that had spent years at in a gym. Perhaps he'd been a boxer, because his nose had seen a few punches in its time. Appearances aside, Harry McCarthy was very welcoming. One thing you learn when playing cards is to look out for partners. Two or more players secretly playing together is a recipe for heartache. It's one of the quickest ways to get ripped off in a card game. Frank started off playing carefully, feeling out each of the players, looking for signs he was being scammed.

Harry and Chris were, by far, the most-aggressive players at the table. Mind you, they went head to head against each other as often as they took down anyone else. It seemed Chris wanted to prove his worth to the old man, while his father wasn't willing to let the top seat at the family table go just yet. The rest of the players were all good players, Ben Wiseman aside. After half an hour, Frank was happy it was a clean game and began enjoying himself. The cards flew, as did the time. Before long, Frank had to visit the bar for more chips, but it was all in good fun. Just a couple of quid, he assured himself.

"That's it for me, lads," Frank said, when it was about seven. He had a few chips left but had lost at least five hundred euro during the game. It was a lot, but he could afford it.

"Hard luck, Frank. You play a good game," said Chris, shaking his hand with the tiniest a hint of smarminess in his voice. "We're here most Fridays, if you want a chance to win your money back." Frank kept shaking Chris's hand and kept a smile on his face, but he couldn't deny the sting of the little shit's words. He waved good-bye to the men at the table and nodded to Greg behind the bar as he left. He'd only got a hundred yards down the road when his blood began to boil at the snide comment Chris had made. Good sense and cowardice kept him walking toward his car.

The following week, Frank was back. The game started well for him, with Frank winning back more than he had lost the previous week. He was getting a feel for the players and how they played the game. By half past six, he had a sizeable stack of chips sitting in front of him. Over and back, the game swung, and the hours passed quickly. The banter was good natured, and drinks flowed. That was when the poker gods smiled. Frank opened the betting with two pair, aces and tens, a good hand when you were playing with a full deck. Everyone stayed in. Frank flung his dud card away and was dealt a fresh one. He shuffled his hand, backs up, before slowly spreading them close to his chest. Out peeked the ace of spades. Full house! Play it cool, Frank, play it cool, he thought to himself. Now was the time to make Chris pay for his cockiness, and he was going to make him pay big time.

Harry had dealt. Frank was on his left, so he had opened the game with his original two pair, and Sean had stayed in but changed no cards at the burn, so he had either a full house, a blue, or a run. Frank's house was a monster, so no danger there. Chris had played and bought two cards; more than likely, he was sitting on three of a kind. Harry bought three cards. He could be holding a pair or nothing at all, and he was the weakest of all the players.

"I'll check," said Frank, hoping to disguise the strength of his hand. He wanted to let someone else build up the pot, only to swoop in and clinch it at the end for himself. Sean was eager to bet, and Frank was only too happy to let him. Sean pushed a small stack of chips into the middle. "I'll go eighty euro."

Chris looked at his cards. "It's a nice hand, but not nice enough," he said, throwing them away. Inside, Frank was furious. He had wanted to skin Chris alive on this hand, but somehow, he'd smelled a rat and dodged the trap. Frank had to be careful not to tip his hand too early and let the rest of them out of his sights. This was a once-in-a-lifetime hand, and he had to make the best of it.

Harry stayed in the game, adding his eighty to the eighty Sean had already wagered. The betting was back in Frank's hands.

"I'll see your eighty, with a hundred on top."

Sean whistled. "You think you've got me, Frank?" Sean asked, pausing for a hell of a long time, trying to read Frank's face. Frank concentrated on staying as blank as he could. In the end, Sean counted out a stack of chips and tossed them on the ever-growing pile in the middle of the table. "Your hundred, with another three hundred."

Harry looked at his cards. Frank was sure he'd fold, but when Harry surprised him and shoved over the extra chips, Frank knew the pot was his. There was no way either Sean's hand or Harry's could beat his. He counted up what he had left in front of him and pushed it all into the middle.

"Your three, with two hundred and eighty on top," Frank said.

Sean sat back in his chair, locking his fingers under his chin, while he looked at the mountain of chips in the middle of the table. Frank felt sweat break out on his forehead when Sean sat forward. "Your two hundred and eighty, with a thousand more." Sean pushed in all his chips and added a fold of notes on top, which he produced from his jacket pocket like a magician pulling a rabbit from a hat.

"For Christ's sake, Sean, I can't cover that," said Frank, realising that he had been outflanked.

"It's no limit, Frank. If you can't cover the bet, you are out," Sean said.

"I just don't have that kind of cash on me," Frank said

"Not good enough, Frank. Cash on the barrel head, or no bet," Sean said, delighted he was going to steal the pot.

Harry quietly pushed his chips to the middle while the other two men argued. Frank was on the verge of throwing in his cards when Harry said, "I'll lend you the money if you want it, Frank." Harry dipped into his pocket and fished out a thick brown envelope stuffed with notes. He counted out twenty fifty-euro notes. Frank stared at the bundle of notes and said, "Can you make it two grand?" Harry shrugged, and dipped into the envelope again, adding more notes to the bundle, handing it all over to Frank, who promptly dropped the whole lot on top of the stack of chips, making this a life-changing pot.

"Back to you, Sean," Frank said. Sean knew he had just been shot with one of his own bullets and collapsed back in his chair.

"I'm out." He spat, throwing his cards on the table face up, showing a run to the king. Frank let out a little yelp of joy as he reached for the chips.

"Hang on, Frank. I'm still in," said Harry, who dropped another bundle of notes on the massive pot with a smile. "I'll see you."

Frank laid his cards on the table, showing everyone his aces and tens full to the brim. "Sorry about that, Harry, but at least some of it's still yours."

Harry looked resigned but calm, as he picked up his own cards "No, it's all mine," he said, throwing down four deuces.

Frank felt like he'd been kicked in the balls. He watched as Harry restuffed his envelope with all his cash, and more besides, raking a mountain of chips to his side of the table. The chips covered so much of the table in front of him that Harry had difficulty stacking them, so he shouted to the bar. "Greg, can you cash me out?" He walked away from the table, beckoning Frank to come with him. Frank's legs felt like jelly, but he had no choice but to follow Harry across to the bar.

"Don't feel too bad, Frank. It's only money." Harry said, smiling.

"Yea," Frank agreed, not sounding glib. "I'll have the two grand for you in a few weeks."

"Ah, Frank, what do you take me for, a charity? In two weeks, you'll owe two thousand eight hundred euro."

"Eight hundred for what?" Frank exploded.

"We all have to make a few quid somehow. It costs to borrow, Frank."

"Eight hundred is extortion!"

"I don't like that word," Harry said coolly. "It's called interest. Twenty percent a week, Frank. Industry standard. My industry." Harry's voice was quiet, which added to his menace.

"What if I can't get it all?"

"The juice flows on what you owe. Any interest that builds up, twenty percent on that, too," Harry said, his eyes hard as flint. Like a flash, he was friendly again. "Look, I'm a reasonable man. Pay off the money this week, and it is only two four you owe me. I'll even start your clock from tomorrow. Can't be fairer than that now, can I?" he said, waiting for an answer.

"Guess not," Frank eventually said.

"Good man. Just one more thing, Frank. Pay something every week. That's a golden rule," Harry said, laying a hand on Frank's shoulder. "If you miss a week, I'll be coming to collect, and you don't want that." The hand tightened painfully on his neck. The meaning was clear.

That was two weeks ago, and Frank hadn't gone back to the bar again. He wasn't a regular there, and he didn't remember telling them anything during the games other than that he was an estate agent. Frank figured, as Harry wasn't out any cash, he'd let it go, sooner or later. That was until today. A letter was hand-delivered to his office while he was out.

Inside the envelope was a simple slip of paper with an equally simple message: *Frank, I keep missing you. Harry*

"Jane, who left this?" he asked the office secretary.

"Oh, yea, two friends of yours called. Did you not know them?" Jane said.

"Not really. Don't give them any information if they call again, okay?" he said.

"Sure," she said. "They looked a bit on the rough side, now you mention it."

When Frank left the office, he was sure a black BMW had been parked across the street. When he saw the car again on the motorway, Frank was sure it must have been Harry coming after him. Now that Harry knew where he worked, there was no way of walking away from the debt. He'd have to figure something out, but the biggest problem was, he had no money. Not a penny. Harry had to realise he couldn't get blood from a stone; after all, he wasn't a complete fool.

"Frank, did you take the chicken out?" Barbara called from upstairs.

"Shit!" he said, jumping off the chair to open the oven. The bird wasn't burned, well, not too much.

"Yea, it's on the counter," he called. "I'll run down and pick up Enda." Frank said grabbing his jacket and running for the door, trying to make good his escape before the impending nagging over the burned bird ensued. Outside, parked behind his car, was the black BMW with Harry McCarthy sitting on the bonnet. Harry smiled at him as he shuddered to a stop, still holding the door half-closed behind him.

"Did you think you were going to be hard to find?" he asked. "Big mistake, Frank."

Chapter 2

Mary Sweeney stood inside her sitting room window, watching the man loitering outside Frank O'Shea's house. She was on the verge of phoning the O'Sheas when Frank come out. It was hard to be sure, but he didn't seem overjoyed with his visitor. A few minutes later, both men got into Frank's fancy new car.

Mary wasn't a nosy neighbour. She just happened to see the man and didn't like the look of him. He looked like a thug, though perhaps he just had the bad luck to be born with a face like a bulldog chewing a wasp, but that's rarely the case. Mary knew from bitter experience that if it looked like trouble, walked like trouble, sooner or later, it was going to be trouble. Even though she had more than enough strife in her own life, it was difficult not to worry for other people. You were never sure what was going on behind the neighbours' closed doors. She'd actually been watching for her own husband. She liked to be there to see Pat arrive home, not because she was lovestruck, just the opposite. It gave her a chance to see his humour. If he slammed the door of his van and stomped into the house, she knew it was going to be a rough night. Those few precious seconds allowed her to ready herself. Pat's moods were like storms coming in from the ocean, sending waves of bad-tempered fury crashing against the harbour wall. Sadly, that was she.

Mostly, the days passed in sulky silence, not happy but not raging, either. The majority of Pat's life, and subsequently hers, lay somewhere between happiness and misery. She had taken slaps and punches over the years, but they were few and far between. Most of the abuse she suffered at the hands of her beloved was mental. One night ten years ago, she'd discovered Pat was basically a complete coward. After years of withering under his sharp, unhappy tongue, that came as quite a surprise.

That particular night, he'd come home flaming drunk. It didn't take long for a row to start, and escalate to the level of World War II. She'd made some comment or other, stinging his pride, and he'd punched her hard, in the stomach.

She'd crumpled to the ground, the wind sucked out of her. Something in her mind had snapped. She'd struggled to her feet and felt rage thunder through her veins. Mary launched herself at him, with a strength she didn't know she had. She'd lashed out at him, clawing his face, raining blows down on his head. Pat cowered in the corner until her red mist cleared. She'd stood over him, hands fisted and trembling, shocked at herself, at what she'd done. The startling fact of the matter was, she'd loved it. She liked seeing him cower and the power she felt.

Then other feelings came: shame, worry, disgust. She stood above her fat, witless husband and felt sorry for him. Pat had bolted for the door, escaping into the night. Hours passed. Mary's feeling of victory faded, and the spectre of worry descended. What if she'd gone too far? Would he leave her? How would she cope with the house, the bills, and the kids? Long into the night, she waited, but Pat didn't come back. When he turned up the next morning, Mary felt a wave of relief wash over her. Pat never again mentioned what had happened that night, but he looked at her with new eyes, spiteful eyes. Just enough fear there to keep his fists to himself—well, most of the time.

If you tell people your husband hits you, they react with horror and say things like, "how could he?" or "You must have been terrified," or "Get out of there. Just take the kids and go." But go where? All those do-gooders' intentions would vanish into the ether if she turned up on their doorsteps with her brood in tow. Mary was above all things a realist. She'd finished school, just about, but she'd never had a job, aside from being a wife and a mother. Where would she get money from, if she ever left him? Pat might look after them, but Mary knew he'd more than likely drink every penny that came into his hands. Pat is a weak man, with a weak mind, and no morals to speak of. She didn't love him, but she could put up with him. What alternative had she? Prince Charming wasn't waiting in the wings to sweep her off her feet. It was laughable, considering she now tipped the scale at fifteen stone. On the day she married Pat, she was a mere slip of a thing, weighing in just over eight stone, despite being encased in the most-hideous toilet-roll-holder of a wedding dress. Pat was all she had wanted that day and all she was getting now. Her bed was made; she'd have to lie in it.

Her kids didn't understand what it was like to have no options. They thought families should be ideal, and were well aware that their family fell far short of that mark. It was impossible to hide the rows in such a small house, not that Pat ever tried. That's what hurt her the most. He seemed to want the kids to watch as he undermined her. He tried to make her look stupid, or at least more stupid than he was, every chance he got. The more the kids saw, the worse he became. Most of the time, it was easier to say nothing, but now and again, she just had to fight back. Then they would argue, raging at each other, until one or other of them stormed off.

Mary had told her mother what Pat was like a few years after they had gotten married, and her mother had said, "That's men for you." She had also told Mary how lucky she was to have landed a man that would put food on the table and not go whoring all over town.

Not everything that had come out of her marriage to Pat was terrible. She had been blessed with three lovely kids. Angie was nineteen and full of spirit. Then there were her boys: Johnny, twenty-one and in the army, and Billy, who was eight.

Billy was upstairs doing his homework—at least he should be doing it, but Mary would bet he was playing on his Xbox. Billy was taking after his father, a bit thick. Thankfully, unlike his father, he was a good lad. Mary knew that Billy would be labouring for Pat long before he finished school, which was no bad thing. School and Billy went together like a bicycle goes with a goldfish. Pat was a builder and had a good business. He wasn't greedy or clever enough to rip off the customers, which earned him a reputation as a decent bloke. He wasn't the fastest builder on the planet, but he got the job done, and he mostly did a solid job. He did all his own carpentry, block laying, and plastering. He left the plumbing and wiring to the pros. Sometimes he'd do gardens as well. She had to give him this much, he was a hard worker. Sadly, he was a hard drinker as well. The booze was his downfall.

Pat's battered transit turned into the top of the road. He drove past Frank O'Shea and his friend, who were getting out of Frank's Lexus. Pat pulled the van to a stop a couple of feet from the sitting-room window. The dashboard was a blizzard of crumpled dockets, empty coffee cups, and cigarette boxes. The outside of the van was just as dirty as the inside. Some smart arse had written, "I wish my girlfriend was as filthy as this van" in the dust along the side. Pat levered himself out and waddled toward the front door. Pat was carrying an extra couple of stone around his middle, his belt never knowing which side of his butt to settle on, above or below the crack. He seemed to be happy today, or at least what passed for happy in Pat's world. The signs were it was going to be one of the good nights.

The front door opened, and she heard him dump his boots in the hallway.

"How was your day?" she asked, turning on the TV. Pat came in covered in concrete dust, leaving a trail wherever he went. He collapsed into the reclining armchair, which was his throne, taking the remote Mary offered to him.

"Same as always. The O'Brien guy paid for his kitchen at last. Four times I had to call around to his house. Some people are so tight," Pat said, surfing the channels, looking for football.

"Dinner will be a while yet. Do you want coffee?" Mary asked, walking through the French doors separating the kitchen and the sitting room. Pat had installed the doors a few years ago. He said they would give the house an open feel, but Mary knew it was so he'd be closer to the fridge. Pat had knocked through the wall and hung the doors in no time, but that was where the work stopped. He still hadn't filled in around the frame or painted the walls. Mary would have done it herself, but that would have sparked off another fight. Why is it that a builder's house is the one that never seems to get finished?

"Do you want coffee?" she asked again, as he hadn't bothered to answer her the first time.

"Why not? Bring in some biscuits," he said.

"Did you see that man talking to Frank O'Shea?" Mary asked as she handed him the mug of steaming coffee, milk and sugar added, stirred and all.

"The one with the BMW? Yea, I spotted him," Pat said, sipping the coffee and reaching for a chocolate digestive.

"Did he look all right to you?"

"I don't know, do I?" Pat snapped. "I don't go poking my nose in where it's not wanted. You should take a leaf from my book and mind your own business." She didn't push it further. Pat was like that. Ask him something simple, and he backed into the corner, snarling.

The front door clattered open as Angie blew into the house. She was a force of nature, that girl. Whatever she did was big. Her mistakes were huge; her celebrations even bigger. Those kind of traits on some people could be grating, but on Angie, extravagance seemed to suit her. Her personality shone all the brighter the bigger her actions got.

"Don't slam the door!" shouted Pat.

"The wind caught it," she said, throwing the comment over her shoulder as she flounced past him, wallowing in his chair like a stranded walrus.

"What's for dinner?" she asked, pulling open the fridge. She rummaged through the packets and pulled out a slice of cheese to munch on as she continued her search for something tasty.

"Pork chops," Mary said, putting a pan of frozen vegetables on the hob.

"You know I don't like chops. Is there anything else?" She sulked.

"Your father likes them, and no," Mary said. Truth be told, she liked them more.

"It's always what he wants," Angie whinged, looking with distain at the open French doors.

"I heard that!" Pat shouted from the sitting room over the roar of the football game.

Angie rolled her eyes to heaven. She slammed the door of the fridge closed and bent to look in the oven, finishing off the slice of cheese. Having satisfied herself that the oven held nothing of interest, she turned to Mary.

"I am going to town with Suzy for a while, so I'll have mine later." Angie half walked, half jogged out the door and dashed up the stairs. It was amazing she could walk in those platform shoes at all, never mind run. A few minutes later, Mary heard the bathroom door slam and the shower start.

"Not again," she heard Pat say, and she could hear the leather squeal in protest as he pulled himself out of his chair. He thundered up the stairs, the timber treads shuddering under his substantial weight. Mary heard him banging on the bathroom door.

"Angie! Angie, don't use up all the hot water. I haven't had a wash yet."

"Pat, leave her alone!" Mary yelled.

"Shut up! Don't tell me what to do in my own bloody house!" he yelled.

Mary moved to the bottom of the stairs and saw the bathroom door open. Angie appeared with a towel draped around herself.

"Are you happy now?" She pushed past her father, dripping water all over the landing, the towel barely covered her ass. Mary went back to the kitchen. Why did every day have to be like this?

When dinner was ready, Mary portioned food onto plates and placed a big bottle of Coke on the table before shouting, "Dinner's ready!"

Billy bounded down the stairs. He was a bottomless pit of a boy. You could throw food into him all day long. Pat barged in, grabbed his plate and a couple of cans of beer from the fridge, taking the whole lot back to the sitting room. Mary picked at her meal while watching Billy wolf down his dinner.

It wasn't long before Angie vanished out the front door in a fog of hair spray and perfume. "Don't wait up!" she called on her way out.

What was the point of waiting, anyway? Half the time, she didn't come home at all. Running around Dublin with that slapper, Suzy. God knows what they got up to. That's not completely true, God knew, but Mary also knew. She just didn't like to think about it.

Mary felt invisible. Accepting her life wasn't the same as liking it. She'd had dreams once. Sometimes, after a soppy movie or a good book, she would feel them trying to dig their way out of the corner of her mind, where she had buried them. If she let her dreams out to wander the hopeless wasteland of her life, she'd surely go mad, stark raving mad.

"Thanks for dinner, Mom," said Billy, racing back upstairs to his video game.

She smiled to herself. Maybe she wasn't invisible to everyone. "You're welcome, Billy," she whispered. Billy was a good boy, but he still left the dirty dishes for her. Pat would leave his plate beside the chair, where it would grow roots before he thought to bring it to the kitchen sink.

Mary started washing the dishes by hand. She'd asked Pat for a dishwasher time and again, but he said why waste money on a thing like that, when they had a perfectly good sink in the kitchen. What he meant was, why waste money on a dishwasher when he'd married one years ago. Mary cleaned the kitchen and the cooker, and took out the rubbish. She swept and mopped the floor, and started on the mountain of ironing while the radio kept her company. Friday was a great night for music. The station she listened to did a night of eighties pop. She ironed and swayed to the songs of her youth, forgetting about her aching hips or how long it took to get out of bed in the morning. It was as close to being young as she was ever going to get. Mary remembered school dances and the boys she'd kissed. It seemed like only yesterday. Hard to imagine that was thirty years ago.

When the football game finished, Pat visited the kitchen to take a can of beer from the fridge. He couldn't even sit on the toilet without a can in his hand. A while later, she heard the shower start to run.

Mary knew Pat would leave a trail of smelly socks and dirty underwear as he went. She knew he would slop water all over the floor and leave the bath filthy. She was back to being invisible again. She hovered the sitting room while it was empty. She was just putting the hoover into the press under the stairs when Pat descended them. He was at the door before he noticed Mary kneeling in the hallway press.

"I'm going over to Andy's for a while."

"Okay. See you later," Mary said, looking forward to getting the house to herself. The front door slammed shut as Pat left. He hadn't event waited for her answer before vanishing into the night. She finished cleaning up the mess Pat had left upstairs before settling down with a large glass of wine, not that anyone could blame her.

From Billy's room, the sound of rapid gunfire and screams let her know she wasn't alone. The only thing that would bring Billy downstairs again would be the fridge. She took a gulp of her wine, then topped the glass up to the brim. She didn't like the taste of wine, but she needed dullness in her mind to be able to sleep. Wine was just the thing to knock her out.

How many nights had she lain awake waiting for the sound of a key in the door? The halting steps climbing the stairs? On the good nights, he'd collapse into the bed, fully clothed and snoring in seconds. The bad nights, he'd paw at her roughly. He didn't even want her undressed. He'd pull aside anything that was in his way before forcing himself into her. Whether she was ready for him or not didn't matter to Pat. She would fondle him, stroke him, and make noises she knew he liked. Anything to speed things up. He seemed to like it best when it sounded like he was hurting her, which most of the time, he was.

Anything to get it over with quickly. Sometimes he was far too drunk to come. Those were the worst nights. He would buck and rut at her with his thick, brutal penis, until the futility of it all penetrated his drunken mind. He would pull his shrinking member out of her, leaving her sore and frightened. She knew that it was best to say nothing. He blamed her for his failure. Once, she'd tried to console him, which resulted in a shiny black eye and a bloody nose.

These days, wine was her friend, knocking all sense and feeling out of her long before he could do the same. Mary raised her glass in a toast. "To grapes and small mercies," she said to no one in particular.

Chapter 3

"You don't look happy to see me. Why is that?" asked Harry, walking up the driveway. All of a sudden, Frank felt his bowels go watery.

"I was coming to meet you, Harry. Honest," Frank said.

"I was sure I said pay every week, or I was coming to collect. Guess what, Frank? I'm here to collect," Harry said, walking toward Frank, only stopping when he was uncomfortably close. Harry buried his hands in his jacket pockets and looked around, as if he were bored.

"I don't have it yet," Frank said.

"You have something," Harry said, matter-of-factly. Frank dipped his hand into his back pocket, taking out his wallet. Harry shook his head in annoyance.

"Not here, where the world and his dog can see. Get in the car."

Frank had no choice. He pushed the button on the key, and his friendly Lexus chirped. Harry walked around to the passenger side and got in. Frank took a bit longer before he got up the nerve to slide into the driver's seat. It was warm, so Harry lowered both driver's and passenger's windows with the buttons on the dash. Despite the heat, Harry kept his jacket on.

"You must take me for a right mug, Frank. Did you think you were the invisible man? I could have been here last Monday, you fuckwit," snarled Harry.

"I swear, if I had the money, I'd have paid you. I'm broke, flat busted," Frank reasoned.

"I don't give a shit. You borrowed from me. You gambled my money, and you lost." Each *you* hit home with a steely tone. Frank knew it was true, but what could he do about it? Even Harry must realise a man with no money can't pay. That realisation gave him confidence that his argument would be meet with reasonable ears.

"You got all your money back and more. You're not out a penny. I can't pay you what I don't have," Frank said, shrugging his shoulders. Harry shook his head, like he had expected Frank to say exactly that. He leaned forward and opened Frank's glove box. He rummaged through it like he had every right in the world to do so. Frank felt the little hairs on the back of his neck start to hackle with anger, but his fear kept his mouth in check. What did Harry think he was going to find in there, gold bars? He shuffled through the insurance papers, garage receipts, like he were at a thrift shop.

"You're going to pay, and that's a fact," said Harry. "It might take a year, ten years, your whole life, but I'll get what's due to me."

"Are you threatening me, Harry?"

"Absolutely. Wasn't I clear enough?" he said, with a smile.

"You can't go around threatening people whenever you don't get your way," Frank said.

"Think of it as a promise, you plank," said Harry, with a stony face.

"I've had enough of this," said Frank, his expression someplace between disbelief and anger.

"If you even think about doing anything stupid, like going to the cops, or God forbid, legging it, then your family will pay. Do you understand that Frank? You'll never escape from me. Never," Harry said with menace, stopping Frank before he got out of the car.

"If you go near my family . . ." shouted Frank, grabbing Harry by the jacket. Harry didn't bat an eyelid. He just held Frank's stare, with an easy confidence that Frank could never attain. Slowly, Frank let the jacket go, clearly having lost the battle of wills.

"Open your wallet, Frank," Harry said calmly. Frank had little choice, and eventually, he did as he was told. Harry took out the notes that were inside and counted two hundred and fifty euro, still managing to look disappointed.

"Have you more in the house?"

"No," Frank said. The last thing he wanted was this guy going through his house, like he had gone through the glove box. "Here, take this." Frank held out a credit card. "There is a grand credit on that."

Harry laughed, refusing the card with a wave of his hand.

"You must be joking. Ten minutes after I'm gone, that thing would be reported stolen, and I'd end up nicked for using it. I thought we'd clarified that I'm no fool, Frank. Cash only." Harry waved the little fold of notes in Frank's face. "This is for my time coming out here to find you. I hate the country, Frank. Did I ever tell you that? It's all cow shit, grass, and gobshites like you. Don't make me come out again. I expect to see you at the pub by six next Friday, not a second later. As long as you have three thousand and fifty-six euro for me, you'll never see me again."

"I thought it was two thousand eight hundred," Frank said, stuttering over the words.

"Interest on interest, Frank. It adds up. Are you sure you're an estate agent? You seem a bit stupid," said Harry, stuffing the notes inside his jacket pocket. Frank hated being called stupid, and hated even more that he could do nothing about this. He was relieved that Harry was leaving. Anything else didn't matter at this particular moment.

Harry got out of the car, leaving his door open, and walked around to Frank's side of the Lexus. He half-opened the driver's door and leaned against the roof, like the two men were old buddies who had stopped for a chat after bumping into each other on the road. Harry noticed a young woman walking along the footpath toward a house farther along the lane. His face made no secret of the fact that he would like to do some deeply perverted stuff to her. Frank felt his stomach churn at that look. Harry didn't care who he had in his sights, a man, a woman, or even a kid. The only thing that mattered to Harry was that he got what he wanted. Frank had an inkling that the harder it was for the giver, the better Harry like it.

The girl spotted Harry ogling her as she drew level with the back of the car and gave him a filthy look. Harry responded with a lecherous grin and a lick of his lips, to which she flipped him the finger.

"Saucy cow," Harry said with a snigger. "She's a fine-looking thing, with lovely perky tits, Frank. I wouldn't mind bumping into her down a dark alley some night." Harry had said this loud enough for the girl to hear, and he punched Frank in the shoulder in mock affection. Harry watched the sexy bounce of her ass, jiggling its way down the road like a dog eyes a bone.

"Nice neighbours you got, Frank. Ever give her one?" Harry laughed once the girl had gone. He bored his eyes into Frank's disgusted face. "No, of course you haven't. Stupid question, really." Like a switch had been flipped inside Harry's head, his face morphed into a mask of hate. "Don't you ever put your fucking hands on me again." With amazing speed and strength, he put his hand through the open car window and grabbed Frank's wrist. With a savage twist, he bent the hand until Franks fingers were wedged in the open jamb of the door. Then with all his might, Harry slammed the door on Frank's fingers, giving the door a solid kick for good measure.

As Harry walked toward his car, Frank's cries of agony rang in his ears. He didn't give a damn about Frank, or how badly injured he might be. Harry wasn't built like that; he could do things other men would never do. Business was business, and Harry knew fear was the key to getting what he wanted from life. He didn't always have to get this nasty, but the truth of the matter was, Harry liked it. The more brutal he was, the more control he had, and this guy was in his pocket, deep.

Climbing behind the wheel of his BMW, Harry pulled away from the curb. He still couldn't get over the brass balls on that bird. She'd actually flipped him the finger, sexy bitch.

Chapter 4

On the kitchen table at Four Honeysuckle Lane, Tim Murphy was churning through a mountain of paperwork, or at least, he was trying. His wife, Martha, was in the living room watching a talent show on TV, which was a little distracting, but the real problem was the noise coming from next door. The new neighbours seemed to be holding a bloody concert or something. Loud singing, laughter, and music drifted across the narrow boundary, destroying Tim's peace. They had moved in only a couple of days ago, and they were having parties already. Tim had a good mind to call the cops, but that would only make things worse in the long run. They were going to be pests, Tim just knew it. He was a mortgage broker for one of the three big banks. He had mounds of paperwork laid out about him because he wasn't going to be happy until he was branch manager, or higher.

Most people did the bare minimum, which is why they stayed chained to the same old desk, year after year until they were laid off, retired, or dropped dead from boredom. Tim had ambition, far too much of it to settle for anything less than success, but he knew it was work that made dreams come true, nothing else. Because of that, Tim took extra courses, all on his own time. The amount of work he cleared through his desk seemed impossible, and others commented on it. In reality, it was because of hundreds of extra hours he put in long before others got to the office, or late into the night at this kitchen table, that made it all happen. It was a price that had to be paid for success.

The bank was the first place he'd ever felt better than anyone else. Up to then, he'd been a Billy-no-mates. In school, he was bullied, and in college, he was ignored; it was hard to pick which was worse. If he was being honest, he was still a Billy-no-mates, but at least he was successful. Tim was sure that if the kids who went to school with him and the girls who shunned him at college could see how well he was doing, they would be green with envy, all of them. New BMW sitting in the driveway, great new house, but mostly, he had Martha. None of them would ever have a woman like Martha.

Martha was his ultimate prize. Sitting only feet away, she was a woman of such spectacular beauty that she could cause fender benders just by crossing the street. Her long legs supported a body designed by a perverted genius. She'd done some modeling in the past, but since they had gotten married, she hadn't had the time. Wherever they went, men looked, and kept looking, at her. Tim enjoyed the attention, but feared it at the same time. He worried that someone was going to steal her away from him. He felt compelled to protect her, give her everything she needed, so she'd have no reason to stray. He would never let her get away, that was for sure.

When they met, he was attending a conference at the five-star, Westbury Hotel, where Martha was a receptionist. Back then, he drove a beat-up old Porsche, but the keys looked mighty impressive when left on a counter. The hotel was the kind of place where a coffee cost a fiver and a steak as much as Tim's weekly rent. It was just as well the bank was paying his bill, or he would have starved. That fateful day, Tim strode to the reception desk with a swagger he rarely felt. His beloved car keys dangled from his hand, and he'd slung a faux leather suit carrier over his shoulder. He dreamed of being able to afford such a life, all the time. He dropped his car keys on the counter, and there she was. He couldn't keep his eyes to himself while filling out the registration card; she was breathtaking. Her eyes were the clearest blue, so sharp, they could cut diamonds. As they flicked over the Porsche emblem, Tim swore her pupils dilated just a little, a tiny reaction not lost on him. She chatted happily as he finished jotting down his details.

"Are you with the conference?" she asked in accented English.

"I must look like a banker," he said with a smile. "I can't wait for the weekend to get out of the city for a while. I have a trip to Galway coming up." He felt like he was rambling in the presence of this beautiful creature, he was defiantly lying, because he'd no such weekend ahead of him. In reality, his weekend would be spent yet again catching up on paperwork in his tiny flat.

"That sounds fantastic! I love Galway. I'm sure your wife will love it," she purred, taking his completed registration form.

Tim smiled and tipped his bare wedding finger. "Just a golf weekend. Mrs. Murphy hasn't come along yet."

"I'm sure you have girls fighting over you," she said with a cheeky wink, then gave him his room key and all the information he needed to find his way around the massive hotel. He was besotted with her before he ever left the desk; he hung on her every word. He could have listened to her reading the phone book all day long. The encounter was over far too quickly. As he left the desk, Tim knew he had to see her again and thought of one more question to ask her.

"Can you recommend a nice restaurant in town for dinner tonight?"

"I hear that Unit One on Beckett Road is fabulous," she said.

"Great. Perhaps you'd like to come along, that is, if there isn't someone waiting at home for you?" he said impulsively.

She looked at him openly for a long moment. He was sure she was going to laugh in his face. Butterflies went mental in his stomach. He'd never been so bold with a stranger, a friend, or any woman before.

She blushed slightly, saying quietly, "That would be very nice, but don't tell anyone. We're not supposed to socialise with the guests." Then, in a louder voice, she said, "I'll book a table for you, sir, and give you a call in your room to let you know the time."

Tim walked away from the counter in a cloud of ecstasy. He couldn't believe he'd been so forward, or that it had worked. He felt like Superman as he rode the lift up through the building, as if he were flying. A few minutes after he arrived in his room, the phone rang.

"Mr. Murphy, this is Martha at reception. I've booked a table for you at nine tonight. The booking is for two, if that's still okay?"

"Fantastic, Martha. I'm so looking forward to it. Can I pick you up somewhere?"

"Can we meet there? The concierge will give you directions," she said, in hushed tones. There must have been someone listening nearby.

"Perfect, I'll see you at nine."

"Oh . . . Mr. Murphy?"

"Yes?"

"Thanks," she said. The tone of that last word was a world apart from the rest of the conversation. It was like molten gold dripped into his ear, making him the richest man in the world. He looked at himself in the full-length mirror. A young businessman in a stuffy suit looked back at him. On the bed lay his suit carrier with duplicates of what he already wore. This wouldn't do, Tim thought to himself. This wouldn't do at all. He draped his conference pass around his neck and left the room in a hurry.

Back in the hotel lobby, Tim followed the signage toward the cavernous banqueting suite, joining a herd of suited men queuing at the obligatory registration desk. Tim signed in, collected his conference pack, and entered the vast arena, crammed full of businesses trying to flog their wares to the gathered bankers. It was as busy as a train station, and just as noisy. One quick round of the room, shaking hands, saying hi to colleagues, and then moving on as quickly as he could. An hour later, Tim slipped out of the conference centre and out of the hotel. No one missed him for the rest of the day as he went shopping for something more suitable to wear on his unexpected date.

That night, he arrived at the restaurant in expensive shoes, designer jeans, a designer shirt, and a sports jacket. Tim couldn't help feeling like this was sprinkling diamonds on a dog turd as he struggled to get used to the feel of his completely new wardrobe. He was sure the girl would stand him up. The more he thought about it, the surer he got; a woman like that had no business with a nerd like him. She was probably sitting at home with her buff boyfriend, laughing at the fool he was making of himself. If they only knew he was wearing a completely new outfit that cost more than all his other clothes put together, the pair of them might just expire from mirth.

Tim was on the verge of leaving, beginning to feel as much of a prat as felt he looked, when she walked in. Martha stunned the entire restaurant into a hush. She looked like a supermodel. Tim's heart raced in his chest, as this vision of beauty strode across the restaurant to join his table.

She wore an extra-tight, black pencil skirt under a white blouse, which showed her perfect neck and the edge of the most-succulent breasts he'd ever seen. She was beyond beautiful. She was a goddess. He stood to welcome her, holding out her chair with shaking hands. Once she was seated, he tried to catch the attention of the waiter, which wasn't difficult, as every man in the place was already watching Martha. Tim felt a bit short of breath as he retook his seat. Was this beautiful woman actually here to have dinner with him? He couldn't believe it himself.

"Thanks for coming. I hate eating alone," he said, trying to act cool, but he thought it came out sounding stupid. He flushed bright red at the sound of his own words and was tongue-tied for an age. In the end, he extended his hand and said, "I'm Tim."

She shook his hand and said, "I know. I checked you in, remember? My name's Martha." Her smile made him relax just enough to stop him from having a coronary, right there and then. Tim could never remember being so nervous. They sat, and he searched for something to say, but his well of words came up dry. Martha must have sensed how nervous he was, because she took the lead in the conversation and asked him about the conference, his job, and his family, among countless other subjects. Her easy manner and twinkling laugh helped him relax.

That was the start of something wonderful. The night went incredibly; they were one of the last couples to leave the restaurant. They walked along the edge of the river, under a canopy of trees swaying in the gentle evening breeze. Each step they took drew Tim closer to the end of the night, so he took each stride with exaggerated sloth. Despite Tim's best efforts, the taxi rank arrived far too quickly, and it was time to say good night to this wonderful, extraordinary woman. He was sure that she would jump into the nearest taxi and leg it, but she surprised him by doing nothing of the sort. Instead, she stood with her back to the taxi and turned her full attention on him, clasping her hands in front of her demurely.

"I hope you enjoyed yourself," she said.

"One of the nights of my life . . . No, the best night of my life," Tim said, amazed by how flattering it sounded instead of geeky and weird.

"Sweet." She laughed, leaning in to kiss him on the lips.

"Wow," he said out loud, when her lips left his.

She laughed and opened the door of the taxi, pausing before she got in to say, "See you tomorrow, I hope."

That was the start of something he never could have expected. Tim did see her the next day, and every day until he left the hotel. Afterward, he continued to keep in touch with her, never leaving a day go by without a text or a call. Over time, Tim took Martha on weekend breaks, which grew into holidays together. Basically, he lived the life he always dreamed of having, with his dream woman by his side. Tim was forever expecting for Martha to say she was leaving him, dreading the day she would walk out the door, but it never came.

After they'd been seeing each other for a year, he proposed, again expecting to break the spell. But it was the best decision he ever made. She said yes.

They got married in Wroclaw, in the spring. Tim was the happiest man on the planet, the day she walked down the aisle and stood by his side. She had given him so very much, more than he thought any woman would ever give. He needed to be the husband she deserved.

That was Tim's version of their story. Martha's version, her private version, was basically the same, with one or two notable differences. The truth was that she didn't go weak in the knees when Tim came walking across the lobby, or even swoon at his clumsy advances. He looked like a little boy in his father's suit when she first set eyes on him. What she had seen in great big capital letters was money—or the prospect of money. She saw his car keys and that he worked at a bank. Okay, he was young and hadn't got there yet, but he would. Martha could tell. This was a man that could give her what she needed.

Martha had been working at the hotel for three years and had gone through a string of men, some Polish, some Irish. Most worked with her. She'd even had a fling with a married manager, which was a huge mistake. The affair ended badly, and the guy turned on her. He thought his wife or the staff would find out about them and began making her life miserable to drive her out. Martha told him she would say nothing, but that wasn't good enough. He didn't come right out and say it, but he wanted her to quit and did everything he could to make it happen. He wanted rid of his dirty little secret. It was only a matter of time before he got his wish. On several occasions, she nearly gave in, but she needed the job too much. When Tim showed up at the desk and asked her out, it was an amazing stroke of luck. His timing was impeccable.

Martha knew she had power over men. Only a fool would have been unaware of the way they looked at her. They lusted after her body, which was a blessing and a curse. Most of the time, they made her feel like a piece of meat, or some prize to be fought over. Sex was all it was ever about with them. She had that market cornered. She knew she could have anyone, any time she liked. If she was completely honest, sex was nearly always a disappointment. In the end, her evening with Tim had been a huge surprise. He had been gentle and kind with her. He listened, unlike most men, who pretended to listen while staring at her boobs. When he walked her to the taxi, she let him kiss her on the lips. It was the way he had looked at her after that kiss that won her heart. She never remembered any other man ever looking at her the way he had that night. In his eyes, she saw real love, for the very first time, and it was delicious. She was starving for that look, and wanted more, so she agreed to see him again.

It went from there. Tim took her on trips, nice nights out, meals, and holidays. Every time he laid eyes on her, his face exploded with unbridled adoration. She was addicted to that look, and the fact that this man would do anything for her. He would never stray, never leave her for a younger set of legs, or bigger pair of tits. It might sound silly, but it mattered, mattered much more than his looks, his house, or his body—to her, at any rate.

Tim asked her to marry him, which took her completely unawares. She'd known he wanted to marry her, but she never expected he'd have the nerve to pop the question. She remembered that moment with mixed emotions. He'd stopped in the middle of a walk through the park and dropped to one knee. Luckily, there was a bench close by, because her legs went to jelly. She was shocked, but her heart didn't flip with delight. It flipped with fear. What should she say? "Yes," and be his wife forever? "No," and break his heart, destroying all the good things that were happening in her life? There was another option: Say "Yes," and buy a little time, which was exactly what she did.

A strange thing happened over the next few days. She fell in love. She fell in love with the idea of being married, being Mrs. Someone, of security and happiness that couldn't be taken away. She spoke with her mother on the phone to ask her for advice.

"Will this man make a good husband?" asked her mother. That was the right question, not whether she was in love with him, or was he handsome, or good in bed. Martha knew Tim would be. Coming from a life of hardship tends to knock romance on its ass. Marriage is a deal, a deal between two people who each get something from the arrangement, a bargain. In this particular bargain, Tim got beauty, and she got security. Martha realised what Tim proposed was a good deal, a deal with an honest, reliable partner, one she would be lucky to find again. Martha willed herself into love, and it worked. As she said her vows on her wedding day, she meant each and every one.

It had been more than five years since she had said those vows, and how her world had changed since then. The truth of the matter is, she got everything she'd expected. Tim was a loving husband who never thought of cheating on her. He treated her well; he gave her a fine house and a comfortable life. What she hadn't counted on were the things she'd have to give up. She left her job when they moved into the suburbs and lost touch with many of her friends. She was no longer the Martha she had been; now she was one half of Tim and Martha, one never seen without the other. Over the years, the trips had dwindled away until they were a rare gem in a life of constant routine. Dinners out were few and far between; even walks together were things of the past. Tim got sucked more and more into his work and the act of making money. Martha once had gotten so frustrated at his dedication to his form-filling that she actually thought he should've married his calculator. Every night was the same thing: Work, work, work. She felt so abandoned, even now, sitting only a room away from her husband. She was alone.

When the house next door was sold, Martha was delighted. The prospect of making new friends was like a lifeline to her. She couldn't wait to see who would move in. Martha only prayed they wouldn't turn out like the guy who rented the eyesore of a house on the bottom of the row. People who rent never take pride in their homes. It wasn't fair that she was faced with a weed strewn yard and a half dead hedge, every time she walked out her own front door. She shouldn't have to look at something like that after paying so much for her own house. Martha had gone as far as posting a note through the letter box of the house, and knocking on the door, of course she never heard anything from the man.

The weeks went by without seeing anybody at the house next door. The only indication of the change in ownership was the "For Sale" sign vanishing from the side of the house. A car appeared now and again, but she never caught a glimpse of the owner. A few days ago, a delivery company had arrived with belongings, but the owner wasn't to be seen. Martha's dreamed-for prospect of a new best friend looked less and less likely with each ghostly appearance. Tonight was the first time there was any sign of life. A few strange cars arrived, and the music had begun an hour ago. She was on tenterhooks, dying to see what and who was next door.

Martha suggested to Tim that they should call around and introduce themselves, but Tim said he was too busy. She knew the growing noise of the party was driving him nuts in the kitchen as he scribbled out his forms. Serves him right, him and his flipping calculator, she thought. It highlighted how lonely she was that she was actually jealous of a calculator. She noticed the little vein on the side of his head bulging. It only did that when he got annoyed, or was having sex.

The doorbell chimed.

"Can you get that, Martha?" Tim said. She padded toward the front door on bare feet.

When she opened it, a man she'd never seen before lounged casually against the frame. He had long flowing hair, which suited him. He wore a shirt that billowed in the evening breeze, revealing a hairless chest. He wore two or three leather cords around his neck, one of which held a black timber cross, and on his wrists he had leather bangles. He looked like he had fallen out of the pages of a magazine.

"Hi," he said with a huge smile. "I am Ogie. I moved in the other day. I thought I'd come introduce myself."

"Hello, I am Martha," she said, holding out her hand. His eyes moved from her face to her hand, taking in her chest during the journey from point A to point B. Just the brush of his eyes over her body caused electricity to tingle through her skin. He raised his hand, but it wasn't empty. He held a bottle of wine, which he threw in the air with a flick of his wrist, deftly catching it in his left while taking her outstretched hand with his now-empty right.

"Good reflexes," she said.

"I'm a drummer, so I'm good with my hands," he said with a smile. Ogie offered the bottle of wine. "For you."

"Thanks," she said, knowing he was flirting, but she couldn't help being flattered by it. "Let me put this away." She took the bottle from Ogie's hand and deposited it on the table at the end of the hall. Martha found herself liking this man. There was something naughty about him that was infectious. She became aware of an extra swish in her hips as she walked. She liked the feeling and went with it, sensing his eyes on her as she moved.

"Tim, come meet our new neighbour."

Tim appeared, carrying his highlighter. "Hello," he said, pumping Ogie's hand.

Martha liked the slightly embarrassed way Ogie looked, now that he was face-to-face with her husband. Like any good showman, he recovered quickly. Tim rattled off questions like he was conducting an interview, which Ogie answered with warm humour. Once Tim had Ogie's life story archived in his brain, he asked, "So, you're a drummer?"

"Don't worry, guys, I won't be practicing here, if that's worrying you. In fact, I don't even drum in the band anymore. I got promoted to lead singer. We've got a new guy on drums. The band has a place in town where we keep our gear and practice. The gang are all over tonight. They'd love to meet you."

"I'm not sure. I've a lot on," Tim said, looking with concern toward the kitchen.

"No worries," said Ogie, backing down the path. "If you change your mind, come on over. The door's open. Nice to meet you both." He waved before Tim closed the door.

"He seems okay," said Martha.

"Yea, I hope he's not going to be partying like this every night. Once in a while is one thing, but if it going on all the time, we will have to have some words," said Tim, walking toward the kitchen and his precious paperwork.

Martha went back to the sitting room. One way or the other, they were going to that party; she just had to pick her moment carefully. About an hour later, Tim came in with a beer in his hand.

"What's on the box, love?" he said, pawing at her thigh.

"'X Factor,'" she said, knowing he hated the show.

"Oh, God, is there anything else to watch? I hate Simon Cowell," Tim whinged.

"Afraid not. Want to have a look?" She handed over the remote.

"No, thanks, I'm not in the mood for telly, anyway," he said. "What did you think of our new neighbour?"

"He looked a bit wild to me," Martha said, knowing it was what Tim would be thinking.

"I thought that myself. Did he say if he was married?"

"He didn't mention."

"Can you imagine the kind of crowd he hangs out with? Probably a gang of womanising druggies," Tim griped.

Martha saw her opening and went for it.

"You could be right. If all his friends are there tonight, it would give us a chance to see what kind of people will be coming and going from the house. We would be better off, knowing what we're dealing with," she said.

"I agree," Tim said.

"Do you know what we should do?" she added.

"No. What?"

"He's invited us over. I think we should take him up on him up on the offer." She sat forward, looking him full in the face to reinforce her point.

"Do you think we should?"

"What better chance will we get? We could be watching them come and go for months without getting another chance like this. If they're going to be a problem, I'd rather know now," Martha said.

"Okay, half an hour, and I'll be finished. We can go 'round then."

Bingo! He'd fallen for it, hook, line, and sinker. She bounced off the couch. "I'll have a quick shower," she said. "Why don't you change your clothes and let them know they're living next door to classy people?"

Martha laid out a top on the bed. The jeans she had on were fine; no point in going overboard. She kept remembering the cocky way Ogie leaned against the door while they talked, the way he made no secret of his admiration of her body when he looked at her. His actions would have seemed arrogant on anyone else, but on Ogie, the cloak of confidence he wore suited him. It was a gentle assurance that changed the world around him.

Martha started the shower running and was just pushing her knickers down when Tim came into the room. He rummaged through his side of the wardrobe for something to wear. She couldn't get Ogie out of her mind. How could a man she had seen for a moment have this effect on her? She relished her secret arousal, knowing it had nothing to do with the man in her bedroom. She moved around the room, fantasising about Ogie. Having Tim right there only heightened her pleasure. It was role play for one. Heat flooded her body, flushing her skin; she was sure she could smell the musk of sex wafting off her. Martha escaped into the privacy of the shower to savour the moment.

By the time she got under the flowing water, she was a puddle of frustration. The jets of spray massaged her skin like a thousand tiny hands. She soaped herself with vigour, her fingers delving between her legs in the process. She was so turned on, she could feel each tiny fold of skin as a finger-tip passed over her clitoris.

Martha jumped when the shower door opened behind her; she felt Tim's hands exploring her body from behind. His already erect penis pressed against her. She moved her feet apart, knowing instinctively what he wanted. Tim had no imagination when it came to making love—he was as erotic as a toaster—but tonight she wanted to be taken, and Tim would have to do. His breath shortened, and his strokes quickened. Martha closed her eyes, letting the water flow over her face. She concentrated on the warm thing between her legs, willing herself to climax, but it wasn't to be. She felt Tim stiffen and shudder as he came inside her, leaving her aroused and unsatisfied. He panted like a winded old pensioner, his penis withering. She wished he would pull out and leave her alone, so she could finish for herself. Instead, he turned her around to kiss her on the lips, clinging to her in a lovers' embrace. Martha hugged him back and wondered if the bargain she had agreed upon was such a good deal after all.

Chapter 5

The last house on Honeysuckle Lane seemed to brood. Its windows in near constant darkness, the house looked upon the comings and goings of its neighbours with sinister eyes. No flowers grew in the yard; the grass long ago had been replaced with lifeless concrete. The house was rented by a single man, who kept himself to himself. He slipped in and out so quietly, he might as well have been a ghost. The car in the driveway was a six-year-old Mondo as forgettable as its owner. Brendan Roche had lived among the people of Honeysuckle Lane for three years, but had not yet talked with even one of his neighbours. They had seen each other, exchanged glances, but Brendan doubted any of them would know his name. Most of that was due to Brendan's unsociable nature, but it was also a feature of suburban living in a modern society. Keep your head down, don't get involved, and look out for number one. Brendan was tall with drab, receding hair; he wore oversized glasses and dressed in off-the-peg suits found in the cheaper department stores. He wasn't, by any stretch of the imagination, a dedicated follower of fashion. His height was exaggerated by his slender build, and he often walked hunched over, as if shrinking from the world. His eyes constantly rolled in his head, as if on the lookout for predators. Brendan knew he was all but invisible to those around him, but he never missed a thing.

  Brendan thought of himself as a watcher. He would stand in his darkened house for hours, spying on his neighbours. He watched those he worked with, day in and day out, but mostly, he watched people who ignored his presence completely carrying on their daily lives in the city. Dublin was like one huge invisibility cloak thrown over him. Brendan had found it strange when he first moved to Honeysuckle Lane. It was quiet, isolated, and he began to feel hemmed in almost straightaway. The house was fronted by a tall hedge that cut off his view of the world. In the middle of the night, he poured salt on the roots of the hedge, and within a few days, the lush, green leaves turned brown and died. The landlord came a few weeks later and cut away the lifeless skeleton and replanted it, but nothing would grow. In the end, Brendan had an unfettered view of his private universe and began to feel at ease once more. It was a few months after he first moved in, that Brendan began to get the feeling his presence on Honeysuckle Lane had not gone as unnoticed as he had imagined. He began to see people watching him as he drove in and out to work. Soon, the looks became less friendly and more disdainful. That was when the letter arrived asking that he do something to improve the look of his garden. They even had the audacity to come knocking on his door one evening, but Brendan refused to answer it. He knew the ring leaders were the suck-up young couple in number four and the O'Shea woman in number two. He could tell by the way they looked at him anytime they happened to cross paths.

Tonight, like all other nights, he watched the activity on his lane. In the corner of the room, his computer glowed coldly. Brendan had seen the altercation between the O'Shea man living up the street and the thug from the BMW. He had seen the car door being slammed on Frank O'Shea's fingers and barely had flinched. Brendan felt little compassion for his neighbour, even though he knew he should. Mr O'Shea had not done anything directly to him, but his wife looked down her nose at his presence on the lane, which made him guilty by association. To Brendan, this altercation was just something interesting to watch. Brendan was different from other people and he knew it. He often wished he had been made the same as everyone else. He envied them, their small brains and their abundant emotions. Brendan was sure that was the reason others seemed to shun him. They must sense he was different.

Brendan knew he never belonged to this world. He was a puzzle piece with nowhere to connect. He'd been alone all his life. People had the ability to be so very cruel toward those who were different. Life as an infant had been easy, given he had a loving mother and a busy father similar in nature to himself, slightly introspective. It was when Brendan had started school, his torment began. It was like being thrown to the lions. For years, he was taunted, bullied, and despised. He never felt safe. He'd wanted to run but had nowhere to go. Instead, he learned how to hide.

Brendan couldn't tell the exact moment he first felt his inner self. It had all happened very slowly, a whisper at the time. The first clear memory he had of something greater dwelling within him was one evening returning home on the school bus, he would have been about fourteen years of age. It had been yet another day of torture at the hands of troglodyte students and masochistic teachers. They called him Lurch because of his height. That day, the ride home was even more unbearable than usual. Behind him, a group of morons were amusing themselves by kicking the back of his seat. In the end, he lost his temper and turned, intent on confronting them, but words failed him. All he did was stare.

"What you looking at, dork?" a flat-faced throwback shouted at him. Brendan held the eye of the bully. He felt he was winning when a fist shot at him. Brendan flinched, and in the face of the enemy attack, he failed.

Kids are like wild animals; they sense weakness, and they can smell blood in the water. The pack of thugs tore into him, shredding his flesh and his dignity. They punched the side of his head, making Brendan's ears hum. He tried to shrink deep into the corner of his seat while punches rained from behind, but there was no place to hide from them. The attack seemed to go on for ages, but in reality, it only lasted seconds.

Even after the blows had stopped, Brendan kept his head bowed, covering his stinging ear with his hand. It was then that he heard something, a word, distant, whispered by an unfamiliar tongue. It tinkled, like crystal chimes stirred in a summer breeze, an unworldly sound. He couldn't quite make out what was being said. Yet the feeling of a separate reality existing inside of him was undeniable. Brendan willed his mind to be still. He focused it like a beam, searching through the dross of his thoughts for a precious treasure. What was the word? What is this place? Brendan felt tiny inside his own mind, like a lone person standing in the middle of a vast, undulating plain of grass, dancing in a warm wind that carried with it a distant sound.

The harder he tried to find the source of this wondrous noise, the bigger his mental world grew. A realisation struck Brendan: It was imperative that he know what word was being spoken. He did not know how, or why, but he knew his very sanity depended upon that word.

Finding the sound wasn't proving easy and to make matters worse, the realm of his mind chose that moment to expand exponentially, while he remained tiny. It was like being shown paradise, just to have it whipped from his grasp at the last moment. He heard the word again. At last, he got a bearing. Brendan moved forward in his mind, racing toward the sound. He felt the word rather than hear it. Again, it came, clearer this time: *Bag*.

In that second, Brendan saw the light. The voice wasn't part of him; it felt completely alien. *Bag*, it said again. Brendan felt so alive, like he had never felt before. From where he cowered, Brendan saw a green satchel dumped under the seat ahead of him. As the bus began to slow, the bully behind him got ready to leave, punching him one last time. Brendan stretched out his foot and nudged the bag, just a few inches. It happened in a microsecond. The driver pushed the brake a bit too quick, and the bully lost his balance and stumbled forward. His toe caught the edge of the satchel, sending him crashing face-first into a handrail. A fountain of blood accompanied his scream of pain. His mouth was a carnal, red slash, with teeth sheared off at the gum line.

Brendan knew it had been preordained. More than that, Brendan had been the tool of destiny, the bringer of retribution. He felt nothing for the bully as he stepped over him to get off the bus. In the years that followed, the voice appeared once or twice, but mainly, it remained mute within him, content to watch the world through Brendan's eyes.

Something else Brendan had seen today was how the thug that had crushed Frank O'Shea's fingers had ogled Angie Sweeney. While he would gladly have stood by and watched that throwback do anything his inbreed heart desired to Mrs O'Shea or that young bitch at number four. The thought of the man's eyes on Angie drove him to distraction. For three years, he had been living next door to that girl, and for three years, he had been watching her comings and goings. In the beginning, he had thought nothing of it. She came and went, day after day, a silent visitor passing through his world. As time passed, and the girl grew before his eyes, his interest in her deepened. It was not long before he was waiting for her specifically to come into view. He catalogued her clothes, her friends, and her movements as meticulously as any astronomer logs the movements of the stars in the heavens. And like any astronomer, he began to fall in love with his star.

There was something vital about Angie, something that Brendan couldn't see in others. She was different, like him. She was special. Seeing that vile piece of shit leering at her, speaking to her, filled Brendan with rage. Even seeing that she angrily flipped him the middle finger did little to dampen his anger. He wanted to hurt that man and hurt him badly. Sadly, Brendan was a man of passion but few actions.

Later in the evening, Angie appeared from her house dressed for a night out. She was a young woman, after all. Why shouldn't she dip her toe into the waters of the world? Brendan reasoned. Her hair was still wet from the shower, her skirt too short for Brendan's liking, but that was the fashion of the day. Brendan watched her walk away and felt aroused.

A word echoed in his mind: *Tramp*.

Brendan frowned. It had been many years since he had heard anything from his inner self—so long, in fact, that Brendan wondered if it even existed any longer. But his surprise was only surpassed by his annoyance at the word it chose to utter.

"Not a tramp," he mumbled to himself.

Tramp. Trash. Whore, the voice answered, more forcefully.

Brendan had to agree that the girl's family was despicable. Her obese, slobbering, dullard of a father, with his knuckle-dragging tendencies; the passive weakness of her mother; and the fool of a brother. None of that could change the way she sent jolts of electricity through him. None of that could change the fact that she was special, a fact which his inner self was clearly ignorant of. He tuned out the distant words, and watched her leave.

Harlot, the inner voice said thinly, far more distant than before. It was vanishing once more into the ether. Brendan was glad. He moved away from the window toward his computer once Angie had vanished from sight. He massaged his temples and closed his eyes.

When Brendan opened his eyes once more, he got to work on his MacBook. His fingers flew over the keys like liquid mercury. The digital world was a place where he was completely at home. Everything made sense; everything had a rule. Brendan was something of a savant when it came to programming. Nothing was safe from his touch; nobody was out of reach.

Tonight his virtual hands caressed Angie, and she didn't even know it. There was more than one way to watch people these days. As George Orwell had predicted, Big Brother is watching us. Always.

Chapter 6

Tim and Martha crossed the few feet to Ogie's door. The sound of singing and laughter oozed into the evening air. Tim knocked, but there was no answer. It was clear that they couldn't be heard above the noise. If it was up to Tim, they'd have stood there till Hell froze over, so Martha pushed the door, which was open, just like Ogie had said it would be.

She poked her head in tentatively and said, "Hello?"

The party clearly was taking place in the kitchen, judging by the wall of noise coming from that direction. The downstairs bathroom door opened suddenly, and a stunning woman appeared in the hall. The woman was shocked to find Martha looking in the front door but quickly gathered herself.

"Oh, hi?"

"Hi. Ogie came round earlier and invited us over. I hope that's okay. I'm Martha, by the way, and this is my husband, Tim. We live next door."

"I'm Annabelle. Come on in," she said, holding the door wider for them to enter. Martha had in her hand the bottle of wine that Ogie had given them, and Tim had a bottle of vodka. Martha held out the bottle for Annabelle, which she took with a sly smile.

Annabelle led the way into the kitchen. About fifteen people were sitting around in a relaxed way. One or two women were sitting on men's knees. A handsome guy was playing "American Pie" on the guitar. The tabletop was littered with beer bottles, dishes of chips, and ashtrays. Plates from an earlier meal were stacked on the draining board, clearly not going to be washed tonight. Ogie spotted Tim and Martha and came over to greet them as the sing-along continued.

"Hi, guys! Great you could come," Ogie said over the howls of "Bye, bye, Miss American Pie.' Tim shook hands with Ogie and handed over the bottle of vodka. Martha spotted Annabelle dropping the bottle of wine she had given her with a dozen other identical bottles and felt embarrassed.

"Thanks so much. You shouldn't have gone to the trouble. What can I get you to drink?" Ogie asked, putting the vodka to one side.

"Glass of white would be fine for me," said Martha.

"A beer, if you have it," said Tim.

"Coming right up," said Ogie. The house was very much like their own but a little empty. Martha could see a stack of moving boxes, not yet opened but piled up in the sitting room. The only thing fully functioning seemed to be the sound system. Martha would never invite people to a housewarming party until everything was perfect. That was just the way she was. Ogie seemed to have a more laid-back attitude.

Martha found herself wondering what part Annabelle played in this arrangement. She seemed to be more than just a guest. It was hard to describe, but she had a proprietary air about her. Still, there was no sign of a woman's touch to the house, or furnishings. Ogie came back with a cold bottle of Budweiser for Tim and a bucket-size glass of wine for Martha. The song was coming to an end, which cued a thunderous round of whoops and applause. Ogie guided them toward the table, where a few people were giving the new arrivals inquisitive looks. This was a tightly knit group, anyone could tell. Being accepted might not be the easiest of things. On the other hand, they all seemed like lovely people, not a strung-out heroin junkie in sight, which would make Tim sleep happier in his bed.

"This is Tim and Martha, from next door," Ogie said. "This is the gang." The table erupted with greetings, each friendly handshake shoving another aside. It was like being mauled by a dozen happy toddlers. It only lasted a few moments, but Martha felt winded yet delighted by the warmth of this group, a feeling that she had never expected. It made her smile like a loon. Soon, they all launched into a wild version of "Delilah" by Tom Jones, and Martha felt like she was now, truly, one of the gang.

The music and singing were fantastic. Martha could tell they were professionals. Two chairs were added around the table for the new arrivals, and a cunning little red-haired man managed to cut Martha away from the herding arms of Tim, who was left sitting alongside a girl in her thirties with pigtails and a tiny schoolgirl skirt. She looked like a mother trying on her daughter's clothes.

Martha soon learned that the name of Ogie's band was Pigmy Moon Child. Only one other member of the band was at the party. The others were friends of Ogie's from college. The little ginger guy described the band's music as contemporary rock, not that Martha had a clue what that meant. He told her they had two albums and a college following, which kept the band constantly on the road. Martha knew she had broken another heart by the way the little man looked at her.

"How long have Ogie and Annabelle been going out?" Martha asked her new admirer.

"They're not together, but I'm sure she'd like to be."

So, thought Martha, Annabelle was trying to pin down the wild and delicious Mr. Ogie. You couldn't blame her, really. If Martha were single, she'd be doing much the same thing.

For the rest of the night, they all chatted, laughed, and sang. The little red-haired man was never far from Martha's elbow, watching her with puppy-dog eyes and hanging on her every word. Tim gave a few knowing looks but seemed to accept the attention as inevitable. The hours flew in a blink of an eye, and Martha felt the wine start to take effect. She looked around and saw Ogie leaning against the kitchen counter, singing along with the latest song to be favoured by the group, while holding a tumbler of Jack Daniel's with ice, Coke not required.

Martha excused herself to use the little girl's room. On her way back, she glided over and propped herself alongside Ogie.

"I wanted to thank you for inviting us tonight," she said, leaning in close, brushing her bare arm against his in the process.

"I'm not sure your husband agrees," said Ogie, smiling. He motioned toward Tim with his glass, making the ice tinkle in the amber liquid. "Vanessa seems to have her claws in him. She is probably boring him rigid about her divorce."

"I wouldn't worry too much," said Martha with a smile. "Bored rigid is his natural condition."

Ogie gave a belly laugh and said, "I think we're going to get on, Martha."

"So, who is living here with you?"

"Just me. It is far too big, I know, but I had to invest in something, so it might as well be something I could use," said Ogie. He was aware of her skin brushing against his; the touch lingered longer than a simple brush. He knew she was flirting with him. After all, he was the king of flirting himself. But look at her, thought Ogie. She's a goddess. Perhaps that was just the way she was with everyone.

"Why aren't you married?" she asked, taking him by surprise.

Ogie could have told her he wasn't the marring kind, or that he wasn't really a grown-up, or that he didn't treat women very well, all of which were true. But instead, he said, "I guess I'm still waiting for the right woman."

He watched Martha melt a little more. She leaned in, turning her head demurely. Ogie knew now for sure, she fancied him. He could hear the cogs in her brain whir as she added these new dimensions of his personality to what she already knew. He knew he had her on the hook, but playing the fish was half the fun.

"Come on. Let's save poor Tim," he said, talking her by the elbow, letting his fingers run slightly up the inside of her arm, where the skin was soft and warm. He held the touch for a fraction longer than necessary. Ogie was sure he could feel her temperature rise in his grip, and she did nothing to disengage his hold. He soon manoeuvred himself into the conversation to which Vanessa was subjecting Tim, steering Vanessa away from the depression she'd suffered after that asshole of a husband left her for his secretary, of all things, and onto more fun topics. Martha could see Tim warming to their host before her eyes.

The four of them eventually gravitated away from the main group; it ended up as a party within a party. Vanessa thought that Ogie was flirting with her. Tim was enjoying Ogie's company enormously, being one of the boys for a change. Martha was throwing in very subtle flirts of her own toward Ogie. Only Ogie truly knew what was happening—or so he thought. Across the room, Annabelle watched from the corner of her eye. A woman knows when someone is moving in on her man, and Annabelle did not like the look of Martha one little bit. A woman that good-looking, and that unfulfilled, was a dangerous distraction to any man, let alone Ogie.

It was late when Tim looked at his watch and said, "It's time to go." Martha was in no mood to leave, but what could she do? Tim shook Ogie's hand, while Martha delayed, looking for her purse. Tim vanished out the front door, towards home. Martha took her opportunity in the hall. She embraced Ogie, and gave him a lingering kiss on the cheek. She kept her arms around him after her lips left his skin, and asked quietly, "Is Annabelle your girlfriend"?

She felt his little finger move down and stroke the top of her ass, through her tight jeans. "We're just friends."

"She was watching us earlier, I hope you're not in trouble," she said, with a naughty smile.

"Nothing I can't handle," said Ogie, releasing his grip on her. Ogie leaned out the front door and waved, as Martha followed Tim across the strip of lawn dividing their driveways. "'Night, Tim, Martha. Thanks for coming."

Once they were gone from sight, Ogie closed the door. Only Annabelle was left in the house. She was in the kitchen, tidying up. Ogie took her by the hand and led her upstairs. Not a dish was touched that night, because Annabelle was the kind of friend that came with lots of benefits.

Chapter 7

Frank's hand was a mess. After Harry had driven off, Frank had staggered into the house and packed it in frozen peas. Barbara heard the door and came downstairs.

"What happened?"

"Wind caught the door and slammed it on my fingers," he said with a wince, hoping she wouldn't notice that there wasn't a breath of wind outside. She didn't.

"Here, let me look at it," she said, taking hold of his wrist.

"Ow! Don't poke at it."

"That looks bad. Do you think it is broken?" she asked.

"I don't know, it's killing me," he said, pulling his hand out of Barbara's viselike fingers. His mother had been just the same, the bedside manner of a butcher. Deep down, he thought both of them did it on purpose, taking satisfaction in making him jump. Sadists.

"You'll live," she said, managing to sound let down. "Did you pick up Enda?"

"Does it look like I did?" Frank said, waving his injured paw in the air.

"Come on, we'll get him up on the way to the hospital," she said, lifting the car keys from the table. Frank hated it when she treated him like one of the kids. They found Enda waiting outside the school before making made the short trip to the hospital. Frank whinged all the way there. Barbara's heavy sighs made it clear she thought he was being a little girl. She pulled up at the emergency entrance, letting the car idle.

"Are you not coming in?" he asked.

"You'll be ages, and the kids haven't had dinner yet," she said, staying behind the wheel. Frank was finding this hard to take in, being jettisoned at the door like the victim of a drug overdose. He got out of the car, not believing she actually was going to leave him.

"Give me a call when you're ready to come home," she said.

"It might be quiet, why don't you come in and see," Frank asked, not wanting her to go but reluctant to sound whinging.

The car behind them revved its engine. She leaned over, pulled the door closed, and was gone. Frank watched her drive away like a spanked toddler, his bottom lip sticking out just a little.

In the end, Barbara had been right. He waited four hours, and there was only one other person in the emergency room. The x-ray showed nothing broken. In the end, they just bandaged him up and said take a Panadol. He could have done that himself, saving a numb bum and fifty euro more on his credit-card bill.

All day Saturday, Frank stayed in the house. Barbara did her level best to drive him out into the world with a barrage of nagging but failed. Frank felt like the victim of a mugging. He was scared to go outside, even though the rational part of his mind knew there was nothing to fear. When he thought about it, he was a victim. Look at what Harry did to his hand. He was better off staying out of the way.

By evening, Barbara had had enough and went down to the tennis club for a game of doubles. Frank thought about going online; he might be able to win back his money. He got as far as typing in the credit-card number, but he stopped short of pressing the Return key. On some level, he knew it was only going to make things worse. Still, his finger hovered over the key. One little push, and everything could be fixed. One good night, and he could pay off everything. He slammed the laptop closed so hard, he heard the screen crack. His hands were shaking. He needed a drink. Three large whiskies later, Frank's head was spinning. By the time Barbara arrived home, he had fallen asleep on the couch, the empty glass still clutched in his good hand.

She smiled at him. He looked like an overgrown kid when he slept, with his chubby little cheeks and the way he made little-boy snores. She was going to leave him where he was but thought better of it. If he spent the night on the couch, he would be stiff and grumpy tomorrow. Taking the glass from his hand, Barbara shook him gently.

"Time for bed, sleepyhead."

Sunday had always been Frank's favourite day of the week. A Sunday newspaper, sitting in front of the TV, the kids playing outside—well, that bit might be in his head, but the best thing was a mouthwatering Sunday roast steaming in the middle of the table. No one could match Barbara for her Sunday roast: Beef joint, pink in the middle, smothered with gravy so rich, it should come in an armoured van. Then there was the Yorkshire pudding. Frank loved Yorkshire pudding.

Today was different. Even the stomach-bubbling smells wafting from the kitchen couldn't shake his troubles. Harry's payment clock was ticking loudly in Frank's head.

Frank was a dummy but not totally stupid. He knew that the only way to get rid of Harry was to pay him off in one big lump. He needed to get all the money together now, or he'd be paying that scumbag off for years. Twenty percent interest a week! How the hell did he allow himself to get suckered like that? Where could he lay his hands on four grand in cash before Friday? He could sell the car, except he needed it for work, and what would he tell Barbara? What about selling something else? Frank looked around, and all he could see was overpriced knickknacks not worth dusting. What about a loan? Would the bank give him a loan? Frank thought about the maxed-out credit cards filling his wallet. They would have all the records; no one was going to give him a real loan, and another loan shark would only make things worse.

He had one hope, a slim one, but a hope nonetheless: his brother, Richard. Frank knew when it was time to back a long shot. He pulled out his mobile and dialed his brother's number.

Richard picked up on the fifth ring. It sounded like he was outside.

"Hi, Rich. It's Frank. Can you hear me?"

"Frank, no need to shout. I can hear you fine," Richard said. In the background, the wind was howling, as if he were standing on top of Mount Everest.

"Just wondered if you fancied buying your little brother a pint?"

"Ah, can't. I am playing golf with the lads," Richard said.

Frank should have known. Richard played golf every Sunday.

"What about when you're finished? I can come meet you?"

"Hold on." Everything went quiet. Frank heard the thwack of a golf club, followed by distant voices. Richard came back on the line. "Okay, Frank, meet you here in about two hours."

"Thanks, Richard, it's—"

The line went dead.

Frank looked at the buzzing phone in his hand. Typical of Richard, the arrogant twat, who did he think he was? Frank had to pull himself back from that thought. He couldn't afford to be angry with his brother. After all, he was the one person who just might be able to help him.

Frank flicked through the TV, rustled the paper he had already finished reading, and paced the room. He managed a full forty minutes before he could wait no longer. He bounced off the armchair and grabbed his jacket.

"Barb, I'm just nipping out for a pint with Rich. Won't be long."

"Frank! Dinner's nearly ready," she called angrily.

"Put mine in the oven. Won't be long," he said, slamming the door behind him.

On the drive to the golf course, Frank thought about what he would say to Richard. No matter how he worded the situation, he came out sounding pitiful. Richard was the most-conservative guy he knew. "Money doesn't grow on trees" was more or less his motto. He spent what he could afford and always had a little something put away for a rainy day. That was the bit Frank was counting on. He had to appeal to Richard's brotherly love, wherever the hell he kept that hidden. Perhaps he should tell Richard the whole story, about the cards, the money he lost online, as well as Harry. Perhaps he should he just lie. The truth was, Frank could lie to beat the band, but he reached the golf course before he could think of a good one.

In the car park, he saw Richard's Audi nestling in the shade of a chestnut tree, clean but far from new. The car park was busy, but it was a sunny Sunday morning. Mercedes dotted the place, contrasted by a painter's van and a ten-year-old Astra. After all, this was a community golf course. Richard was a working man, even if he loved this gentrified pastime.

Frank went through the gate and down the path to the clubhouse. The bar opened onto the eighteenth green, where people could sit around watching that final putt. Nothing like a crowd to add pressure. The day was warm, so a lot of people were outside. Frank spotted Richard on a bench with three men, sipping pints of lager, surrounded by golf bags. He waved but waited where he was. The last thing Frank needed was an audience for this particular conversation. Richard waved back and excused himself.

"Hi, Rich. How was the game?"

"Hit and miss. I had the chance of an eagle on the sixteenth," Richard said. "Do you want a pint?"

"Go on so," said Frank. They went into the clubhouse. Frank found an empty booth while Richard got the drinks.

"What is all this about?" Richard asked, plopping a dew-dripping glass in front of Frank.

"Can a man not have a pint with his brother these days?" Frank asked.

Richard didn't suffer fools and didn't beat about bushes. He went straight through them with a chainsaw. Folding his arms, he gave Frank a look that said, "Pull the other one."

"Okay," Frank conceded. "I need a favour."

"How much?" Richard said abruptly.

"I didn't say it was about money," Frank said indignantly, mostly because Richard had hit the nail on the head.

"How much?" Richard asked again, his face set hard.

"Four grand."

"Four grand!" Richard sat back in his seat. "Phew! What do you want four grand for?"

"Things have been bad. It's work. The commissions have dried up, but the bills keep falling on the mat," Frank said.

"Sounds like you need to make a few lifestyle changes, Frankie. I don't have that kind of money," Richard said, taking a slug of his beer.

"It's gone beyond making a few cuts, Rich. I owe a lot of money on the credit card, more than one credit card. The interest is huge. I can't get out from under. I really need some help."

Frank could hear the fear and desperation in his own voice. As Frank watched his brother, he realised Richard would have made a terrible card player. Every emotion showed on his face. Frank watched his brother mull over the problem. He could tell the moment Richard came to a decision, and the pain it caused him was etched all over him. Long before he said a word, Frank knew his long shot had come in dead last.

"I'm sorry. I really am, Frank. Things haven't been easy for me, either," Richard said, his tone softer. "I just don't have the money."

"I understand. I had to ask," Frank said, playing the sympathy card one last time.

"I can let you have a couple of hundred. If I had more, I'd give it to you," Richard said sincerely.

"I know you would. Look, don't worry about it. I'll get things sorted," said Frank. Inside, he felt like crying. But he also felt embarrassed and ashamed at what he had become. He was begging from his own brother, for God's sake. How much lower could he get?

They finished their drinks, trading awkward chitchat, neither wanting to be there at that moment. Not quickly enough, the drinks were finished and they could leave the clubhouse. On the way out, Richard picked up his golf bag. On the walk back to the car park, Frank let the worry boiling inside him bubble to the surface. It must have showed on his face because Richard noticed and stopped beside his car. He looked at Frank with concern.

"Are you sure it's just money? You don't look yourself," Richard said, propping the golf bag against the Audi's boot.

"I've been stressed, worrying, not sleeping," said Frank, rubbing his forehead. "I haven't told Barbara yet. Can we keep it between us for now?"

"You can't go burying your head in the sand. Stuff like this won't vanish," said Richard, popping the trunk and swinging his bag into the cavernous opening. It reminded Frank how easily a body could vanish if one were of such a mind.

"I know you, Frank. You'll try and wish it all away," Richard went on. He had the measure of him. It had always been Frank's way to duck and run when things got sticky. So far, it had worked just fine.

"I won't," Frank said.

The brothers parted with a wave; they weren't a hugging family. Frank drove home with rocks in his stomach. He had no idea what to do now. The future loomed in front of him like a huge black hole, as the ground slipped out from beneath his feet. The thought of going home, eating roast dinner, and pretending that everything was fine sickened him, but he had to do it. He couldn't let Barbara know what had happened. It would kill her.

Suck it up, Frank, he told himself. He needed to buy some time. He had to gather whatever cash he could before next Friday and hope for the best. After Harry's last visit, Frank knew running wasn't an option. He'd been stupid to think he could threaten a loan shark. They did the threatening; Frank did the trembling. That was the arrangement. His tender hand, resting on the steering wheel, was proof that Harry McCarthy was capable of far worse than threats. Richard had been right about one thing: Standing still was no longer an option.

Chapter 8

Brendan woke in the early hours. His head seared with blinding pain. These headaches were coming more often. The doctor had diagnosed migraines, but Brendan knew he was wrong. Brendan knew it was the effect of his mind expanding, growing pains of a kind. He had played along with the diagnoses because the drugs he got helped to dull the pain. Brendan struggled out of bed and into the bathroom. He slid open the mirrored front of the medicine cabinet, knocking bottles of tablets over as he rummaged for his painkillers.

The cabinet was awash with sleeping pills and antidepressants, as well as a cacophony of painkillers. Brendan knew he was stronger than most men, which had the damning effect of making his suffering so much more difficult to control. Instead of going to one doctor, Brendan visited half a dozen, collecting prescriptions from all of them, stockpiling the pills until he really needed them. Brendan poured three into his palm and swallowed them dry. As he waited for the drugs to take effect, Brendan leaned against the bathroom sink, looking out on the world. The sky was turning pastel in the moments before dawn. The fog in his brain started to clear. Brendan heard something echoing in the corner of his mind. He had never heard the voice come again in such a short time. He listened, but it was gone. It must have been a trick of the medication, or a memory of sorts. Brendan washed his face and tried to wake himself up a little.

When he went downstairs, the screen of his laptop still glowed, which reminded him of his activities the night before. Computers weren't only his passion; they were his profession. The Internet was truly the new church of man. Months ago, he had begun researching Angie, hacking into her accounts, spying on her virtual life. He even had bugged her phone and invaded her e-mail. Like all people, Angie felt she was completely secure, sharing her most-intimate information across the Internet. Little did she realise that social media was, quite literally, an open book to a person like him. It didn't take long before watching wasn't enough. He wanted to reach out and touch her, hold her, talk to her, even influence her. In reality, the time wasn't right, but on a computer, he was God, and God could do anything.

He'd opened a Facebook account using the name Tina Ryan. He added an out-of-focus shot of an eighteen-year-old girl, normal-looking, mousy, wearing a hat and glasses at some random festival. She could be anyone in the right light. Brendan registered her school as St. Mary's, the one closest to Honeysuckle Lane. He surfed students and recent ex-students, picking the dullest, most-nerdy-looking ones. A few friendly messages later, Tina's—and his—circle of friends began to grow. It was amazing how many kids added him back without even checking who she was. Soon he was copying posts to his timeline, building up a virtual life for Tina. He skipped and hopped from person to person, not sending more than a couple of messages to each, all the time circling closer to Angie. When he felt he had enough backstory built, he sent her a friendship request and waited. It was one of the happiest days of his life when he received the notification that Angie Sweeney, age nineteen, single and loving it by the photos she posted, accepted his request.

Brendan now had access to her friends, to her message history. She'd even posted a copy of her exam results with all the official contact information on the top. More important, they were now actually friends. Granted, she did not know the full extent of who he was, but the essence of Tina, and the essence of him, were fundamentally the same, were they not? Brendan watched as she talked to others. He was now able to comment on their posts, to interact in a real way with her. He recruited new people from the outskirts of her circles, enough to seem familiar but not enough to draw attention. He discovered she worked in a café not far from his office, but he had not been able to build up the courage to visit her in the flesh yet, or to approach her as Brendan. He needed more time for that, he needed a key to unlock her life. The search for the key was no closer this morning, after another fruitless night of nightclub photos and drunken status posts.

The voice had been different last night. It seemed to be more powerful, louder. It worried Brendan slightly, but intrigued him in the same instant. Over the years, Brendan had worried about the issue of his inner self. He had come to some conclusions. He was sure that the voice he heard was not his but another's, an echo from the past or even the future. Either was possible. While being benign, this entity wasn't without power. It held some sway, over him and others, but it had its limits. During its celestial wanderings, it could smell, hear, speak, see, think, and interact at all levels but one. Touch was reserved for this reality alone. Brendan had the impression that the voice both suffered from and resented this limitation. While Brendan could experience the brush of velvet skin, the hard bite of cold steel, or the warmth of licking flames, he felt sure that the voice only could watch with envy.

Recently, Brendan became aware of patterns in things he encountered that could not be explained away as chance. This morning, he wondered if they might possibly be side effects of the power growing inside him. On the streets, Brendan saw things to which other people were oblivious: People and objects moving in patterns, forming triangles, squares, even stars. Moving in symmetry, guided by an unseen hand. Brendan was sure this power could be sensed in the swaying of branches, the flights of birds, even in the numbers of letters in a name. Brendan could see the hand of something at work, and he was delighted by it. Only this morning did he begin to wonder if he himself were not the power bringing about these things. That may answer why he was the only one who seemed aware of their existence at all.

Brendan had always believed that whatever he was hearing to be benevolent, but the filth it had cast before him about Angie was worrying. Could there be a malevolent taint to these promptings? Since Brendan had begun his surveillance of Angie, the occasional word he heard had taken a decidedly jealous inflection, perhaps even evil. The pain he sometimes experienced as a result of his special gift served as a warning that he needed to proceed with care. Brendan went back to the bathroom and took two more painkillers. He looked in the mirror and felt like young Icarus, about to fly too close to the sun and run the risk of exploding into flames.

Along with the headaches, Brendan had to endure other trials because of his special position among men. Isolation was the one that hurt the most. Brendan had to act normal, to seem normal, while knowing he was extraordinary. Brendan dismissed religion as the scribblings of children trying to recreate a masterpiece, simply a blunt tool of those unworthy of divinity. Brendan knew that only a few, perhaps only he, had been born with the ability to truly understand the essence of the universe. He wasn't sure what was becoming of him, but it was the beginning of an epic revelation.

The pills took hold, and Brendan began to feel better. He showered and dressed for the day. He couldn't face food but managed a glass of juice. He gathered his belongings and left the house, long before the morning rush hour. Even now, he noticed patterns in the light traffic. A red car sandwiched between four black ones, all moving along as if chained together. He got to the office block before anyone else arrived and began untangling lines of corrupted computer code, thus making modern life possible.

This, thought Brendan, was what the world saw of him. A man who could talk to computers, a bland and depthless persona. In truth, Brendan wrapped it around himself like a security blanket. It kept mankind at bay while he existed within its safety. Occasionally, the passion he held prisoner spilled out, causing problems. It was another price he had to pay for standing above humanity. It was the cost of hiding. For the rest of the morning, he installed programs in computers all across the globe. His digital fingers reached thousands of miles across continents to code servers and design systems that controlled everything people took for granted in their day-to-day lives. He was the unseen master of an electronic universe.

Brendan didn't do chitchat at work or at any time for that matter. Even in this Babylonian skyscraper of nerds, he was the most-aloof of them all. His colleagues thought he was beyond peculiar. The way he looked into space, his fits of rage, and the way he stood far too close when talking and kept eye contact long afterward was creepy. Despite being aloof and isolated from his colleagues, Brendan knew more office secrets that the greatest watercooler gossip in the place. Brendan knew that Linda Jameson in accounts was having an affair with a married director of the company. He knew that the smiling little shit in the next cubicle spent half his day looking at naked girls who were far too young to be legal. Brendan knew all this, not because anyone told him, but because he'd installed a trapdoor program in the main server which allowed him free access to all parts of the company's computer network, even the company bank accounts. Brendan had access to every e-mail, every file, deleted or not. If knowledge was power, then he was all-powerful.

Brendan would've been fired long ago for his strange behaviour if he'd not been such a genius at coding. To Brendan, the work was infantile. The complex lines that flashed across his screen glowed white-hot in his mind's eye and were as simple as a nursery rhyme. He made connections no normal man could make. He fixed problems that others overlooked. Throughout the morning, he worked at impossible speed. By two-thirty, he had cleared a week's workload. It was time for a project of a different kind.

Brendan flashed off an e-mail to the office manager, Mr. Pulter, saying he was going to a funeral, before leaving the building. Brendan strolled through the warm afternoon streets. The café Angie had mentioned on her Facebook page was only a few blocks away. He knew it was time to meet her, face-to-face. His stomach was a knot of anxiety. When he got to the café, he could not make his hand open the door. He wanted to go in but feared what might happen. He was opening himself up to ridicule, and hurt, by showing his feelings for the girl.

The café was jammed with small tables and wicker chairs, but most of the customers ordered, accepted their food and left. Huge coffee hoppers, muffins, cakes, and deli rolls vied for space on the counter. If anyone actually took the time to sit down, they never stayed long. It wasn't the kind of place you settled down with a good book to pass a few hours. Brendan turned away from the door looking for a dark, safe place to assess the café before making his final decision. Thankfully, the entire front of the building was made of glass, and across the road was a bar with a sidewalk-seating area. From there he could watch and not be seen.

Brendan walked across the road and sat at one of the tables, but it was not quite right. He needed some window dressing. Brendan went inside the bar and ordered a pint of lager and a sandwich. He lifted a newspaper from the counter without asking permission, going back outside to settle himself on the uncomfortable pavement furniture. From the corner of his eye, he had a perfect view of the café and waited excitedly to catch a glimpse of Angie. Minutes ticked away, his food arrived, but there was no sign of Angie working in the café across the road.

He was starting to think she might have had the day off when she appeared, carrying plates to a table inside the window, smiling as she delivered them. Brendan delighted in the fact that he could watch her every move with impunity. The word *voyeur* didn't sit well with him; *watcher* was a nobler title. Brendan nibbled his sandwich and for nearly an hour, he observed Angie clear tables and serve customers. She weaved between chairs with liquid grace, her youthful legs filling out her skinny jeans perfectly. The white apron she wore suited her—it accented her slender waist—but by far, her most-alluring feature was behind her. Every time she turned her heart-shaped ass toward the window, Brendan felt electricity course through his body. He imagined possessing her, having her do anything he wanted. He felt himself harden and did nothing to hide his erection. There was no one to see it, but even if there were, he wouldn't care. People's opinions were unimportant to Brendan. Did the farmer ask the chickens for their opinion before swinging the axe?

Still, Brendan was feeling a pinch in his back from sitting on the hard chair. He had just made up his mind to cross over to the café when a man in his early twenties entered. Angie stopped what she was doing and smiled at him. Brendan forgot about his back. There was something different about this guy. Brendan could read it in the way he moved. The man didn't go to the counter. He walked directly to Angie and smiled right back at her. Brendan felt his erection wither and his rage awaken. Angie slipped close to the man, planting a quick kiss on his lips. His hand slipped down her back, resting on her perfect bum for a second, perhaps longer. In Brendan's mind, time slowed. His eyes zoomed in until he could see every hair on the man's fingers as he groped his girl, his Angie. Brendan bathed in an uncontrollable torrent of wrath, but shock prevented him from moving. The man's lips left Angie's, leaving tiny thread of saliva connecting their mouths. In Brendan's heightened awareness, he could see every detail, even the light twinkling through their body fluids, bejewelling their entwined essences.

Brendan's fist tightened around the base of his pint glass. He imagined shattering the glass into the young man's handsome face, grinding it into the soft flesh until he was unrecognizable scarlet chum. No woman would let him touch her ass then. Just when Brendan felt he could take no more, a man behind the counter gestured at empty tables strewn with cups. The young couple kissed again, and the young man walked from the café into the flow of afternoon shoppers.

In Brendan's mind, the voice hissed into life. *Tramp*, it said. This time, Brendan didn't contradict it.

Brendan kicked the table out of his way, sending glass and crockery crashing to the cobbles. He flung a tenner on the ground beside it and stalked after the young man. The street was filled with shoppers and schoolkids. The young man slalomed between the throngs, only to vanish into a tall building at the end of the block. Brendan lengthened his stride, putting on his overcoat as he entered the building through doors embossed with the names "Brady, McCarthy, and Doyle."

Brendan saw the young man stepping on the elevator and called to him, "Hold the lift, please." To his credit, the young man put his hand between the closing doors. Brendan got on, smiling his thanks. He looked at the buttons, noticing that three was glowing. Brendan pushed four.

They rode up in silence. Inside, Brendan was far from silent. He raged against everything that the man represented. He was young, good-looking, athletic—everything that Brendan wasn't, everything he had wanted to be. If this weren't enough, this slimeball wanted to take the one good thing Brendan had in his life. Brendan wouldn't stand for it. He'd put a stop this guy one way or the other, no matter what the cost. The doors pinged and slid apart on level three, revealing an open-plan office not unlike his own.

"Good-bye," said Brendan to the young man, as he stepped off the lift, meaning it in every sense of the word. They young man smiled over his shoulder at Brendan and walked away.

Brendan rode the lift up one more floor but didn't get off. Instead, he studied the buttons; they were numbered one to five but also B. Brendan pushed the B button, hoping it was a car park. Sure enough, the doors opened revealing an underground garage, packed with cars. Brendan studied the interior and saw only one car exit. It rose up, joining the street toward the front of the building. He also spotted a couple of cameras and a pedestrian fire exit. He rode the elevator back up to the lobby and left the building.

The voice echoed through his thumping brain. *Wait. Watch*, it chanted again and again. Never before had Brendan experienced the voice so consistently, or so loudly. It was like someone standing behind him, whispering into his ear. The presence was getting stronger. There was no denying it. Maybe it was an angel sent to help him in times of trouble. This situation certainly qualified as stressful.

It was only 4:00 p.m. The guy would be at his desk for at least another hour. A plan was forming in Brendan's head for which he needed to get a few things, but they were easy to find. It felt good to take action. The thought of the man's hand resting on Angie's skin steeled his conviction. Brendan walked through the swarm of shoppers with a mission to complete.

Brendan reappeared outside the building at five, this time dressed in jeans and a hoodie. On his feet, he still wore his work shoes, but they'd have to do. His suit and overcoat were bundled in the large shopping bag resting at his feet. Brendan leafed through a car magazine while he lazed on a bench close to the ramp. He was willing to bet a man in his midtwenties would buy a car with his very first paycheck. Half-five saw a flood of people appear through the main doors of Brady McCarthy, and Doyle. Cars queued on the ramp of the car park, waiting to join the evening traffic. Brendan's quarry wasn't hard to spot. He roared up the ramp in a sporty-looking Toyota Celica, silver with alloy wheels but at least eight years old. The car pulled into the traffic with a squeal of rubber.

When the flow of cars leaving the garage petered out, Brendan dropped his magazine into the bag and walked down the ramp, pulling his hood over his head. He fished a can of spray paint out of the bag. On the wall, a security camera pointed at the cars leaving the building. Brendan shook the paint can and gave the camera quick squirt, not enough to black out the picture, but just enough to haze it with spots. At the far end of the basement, another camera got the same treatment. Brendan made sure to keep his head down when approaching and spraying the cameras. He left by the emergency stairs, checking for alarms. There were none, but there was another camera. Again, he sprayed it, hearing the door click closed behind him.

The following morning, Brendan was at his desk before seven in the morning, beavering away at his computer. Everyone arriving to work noticed his early arrival, but no one noticed when he slipped away at about twelve. No one noticed the tall man in a hooded top walking down the ramp into an underground car park a few blocks away. No one took any notice of the heavy-looking sports bag he carried over his shoulder. No one noticed Brendan slipping back behind his desk just before lunchtime. Brendan soon was absorbed in his work, trying to diagnose a niggling problem in a bank's Internet server. It was like that with him. His brain compartmentalised things; doors opened and doors closed, allowing him to function from day to day. How else could a man with a whole universe existing within him cope with the trivialities of life?

On the corner of his desk sat three shiny wheel nuts. No one noticed them, either.

That night, Brendan ate his dinner in front of the TV. When the nine o'clock news came on, a picture of a mangled silver Toyota poking out from under the rear wheels of an articulated lorry led the headlines. Brendan didn't smile or feel sad. He just stirred his coffee, watching the report. When the news was over, Brendan washed his dishes and had an early night. After all, it had been quite a long day.

Chapter 9

The traffic inched forward at a snail's pace. An unmarked Garda car screamed past the stranded motorists, using the hard shoulder. Blue lights flashed while the siren warned of its rushed approach. Up ahead, a thick knot of emergency vehicles had gathered. A traffic patrol car was pulled across two of the three lanes of the motorway, keeping everyone away from the incident ahead. The unmarked unit jinked past the patrol car into the closed section of road while an officer herded stranded cars single file into the outer lane.

Detective Stephen Adams stopped his car and surveyed what lay ahead of him. The air was a mass of flashing lights, mostly blue, and wrecked cars steamed in the middle of the road. People were being treated by medics, disgorged from arriving ambulances. At the head of this trail of destruction stood an articulated lorry, with the remains of a silver car wedged under its rear wheels. Fire crews were trying to release whatever unlucky people were inside. Detective Adams wished people could see what he'd seen before they got behind the wheel of a car. A moment's carelessness, mixed with overconfidence, was all it took to create misery. A quick look was enough to tell him that this one was fatal.

The area around the truck had been sealed off using yellow tape. Standing guard was a uniformed officer. A gaggle of people had gathered around him, watching what was unfolding. Some were occupants of cars involved in the incident; others were emergency people, waiting their turn to help. The officer was doing a good job of keeping them all out of the way. Adams walked up to the officer at the same moment a paramedic crawled into the wreckage of the silver car. His legs wiggled and moved now and again while everyone stood still and watched. After a few minutes, the paramedic wiggled back out. He shook his head in response to an unheard question, and then packed up his gear. The fire crew began cutting through the remains of the silver car to extract the driver.

"Has anyone come out of that?" Adams asked the officer, indicating the silver car being sliced open by the Jaws of Life.

"No, sir, single occupant. Male, I think. It's not looking good."

"Were you the first officer on scene?" Adams asked, taking out his notebook.

"Yes, Sir, me and Garda Stewart over there. He's with the truck driver."

In the grass margin, a heavy man in his late fifties was sobbing, while a uniformed Garda patted him on the back. Adams took down the name and badge numbers of both officers, and made a quick diagram of the crash site. Detective Adams didn't venture into the rescue area, knowing the technical officers would want it as untouched as possible.

"Did anyone get see the incident happen?" Adams asked, when his drawing was finished.

"A Mrs Lucy was driving that blue Micra. She was directly behind the truck when the crash took place. She saw the whole thing."

Detective Adams made a quick assessment of the small blue car parked neatly in the hard shoulder. He couldn't see any sign of damage.

"Where is she now?"

"She is in the ambulance parked at the front of the truck."

"Was she injured?" Adams asked.

"No, just badly shaken. She is well into her sixties. In fairness to her, she was the only one that tried to help the guy in the car. The truck driver was sitting right where he is now when we arrived. We found Mrs. Lucy lying under the truck, doing her best."

"A tough old girl, it would seem," said Adams. He walked around the perimeter of the wreck to find the ambulance in question. He soon spotted Mrs. Lucy. She was a white haired lady, as small as a sparrow, sitting up on the stretcher, her mouth covered with an oxygen mask and a blanket wrapped around her shoulders. Her jacket and blouse were stained with motor oil from lying under the crashed car. Detective Adams knocked on the open door.

"Mrs. Lucy, my name is Detective Adams. I am the investigating officer for this incident. Do you feel up to answering a few questions?"

The paramedic looked annoyed. "Mrs. Lucy has had quite a shock, detective."

Mrs. Lucy rested a liver-spotted hand on the medic's arm. "It's okay, love. He has a job to do. It's better to ask now. At my age, I might have forgotten it all by tomorrow," she said, her words muffled by the oxygen mask. She pulled the mask down, so she could talk better. The paramedic stopped the hissing oxygen with a twist of a red knob.

"Ask away, detective," Mrs. Lucy said.

"Did you have a clear view of the crash when it happened?"

"I did. I saw the whole thing."

"Could you describe what took place, in your own words, Mrs. Lucy?" Adams had his little notebook at the ready.

"I was driving in the slow lane behind the truck. I was keeping well back, because those things are always throwing up stones. I saw a silver car coming up in my mirror. It was going fast in the outside lane, but there was a van ahead of me in the overtaking lane, doing about fifty. When the silver car was level with me, he pulled in beside the truck. That was when it happened."

"That was when the car hit the truck?"

"No, that was when the wheel came off."

"Before the car and the truck collided?"

"Yes detective. As the car pulled into the middle lane, the front passenger wheel seemed to wobble a bit. Then it just came off and bounced down the road. The front of the car hit the ground and went sideways under the truck. It got trapped in the back wheels and was dragged up the motorway. I saw what was happening and pulled my car onto the hard shoulder. The silver car was mangled by the time the truck stopped."

"No other car tipped off the silver car that you saw?"

"No, it happened for no reason. The van on the outside lane kept driving. I heard more crashes, but I didn't see them."

"You've done very good to remember so much, Mrs. Lucy. I understand that you tried to assist the person in the car."

"I did, the poor thing, but it was too late. He was already dead by then."

"What made you think that?"

Mrs. Lucy gave a little chuckle. "All you see is a silly old lady, Detective Adams. I was a nurse for nearly forty years and have seen more dead people than you've had dinners. When a head is twisted completely in the wrong direction and hanging like a discarded yo-yo, the outlook isn't good."

"Sorry, Mrs. Lucy, I should have known better," said Adams with a smile. Once he had all the important information recorded in his notebook, Adams handed Mrs. Lucy his contact card. "I'd like you to come down to the station when you're feeling up to making a full statement, if that's okay?" She nodded and replaced her oxygen mask. She looked tired, but her mind was razor sharp.

Adams liked Mrs. Lucy. One tough little lady, indeed. He walked back toward the rear of the crash, skirting between the tape and the slow-moving motorists. He could see a van with *Technical Division* stenciled on the side had arrived and parked near his own car. A team of men in white, now added to the crowd standing outside the tape. They were already on the job, taking photos of the scene even while the emergency crews were working. Some press people had appeared and were filming. The last thing anyone needed was pictures of this showing up on the news, before he'd got a chance to inform the next of kin. It would make things a dozen times worse for them.

Adams was distracted when a passing car veered directly at him. The driver was busily trying to see what was happening, not watching where he was going. The driver saw Adams just in the nick of time and wrenched his wheel to the right. Adams pounded the bonnet with his fist, as the front bumper passed inches from his leg.

"Gobshite!" he shouted at the driver. Goddamn rubberneckers were lethal. People were ghouls.

"Lads," Adams shouted at the men in white. "Can you get the screens up before one of these fools kills someone? And can someone get those cameras out of here, please?"

In minutes, a portable screen was erected, blocking the view of the rescue attempt from passing traffic. The press were herded right back to the edge of the incident area, objecting strongly as they went. Everyone knew it was less a rescue operation and more a body recovery by now.

Adams interviewed the truck driver, or at least tried. The man wasn't much help. He said the first thing he knew about anything was when he felt the car hit his trailer. That was as far as his story went, because he started blubbering and had to be given tranquilisers by the doctor on site. The truck was fully loaded, carrying over forty tonnes of cattle feed. Nothing was going to stop that weight.

Eventually, the driver's body was freed from the silver car. Mrs. Lucy had been right; the young man never stood a chance. The body was loaded on an ambulance, which drove away under blue lights. The technical boys were now allowed to examine the car, while the firemen took a break. A little over an hour later, the car was winched free of the truck. More patrol units arrived, and Adams sent the extra officers to take details on other crash victims. Thankfully, today only one name would be added to the list of road deaths: Tony Kelly.

Adams found the head technician photographing gouge marks in the tarmac a hundred yards behind the truck.

"The eyewitness said the front wheel fell off the car before the crash. Have you heard anything like that before?" Adams said, kneeling to get a better look at the marks on the road.

"Can't say I have. Blowouts, yes. A wheel falling off, no."

"She seemed like a reliable witness. Keep it in mind when you're looking at the wreck."

"Did she happen say how the silver car was driving?"

"She said it was coming fast in the outer lane, then it made a sharp lane change. That was when the wheel came off, and the car went under the truck."

"We'll let you know what we come up with," the technician said, starting to take photos once more.

It was another hour before the wreckage of the silver Toyota was loaded on the back of a flatbed truck and taken to the technical lockup for a detailed examination. The lorry was photographed and examined at the scene before being driven away by a Garda driver. Tony Kelly was on his way to the hospital, not that it would do him any good. The next bit was the hardest part. Adams braced himself to contact the young man's family.

This part of the job was enough to make him consider leaving the force and taking up gardening, or something equally dull. He reviewed his notes, making a few final scribbles. Tony Kelly, age twenty-four, never to see twenty-five. What a waste, he said to himself. Beside the name was a home address on the west side of the city. He sat in his car and called control. He gave them the address and requested a woman officer, with counselling experience, to attend with him. As he started the car, a fireman was sweeping the last of the glass off the road. Once that was gone, no sign would remain of what had happened. Adams thought the world should be different somehow, or should it? For the Kellys, nothing would ever be the same after today. He knew he was about to wreak havoc on their lives. It was turning into one of those days where he wished he'd stayed in bed.

Chapter 10

If Tim mentioned the London trip one more time, Martha was going to strangle him. Some guy in Cork should have been going, but he broke his leg playing football. One call from head office, and Tim jumped to attention. He practically bounced into the kitchen after work, unable to keep the news to himself. Sometimes he reminded her of a toddler, an annoying one, at that. Tim said it looked even better, because he had been able to step in at the last minute. He thought he was so clever, making a song and dance about leaving Martha home alone in the process, appearing to make an even-greater sacrifice. He was even more delighted when they offered to make the airplane ticket for two. Tim genuinely thought Martha would be delighted with the prospect of a trip to London. What she actually felt was that it showed just how little Tim knew her.

Yes, Martha would love a trip to London, but not to attend some banker conference. London was for shopping, seeing West End shows, and expensive meals. What Tim was offering was more like a prison sentence than a holiday. She had been dragged along to these things before, and they sucked. Stuck in a hotel room for hours on end, no one to talk to, no one to go anywhere with. Then there were the corporate dinners. What a nightmare they turned out to be! Pinned between lecherous drunks and stuffed shirts, Martha couldn't figure which type she despised more. Nope, like it or not, Tim was going to London alone. She had to find the right time to break it to him. They hadn't gotten to the stage in their marriage that allowed her the luxury of complete and open honesty. Telling Tim would result in a row and days of sulking. Martha was sure she'd find a way out if it; she just had to seize the right opportunity.

Tonight Tim had even more folders with him than usual. He didn't even eat with her. Martha took her plate and ate alone in front of the TV. The news came on just as she finished her meal. The horrific image of the silver car, twisted beyond recognition under the rear wheels of a truck, was awful. Why do they insist on showing stuff like that at dinnertime?

She washed the dishes and tidied the kitchen. The evening was delightful, a perfect summer day for a walk on the beach or a barbecue. She looked at Tim working away, still in his suit, and knew there was no chance of either happening. She looked out the kitchen window at the back garden. She noticed how wild it was looking, realising that she'd been neglecting it lately. Weeds were popping up everywhere, some bigger than the flowers struggling to bloom. Compared to the incessant clicking of Tim's calculator, weeding seemed like a pleasant option. When gardening looks attractive to a girl, something's got to give.

She changed into old clothes and opened the little timber shed at the bottom of the garden. She pulled out the wheelbarrow, still loaded with tools from a few weeks ago. There were some dried-up husks of weeds littering the bottom of the barrow that she had forgotten to dump the last time. Martha pulled on her gardening gloves and set to work. Physical labour was somehow soothing, like meditation. Martha was deep in thought as she tore the dandelions out of the ground, tossing them into a wheelbarrow on top of their mummified cousins. She couldn't stop thinking about the trip to London.

Tim said she would go, without even checking with her. She ripped a plant from the ground.

He could have called her. Another weed had life yanked out of it.

He should have asked. A nettle died a violent death.

Martha was getting more and more annoyed as the one-sided argument dominated her brain. The evening sunshine was warm, making her sweat. She sat back on her haunches, taking a breather. From the corner of her eye, she noticed the curtains in the upstairs window of Ogie's house stir. She continued her chore, pretending she hadn't seen the movement but kept a discreet watch on the window. The curtain moved again. Martha was sure of it this time. She thought she could see a person hovering just out of view.

She stood and pushed the barrow a few feet farther along the fence separating the two properties. She hoped Ogie was watching, not Annabelle. Martha dropped the barrow and rubbed away the sweat from her brow. She was feeling hot, so hot, in oh-so-many ways. Martha pulled the ends of her white blouse free of her jeans, turning slightly toward the window as she ripped the shirt studs open, using the tails of the open shirt to waft cool air across her naked belly. The middle of her tiny lace bra was revealed, cupping her boobs expertly into perfect cleavage. Her skin was blemish-free and lightly tanned, her tummy completely flat, with the hint of washboard muscle lurking underneath. Martha was proud of her figure, even though she would have liked bigger boobs.

She gathered the ends of the shirt, rolled them together and knotted them tightly under her breasts, doing up only one higher button, to keep the thing together. She returned to the job in hand, this time standing rather than kneeling. As she worked, she swayed, keeping her long legs planted about a foot apart. She rolled her hips as she reached farther into the flower bed. It was an uncomfortable way to work, but her stance was loaded with suggestion. It was a pose of exposure, a stance of wanton abandon. She could feel eyes on her, moving over her body, taking in the full roundness of her ass. Those eyes could belong to either Annabelle or Ogie; it didn't matter anymore. It might be even more exciting to think of a woman spying on her, indulging in forbidden fantasy. Martha imagined what he or she might be doing while they watched, and got even more excited herself. The cool evening air tickled her bare skin, making tiny hairs quiver. It seemed weeding could be quite a turn-on, after all. When the sun sank low in the sky, Martha decided she had enough and went back inside.

"What were you doing, honey?" Tim asked.

"Weeding."

"Hum," he said.

She knew he wasn't listening. She should have said, "Waving my ass at the new neighbour" to see what he'd say then. Probably, "Hum."

Martha went to the sink and washed her hands, scrubbing the clay from under her nails. She popped a bottle of beer, placing it beside Tim, and poured a glass of wine for herself. She resigned herself to another night alone in front of the telly. She was thinking about the trip to London, but a tingle between her legs was too much to ignore.

"I am going for a shower, Tim. Are you coming?"

"Wish I could, babe, but I have too much to do."

Martha smiled to herself. This time, she knew the climax of the night was in her own hands. She climbed the stairs two at a time.

Chapter 11

Angie was fluttering around the near-empty café, wiping down tables, when a news programme came on the TV. The night had been very quiet. Angie wondered why the owner persisted with opening in the evening at all. Tonight there had been only one customer, an older man eating pasta and reading a book. He ate slowly. Angie felt sorry for him. He looked like he'd nowhere better to go and no one to care where he went. She happened to glance at the TV when a car appeared on the screen, mangled under the wheels of a lorry. God help whoever was in that, she thought. Something about the image poked at her memory. She moved closer to the TV, noticing the red parcel shelf hanging askew from the back window, as if it were a panting dog's tongue. Tony drove a silver car.

Angie's eyes grew wide, remembering the fuss he'd made the day she'd glued red novelty material on the back window shelf of his car. She thought it looked cool; he'd said it was girly. The lone customer nearly choked on his pasta when she started screaming. The chef came rushing into the restaurant. Despite their efforts, the waitress wouldn't stop screaming. With no idea what to do, the customer called the emergency number and gave the address of the café. The chef was from someplace in China and only knew a few words of English. Angie was still howling when a squad car pulled up outside, soon joined by an ambulance, as the customer had told the emergency operator that a girl was having a fit.

A female officer tried to calm the girl, and eventually got her to drink some tea, while her colleague contacted the owner of the café. The ambulance left, as it was clear Angie wasn't actually having a seizure. It was difficult to understand what had caused the girl's meltdown. She kept saying the name "Tony" and something about silver and red. It was all too much for her. The officer thought she might be having some type of mental breakdown, or a bad trip. He checked her arms for track marks and her pupils for dilation, but she was clean. As the warm tea worked its magic, Angie became more lucid. Slowly, the officer pieced together what had happened. Tony was her boyfriend. The girl had seen a car crash on the TV and was sure it was the boyfriend's car. Whether she was right or wrong, Angie was in no state to be left here alone, never mind continuing to work. The officers decided it was best for her to go home.

Angie didn't want to go. She wanted to be taken to the scene of the crash, so she could know for sure. The officer tried to explain that wasn't possible. Everything would've been taken away by now.

"Do you have a car?" asked the female officer. Angie shook her head, sending tears sliding sideways across her cheeks.

"How do you get to work?"

"Bus," she sniffled.

There was no way she was able to manage a bus ride home, so the officer got her address and phone number. She rang the house and spoke to Angie's mother. With nobody available to pick her up, the officers had no choice but to drop the girl off at Honeysuckle Lane. During the journey, Angie began shaking, as her body went into shock, the officers wrapped a blanket around her to keep her warm. Mary Sweeney was waiting at the house when the squad car pulled up.

"You may need to get a doctor for her," advised the female Garda, as she handed over Angie.

Mary folded the sobbing girl into her loving arms and hurried her inside. "Thanks," she said over her shoulder to the departing officers.

Once inside, Angie's defences crumbled entirely. Her body shook with enormous sobs. The only thing Mary could do was hold her little girl and let her cry.

"Tony's dead," Angie bawled.

"We don't know anything for sure yet, sweetheart," Mary soothed.

"I spoke to him a few hours ago. He was playing a match tonight. Now his phone is off. I've tried a dozen times to ring him. It must be him."

"You don't know anything for sure, baby. There are thousands of cars just like his on the roads, and there might be any reason for his phone being off. If it was Tony in the accident, he could be perfectly fine. We've got to keep hoping for the best."

Mary had seen the pictures on TV, and if Tony's car were involved, she knew they needed a miracle, not hope. Mary suggested they try and call Tony at home. A neighbour picked up the phone and explained that the police were there.

When Mary hung up, she broke the news to Angie, and cried as she saw her daughter go to pieces in front of her eyes. The house was filled with grief, so bitter, so deep, it could only flow from the broken heart of youth. Mary rocked her daughter for a long time as she poured out her pain. Tony was a nice young man. Mary had met him a few times. She never thought he was The One, but tragedy seemed to make love deeper and faults vanish. Angie was at that age where life is its most vibrant. Young love burns fierce, but like all such flames, it vanishes quickly. Mary worried for her little girl. Angie had a flinty exterior, but it was only that, a façade. Mary knew her daughter was a tender girl at heart. No child thinks a parent can understand them. The truth is, a parent understands like no one else can.

Billy was in his room. Pat was still at work, so they had the place to themselves. Eventually, Angie's sobs died into sniffles. Mary gave her a brandy and had a large one for herself. Angie sipped the golden liquid, letting melancholy settle heavily on her shoulders. Angie said she knew nothing would ever make her smile again; her love had been crushed by an eighteen wheeler. It sounded like a lyric from a country-music song.

"Why don't I make you a bath?" suggested Mary. Angie nodded, weary from loss.

Mary went upstairs and started the water flowing. She added a good dollop of bubble bath she kept hidden for herself and turned on the emersion to heat more water. Soon, the little bathroom was filled with a cloud of sweet-smelling steam. Mary led Angie upstairs. She heard her girl slip into the water, making a noise somewhere between a sigh and a sob. Mary knocked and pushed the door open a little. She laid a stack of towels on the laundry basket and picked up Angie's work clothes.

"Call if you need anything," she said, closing the door, giving her girl space and time to grieve.

When Pat eventually came home, he thought the whole thing was being blown out of proportion.

"Christ, Mary, they've only known each other a wet week," he said, leaning against the cooker, covered in concrete dust.

"That's not the point," snapped Mary, sounding tired and cranky. She bit her tongue. The last thing Angie need was their arguing again.

"What's for dinner?" he asked, opening the oven. His dim brain didn't register that his huge ass should have been on fire if the cooker was on.

"I've not had the chance to make anything. Why not have a few pints down the pub and a Chinese?"

Pat didn't have to be asked twice. Given the choice between teary women or the pub, there was no contest. Mary was glad he'd be out of the way. At times like this, Pat was neither use nor ornament. She rustled up chips and fish fingers for Billy; she couldn't get Angie to eat anything. Mary could hear Angie crying upstairs, and there was nothing she could do. It broke her heart.

Chapter 12

The alarm cut through Martha's dreams. Tim threw off the covers, flooding the bed with cold morning air. He opened the curtains. The sun was already up, despite the early hour. He kissed her on the forehead before peeing loudly in the bathroom en suite. She rolled over, burying her head into the pillow, trying to block out the sound. A rasping fart still managed to penetrate her sanctuary, making her grit her teeth.

Tim was sitting at the kitchen table, munching on toast, checking the news headlines on his laptop when she came downstairs. In the corner of the kitchen, a percolator bubbled, filling the kitchen with the aroma of brewing coffee. That smell was one of Martha's favourite things. Growing up in a cramped apartment deep in industrial Poland, their only luxury had been a coffeemaker. Every few weeks, her mother would buy fresh-ground coffee, and that smell would fill the apartment. Martha poured herself a cup and topped it with a dollop of whipped cream, the delicious smell bringing back memories of home.

Tim eventually looked up from his computer. "Terrible car crash on the motorway yesterday."

"I saw it on the news," Martha said, remembering the pictures.

"The police are treating it as suspicious," Tim said and read aloud the rest of the latest press. Soon the crash was lost among countless other baying headlines.

Martha had nearly finished her coffee when Tim said, "Will you ask Kevin for next week off? We need to get organised for the trip."

Kevin was Martha's boss, who, as it happened, Tim detested. The reason? Jealousy, pure and simple. Tim thought Kevin fancied her. Kevin did fancy her and made it very clear he'd like to do something about that feeling. Martha had no problem in handling Kevin. It annoyed her that Tim didn't think she was capable of making her own decisions, that she would be swayed by every man that looked at her with lustful eyes. She wished he could spend one day in her body; then he would know that happened to her a thousand times a day. However did she resist them all? It was typical of a man to think that a woman was ignorant of such things. Women are the masters of reading signals.

"Sure," Martha said, with no intention of asking at all.

She wasn't going to London, and that was that. She refilled her coffee and took it upstairs with her to dress. Martha was looking forward to today because she'd arranged to meet Ann for lunch. Ann was her best friend and had been maid of honour at her wedding. She dressed in a tailored pantsuit and an open-necked blouse finished with a gold-and-diamond pendant. She looked great, and she knew it.

"Are you ready?" Tim shouted from the bottom of the stairs. It was still only 7:15 a.m., but he was itching to leave. Martha would be hanging around for nearly forty minutes, waiting for her office to open, all because Tim liked being early.

"I'm coming," she snapped, descending the stairs. Her outfit wasn't lost on Tim. His eyebrows arched.

"Lunch with Ann," she said, by way of explanation.

"You look lovely," he said with a smile, but behind it, Martha could see nervousness in his eyes. Tim's growing insecurities were getting to her. She'd done everything she could to make him believe she was trustworthy, and she was trustworthy. No matter what she said or did, he worried. At first, it was nice, but now, it was plain irritating. He always needed to be with her, and it was suffocating. She knew if they were going to survive as a married couple, things would have to change.

The journey into the city passed in comparative silence, the radio filling the void. Tim dropped her within walking distance of her office, but it was still only eight. She had a key for the office but didn't see why she should be at her desk an hour before she was being paid.

Martha passed the time by reading a magazine and sipping coffee in a café surrounded by morning commuters. She missed living in Dublin city; it had a life of its own. The streets were veins that surged with people—rich, poor, elegant, grubby—and they all had a place. She needed to feel the grit of the city under her nails again, to get down and dirty in humanity. At a quarter to nine, she folded her magazine and walked the short distance to her office.

Martha arrived bang on time, taking up her position at the reception desk as the phone rang for the first time. The work was tedious and thankless. Kevin swaggered in at ten to ten.

Throwing his coat across the photocopier, he winked at Martha. "Morning, sexy."

"Morning, Kevin," she replied. The truth about Kevin was, he wasn't terrible-looking, and he wasn't even that lecherous. He just tried too hard. Kevin was always going to be a little fish in a very little pond; even he knew that deep down. He spent way too long hanging around her desk and far too little time working, but that was his problem, not hers. Martha liked Kevin and didn't mind his crude jibes too much.

Martha had no intention of mentioning the London trip to him, mostly because she was afraid he might give her the time off. As it happened, a big contract came in that morning, which would mean overtime. It was a gift from the gods. It gave her the ideal reason to stay home. When lunchtime approached, she knocked on Kevin's door.

"Come in."

Martha opened the door and dropped some faxes on his desk. "Is it okay if I take an extra hour for lunch? I'll make it up during the week."

"I can't see why not, but you owe me one," he said with a wink.

"I'll be as quick as I can, Kevin, thanks," Martha said, rushing out the door without the slightest intention of coming back a minute before necessary.

Ann had chosen a fantastic bistro by the canal. Elegant tables occupied an expanse of granite paving between the canal and the restaurant. Waiters in ankle-length aprons danced a practiced tango between the tables, silver salvers flashing in the midday sunshine. It was slightly chilly in the brisk breeze, even so all the tables were occupied. A single gull perched on a concrete bollard; colourful narrow boats chugged past sedately.

Martha scanned the tables, searching for Ann. When she spotted her sitting alone at a table near the water's edge, Martha felt like running over and hugging her. The feeling shocked her. She hadn't realised just how starved of friendship she was becoming. Ann saw her and waved. She was wearing a beautiful sweater with a diving neckline framing her perfect cleavage. Everything she wore accented her perfect cleavage. As she crossed to the table, Martha felt men's eyes following her.

"It's been so long. How have you been, girl?" said Ann when Martha sat down.

"Way too long. This place is divine! However did you find it?"

Ann smiled a wicked grin. "I have my ways. Do you have to go back after lunch, or can we squeeze in some retail therapy?"

"You never know. Traffic might be murder." Martha laughed.

A waiter appeared at the table with a bottle of wine and some menus. "I hope you don't mind, but I ordered a bottle for us," said Ann.

"When have I ever refused a glass of wine?" Martha giggled, holding out her glass. The cute waiter filled up their glasses and left the menus open on the table.

"So, what's good to eat?" asked Martha.

"Everything, darling, particularly the waiters," Ann said with a giggle.

"Ann, you're wicked!"

Over lunch, they discussed old friends and even-older enemies. Since Martha had left the hotel, Ann had been promoted to front-office manager. She loved her new position, but she missed the rapport with the girls on the desk. The rarefied heights of middle management were not all they were cracked up to be, but the money was good. Martha missed being part of a team as well. It highlighted how isolated she had become since she had married Tim. Hearing about babies and parties people were having left her green with envy. Each story felt like a tiny sting.

At last, the conversation turned away from the goings-on at the hotel and focused on Martha. Compared to the hustle and bustle of Ann's life, Martha's seemed positively dreary.

"How's Tim?" asked Ann.

Martha shuffled the salad around her plate, trying to find the words to answer. It was plain to see the stress etched on Martha's face, and Ann was concerned before Martha had a chance to say a word. Ann had never been a huge fan of Tim's. She'd always thought the whole thing would end in tears.

"Want to talk about it?" Ann asked after a moment.

Martha didn't respond straightaway. As long as the problem was only in her mind, it mightn't be real. For some reason, Martha was sure if she began talking about her feelings out loud, the whole sorry mess would condense into a huge millstone, dragging her marriage to the bottom of a sea of tears. In the end, her need to unburden herself overshadowed any fears she held.

"I think I have made a terrible mistake," Martha said at last, setting down her fork. Ann sat back, waiting for the rest of the story. She knew Martha well enough to know once the first breach of her defences appeared, it would not take long before the wall burst and the whole thing would come flooding out.

"Tim's so boring," Martha said after a moment's thought. "We do nothing anymore, at least, nothing I want to do."

"Have you talked to him about it?" Ann asked, easing into her role as sounding board.

"That's the worst part. I'm not sure I want to," Martha said. The genie was out of the bottle, good and proper. Martha felt tears welling up in her eyes, but she managed to hold them in check.

"Every couple has hiccups. Getting used to having a person in your life isn't easy," Ann said, despite her reservations about Tim. Ann thought he'd rushed Martha into marriage, sweeping her along so she wouldn't have time to see what was happening. He was still a nice man, and being a bit bored wasn't the end of the world.

"Perhaps. I don't know. I'm not sure. I'm not sure of anything," Martha said. She lost the war with her tears and felt them cascade freely down her face. She dabbed them away with her napkin, smudging her makeup. Martha tried to regain control with a few deep breaths and folded her hands in her lap while Ann took a sip of her wine and looked sadly at her. Martha had no idea where the conversation was going or what was going to come out of her mouth next. It was an unnerving feeling not to be in control of your own mind and body. She looked forlornly at her oldest friend, hoping she'd find some answers in her concerned face. It took a second for her brain to realise she was speaking again. Martha heard the words tumble from her lips and was as surprised as anyone to hear them.

"The only thing I'm sure of is that I'm miserable, and that has to change."

"Babes, if being married to Tim is making you this unhappy, you can do something about it. What's the worst that would happen if you left him?"

"He's a good man, a very good man. I would be hard pushed to find someone who treats me better," said Martha, instinctively jumping to the defence of Tim and her decision in picking him.

"Are you trying to convince yourself or me?"

Martha said nothing. There was truth in both parts of that sentence.

"Tim is good at giving you things, but can he make you happy? Is he the man you'd want if both of you were penniless?"

"What are you saying? Are you calling me a gold digger?" Martha snapped, sensing an insult.

"God, no! Never! Look, Martha, I know how hard things were for you. It's a very easy to get security and love mixed up. Tim was, and is, the safe choice, as much from an emotional point of view as any other. You knew he'd never let you down. We all have to make compromises when it comes to choosing people. I just don't think you gave enough thought to your own feelings when you said yes to Tim."

Martha looked around. Things were ganging up on her, the words and the advice. It was all too much too soon. She needed time to think. She hadn't intended on making life-changing decisions over lunch. Could the world change so much between the starter and dessert? Perhaps the changes had been happening all along, and she hadn't noticed.

She took a sip of her wine and scanned the tables. Like a beacon, a couple in the corner stood out. It was the way they looked at each other. They had eyes for no one else. That was what her heart wanted, but her mind was too cynical for all that clichéd rubbish. You can't eat love; it won't keep the rain off your head. Love makes things complicated. Having said that, a life without love was a daunting prospect. Martha knew she had settled for a marriage of like, not love. The question now was, would it be a decision she could live with?

"You might have a point," Martha conceded. "Don't get me wrong: I'm not ready to throw in the towel. What I'm saying is that I need things to change, and I've to figure out a way of changing things without destroying what I have in the process."

Ann gave a short laugh. "If you figure that out, write a book and make a million."

The joke broke the tension, and Martha smiled. "I just might, you know. Tim's going to London next week. Could we go out one night, some girl time? I think I need to let my hair down."

"Best idea you've had all day," said Ann, beaming from ear to ear.

Chapter 13

About the time Martha was saying her good-byes to Ann, Frank O'Shea was watching a horse he'd backed come in dead last, again. He'd been backing long shots all afternoon in the hopes of getting one big win. He crumpled yet another betting slip and let it fall from his hand. The floor was swimming in discarded betting slips, like a sea of broken dreams. Frank didn't think of himself as a bookie man. The places depressed him. They were dank and reeked of desperation. Mostly, it was the sight of the other customers that put him off. So many hopeless people shoehorned into one little room, the places sucked the life out of anyone that went inside their doors. No, Frank was a sporting man who happened to have had a bad run of luck. The only reason he was here at all was Harry bloody McCarthy. The man was a cancer on humanity, just as real and twice as dangerous. The thought of Harry and his looming deadline was making him desperate. In the last hour, Frank had seen a hundred euro disappear into the bookies' till, leaving him a hell of a lot worse than he'd been at the start of the day.

Three more days until his payment was due, and Frank hadn't a brass razoo. Richard had been no use. His current account was so far into the red, it practically glowed. Only one of his credit cards begrudgingly worked, and the euros were dribbling away on that. Frank's hand throbbed, reminding him that running was a painful option. He had been reduced to a mug's life of chasing long shots, praying for a big payout to save the day.

Frank should have been showing an apartment right about now, but the client cancelled on him at the last minute. Yet another disappointment in a disastrous day. Frank knew he was wasting his time showing houses to people most of the time; they either hadn't the means or the motivation to buy. With the latest letdown, the last chance of him making his commission flew out the window. He was sunk completely. He'd even started calling sellers, suggesting they should drop their prices if they wanted to make sales. He'd been on his way back to the office to call the apartment owner when he spotted the bookies. Before he knew what was going on, he was cheering on a horse in the one-fifty at Chepstow. That had been three races ago, and his wallet was now completely empty.

Frank approached the counter, where a heavy woman held out her pudgy hand to accept a winning slip.

"No luck this time," Frank said as cheerfully as he could.

"Next one might have your name on it," she said, withdrawing her hand.

"I've a horse running that I really fancy, but I left my bank card at home. Do you open accounts?" Frank asked.

The woman's face hardened, knowing what was coming. "No credit. Sorry, guy."

"Really, I come in here all the time. Just a small limit?"

"Nothing I can do. Sorry."

"My money was good enough, up to now," Frank said getting annoyed.

"If you'd won, we'd have paid out. Do you know how many people want to bet on credit? If we did that we would be the busiest bookies in town, and closed in a week."

"That's bullshit," snapped Frank backing away from the counter and storming out of the shop. Frank trudged towards the office in a black mood. He was more annoyed with himself than the woman behind the counter. Why'd he gone into that place at all, look at all the money he'd lost and what the hell was he thinking of looking for credit? He knew she wouldn't give him any. He'd sounded like a looser.

As he turned the corner he noticed a black BMW parked outside his office door. It stopped him in his tracks. He ducked into a shop and scanned the area. The car looked like Harry's but to be honest, Frank had been seeing Harry in every face he passed. He waited at the top of the road, looking for trouble, and watched for a while. Harry was nowhere to be seen, and the car was empty. Frank couldn't loiter in shops all day. Perhaps it wasn't Harry's, after all, but his gut twisted with anxiety. Frank made a dash for his office, his head swivelling on his shoulders, checking every doorway he passed for that ominous black jacket. He climbed the limestone steps to his office two at a time, bursting through the door and practically falling into then waiting area.

Inside, Harry and his mutt-ugly son were lounging on a sofa, each with a coffee steaming happily in front of him.

"I was just going to call you," said the office secretary. "Mr. McCarthy wants to view the house on Davis Road."

Harry said nothing but raised an eyebrow in amusement at the stuttering mess Frank had turned into.

"Ah, ah, I wish you'd called me, Betty. I've another viewing in half an hour," Frank said. "Perhaps someone else can take you?"

"Mr. Keating is going to do the Stackville Street viewing," Betty said unhelpfully.

"Isn't that grand?" said Frank, beaming a smile at Harry and getting a stony stare in return. "Let me get the keys."

Frank vanished into his office. He sat at his desk, trying to get his head around things. He still had two more days before his payment was due. Why was Harry here? Frank took the keys for the Davis Road property and braved the front office.

"Right you are, gents," Frank said, leading the way out. Harry and Chris fell in behind him.

Harry stopped beside his car. Frank walked toward his own.

"Why don't you ride with us?" Harry said.

"You're all right. I'll follow you," said Frank.

"Get in the car, Frank." Harry stood by the driver's door but didn't get in. There are requests, and then there are orders. This was an order. Frank walked back to the BMW and opened the passenger door. It took all his willpower to force his body into that seat. Chris tumbled into the back while Harry slid himself onto the comfortable leather of the driver's seat. Frank was so sure getting into this car would be the last thing he'd ever do, he couldn't get his shaking hand to pull the door closed.

"Shut the door like a good boy," said Harry. Frank eventually slammed the door closed and sealed his fate.

The leather was comfortable, which wasn't the way he imagined a gangster's death car should feel. A ride to a beating, or worse, shouldn't be cushioned by expensive heated seats. The harsh, cold metal of a van floor would be much more suitable to Frank's terror. He listened for the clank of iron bars in the boot but couldn't hear anything. What if there were shovels in there? Or a gun inside Harry's jacket? Why did he get into the car at all? Leather, heated or not, couldn't stifle the shiver that ran through his body. He had no idea what was coming, but it was going to hurt, and there was nothing he could do about it now.

"What's going on, Harry? Why are you here?"

"To see a house, Frank, and do a little business."

Frank could only sit and pray as the powerful car eased through the light traffic. To Frank's surprise, Harry eventually turned onto Davis Road and pulled up outside the dethatched Georgian house standing on a full acre of private garden that Frank was trying to sell. The asking price was two point three million euro.

"What's all this about, Harry?" Frank asked again, not believing for one minute that it was really about buying the house.

"I told you, I want to see this house. So why not do your job, or give me the keys and I'll take a look myself," Harry said without an ounce of humour.

Frank climbed from the car and opened the side gate. Harry and Chris followed along behind him. Frank walked up to the front door and rang the bell, but there was no answer. He flipped open his briefcase and took out the keys and alarm code. He slid a long brass key into the lock and twisted it. The door swung open silently, but seconds later, the air was filled with a high-pitched whistle. On the wall was a white alarm panel. Frank flipped down the plastic cover and punched in the code he had written on a tag attached to the key. A long beep told him the system was disabled. Harry and Chris followed him inside.

"Lead on, McDuff, and don't rush. We want the full tour," said Chris, speaking for the first time since they had left the office.

Frank showed them through the whole house. It wasn't a quick showing. Chris and Harry looked at everything. Frank noticed both men kept their hands firmly wedged in their pockets. In the end, they seemed satisfied.

"Give us a minute, Frank," said Harry as the two men left the house. Frank stayed behind to lock up. They leaned against their car, talking. After a few minutes, they got in and started the engine. Frank walked out the side gate and got into the backseat with reluctance.

"Are you interested in the house?" he asked.

Chris turned around in his seat and said, "We're very interested, Frank. Couldn't you tell?"

"It's on the market at two point three million, but if you went with an offer of one point nine, you might clinch it," Frank said. Could it be possible they weren't pulling his leg, after all? The commission on a sale this big would solve everything. Harry would end up paying himself off.

"Chris said we were interested in the house. He never said we intended paying for it," said Harry without turning around, his fingers tapping on the steering wheel angrily.

"I'm not with you."

"Have you got my money, Frank?"

"It's not Friday yet," Frank said, his voice choking a little.

"That's a no," said Harry with a sigh. "I can see this is going to get messy for you."

"Don't worry, Harry, I'll have it by Friday," Frank rushed to reassure him.

"I'm not worried. You should be. How's the hand?"

Frank said nothing, but the threat was clear. "I'll have it," he said quietly.

"How would you like to make your eight hundred euro interest payment?" asked Harry.

"I'm listening," said Frank, wary of a trick.

"Give me a copy of that key and security code. Not much for eight hundred," said Chris.

"You're going to rob the place!"

"Spot on, Frank. Welcome to the conversation," said Chris, his voice heavy with sarcasm.

"I can't do that. You're crazy."

"We are going to do it, Frank, with or without you," said Harry. "We've seen all we needed today. The only difference is, with the code and key, it will be a little quicker, a little quieter. That is worth eight hundred euro to us."

Frank said nothing. He was having difficulty coming to terms with the jam he had gotten himself into. He was in debt up to his eyeballs, and now it looked like he was going to be dragged into a burglary. He couldn't do it. No way.

"Tell you what, Frank," said Harry. "You think about it on the way back to the office."

"Okay," Frank spoke into his chest.

The car ticked over but didn't move. After a few seconds, the car was still standing stock still. Frank lifted his eyes from the floor and looked straight into Harry's eyes, which had taken on a sheen of madness. "Out!" he barked.

Frank threw himself out of the car. He was hardly clear when Harry put his foot down and speed away in a squeal of rubber. Frank had a five-mile walk ahead of him to think of a way to get out of Harry's proposition.

Chapter 14

Detective Adams was reading over the witness statement Mrs. Lucy had given earlier in the day. His impression of the woman only had been reinforced. She'd recounted the whole event nearly word for word as she had on the day of the crash. Mrs. Lucy still was absolutely certain that the wheel of the Toyota had fallen off, causing the wreck. As soon as he'd finished reviewing the details, he added the statement to the growing folder of paperwork being garnered on Tony Kelly's case. Adams intended to contact the technical unit next and see what information they'd gathered from the examination of the crashed car.

He was about to dial the forensics division when his mobile rang. "Detective Adams," he said, distractedly holding the phone in one hand.

"Detective Adams, this is James from forensics. We spoke yesterday at the car crash on the motorway, the silver Toyota Celica."

"I was just going to call you. What did you come up with?" said Adams, flopping back into his swivel chair.

"The full report will be sent over later today, but the long and short of it is, the crash wasn't an accident."

"That tallies with witness accounts of the incident. Have you confirmed it beyond doubt?"

"The front passenger wheel had been deliberately interfered with. Three of the four nuts had been removed and were not found at the crash scene."

"Is there any possibility that they fell off earlier in the journey?"

"One nut, sure. Three, very doubtful, but that's not why we're sure it was deliberate interference."

"Go on, I'm listening," said Adams, fishing a pen from his desk drawer.

"What we found at the crash site were the decorative nut covers that should have been covering the wheel nuts. The car had a set of custom-alloy wheels; the steel nuts are covered with chrome vanity caps. Three of the caps had traces of superglue. The glue wasn't fully set. It had been applied to the nut covers within twenty-four hours of the crash."

"Let me get this straight: Someone removed three nuts and glued the empty covers back in place?"

"Correct, detective. The wheel hub shows residue of glue over three of the nut holes. The damaged section of the wheel had no glue residue. Because only one nut was holding the wheel on, it was under considerable strain. When the driver made his aggressive overtaking manoeuvre, the one remaining nut sheared off."

"When will the full report be ready?"

"It should be on your desk first thing tomorrow."

"Thanks for that, James. Talk to you soon," Adams said, hanging up.

Adams tapped his pen against the growing pile of paperwork. Okay, he thought, what are the facts? This wasn't an accident. Could it have been human error? It didn't seem likely. The glue residue made the element of premeditation clear. Was it murder? It could have been manslaughter, a lazy tyre change in a cheap garage, but again, an unlikely angle. Adams ran the facts over and over again in his mind, and each time he came up with only one answer. Someone wanted to hurt Tony Kelly and hurt him bad.

What about the victim? Was there something Adams wasn't seeing there? Junior accountant, nothing particularly responsible. His bank account was skinny but not starving; no big transactions in the last six months. A few small loans, all paid up to date. Nothing to indicate he was in financial hardship. That left Tony's family, friends, and lovers. Did any of them have a reason to want to hurt the young man? There was only one way to find out. It was time to get to know Tony Kelly a bit better.

Adams went to the chief inspector's office to update him on the information he had just received. When he walked out of the inspector's office half an hour later, he found he was heading up a small investigation team. Tony Kelly's death was now officially being treated as suspicious. The team that the chief had assigned to Adams consisted of Detective Joan Sims, Detective Kevin Dolan, and himself.

Sims was a recently promoted officer and still wet behind the ears, but eager to make a big impression. Adams had worked with her once or twice recently and found her clever and hardworking. Dolan, on the other hand, had plenty of experience at twenty years older than Adams, but was too close to retirement to care all that much about chasing bad guys. He was a clock watcher.

Adams knew it was pointless to try to get more people on the case. The powers that be only took out the cheque book when a case made the front page of the newspapers. This one was chicken feed, the same as the team he'd been given.

Adams called the Kelly family and arranged to meet them a little later. Dolan was out sick today, but Sims was around the station somewhere. Adams tried her mobile and found it powered off. He left a message on her desk, telling her to follow him to the Kellys' address, and left the station alone.

The traffic was surprisingly light, and for once, he wished it had been fierce. He was dreading looking into Mrs. Kelly's eyes, already brimming with pain, only to add more suffering. Having to tell her that Tony's death hadn't been an accident was going to be incredibly hard. They were good people who did nothing to deserve such heartache, as far as he knew.

He knew he would need to question them about Tony's life, his friends, his enemies, his problems, and his everything. It would be like raising Tony from the dead, only to bury him over and over again. Above all, he knew it had to be done. In that house might be the first clue to catching Tony's killer. Others mightn't recognise the tiny piece of information that could unlock the secret of Tony's death, but he was good at spotting the wrinkle in the fabric of life, the part where the two edges of reality nearly joined but not quite. It might be a letter, a strange phone call, a new friend, an old grudge, a bad habit. Adams had no idea what it might be, but he'd find it. He had to find it, because once a man started killing, not much would stop him. Someone had done this to Tony Kelly. Someone had taken his life, and that someone had to be caught.

The miles vanished with worrying ease. Things were going too well; it gave him the shivers. When he got to the Kelly's house, it was a veritable hive of activity. Neighbours and family members were coming in waves, breaking on the walls of their grief, wearing them down, lulling them with normality. Adams waited outside, gathering his thoughts. He took only a moment. His path mightn't be easy, but it was clear. He squared his shoulders and approached the door. It was ajar, but he knocked, anyway. Mr. Kelly opened it, two days' beard growth on his chin and a world of pain in his eyes.

"Mr. Kelly, I'm Detective Adams. I called earlier."

"I remember you," he said in a tired way, not friendly, not hostile, either. "I'll never be able to forget," he added, the weight of the world in his words.

"I need to speak with you and your family. There are details to discuss."

"Come in," he said, standing aside.

"It would be better if it were just close family, if you don't mind."

"Okay," he said, his forehead creased. Mr. Kelly knew there was something coming, and it wasn't just a discussion of details. Adams waited in the sitting room while the Kellys saw their callers out. It was just Mr. and Mrs. Kelly in the sitting room when Adams broke the news. What followed was everything he dreaded: Mrs. Kelly broke down completely while Mr. Kelly raged and then comforted his wife. Thousands of questions, with no answers to give, no answers needed. Adams let it all come out and gave as much sympathy as he could.

The arrival of Detective Sims was a godsend. Sims was in her midtwenties with a face that looked thirty. She had a sturdy build, like a female rugby player. She was lovely, actually, in the way aunties are lovely. The first thing she did was to go straight into the kitchen and make tea. She got Mrs. Kelly to show her where things were, distracting her from her grief. This gave Adams time alone with Mr. Kelly. He asked the questions he needed to ask, and Mr. Kelly answered them in a hollow voice from the depths of despair. It was not long before Adams was convinced that Tony—the whole Kelly family, for that matter—were perfectly normal. No history of criminality, no drugs that anyone knew of. No enemies, good jobs, a hardworking, loving family. Everything you'd want in your own family, but a nightmare for a detective working on a murder case.

Mr. Kelly took Adams upstairs and watched as he searched his son's belongings. Adams turned up nothing except a few porno magazines stashed under the bedside locker. Mr. Kelly laughed when Adams suggested getting rid of them before Mrs. Kelly saw them. "Sharon found them years ago. We had a right laugh over that. She never told Tony, because it would only embarrass him. He was a normal young lad. It would be weird if he didn't like a few naughty books."

Adams slid them back under the locker and scratched his head. Mr. Kelly was right. Nobody should have wanted to kill this kid. Adams would have to look further for an answer. Mr. Kelly gave him the names and numbers of Tony's mates and his girlfriend, Angie.

They went down to the kitchen, where they found Mrs. Kelly and Sims in the garden, looking at some potted plants. Mrs. Kelly was telling Sims in great detail about the flowers. Adams knew she was blocking everything out right now. It would be pointless and cruel to question her. He would do it tomorrow, or the next day if necessary. Adams was happy that Mr. Kelly had given him all the information he could right now.

When it was time to go, Adams told the Kellys how sorry he was and promised to do everything he possibly could to find who had done this to Tony. Mr. Kelly shook his hand on the way out the door and looked him directly in the eye. "You've to find him, to make sure he'll never do it again."

When the detectives were back on the pavement, Sims lost her motherly look and became all business. "Did you manage to turn up anything?"

"Nothing. They are so normal, it's abnormal."

"Same with her. What do you want to cover next? Friends, girlfriends, work?"

"Let's start with the friends." Adams split the list with Sims before heading off in separate directions, agreeing to meet back up at the office by six.

Chapter 15

Brendan was having a hard time concentrating. An open-plan office was never a private place, but today was beyond a joke. From a cubicle close by, the nasal braying of a woman cut through the air like a chainsaw. For twenty minutes, he'd been subjected to her one-sided conversation, and he was near the breaking point. What was worse, she occasionally burst into a snorting laugh that cleaved his thoughts like an axe. It seemed one voice in his brain wasn't enough torture.

Brendan's feeling of satisfaction at having gotten rid of his rival for Angie's affections had been short-lived. He had gotten very little sleep since the crash. Every time he tried to close his eyes, a thousand thoughts raced across his mind, waking him again. He felt weighed down by excitement, worry, and anticipation. The combination of emotions were frying his brain. Now, he was tired and irritable, and having difficulty containing his anger. In his weakened state, the voice inside had started to whisper at him more often until if felt like the voice plagued him twenty-four hours a day. It hinted he'd forgotten something, something trivial that would lead to his downfall.

At first, Brendan had been able to dismiss these accusations as natural doubts. He knew he'd been careful, sure in his own superiority, but the voice wouldn't let go. It poked and prodded, eating away at his confidence. He had mentally retraced his steps, trying to recall any slips he might have made. The more he thought about his actions, the more frustrated he became. What he had believed to be a perfect crime now seemed so full of holes, it was barely a plan at all.

Brendan massaged his temples, trying to control himself, but the annoying power of the woman's voice was unbelievable. Brendan glanced at the *Irish Times* on his screen. The story showing added to his distress: *"Car Crash Fatality Investigated As Suspicious."*

Members of the public are requested to contact the Store Street Gardaí Station if they were in the vicinity of Brady, McCarthy, and Doyle Accountancy Offices on Angier Street on Monday, 13 June, between the hours of ten a.m. and five p.m.

Brendan was worried. It wasn't just being caught that worried him. It was being caught before he was finished. He needed more time. He had things to do, things to conclude.

Perhaps he'd been noticed by some passerby, someone that knew him, or might recognise him from his daily commute? He had to admit it was possible but unlikely. He felt nothing for the man he'd killed besides a small level of satisfaction. He had been an obstacle, and now he wasn't. Brendan thought the chances of being caught were slender, but that didn't mean he could be complacent. Alone, people were stupid, easy to manipulate. En masse, they could be deadly. The clothes and tools in the sports bag back at his house were bothering him. They were the only things directly connecting him to the crash.

Sitting on his desk were three wheel nuts, lined up like little soldiers. He picked one up and ran it through his fingers, enjoying the cold, greasy feel of it. Another volley of honking laughter cut through his thoughts. Brendan dropped the nut on the desk. He had had enough. How could anyone be expected to concentrate?

He strode across the office, zeroing in on the source of the noise. A hefty woman in a cheap blue suit was swivelling in her chair, playing with the cord of her phone. Brendan entered her cubicle. Reaching across her, he slammed his finger on the cradle of the phone, terminating the call.

"What the hell?" She looked at him indignantly. Brendan felt hatred rise from his gut as he looked at her. He felt contempt for this miserable waste of a human life. Gripping the armrest of her chair, he spun her she so she must face him, his arms holding her captive. He leaned incredibly close, coming eye to eye with her. She leaned away from his face until her head touched the chair and could go no farther. Her expression changed from one of shock to one of fear. Brendan loved that look. He'd never caused anyone to be terrified in his life. It fueled his rage, and he loved the feeling of power.

"Stop your inane drivel, woman!" He spat in her face. His cold eyes held her gaze for a long time: eventually, he stood up and went back to his desk. The woman fled the office in floods of tears. At last, it was quiet, and Brendan could think.

He had been working only ten minutes when his phone rang, "Yes?" he snapped.

"Brendan, could you come to my office, please?" Brendan recognised the voice of Brian Pulter, the area manager.

"Can't it wait? I'm very busy right now."

"No, it can't wait."

"All right, I'm coming." He sighed, hanging up. Brendan took the lift up a few floors and walked along the corridor to the manager's office. The door normally stood open, but today it was closed, and the secretary's desk was vacant. Brendan's hand hovered over the handle. He wanted to walk in, but a simple door was holding him at bay. It galled him to knock, but knock he did.

"Come in."

Brendan opened the door and went inside. The first thing that struck him was how untidy the office was. He was left wondering how the man would work with a landslide of papers on his desk; it was such a mess. Brian Pulter wasn't paying attention to any of his accumulated files. He was sitting in his chair, waiting for Brendan.

"Sit down, please, Brendan," he said, gesturing to the seat on the far side of the desk.

"I'd rather stand. Will this take long?"

"That depends. What did you do to Janice?"

"Janice?"

"Yes, Brendan. Janice Potts."

Potts? That must be the lardy woman's name, not that her name mattered. None of them mattered, as long as they weren't getting in his way, or on his nerves.

"She was screaming into the phone, distracting everyone. I only did what you should have been doing, ensuring a constructive working environment. This is an office, after all, not some all-day social club," ranted Brendan.

Brian Pulter stiffened in his chair. Any conciliatory tone in his voice was gone when he next spoke.

"Ms. Potts happened to be on a call to a very important client. You could have lost us a great deal of business," Pulter said, leaning forward in his chair.

"Preposterous! Clients come to this company because of what I do, not to chitchat with the likes of her," Brendan said dismissively.

"Brendan, you've to remember you're part of a team. We all need to work together. Your behaviour was unacceptable. You'll have to apologise to Janice."

"I'll do no such thing. I've nothing to apologise for."

Pulter's voice was steely cold. "You *will* apologise."

Brian Pulter enjoyed confrontation. He'd played rugby when he was young; admittedly, the toned teenage body he'd once had was now covered by years of good eating, but the appetite for a fight was still there. He wasn't the slightest bit intimidated by the tall gangly figure of Brendan, just the opposite. Brendan was the one feeling uncomfortable. Nobody had made him feel this small in years. Brendan began to bounce on his toes, his body struggling to contain the urge to escape. When he felt attacked, it was flee or fight, so Brendan lashed out.

"Don't command me. Who do you think you are? Your job here is to facilitate me! I am the talent in this business. My abilities are the product. Without me, you'd have nothing! Do you get that? *Nothing!*"

The office manager was taken aback, but not for long. "I seem to have no choice. You're suspended on full pay, pending an investigation into the incident. You will—"

"You can't suspend me!" shouted Brendan.

"I can, and I am. As I was saying, you're required to attend this office on Monday, time to be confirmed. You may have one colleague with you."

Brendan stormed out of the office, leaving the door standing open behind him without answering or letting Pulter finish his sentence.

Snivelling bureaucrat, he thought to himself, as he stomped back to his cubicle. In his imagination, the voice rose from the depths and laughed at him. He was being mocked even by his own body.

Brendan shook with rage. Unable to control himself any longer, he swept his desk clear of everything, sending his screen and printer crashing to the floor. All around the office, heads popped over partitions like a herd of gophers—except for Janice Potts. Just as well, she kept her head down. He'd make her pay for this indignity, her and that creep, Pulter. She was probably in his office right now, sucking him off under his desk. Brendan lifted the wheel nuts from where they were spinning on the floor and stuffed them in his pocket. Grabbing his coat from the back of the chair, he stormed out of the office. All the gopher heads followed his progress, mouths agape.

"*What?!*" he roared, forcing the nearest office gophers to dive back into their holes.

The rage stayed with him, the whole way back to Honeysuckle Lane.

The journey was torture; the voice kept laughing. Once he was safe inside his house, he closed all the curtains, shook out a handful of sleeping pills, and swallowed them all. He needed to sleep, and if he didn't wake up, how bad would that be? Brendan crawled under the covers, where it was just him and the voice ringing in his ears. He would deal with the rest of the world later.

It was dark when Brendan came around. He was groggy but felt better for having slept. A quick check online showed the investigation into Tony Kelly's death seemed no farther along but the Garda would hardly put up hints that they were getting close. Brendan needed to get rid of everything connecting him to the car crash. Using rubber gloves, he wiped down the tyre iron and the nuts. He soaked the clothes in bleach, checking the pockets for anything such as receipts. Everything went back into the sports bag. He had made the purchases in cash, leaving no transaction trail.

It was late when he got into his car and drove twenty miles to a secluded area along The Royal canal. He parked near a block of apartments and walked along the overgrown towpath. The sun was setting and the street lights were just starting come on. After a while, he found a bridge that arched over the path, shielding him from prying eyes. He looked in both directions before slipping the bag from his shoulder. He put on disposable rubber gloves and wiped down the bag with a solvent-soaked rag, removing any fingerprints that remained. He tossed the bag and the rag into the water, the weight of the tyre iron dragging it quickly under the surface. A noise behind him made spin around. A jogger was bearing down on him, dressed in black Lycra, making her nearly invisible in the gloom. She didn't look at him as she passed, but Brendan was sure she had seen him throw the bag in the water. She jogged away into the distance.

Had she had seen his face? Would she reported what she'd seen? Or if the bag was discovered by accident, would she be able to give a description of him? If she couldn't describe him, it wouldn't matter if the bag was discovered or not. Brendan had no choice but to do something about this new loose end, so he followed her. Farther along the path, he found a bench backed by dense bushes. The area was littered with empty beer bottles; it looked like a hangout for winos. A gap had been made in the bushes, and it smelled like a toilet. From behind the bushes, Brendan was completely hidden, but he could see the path clearly enough through the leaves. His shoe pumped against some loose rubble from the retaining wall rising above the treeline. Brendan selected a half brick, hefting it in his hand, testing the weight. It was a crude weapon, but it would have to do. He waited motionless behind the bush, like a panther waiting for prey, doing his best to ignore the stink of human waste all around him.

After quarter of an hour, he heard the soft padding of runners on pavement, as she appeared out of the gloom, like a spectre. Brendan tensed; it was the same woman, returning along the path. Brendan tightened his grip on the brick. As she jogged past the bench, Brendan slipped from his hiding place. In a few quick strides, he was directly behind her. The blow landed above her right ear, dropping her midstride. There was a surprising crunch embedded in the sound of the impact. Brendan knew he'd hit her hard, but he thought it would take more than one blow to knock her out; he mustn't know his own strength. With his still-gloved hands, he grasped the woman under her arms and dragged her behind the bushes. Her body shuddered in his grip as she was racked with spasms. He pressed a hand over her mouth and nose until she grew still.

Unlike with the man in the silver car, Brendan felt completely connected to this woman as she stopped existing. He savoured every twitch as her soul was ripped away from her body. He found he was breathing hard and could feel the blood surging through his veins. He'd never felt so powerful, so invincible, so turned on in his life. Brendan knew he'd crossed a threshold, leaving behind the man he'd been. He was changing into something more majestic, more terrible. A man to be feared and respected. No longer was he one of the herd. He stood above them all now, like a king, like a god.

Brendan had to keep control. He couldn't let his emotions run away with him. He realised he needed to be careful; he must think about what he was leaving to be found. What would the police think when they found this body? Why would a woman be killed on a lonely towpath? For sex or money were the most-likely answers. Sex was always a good reason. In reality, it was a half truth; killing her had been better than sex. It was an ideal way to muddy the waters and confuse his pursuers. Brendan ripped open the woman's running top and pushed up her training bra, revealing small, hard breasts tipped with dark-brown nipples. Brendan couldn't resist running his hands over them, stroking the skin, as it began to pale to a bluish hue. He felt himself get hard. Was it her flesh? Or the scent of death in the air that turned him on? Both, perhaps. He slipped his gloved fingers inside the Lycra leggings and pulled them all the way down to her ankles, revealing the woman to be completely shaven.

Any erotic thoughts were swept aside by the bitter realities of death. In her final moments, the woman had soiled herself; the smell of urine and faeces assaulted his senses, making Brendan cover his mouth and nose. He jumped back from the body, staring at the dead woman in disgust. He looked about and noticed the half brick lying on the path on the far side of the bushes. He checked there was nobody coming before he slipped out and retrieved the brick. Just as quickly, he was back behind the bush again. Brendan rolled the brick in the dirt where the drunks had been pissing, adding as much filth and DNA as possible, while his gloves kept his own DNA in check. He dropped the brick conveniently beside the woman's head. He spread the woman's legs wide, exposing her to the world. He pinched her breasts and nipples hard, leaving marks he felt would be viewed as marks of passion. He couldn't bring himself to touch the filth-stained area of her crotch; instead, he picked up a discarded Budweiser bottle, pushing it all the way home until the neck rested against her pubic bone. He stood back and looked over his handiwork. Brendan was annoyed with the woman for voiding herself, ruining what should have been an exhilarating experience. He thought of Janice going down on a gloating Mr. Pulter, and rage rose in his chest. The nameless woman's face melted and transformed before his eyes, becoming that of the hated Janice. He viciously kicked the bottle, shattering it inside her as blood seeped from her most-private area.

Brendan walked casually back to his car, the gloves now floating, like countless other pieces of rubbish, in the filthy water of the canal. He'd never felt so alive. His mind turned to Janice and Brian Pulter, another two that were making his life difficult. How simple it would be for him if they just stopped being.

By the time he got to his car, a plan had hatched in his mind. Brendan felt focused again.

Chapter 16

Tim flew to London on Wednesday evening and Martha drove him to the airport—no, not quite. Tim drove to the airport; she was just about trusted to drive the car home. It was typical of him. The car would've remained in the short-term car park, except she needed it to get to work for the rest of the week. The drive home was an awakening. She could feel tension lifting from her shoulders as she zoomed along the M50. The radio, tuned to a rock station, was playing at nightclub levels. Martha smiled happily as she tapped her fingers on the steering wheel. She felt like a kid on the first day of the summer holidays, a kid with a free house for the weekend. The feeling only got stronger when she opened her front door.

The house felt completely different. It felt like her house, not their house. She drew a bath and took it with the door open, music playing on the stereo system downstairs. On the edge of the bath rested a glass of wine. Martha lay back with a contented sigh; the bubbles tickled her chin. Warm water soaked her body, washing away the stresses of the day. When the water started to cool, she toweled herself dry and wrapped up in a fresh robe. It was such a relief to feel like the mistress of her own life. That night, she slept a dreamless sleep, undisturbed by snoring or vanishing bedclothes. When she woke at the same time she did every morning, she began getting out of bed until she realized she didn't have to leave so early. Martha snuggled back under the duvet for an extra hour of blissful sleep.

At work, Martha was a different woman. Her day flew. She was bubbly with clients, and even Kevin got a warm smile. She left the office at the same time she always did but was home nearly an hour earlier than normal. Life was so simple when you didn't have to bend your actions to account for another. Martha spent another luxurious evening in her own company, a simple dinner of salad and pasta with a glass of fine wine. The idiot box in the corner was thankfully silent, replaced with beautiful music. She retired to bed when her body urged her to sleep. Her night was restful and deliciously decadent. Martha awoke from a dream so delightful, she smiled and lay back in the warmth of her darkened room. She let her mind replay the dream while her fingers substituted for the leading man.

Friday went in a flash. She had to rush into work, the first time she had been late in years. A stack of paper was waiting on her desk for typing and filing. She skipped her tea break but was still struggling to catch up at lunchtime. Her phone bleated constantly with a stream of texts from Tim. Martha was looking forward to meeting Ann in town for dinner later that night, but everything seemed to be working against her. She asked Kevin if she could leave early, to which he agreed after a lingering look at her breasts.

Despite her best efforts, it was nearly six when she got the car started. She rushed home, throwing off her clothes and jumping into the shower. A taxi was booked for seven-thirty. She was racing to apply the last of her makeup when its horn blew outside.

Martha still arrived at the restaurant long before Ann. She should have known. Ann was rarely on time for anything. Martha was on her second glass of wine when Ann breezed through the door, filling the room with a fog of Chanel. She slid into the chair across from Martha, throwing her eyes to Heaven.

"I thought I'd never get here! Hope you weren't waiting long." Ann picked up a glass and twiddled it between her fingers in the direction of the waitress, who glided toward the table.

"Can I get you a glass of wine, madam?"

"Today's Friday, honey. Monday is a glass day. Friday is definitely a bottle day," Ann said with a cheeky wink.

The waitress's smile said she agreed.

Dinner was a delight: good food, nice wine, and great company. The empty bottle of Pinot was soon joined by a second. Martha felt more vibrant than she had in years. When they tumbled onto the sidewalk, the night was alive with happy voices. They followed the crowd as it streamed toward the centre of town. They were passing The Cavern Club when Martha noticed a poster. Pygmy Moon Child was heading the bill tonight, of all nights. Martha stopped, like someone had nailed her feet to the floor.

"What's wrong?" asked Ann, when she realized her friend wasn't following.

"Let's go in here."

"Here? The Cube is only around the corner."

"I've heard of this band. I'm told they're fantastic. Come on, Ann, just one drink."

"Just one. If they're crap, we're leaving," Ann said, not bothering to hide the irked tone in her voice.

"They won't be crap, trust me," said Martha, bouncing like a teenager.

The women descended the stairs to the well-named underground club. The bare brick walls were plastered with ripped posters of acts long since retired. The band was already onstage, the music so loud, it vibrated her organs. The bar was packed with Friday-night drinkers. Men in suits rubbed shoulders with students and clubbers. They moved toward the bar, Ann elbowing her way to the front.

While Ann tried to get drinks by waving cash at a frazzled barman, Martha drifted farther into the room, where she had a better view of the stage. The dance floor was packed with sweat-soaked dancers, pushing to get closer to the front. Heat radiated off them like a furnace. Martha breathed in deeply; the air was thick with the scent of people, of youth, of passion. To her, the dance floor was a pool of unrestrained joy. How she wished to dive in! Above them all, like a priest at his altar, was Ogie, his eyes closed as he sang. His shirt open nearly as far as his belt gave tantalising glimpses of his hairless body. There wasn't an ounce of fat on his etched torso, which glistened with sweat. He sang each word as if it came from the very core of his soul, his body moving freely to the music. It was a carnal dance, full of primitive power. Just as the song reached a crashing crescendo, the band fell silent, leaving Ogie holding one crystal-clear note. The dancers stopped, watching the man in the light. Higher, the note rose, held impossibly long. Then, just at the right moment, the band kicked in, louder and fiercer than before. Ogie, exhausted, dangled from the mic stand, causing the crowd to go completely wild. He held the whole club under a spell with incredible ease.

He opened his eyes and stared straight at Martha. He held her gaze. The song flowed, and he picked up his line perfectly, never letting his eyes wander from hers. It was one of the most-erotic moments of her life. Martha felt a nudge on her shoulder, and Ann handed her a glass of wine.

"So, tell me exactly, how you know this band?"

"The lead singer moved in next door to us a few weeks ago."

"And?"

"And what?"

"That man's looking at you like a dog looks at a steak," she said, nodding toward the stage. Ogie was launching into another song.

"Don't be ridiculous," Martha scoffed.

"I'm telling you, he is going to start humping that mic stand if he gets any worse."

"No harm in looking, babe, for him or me." Martha giggled, taking a sip of her wine.

"You can look at as many menus as you want, as long as you eat your meals at home," said Ann sagely.

It didn't take Ann long to become a confirmed fan of Ogie and his Pygmies. They stayed long past one drink. When the last encore had ended, Ogie grabbed a towel and bounded from the stage. He was mobbed by admirers, some men, mostly scantily dressed girls. He shook hands, exchanged smiles, even took selfies, but he never deviated from his journey to intercept Martha.

"Hey, neighbour," Ogie said when he got to the bar.

"Hi, Ogie, you were great!" Martha said. "This is my friend, Ann."

"Lovely to meet you, Ann," he said, taking her hand in his. He gave her a dazzling smile, bringing her fingers to his lips to kiss them. Martha was shocked at how put out she was at such a casual gesture. She didn't like Ogie kissing Ann's hand, or Ann's anything, for that matter. The feeling was so strong, it surprised her.

"This is your new neighbour? I must call round more often!" Ann giggled. Martha liked Ann's reaction even less than she liked Ogie's hand-kissing.

Ogie nodded at the barman. A bottle of Heineken slid across the counter toward him. He frowned, making a circle motion with his finger. Two glasses of wine joined the Heineken. Onstage, the rest of the band was packing away instruments. Ogie said they were letting him skip his roadie duties, as he'd such important visitors. The three of them moved to a booth in the corner of the bar. Over the next hour, Ogie proved to be the most-charming of men. He was funny, attentive, and alluring. Once the equipment was cleared from the stage, the rest of the band joined them at their table. Empty glasses began multiplying in front of the group, the conversation growing more raucous with each passing round. Everyone was having such a good time, none of them noticed the bar staff calling last orders, or the rest of the customers drifting away. It was only when a cleaner started nudging their chairs with a mop did they realize the night was over.

"I know a great club just around the corner. It'll only be getting going. What about it, girls?" enthused Ogie.

"We should go home. It's been a long day," said Ann. *Dry arse,* thought Martha.

"Are you sure? The night is only a pup."

"Certain there is only so much excitement a girl can take," said Ann. Martha was going to secretly beg Ann to come clubbing, right before she fell over trying to get out of the booth. Her little speed wobble told her that Ann was right. It was home time.

"You're not going to drive, I hope?" asked the drummer, helping Martha get her coat on.

"We'll grab a cab or something," assured Ann.

"Last chance, girls," said Ogie, using his most-winning smile.

"I can drop you home. It's on my way," the drummer said to Ann and Martha.

"You're not coming, either?" stammered Ogie, realising that his friend had no intention of hitting the nightclubs.

"Nah, man. Kids, you know?"

"Some night out this is turning into. No point in going by myself. I may as well get a lift. Hope you don't mind a tight squeeze?" Ogie asked. Martha could see Ann getting ready to say, "No, thanks," so she gave her a sneaky elbow in her ribs.

"That'd be lovely. I hope it's not an inconvenience?" Martha asked.

Ogie laughed. "I think we can manage the extra six feet between your front door and mine."

They all piled into the van: two band members plus Ann in the front seat; Ogie, Martha, and the bass player sitting on speakers in the back of the van. It was great fun, the first time Martha had ever ridden in a van, never mind the back of one. The driver took a bend a little too enthusiastically, and Martha slid across the speaker and into Ogie's arms. She didn't exactly jump out of them, either.

"Sorry about that," said the driver, over his shoulder.

"You okay?" Ogie asked Martha, his arms still loosely circling her.

"I'm tougher than I look," she said, not pulling away.

"I bet you are," he said, smiling and letting his hands drop.

Ann was the second stop. She looked nervous, leaving Martha in the back of a dark van with not one but two rock musicians.

"Why not stay with me tonight? I'll bring you home in the morning."

"I better not. Tim said he'd call the house tomorrow. He'd only worry if I'm not there."

"You're sure?" Ann asked, clearly not sure herself.

"Certain. 'Night, Ann."

Soon, it was only the drummer, Ogie, and Martha left. They all sat in the front of the van for the last part of the trip. Martha had a terrible urge to be in the back, surrounded by rattling instruments and Ogie's arms. That would have looked weird when there were two perfectly good seats in the front. The turn into Honeysuckle Lane came all too quickly. Martha thanked the drummer and got out of the van. At last, on the chilly footpath, the two neighbours were alone.

"Tim not waiting up for you?" asked Ogie, looking at the dark windows of Martha's house.

"He's away for the weekend. Business trip to London," Martha said, feeling her face flush a little. She felt silly. Why was she acting like a schoolgirl around this man? If she were honest with herself, it's because he made her feel young again.

Martha nodded toward Ogie's equally dark house. "Annabelle seems to have gone to bed."

Ogie smiled and shuffled his feet. His hands dove into his jeans pockets. "She's only a friend."

"Someone should tell her. I think she fancies the title of Mrs. Ogie."

"I can't see anyone applying for that job," joked Ogie. "I'm too much of a handful."

"Are you boasting, sir?"

It was Ogie's turn to blush. The cool night air caused Martha to shiver a little.

Ogie noticed. "It's chilly. I should let you get inside."

"Thanks for a lovely night, Ogie, I can't remember having so much fun in ages," Martha said with genuine warmth. She leaned in and gave him a peck on the cheek, the second time she had kissed this man since they met. Martha walked up the drive to her door, Ogie to his. His voice stopped her before she got the key in the lock.

"What about a nightcap?"

Martha looked at the key in her hand, and the dark empty house before her.

"Why not?" she said.

Ogie pushed his door wide, allowing her to pass him.

The door to number five closed behind them. Lights came on behind the sitting room curtains, glowing merrily. After a time, these vanished, to be replaced by a glow in the master-bedroom window. The front door remained firmly closed, the whole time.

Brendan Roche watched all this, from his darkened vantage point at the end of the road. He glared at the house waiting for the stuck up whore to reappear. When the light went on in the bedroom window Brendan smiled to himself. "Would you look at that," he said. "It's time for the worm to turn on that particular busybody," he thought. She's not the only one that can send nasty letters.

Chapter 17

Adams found driving into the suburbs during morning rush hour was a great pleasure. The far side of the road was a clogged artery of cars and trucks while he had the open road ahead of him. The radio was playing, and the smell of fresh takeaway coffee filled the car. Sims sat alongside him. They were going to interview Tony Kelly's girlfriend.

"If I win the lotto, Sims, I'll buy a pad in the middle of town and go to work in the country every morning. Imagine that—never being stuck in traffic again."

She was clearly not a morning person because she didn't even crack a smile. She sipped her coffee and continued looking out the window at the cars they were passing. Adams was always in a hurry, even when there was nowhere to go. He must have been born with a lead foot. She turned her attention back to Adams while he accelerated to beat a yellow light on an upcoming junction.

"None of this adds up," she said.

"I agree. There are some fairly massive pieces missing," said Adams, throwing the unmarked car into the junction just as the light turned red. Somewhere far behind them, a horn blared at the reckless manoeuvre. Adams squinted in the rearview mirror. He hated being criticised, and that horn sounded sanctimonious to him. If he was in less of a rush, he'd have pulled over and given the driver's tax and insurance a good going-over, tyres, too.

Talking to Tony's friends yesterday yielded little. They were all hardworking young men or women. Not a shady one among them. The trick with finding the truth was to interview early, get them alone. The first reaction is normally the truth. In all the interviews, not one half statement or slipped word appeared. They were all shocked beyond words, and the shock seemed genuine.

"What's your feeling on the girlfriend?" she asked Adams.

"On paper, she's a princess, but sex can screw things up plenty. Did you know a unit was called to her work on the night of the crash?"

"No, why?"

"Apparently, she was watching the TV, saw the car, and started screaming the place down. Either all very well-planned, or a genuinely upset girl," he mumbled, fiddling with the radio as it went off station.

"The car was as twisted as a pretzel. How'd she know it was his?" asked Sims.

"I don't know. That's one of my big questions. Was she just waiting to act out her part? I'm not sure."

"What about her family?" Sims asked, liking the way the older detective treated her as an equal, sharing information with her and listening to what she thought.

"Father has a few social-order offences, speeding tickets, nothing much. The feeling is that he might be handy with his fists at home. On the street, he's a spineless lump. Mother is a stay-at-home mom, no driving licence, no record. Older brother in the army, all top marks for conduct and performance, but not officer material. Hasn't got it upstairs, apparently. The younger brother is in the same boat, still in school, and lagging way behind the rest of his class. Angie, that's our girl, was a tearaway a few years ago. Some notes on her, but nothing official. Ran with a wild bunch in school; nothing at all on her in the last few years," Adams said, without needing to check any notes. Sims knew as much already, because the notes she had resting on her lap had a full rundown on Angie Sweeney. The truth was, she just liked having Adams talk to her.

"Did the autopsy turn up anything in Tony's system? Drink? Drugs?" she asked.

"Lots of coffee, but that's about the size of it," said Adams. The turn off appeared to their left, and Adams slid the car into it with practised ease. Ten minutes later, they were searching a warren of roads in a sprawling estate for Honeysuckle Lane.

"Why can't they just number the bloody roads instead of stupid bloody names? Honeysuckle, Hawthorn, bloody Hemlock," fumed the detective as he backed out of another dead end.

"I think that's it, over there," said Sims, pointing out a narrow side road that curled back on itself. She was right. Nine detached houses lined up on the left-hand side of the narrow road, all facing onto a communal green.

A black BMW with tinted windows passed them leaving Honeysuckle Lane. The number-plate camera with which the detective's car was fitted picked up a hit. The car was on a watch list, which made the computer console mounted on the dash beep and display a warning notification.

"That's interesting," said Adams, checking the computer display.

"What is it?"

"Harry is a long way from his patch," said Adams.

"Harry McCarthy?"

"The very same. I wonder if he had anything with the kid's death."

"He likes to keep his hands as clean as possible, murder isn't his style. Do you think it might have been a reminder gone wrong?"

"Let's see what young Angie has to say for herself first. It's probably nothing to do with McCarthy, but there is no harm in asking if they know each other," Adams said, looking for house number eight.

***

Frank mulled over what Harry and Chris wanted him to do as he walked back to the office, and constantly over the following day. In the end, when he woke up Friday morning with an empty wallet and no more time, Frank's mind was made up. They were going to break into that house, no matter what happened. What would it matter if he made some money out of it? If they were caught, and they traced the keys and code back to his office, Frank would say they pinched the keys from his desk after viewing the house.

After work Friday, Frank had no choice but to go to the Black Swan. On the way, he emptied the last two hundred euro from his credit card. Frank slinked into the dingy bar. Greg looked up from his newspaper but didn't offer a drink. Greg knew a man without a cent to his name when he saw one. In the far corner, the poker game that had gotten him in so much trouble was under way. Harry was wearing his trademark black-leather jacket, sitting with his back to the door. It was Chris who spotted Frank, standing near the bar.

"All right, Frank, fancy a hand?" Chris said, laughing.

Frank could feel the money in his pocket throb. Every one of his nerves jangled. All he wanted was to put the cash on the table and try his luck; this time, at least, fear overcame his impulses. "Not today, thanks. Just need a word with Harry."

Harry turned his head. "Leave it with Greg. Can't you see I'm busy?"

"It's about the other thing."

Harry looked back at his cards, and threw another fold of cash on the pot. "Sit at the bar, Frank," he ordered.

Frank sat on a stool while Greg continued to ignore him. Twenty minutes later, Harry stood up. He walked toward the toilets, waving at Frank to come along. What is it with this guy? thought Frank. Why can't he have a conversation in public, like everyone else?

Frank followed, dreading being alone with the gangster. The toilet stank something awful, and it only got worse when the door slammed closed behind him. Harry leaned against the sink, his hands forming menacing bulges in the pockets of his jacket. "I hope you've something for me?"

Frank held out the fold of money, which Harry counted at a glance. "Two hundred quid. Are you having a fucking laugh?"

"Two hundred, and I'll get you the keys and codes you want."

"Clever boy, but you get paid after a job, not before, which leaves you light. Can't have that, Frankie *boy*! Not good for business."

Harry jerked his hands out of his jacket pockets. Frank flinched, throwing his arms up to protect himself. He stumbled back, banging against the closed door. Harry didn't hit Frank; he just snatched the folded notes from his trembling fingers.

"Don't hurt me." Even to his own ears, his voice sounded sniveling.

Harry smiled and took a step closer while stashing the money in his front pocket. Incredibly, instead of lashing out, Harry began fumbling with his zipper.

"What the fuck?"

"You got something to say?" Harry said, his right hand half-inside his trousers and a killer look in his eye.

Frank couldn't move. He managed the smallest shake of his head, trying to become one with the door behind him.

"Good," snarled Harry, pulling out his prick. Frank thought it would've been bigger, but small as it was, it was terrifying. Harry leaned close, putting the palm of his hand against the door. Frank felt wet warmth spread across his thighs, and the pungent smell of urine got a whole lot worse. Frank stood there, letting Harry piss all over him. He was so close, Frank could feel puffs of his breath on his cheek. Frank felt like crying, or being sick, or both.

Harry stood back, shaking himself dry, before putting away his shriveled little dick. He smiled at Frank like they were the best of friends. "Four thousand, Frank. I'll be at your place in the morning for the other thing. Now get the fuck out of my pub. You're stinking the place up."

Frank ran through the bar, the laughing voices ringing in his ears as he went. On the street, he did cry as he ran through the evening crowds.

When morning came, Frank hadn't slept a wink. He was watching every car that drove past the house. It was after ten when the black BMW pulled into his drive. Frank didn't want Barbara asking questions, so he opened the door quietly and slipped out before Harry stopped the car. He had the key and the code Harry wanted. The dark glass of the driver's window slid down smoothly. Frank passed the envelope inside.

"It's all there."

"Will the house be empty this Wednesday?"

"It should be," said Frank.

"Should isn't good enough. Check, and leave a message with Greg."

"All right, all right." Frank said, walking away.

Harry backed out of the drive as a dark-blue Ford turned into Honeysuckle Lane. He knew it was a cop car; he had a sixth sense for the filth. He continued on his way, driving as normal, while trying to see where the unmarked Garda car was heading. What the hell was a city detective unit doing all the way out here? If that fucking toe-rag O'Shea was trying to play clever, he was going to be one sorry motherfucker. Harry drove the rest of the way back to the city in a foul mood, God help everyone.

Chapter 18

Adams knocked on the door of number eight Honeysuckle Lane. Mary Sweeney opened it, still in her dressing gown.

"Good morning, Mrs. Sweeney," Adams said, showing his badge. "Have we come too early?"

"You're all right. Come on in," she said. She wore her dressing gown and pyjamas with an ease that made Sims sure she occasionally spent the whole day in them. Mrs. Sweeney showed them into the front room, then went upstairs to get Angie.

A few minutes later, a pale mess of a girl appeared at the door, dressed similarly to her mother. She was pretty, but it was a harsh beauty. Her makeup-less face was drained. Black rings under her eyes were caused by tears, not age.

Adams introduced both Sims and himself in a kind tone, trying to put the girl at ease.

"I know this is hard for you, but these questions are important. You may know something, and not even realise the importance of it," he said.

"I don't know what I can tell you. I know what people are saying, but I don't believe anyone would want to hurt Tony." At the mention of his name, her eyes brimmed with tears.

Sims turned to Mrs. Sweeney. "Do you think we might get some tea?"

"Of course," she said, jumping to the task like only an Irish mammy can.

When they were alone, Adams continued, "Did you know of anyone that Tony had fallen out with recently?"

"No. No one."

"Even something minor?"

"No. Not that I know of."

"What about money? Did he ever mention any money trouble?"

"He moaned about the cost of his car insurance, but that was about it."

"What about work? Did Tony have any issues there?"

"He liked his job. I thought it was boring, but he said it wasn't like that all the time. He really wanted to get into fund management. He said that was where the big bucks were. He said he was going to buy a Ferrari when he made his first million."

"He liked his cars, then?"

"Loved them. I was always telling him he drove too fast. Once I even made him pull over and got out because he was driving like a fool. I refused to get back in unless he slowed down. He loved the feeling of it, you see, the speed." At this, she broke down again.

When she got herself together, she looked at Sims and said, "I told him it would kill him, and I was right. Why didn't he listen?"

Mrs. Sweeney arrived with four mugs on a tray. Once they all had a steaming tea in front of them, Adams turned to Mrs. Sweeney. "Perhaps it would be better if we spoke with Angie alone."

"Why? Angie hasn't done anything wrong," protested Mrs. Sweeney.

"We are not saying she did, but there are questions of a personal nature we may need to ask. Please, Mrs. Sweeney." Sims ushered the older woman toward the door, her womanly touch working. Adams was glad to have Sims along with him; she was good with people.

"It's okay, Mum," Angie said.

"If you're sure," Mary said, looking at her daughter, then to the officers. Mrs. Sweeney said, "I'll be in the kitchen, if you want me."

When they were alone, Angie looked at Adams and asked, "I'm not in trouble, am I?"

"No, of course not, but there are some questions we might ask that you may not want your mother to hear."

Angie snorted a short laugh. "She knows I'm no virgin, if that's what's worrying you."

"What about drugs?"

Angie said nothing but looked guiltily at her hands.

"Angie, this is about Tony, not you. We need to know if he was involved with anything that may cause someone to interfere with his car."

"So, it wasn't an accident?"

"No, it wasn't, but that's all I can say right now. Did Tony use drugs?"

"Me, not Tony," she said quietly. "I smoked a bit of weed when we first started to go out together, sometimes the odd pill. He threatened to finish with me unless I stopped, so I did."

"Did he argue with anyone else over your habit? Your dealer, for example?"

"Jesus, would you listen to yourself? This isn't 'Breaking Bad.' I smoked a bit of weed, not even that much," she said, getting angry, a classic defensive tactic that Adams was more than used to seeing.

"On the night of the crash, you got very upset at seeing the crash on TV. How did you know it was Tony that was involved?"

"I recognised the car on the telly, and he'd not texted me, like he said he would."

"That car was hard to recognise. I saw it up close, and I couldn't tell the make. How were you so sure it was Tony? It could have been any silver car."

Both Sims and Adams were glued to Angie's features, watching for any sign that the girl was lying. Her answer came quickly, without having to think, and it made her very sad. There was little to make either detective think the girl might be lying.

"It was the red material I'd stuck on the back window ledge that I recognised. How many silver cars have that crap on it? I saw that on the TV, and I was sure," she said.

Adams could see grief threatening to engulf her, and how the girl battled with her emotions, substituting a more controllable reaction: anger. This girl wasn't afraid of a fight, that's for sure. The red-novelty parcel shelf made sense to Adams. He'd thought it looked garish on the night he'd viewed the crash. Not the kind of thing he expected to find in a man's car.

"Okay, what about sex? Was anyone else involved in your relationship?"

"*For fuck sake!*" Angie's raised voice caused the door to open. Mrs. Sweeney clearly had been listening.

"Is everything okay?"

"This dipshit just called me a druggie, and now he wants to know if I'm a slut as well!" said Angie, letting her pent-up emotions overflow.

"It's important we ask some difficult questions, Mrs. Sweeney. Please, let us get this over with," said Sims.

Adams remained silent, looking directly at Angie. As it turned out, Adams's phone picked that moment to spring to life. He excused himself and went into the hall.

"Nobody is casting aspersions on either Tony or Angie. It's important we build up an accurate picture of Tony's life, so we can understand his death," Sims explained to both women.

"I know that. I understand, but you're not listening to me. Tony was a lovely guy; everyone liked him. I don't know what else I can tell you," said Angie, breaking into tears now that her reserves of anger were depleted. Mrs. Sweeney sat beside Angie on the couch, taking the girl in her arms.

Adams popped his head around the door, saying, "We got to go." The phone was still against his ear as he ducked back out again.

"It looks like we've got to leave it there. Thanks so much for talking to us," Sims said to Angie as she stood. She held out her hand toward Angie, but the girl didn't return the gesture. Mrs. Sweeney shook Sims's hand instead.

Just as she was about to leave, Sims stopped. "One last thing: Have you ever come across a man by the name of Harry McCarthy? Or ever seen a black BMW with tinted windows hanging around Tony in the last few weeks?"

"Never heard of him," said Angie, looking up. "Who is he? Do you think he was the one that did it?"

"No, it's just a lead we had to check, and not one that was ever likely to have been relevant. Thanks, anyway," said Sims as she followed Adams out to the car.

"Detective Sims?" called Mrs. Sweeney.

"Yes, Mrs. Sweeney?"

"I've seen a car like that lately."

"Go on," said Sims, walking back into the hall.

"Yes, black BMW. Tough-looking guy with a black leather jacket driving it."

"Do you know Harry McCarthy?"

"No, but I think Frank O'Shea, in number two, does."

"Do you think he is involved?" the woman asked.

"Like I said, it's very unlikely, but as you have seen, he is not the kind of guy you want hanging around your neighbourhood," said Sims. Sims handed over her card. "If you think of anything else, give me a call. Anytime."

Outside, the unmarked car was already running, and Adams was waiting at the wheel.

"What's the rush, boss?" said Sims as she slammed the door.

"We have another body to deal with. A dog walker found it on the bank of The Royal Canal."

"Blues and twos time?"

"Why not?" said Adams, smiling. "If I'm up, everyone should be up."

The screaming siren echoed across Honeysuckle Lane as the unmarked car vanished around the corner in a dazzling display of flashing blue light.

***

The siren cut through Brendan's sleep, like a blade through rice paper. He literally jumped out of bed and raced to the window, expecting to see the house surrounded by dozens of police officers in riot gear. Instead, the lane was empty, with the sound of the siren dwindling into the distance. He let out a breath he hadn't been aware he was holding. His head spun, and his stomach flipped. Brendan felt dizzy, and held on to the windowsill until it passed. He was no longer sure what was real anymore. His head was in agony, and his stomach was in knots.

After the initial high of dealing with the woman last night, he sank, and sank quickly. By the time he'd arrived back at the house, he was convinced he had acted rashly, stupidly. Everything began to close in on him. The more he tried to think, the more confused he became. He felt twisted like a pretzel, inside and out. Brendan was convinced that there were people out there, people who knew what he had done, and who were determined to get him. Every time he turned a corner, every time he felt he had solved a problem, someone else came along to trap him deeper in the mire. They were all out to get him.

After hours of worrying, he did something he nearly never did: He drank. Between handfuls of pills and the empty Jameson bottle, Brendan couldn't remember everything that had happened the night before. His head throbbed, and his mouth was as dry as the bottom of a birdcage. Brendan struggled down to the kitchen. He needed some water. On the kitchen table, he saw his laptop was still turned on. He must have been online last night, after he blacked out. Brendan glugged a full pint of water before turning the machine around to face him. His headache got a hell of a lot worse when he saw Angie Sweeney's Facebook page open on the screen. On the message board was a post made at 3:10 a.m. by Tina Ryan: *Tony is gone. You shouldn't cry. He was never right for you. Destiny intends greater things. All will be clear soon.*

    Brendan must have left the message for Angie the previous night, when he was out of it on drink and pills. Underneath was a string of scathing responses from Angie's friends. Brendan wouldn't have said that if he'd been thinking clearly; he wouldn't have drawn attention to himself like that. What was done was done, he reasoned. None of it would matter soon. Brendan knew he had gone too far; it was time to bring things to a conclusion, one way or the other. He looked at the message again. Now that his course was set, the message seemed apt. After all, it was the truth. Someone had to say it.

    Another streak of brain lightning struck inside his head. He swayed on his feet before deciding that he needed more sleep. He had no work, anyway, thanks to Pulter and his whore, Janice Potts. He may as well go back to bed.

***

The siren didn't wake Martha, since Ogie had done that several times since dawn, but it did stop her from drifting back into an exhausted, delighted sleep. She stretched herself, catlike, in the swirl of silk sheets. The bed was destroyed. Clothes were strewn everywhere. It looked like a tornado had hit the place. Martha had the most-delicious throb between her legs, reminding her that she'd been well and truly fucked. From the bathroom en suite, the hiss of a shower filled the room. Martha looked around at the misplaced ornaments and lamps. There wasn't a surface that she hadn't visited last night on Ogie's erotic tour of the bedroom.

He'd done things to her that she had only dreamed about. He'd made love to her slowly, lovingly. He'd screwed her hard and selfishly. He'd used his tongue, his fingers, his dick in every crack and crevice of her body, playing her as expertly as he'd played the crowd in that dark, sweaty club. After the night he'd given her, she felt owned, a feeling she'd never before experienced. Martha rolled onto her tummy and let her eyes close. She didn't notice the shower stop until she felt his wet, rock-hard body sliding up her legs. The warm trail left by his tongue tracing the inside of her thigh was heaven. He moved higher, spreading her legs, allowing him to access her completely. She felt a rush of blood flood her crotch as her tender lips parted under his touch.

A sudden brush of ice cold against the edge of her libia caused her to shudder. Pain gave way to pleasure, as the tickle of ice on the lip of her vagina awoke desperate, delicious agony. The cold was replaced by licking warmth, refreshing her tired and abused opening. She felt her juice flow, and he drank from her, long and deep. Without opening her eyes, she felt his penis play at her entrance before sliding fully into her. Once again, she abandoned all shame and became his, completely.

Chapter 19

Murder scenes, by their nature, were often hard to reach. Even considering that fact, this one was well off the beaten track. Adams and Sims had to walk along the canal bank for a good fifteen minutes before they spotted the circus of forensic tents in the distance. Dolan was already standing by the barrier tape, waiting for the photographer to finish snapping shots of various patches of mud.

"What have we got landed with now?" Adams asked when they joined him.

"White female, late twenties, maybe early thirties. It looks like a sex attack. Partly undressed with considerable mutilation in the genital area."

"Mutilation? That's unusual." said Adams. Dolan looked over at Sims before continuing.

To Sims, that look was infuriating. It said *detective* on her badge, not shy little girl. Sims hated when her gender set her apart in the force. She had to be better than all the men, just to be taken seriously.

Dolan could see that he'd put his foot in it, and his face reddened. "Yea, it looks like he used a bottle on her. There was some blood, so it may have been broken."

"Christ, that's sick," Adams said.

The crime-scene photographer ducked under the barrier tape, completely covered from head to toe in a white jumpsuit, shoe covers, gloves, and a mask. "She is all yours, detectives," he said, walking away.

The three detectives donned protective clothes similar to the photographer before going behind the tape. Adams let Dolan go in first, holding Sims back.

"Don't pay any attention to him," Adams said with a smile.

"It's okay. I know the score," she said with a wink. Adams didn't release his tender grip on her arm.

"If it gets a little rough in there, there is no shame in taking a break. Just give me a nod."

Sims was touched by Adams's sensitivity. It might be hard, but it had to be done. Sims took a deep breath and nodded.

"Thanks," she said. Adams patted her arm, a friendly gesture, and let her go under the tape.

The assistant pathologist was inspecting the body, with the assistance of a forensic technician. The three detectives kept their distance and let the men work. Judging by her clothes, she was a jogger. It was clear the woman hadn't been dead long. The woman lay on her back, with her legs spread-eagled. Adams felt his gaze linger on the unnatural protrusion from her crotch. Dolan had been right about the bottle. A sample container, positioned between the men working on the body, was already full of test tubes and baggies. The technician took scrapings from under the woman's nails while the pathologist examined her head.

"Care to share any thoughts, doc?" asked Adams through his mask.

"You should know better than anyone, detective. It's far too early to tell."

"I know, doc. Just a few general thoughts, so we can get the ball rolling."

The pathologist sat back. His look said this kind of guessing wasn't what he did, but he continued regardless. "She was hit on the right temple with a blunt object. No apparent defensive wounds. No blood or tissue under the fingernails that I can tell. Considering this, it would seem she was hit from behind. Scuff marks on the back of the runners indicate she was dragged. These marks"—he indicated the area around the nipples—"are not bite marks. No indents. I'd say pinch marks."

"What about the bottle?" asked Sims.

"I haven't made a close examination of that yet. I wanted to leave it in place until we get the body back to the lab. I have a suspicion it may be broken. It's pushed a long way into the canal. That had to be done with some force. I suspect this intrusion occurred post-mortem."

"Why would you say that?" asked Sims.

"Not enough blood," said the doctor, indicating a small pool of dried blood around the crotch area.

"Was there anything on the body, like keys or a phone?" asked Adams.

"Just a single car key, in the pocket of her jacket. The pocket was zipped closed, so we are not hopeful on getting any prints from it."

"Can we take it?"

"Don't see why not. Just sign the release form first."

Adams signed for a single Fiat key. Once outside the tent, Adams drew the other detectives away from the crowd gathering at the barrier tape. "Any thoughts, guys?"

"The key is significant," said Sims, pulling away her mask to take in some fresh air.

"Why so?" asked Adams, letting the young detective have the floor.

"I jog. I have a place near my house that I go, so I normally bring just my front-door key. It is very uncomfortable having a big bunch of keys jangling around in your pocket while you're running. The fact she had a single car key on her would say to me that she drove here. Locked up her car with a key she kept specifically for this reason. Anything else she had like handbag, purse, house keys, credit cards, she'd have left locked in the car."

"That makes perfect sense to me," said Dolan, eager to make up for his earlier gaffe, "and it rules out robbery as a motive."

"Don't go jumping the gun there, Tonto," said Adams. "A mugger wouldn't know she had nothing on her till after he'd bashed her brains in."

Dolan looked embarrassed, and nodded his agreement.

"Let's not overlook anything, even if I think you're right," Adams said, throwing Dolan a bone.

"No, boss," he said, happy that Adams wasn't rubbing his nose in his mistake.

"Let's assume she did just what Sims said. Where would the car be?" asked Adams.

Sims dove right on the question before Dolan had a chance to answer, her young, quick mind racing ahead of the pack. "Looking at the tone of the body, I'd guess she was a regular exerciser, but no long-distance runner. A couple of miles, tops, in either direction."

Adams looked at the area around them. To the left was the canal; to the right, thick undergrowth. Behind this greenery was a fifteen-foot-high wall, topped with glass.

"How far do you think that wall goes?" Adams asked.

"I parked at a public car park about half a mile in that direction," said Dolan. "It's solid all the way back. There were a couple of bridges, but no way onto or off the path."

"We parked at the same place," said Sims.

"Okay, first order of business. Let's find the victim's car," said Adams. He turned to Dolan. "Why don't you go back to where we parked and report in? While you're there, check the car park for a Fiat. Take down all the registration numbers. We can check them out later, back at the station. Myself and Sims will keep going this direction for twenty minutes and see what we find."

"No problem, boss," Dolan said, walking away.

Adams took off his jacket, as the day was starting to get warm. "Let's go for a stroll, Sims," he said with a smile.

Half an hour later, they came to the first break in the wall. A gate that led to a complex of modern apartments, and parked outside the gate was a newish Fiat 500 in white with a red roof.

"What do you know?" asked Adams. He fished the key out of his pocket, pointed it at the car, and pressed the Unlock button. The car's lights flashed, and it unlocked. Adams pressed the Lock button again and called the location to Dolan over his radio, telling him to inform the forensic unit at the crime scene they had found the victim's car.

While they waited, Sims walked circles around the car. "Notice anything?" asked Adams, who was sitting on the edge of a raised flower bed.

"No," she said.

"I did," he said with a smile.

She gave him a puzzled look. Adams stretched out his legs, lying back along the edge of the flower bed, enjoying the sunshine. She raised her eyebrows in place of the question. He pointed a finger straight up in the air. High on the corner of the building sat a tiny glass dome.

"Big Brother was watching, I hope," he said with a smile.

***

Back on Honeysuckle Lane, Martha was doing the walk of shame from number five to number four as quickly as possible. She had just put the key in the lock when the phone in the hall began to ring. She got inside as fast as she could, closing the door behind her. She knew exactly who was on the other end. She steadied herself, trying to make it sound like she just got up.

"Hello?" she answered, in a contrived, groggy voice.

"I was starting to worry, honey. I rang twice already," said Tim.

"I know. I heard, but I wanted to stay asleep. Sorry."

"Are you okay? You sound terrible."

"I think I might have eaten something that didn't agree with me last night. I spent half the night running to the toilet."

Tim gave a sarcastic snort. "Most likely a bucketful of wine, if Ann was involved."

"If you're going to be snarky, I'm hanging up," said Martha angrily, covering her shame nicely.

"Don't be like that, baby. I was only messing with you," he said sweetly. "I wish you were here."

"I miss you, too. I just don't feel myself today. I think I'll go back to bed for a while."

"Okay. I love you," he said sincerely.

"Me, too," she managed, along with "bye" before hanging up the phone.

She did go back to sleep, but it was hardly alone. She settled in between her marital sheets, with the smell of Ogie lingering on her skin. She slept soundly and happily for the rest of the morning.

***

Barbara hurtled through the supermarket, like a woman on a mission. Frank did his best to keep up, with the trolley being buried under the cascade of essential groceries. Parma ham, Brie, fresh French stick, chocolates, and bottles of wine and spirits joined the growing mountain of goods. Barb wasn't the kind of woman who made lists, and Frank was sure it was years since he'd seen a value-brand product gracing their shelves. He was just as sure Barbara couldn't accurately price anything that was flying into the trolley. This weekly ritual bored the socks off him, and he'd long since given up suggesting what to buy. He was the lifter and carrier, nothing more.

Eventually, they rounded the last corner to face rows of empty cash registers. The only two that were manned had long queues. Frank was sure he could hear Barbara's blood begin to boil in her veins. He herd her mumble, "Typical," under her breath.

Frank manoeuvred the trolley behind a large man with a full basket slung over his arm and waited their turn to pay. Barbara was twittering away at him, but the words washed over Frank, like waves over sand. For some reason, all of Frank's attention was grabbed by the large man's basket. It was full of cooked chicken wings, pasties, cakes, and sliced meat, all of which had reduced labels across the original price stickers. From what Frank could see, the whole basket was going to cost less than ten euro.

Slowly, they shuffled forward, one customer at a time. Frank was delighted with his guess when the man's basket came to a staggering eleven euro and forty-five cents. It was stupid, but he got a great deal of satisfaction from his silent victory.

Frank unloaded items from the trolley onto the conveyer belt while Barbara moved past the teller with her selection of hemp multi-use bags. How could four people eat so much in just seven days? thought Frank, as his arms began to ache. The sound that money makes when it goes into a shopkeeper's pocket had long ago changed from *ching* to *beep,* and the *beeps* were flying today.

When the last item skidded across the scanner, delivering a final beep, the cashier glanced at the readout. "That comes to one hundred and eighty-seven euro twenty," she said, in a voice that left no doubt she couldn't care less what the total was.

Barbara finished packing before rummaging in her bag for her purse while the teller waited, with a bored look and an outstretched hand. This delay didn't seem to bother the cashier one bit. She would have waited without a word until the end of time. The queue behind Frank wasn't so forgiving. Hardly suppressed harrumphs speared him in the back of the head. Eventually, Barbara located her purse and flipped a card toward the cashier. She loaded the filled bags into the trolley as the woman swiped the card.

One more *beep* echoed across the shop, this one not so friendly. The next words out of the cashier's mouth made Frank's blood run so cold, it tuned solid.

"Your card's been declined. Have you got another one?"

"What are you talking about? Try it again," said Barbara, annoyed. It must be the machine. Her card was fine. The cashier ran it again, the look on the woman's face saying *the 'machine is fine you snotty cow.'* Frank was wringing the handles of the trolley, praying for all he was worth. The beep was just as shocking the second time it rang across the room. The cashier handed back the card without a word, but Barbara didn't take it.

"You mustn't be doing it right. Do it again."

"I have done it twice already, have you cash, or another card?"

"Let me tell you, there's loads on that card."

"It's not my fault missus, your card's not working."

"How dare you talk to a customer like that, get me the manager immediately," Barbara demanded. Up to now, the people in the queue were enjoying the impromptu floor show, but when it became clear Barbara was going nowhere, their grumbles became less muted and slightly threatening.

"Come on, Barbara," pleaded Frank.

"Come on, what, Frank?" she snapped. "Have you got the cash on you?"

"No," he said quietly.

"Neither do I. It's their flipping machine. They can sort things out."

"Don't make a scene."

"Oh, shut up, Frank."

The cashier came back, talking quietly to a man in a suit. He was nodding and listening but not smiling. He beckoned to another staff member, who opened a third till, letting the waiting customers through this one-woman blockade.

"Let's try this again, shall we?" said the manager, sliding in behind the cashier and swiping the card a third time. Frank knew the beep was coming this time, and was ready for it.

"I am sorry, madam. Your card won't go through."

"It must be your machine."

"It's not the machine, because it is receiving a message from your bank."

"What bloody message?" demanded Barbara, starting to get loud.

The manager handed over the credit-card machine, and there on the screen, she read, *Insufficient Funds.*

"That is absolutely ridiculous," stammered Barbara. "There's thousands on that card, even before the credit limit. Tell him, Frank."

"Let's just go."

"What about the shopping?" asked Barbara.

"Leave it. We can come back later," said Frank, taking Barbara by the arm and steering her toward the door.

"Wait," called the manager. "You forgot your shopping bags."

Barbara twisted in Frank's grip. "Keep the bloody bags! It's the last thing you'll ever get off us, *asshole.*"

Frank tugged her after him, trying to get out of the shop as quick as he could. It was all too late. No matter what he did, the truth was going to come out.

***

The raised voices and slamming of doors outside number Two Honeysuckle Lane reached most people's ears on the street. Mrs. O'Shea was having a full-blown meltdown, standing outside her car in the middle of her driveway. Mr. O'Shea was doing everything he could to calm her down, but that was only making matters worse.

All the noise woke Brendan from his hangover-induced slumber. He got out of bed feeling as stiff as a board. He wasn't used to spending so long resting; it must have been early afternoon. He dressed and went to the kitchen, where the laptop was still turned to the message board and the growing list of comments following his post. Some of the new comments were seriously nasty. Time for Tina Ryan to vanish, Brendan thought. With a few swift keystrokes, Tina Ryan ceased to exist. On the bottom corner of the screen flashed a mail notice. Brendan clicked it open. It was from his office, saying he was required, *required*, to attend a disciplinary meeting Monday at eleven in Pulter's office.

Brendan slammed the laptop closed. He couldn't believe they were doing this to him over some stupid, worthless marketing drone having a hissy fit. Pulter had to be behind it. He'd never liked Brendan, and this was just the opportunity he needed to put the boot in, yet-another drone sent to stand in his way. The directors of the company were only interested in making money, and Brendan was the one raking it in for them. He was sure that Pulter had said nothing to the top brass about what was going on. If he had, it would be Pulter sitting at home on his arse, not the other way around. It was infuriating the way that word, *required*, stuck in his brain.

The voice rose to the surface again, as if it had picked that exact moment to inject its evil into Brendan's head. It snatched the word *required* from the ether of his thoughts and knew it had struck gold.

Required. Commanded. Ordered. It chuckled.

"Be quiet," Brendan said with a note of derangement.

Required. Required. REQUIRED!

"Shut up!" he said, louder this time. Brendan stood and paced the room, holding his head in his hands.

Do as you're told, weakling, toad, useless little shit, the voice taunted.

"*Shut your fucking mouth!*" he screamed, running blindly across the kitchen, holding his head before him like a bowling ball, pain racking his brain. When he collided with the fridge full force, it knocked him out cold. Just as the blackness took him, Brendan heard the voice laugh.

Chapter 20

"Stop shouting, Barbara. Everyone's looking," Frank said.

"I've never been so embarrassed in all my life. You just stood there like some great gormless lump," she said, slamming the car door. She was out of control.

"Please, come inside," Frank said, seeing curtains twitch up and down the lane.

"You know more than you're telling, don't you?" Barbara said, stabbing an accusing finger in Frank's chest.

"The neighbours are looking. Keep your voice down."

"Let them look!" she screamed. "What are you hiding, Frank?"

"I'm not doing this here," he said, walking away and leaving the front door open behind him. Barbara stood where she was, her blood boiling, but there was no point shouting at empty space. She followed him inside, slamming the door behind her.

Frank was sitting in the kitchen with his elbows on the table, holding his forehead.

"What's going on, Frank?" she demanded.

"It's gone."

"What's gone?"

"The money. Our money. It's all gone."

"I don't believe you. Where has it gone?" she asked, her voice loaded with shock.

"I lost it."

"How the hell did you lose our money? It was in the bank!"

"I gambled it, all right?" He jumped to his feet, knocking over his chair.

Barbara was frozen to the spot, eventually shaking her head slowly. Frank was waiting for the next explosion, but it didn't come. Instead, she went into the sitting room and started up the computer.

Twenty minutes later, she came back into the kitchen. Frank was sitting at the table, hanging his head in shame.

"It's more than just gone, isn't it?"

Frank hung his head lower.

"*Isn't it?*"

"Yes."

"You've got one chance, and this is it. I want to know all of it."

Over the next half an hour, he told her about the Internet poker, the bookies, about chasing the money, trying to win it back. Through it all, she said nothing, but her face lost all its colour, fading to grey. When he got to the part about the Black Swan Pub and the card game, he skimmed over the details. He just said that he had lost money to a loan shark who was now putting the squeeze on him.

"How much do you owe him?" she asked.

"Harry? The guts of five grand, but I only lost two."

She shook her head, standing and shuffling to the door, like a woman sleepwalking.

"Where are you going?"

She didn't answer, just walked out.

Frank sat alone in the kitchen for a long time. It was well over an hour before the front door opened once more. He wanted to run into the hall, but his feet wouldn't move. Barbara strode determinedly into the kitchen, sitting down at the table beside him.

"Before I do this, I have to know it's going to be worth it," she said, her face set like stone. "For so very long, I have been missing what we had. I feel alone in this marriage, abandoned. If you want me to face this with you, Frank, all that has to change."

Frank nearly cried with relief. "I swear to God, everything will be different. I'll never gamble again, I swear. I'll get back everything I lost. I promise."

"You don't get it, do you?" she asked, fury burning bright in her eyes. "It's you that I lost, not money, not things. I don't give a damn about the house, the car, or even the money! This family needs the man you were. I need the man I fell in love with."

Frank was humbled and stupefied. He nodded through his tears, knowing that nothing he could say would even come close to matching the magic of those words.

"First things first: You're going into counselling, and I want to hear you say it."

"Want me to say what?"

"I want you to say that you have a gambling problem, and mean it."

Frank said nothing in that moment. He took a hard look at himself. It was easy to say the words, but he had been given the chance to make a clean break in his life, and he intended to make it count. Frank let his heart do the talking for once. When the words came out, he knew he was telling the truth, for the first time in such a long time.

"I know it. I have a gambling problem."

"Give me your wallet," Barbara said, holding out her hand. Frank did as he was told. She emptied all his cards on the counter, and from a drawer, she took a massive scissors and sliced each in half.

"What are you doing?" he asked.

"If you want trust, you need to earn it," she told him.

Frank said nothing but dragged the bin closer to take the dissected plastic, complicit and happy with this destruction.

"The second rule is simple. The next time you bet, me and the kids are gone. Have you got it?"

"I got it," he said sincerely.

"Tomorrow, we go to the bank. Today, we are getting that loan shark off our backs," she said.

After leaving the house, Frank told Barbara everything about Harry, excluding what was due to happen with the house on Davis Road in a few days. Barbara drove their new Lexus into the nearest garage and approached the salesman.

"How much will you give me for that?" she asked bluntly, pointing at the shiny new car.

"As a trade-in?"

"No, just to buy it," she said.

The salesman looked dubious. "We don't buy cars, missus. We sell them."

"What if we were to trade it in against that?" she said, indicating a twelve-year-old Volvo languishing in the corner.

The salesman looked from one car to the other before answering. "Your Lexus is worth about twenty-five thousand. The Volvo is twelve hundred. The difference is twenty-three and change. If you're serious, missus, there is no way I have that kind of money lying around today?"

"Give me five grand and the Volvo. I will trust you for the rest," said Barbara. The salesman looked like he had been slapped.

"For how long?" he said at last.

"Three weeks," said Barbara. "If you have not sold it by then, just give me back the car. You get yours back, and the cash." Barbara held out her hand like a cattle trader. "Do we have a deal?"

The salesman thought for a second, but only a second, and said, "Deal."

An hour after that, Barbara pushed open the door of the Black Swan Pub and walked straight up to the counter. Greg was lounging where he always did, giving the new, unusual customer a wary eye.

"Is Harry here?" Barbara asked.

"Who's asking?" growled Greg.

"I'm asking. Is that good enough for you?"

Greg regarded the woman with a string of pearls around her neck for a moment before lifting the phone. After a quick conversation, he hung up and said, "Take a seat. He'll be here soon."

Barbara and Frank sat in a booth and waited. Fifteen minutes later, the door opened, and a leather-jacketed man entered the bar. Frank elbowed Barbara. "That's him," he whispered.

Barbara stood up, and walked over to Harry. "Mr. McCarthy?"

"Yea, what you want?"

"I believe you know my husband, and he owes you money?"

Harry looked around Barbara, toward Frank. "Yea, what about it?"

"How much?"

"It's nothing to do with you. That's between me and him."

"That is where you're completely wrong, Mr. McCarthy. It is everything to do with me, and you better remember that. I asked you how much you were owed." Barbara sounded like a teacher scolding a child, and amazingly, it worked.

"Four thousand nine hundred," he said at last.

Barbara rummaged in her handbag and started to hand over bundles of cash. Harry held out one hand, then two as the stack of notes mounted. She pulled out a fifth and final wad of cash and added it to the money Harry was holding.

"It's all there. Count it," she said.

"I know what five grand feels like, missus. I don't need to count it," he snarled.

"That is us clear, then?"

"Looks like it," Harry said grumpily.

"I never want to see you again," Barbara said, walking away.

"I'm not that fond of you, either," he snarled. Barbara walked toward the door, and Frank slid out of the booth to follow her.

Harry whispered as he passed, "Nothing's changed. See you Wednesday."

"What did you say?" asked Barbara, from the door.

"Nothing, sexy." Harry laughed. Barbara knew he'd said something, but she wanted to get out of the place. She stormed out of the Black Swan without a backward glance, but Frank knew better. He was still on the hook. He knew his ordeal was far from over.

***

The phone beeped on the pillow beside Ogie's head. His eyes struggled open. It felt like he had just nodded off; his body was leaden with exhaustion. He rolled over and found the phone. He pressed the button, opening one eye and trying to focus on the screen. *Are you coming over for seconds?* it said. Ogie dropped his head back on the pillow. Seconds? Martha was insatiable. The memory of last night was still fresh in his mind, and in every strained muscle in his body. He smiled at nothing in particular, running through the carnal images he had stored in his memory from their last tryst.

He lay there for ten minutes before texting back: *On my way.* If it was being offered on a plate, it would be rude to say no.

Ogie showered for the second time before dressing. It was early afternoon, but his body clock told him it should be morning. Before he opened his front door, Ogie had a moment of doubt. What did he think he was doing? He knew nothing about this woman besides the fact she was stunning, and a complete animal in the sack. He realised that he was still playing by the rule that governed his whole single life: No matter who, no matter where, if she was willing, Ogie was drilling.

He stroked the timber of the door in front of him, trying to decide what to do. Things weren't so simple anymore. He was shitting on his own doorstep, now that he had a doorstep to shit on. He couldn't just pick up and get out of Dodge if the doo-doo hit the fan. Ogie had a massive anchor of brick and mortar around his neck. Despite this moment of clarity, there was something about Martha that Ogie couldn't resist. She was gorgeous, that's for sure, but it was more than that. She had a taste, an essence that was so delicious, he couldn't get enough of her. She tasted like paradise. Ogie's brain was never in charge for long, and the growing need in his jeans soon overruled any sane decision he might make.

He was out the door as quick as a flash, and across the manicured lawn of number four. Ogie rang the bell, and the chime was still echoing through the hall when the door opened. Martha stood there in a see-through wrap, with nothing on beneath it.

"Wow," he said.

"Oh, it's you," she said teasingly, staying in the door.

"You're out of control," he said with a smile.

"You think?" she asked. Her fingers flipped the gossamer robe off her shoulders, letting it drop to the ground at her feet. "What do you think now?"

Ogie stepped into the hall, taking her in his arms. He let his tongue explore the moist cave of her mouth while his hand delved between her legs, his finger slipping into her, on a river of moisture. She moaned into his mouth, and swung the door closed behind them.

Sweeping her up in his arms, Ogie carried her into the kitchen. He sat her naked rump on the table, in the exact spot Tim always chose to complete his paperwork. They kissed with savage hunger for ages before Ogie pushed her away. He gave her wicked look and drew up a kitchen chair, sitting there like a neighbour calling round for tea.

Taking Martha by the ankles, he lifted her feet until they were flat on the table. Stroking upward with slow hands, he massaged the inside of her calves, his fingers running higher until they met the warm, moist skin at the back of her knees. Ogie's hands parted Martha's legs like opening a pair of curtains. His eyes drank in her freshly shaved pubis, framing her perfect, glistening pussy. Martha emitted a small noise, somewhere between a whimper and a prayer. Ogie sat back in the chair, making her wait.

He stripped his shirt off and slipped his jeans down his legs. All this time, he enjoyed the sight of this woman, waiting and exposed, begging for his attention. The tension was getting too much for Martha, who let a hand drift toward the centre of her need. Ogie swatted it away, denying her even that little relief. Forcing her to wait until he felt she was at the pinnacle of her desire, and only then, he sat forward and devoured what she had laid on her table for him.

When Ogie slipped out of Martha's house, he was running late; the guys were due to pick him up at any minute. He was leaving behind a sweat-glistened puddle of a woman. He was amazed how many times he had been able to make love to her. With a fleeting touch, she would draw his manhood from the doors of death, like Lazarus. He had come so often that the last few times, there was nothing left to soil her sheets, or her skin.

No living person had seen him enter or leave the Murphy house, which is not to say his passing went unnoticed. A little red light blinked on the high-definition camera mounted in an upstairs window of number nine. Brendan was out cold on his kitchen floor, but even when Brendan slept, he missed little.

Chapter 21

The Digital Imaging Department in the police station was a long-running joke. When the sign first appeared on the door, it caused giggles to run riot among the rank and file, much to the annoyance of the chief inspector. What wasn't apparent from the door was the tiny proportions of this impressively named department. Completely empty, the room was hardly twelve-feet square. A sweating Adams was now wedged into this space with the equipment operator, Dolan, Sims, and enough computer equipment to launch the space shuttle. They'd been here for hours, running through the camera footage from the apartment complex where the canal victim's car had been found. If anyone had to leave the room, the whole lot of them had to stand up and shuffle about to get the door open.

"How do you work in this shoebox?" asked Adams, half-blind from gazing at the grainy pictures.

"You get used to it," said the operator, twirling dials to adjust the focus of the shots. The victim's car drove into view at ten minutes to ten in the evening. The car-park lights were already on, the weak light reducing the recording to a fuzzy black-and-white image. They watched as the woman, who now lay cold on a mortician's slab, prepared for her run by stretching. She left the car park and turned right on the towpath, running toward her doom with a bouncing stride.

The camera luckily picked up a section of the path near the gate, which gave the detectives a glimpse of everyone that passed. With painful slowness, they let the images roll. Fifteen minutes after the victim left, a couple appeared in shot, coming from the direction of the apartments. They passed the victim's car and continued onto the path. They had a golden Labrador with them, which they let off the lead as soon as they were on the canal path. They turned left, away from the murder scene. A while later, a lone female dog walker appeared, exactly as the couple had, and also turned left. In the twenty minutes that followed, nobody at all passed along the canal.

The next person to appear came along the path, not from the car park, they came into view in the top right-hand corner of the screen. The man walked as far as the gate and turned off the path, walking past the victim's car and then out of the shot. He appeared to be a fairly tall middle-aged man, who had a stoop. He was wearing largish glasses, and there were shiny patches on his head, indicating he had thinning hair, cut blandly. Judging by the direction the man came from, he should have passed the victim running, or at least where the body was found. Adams printed off a still shot, to be used later. He looked like someone coming home from work, by the way he was dressed.

They played the footage all the way through, until midnight. The dog walkers returned within the hour. Several groups of joggers and dog walkers passed both ways along the path, without entering or exiting at the gate. When the time passed midnight, Adams sat back and stretched.

"You can stop it there," he said to the camera operator. On the desk, stills of every person who had passed through the gate or along the path were spread in a fan. Adams pulled the photos of the dog walkers and the tall, stooped man.

"I'd bet a week's wages these people live in the apartments," he said. "Look at this guy. He looks like he's coming home from work. Those aren't clothes I'd wear if I were going for a walk. He looks like a teacher to me."

It was a slender lead to start out the investigation, but it was important to find some witnesses from the area at the time of death. "Get some uniforms, and do a house-to-house survey of the apartments. Give them all copies of these photos," Adams said to Dolan, handing over three he'd selected from the pile on the desk.

Dolan took the photos and tried to get out of the room. Everyone ended up standing and shuffling again.

"What if the killer was already waiting for her on the canal?" asked Sims when Dolan was gone.

"Her in particular?" asked Adams.

"Perhaps, if this was her regular route, or perhaps just any woman."

"It's possible, I guess. Let's have a look at who was hanging around before our girl arrived," said Adams.

The camera operator spun a few dials, and the woman appeared at her car going through her stretches, this time in reverse. Soon, the car backed out of the shot. What followed was a period of nothing noteworthy. Then, out of nowhere, a man walked backward from the right-hand side of the screen, striding backward along the path, through the gate, and across the apartment-complex car park before vanishing clean out of the shot. The time was 9:32 p.m. The operator stopped the footage and played it forward. This time, the same tall, stooped figure that they had seen earlier walked into the shot through the gate and turned right on the towpath.

"Is that our teacher friend again?" asked Sims.

Adams sat closer to the screen. "It sure is."

The operator ran the image forward and backward a few times before Adams said, "Stop it there." Adams pointed at a dark shape hanging from the man's right hand. "He's carrying a bag, see?"

Adams retrieved a photo of the tall man he'd printed earlier. Definitely no bag.

"Nine thirty-two, this guy enters the path and goes right. Nine fifty-four, our victim begins her jog, also going right. No one else passes from that direction on the path until the tall, mysterious stranger reappears at ten-forty," said Adams. The room was practically filled with the sound of cogs crunching in his brain.

"Correct," agreed the camera operator.

"Not a very long walk, an hour and eight minutes there and back, but it puts him right in the middle of our estimated time of death," said Sims.

"This guy could be our key witness or main suspect. Even walking, he should have reached the area where the woman was found," said Adams. The camera operator sat back and let the two detectives talk.

Adams turned in his chair to face Sims. "Why would you take a bag along a canal and come back without it less than an hour later?"

"Because he dumped it," said Sims.

"It could be a bin bag, but it looks too square," said Adams.

"Whatever it was, he came back without it," said Sims.

"I think we should go back and take another look at where they found the car. And take another look along the canal. It might have more than one secret to share," Adams said.

A while later, Adams and Sims were standing in the exact spot the little Fiat had been parked in the camera footage they had watched. They had explored farther along the canal path to the left, away from the crime scene, and found a park riddled with dog walkers. In the apartment complex, teams of uniformed officers were going door to door, taking statements from the residents. Adams checked in with Dolan, and so far, no sign of any of the people from the photos.

"Time to think some more about our mystery bag carrier," said Adams, flipping open his notebook. "One hour and eight minutes on the path. The woman left twenty-two minutes after he did."

"Yes, but she was jogging, and he was walking. Or at least they were, when they left here," Sims said.

"How fast do you think she was jogging, and how fast do people walk?" he asked.

"I don't know. Why?"

"I was trying to figure out how much distance he'd have covered before she caught up with him. Did she pass him before she was killed, or did she never pass him at all?"

"I see what you mean, but you'll never figure that out."

"You said you jog?" asked Adams.

"I did. I do," Sims answered, a little puzzled.

"In exactly twenty-two minutes, I want you to jog out that gate and turn right. Keep going at a steady pace until you see me."

"We don't know how fast either of them were actually going," she said, checking the time on her watch, not particularly keen on having Adams watching her run along in the middle of the day in a pantsuit. It wasn't the most-flattering way to view a girl.

"No, but it's worth a go," said Adams, walking away.

Exactly twenty-two minutes later, Sims jogged reluctantly after him. It was uncomfortable running fully clothed. People stared at her as she passed them on the path. Her heavy leather shoes slapped harshly against the concrete. The path seemed longer than it had yesterday, and even more overgrown than she remembered. There was nowhere for someone to hide a bag, or themselves, that she could see. She spotted everyone coming against her long before she got to them. There was little chance of someone surprising a jogger from the front.

Then the canal curved suddenly. She was starting to sweat as she rounded the curve, catching sight of Adams ahead of her. "Stephen!" she called, stopping him where he was.

She slowed to a walk for the last fifty yards. In the near distance, they could just see the yellow Garda tape, fluttering in the bushes. Adams was standing in the shade of the bridge spanning the canal.

"Did you see any good places to get rid of a bag on your run?"

"Not really, but he could've dumped it in the water anywhere," she said, panting and aware that she was red-faced and sweaty, which made her even more red-faced and sweaty.

"True, if he was dumping a bin bag, full of tin cans. What if he was worried about being seen? Where would you dump something you didn't want found?"

"I think he'd wait until he was out of sight. That was the first bend in the path, or under the bridge. That would be my choice," she answered, looking around her.

"That's what I'd do," said Adams. "If you're right about him wanting to dump something, and assuming our timing isn't miles out, he walks along until he comes to the bridge, is about to dump the bag, and just at the wrong moment, a jogger appears and spoils everything."

"Or she sees him doing it," added Sims.

"That sounds a like a motive to me. Assuming we're right, that is."

Adams looked out across the murky water. It was filthy brown, hiding anything that wasn't actually floating on the surface. He walked up and down the edge of the canal, as if searching for an invisible clue. "What if we're wrong about this guy? We could be chasing smoke here," he said at last.

"That's your call, boss."

He paced up and down some more, stopping all of a sudden. "It's worth checking. We will have to keep the door-to-door enquiries going, of course, but this is too strange to ignore," he said, to himself as much as Sims. Adams flipped open his mobile and punched a few numbers. When the call was picked up, he said, "Sub-aqua unit, please."

***

Brendan woke on the kitchen floor with a lump on his head as big as an egg. He gingerly touched it and winced, but the pain was good. It cleared his mind of everything else. It wasn't good to lose it like that; he needed to keep a grip on things. There was too much at stake. The pain in his scalp acted like medicine for the moment, but it would fade. What would happen then? Would the voice would be back, taunting him again? He need to be ready for what was ahead; he needed to be in control. There was so much that needed to be done and such little time. There were more than one loose end that needed tying up. He had to hurry. He dragged himself to his feet, but his head spun. He steadied himself against the worktop as his swirling vision came back to normal.

Brendan spent the next hour sitting with a cold pack pressed against the throbbing mound on his forehead but still managed to smile. It was the first peace he'd experienced in days. No voices, no doubts, and no worries. He flipped open his computer. The wallpaper was a long-distance shot of Angie Sweeney. Since gaining access to her Internet accounts, Brendan had been able to infiltrate nearly every aspect of her electronic life. He had a programme sending copies of her incoming and outgoing e-mails to a clone folder online. He had access to her phone. He'd even hacked into her message box. Reading her words and listening to her voice brought them closer, he thought.

He'd spent hours reading her posts over the last months, but the newest correspondences sent him into a rage. Even after that fool of a boy had been shuffled from this mortal coil, it seemed that he still was interfering with his plans. Post after post, she lamented his passing, idolising him in memory. Brendan had expected her to grieve for a while, but this was too much. He was a stupid kid, not the love of her life. It enraged him how she put him on a pedestal. Brendan knew he should wait before trying to contact her, but he was running out of time. She was never right for a yobbo like that. Angie was always meant to be with someone greater, someone worldlier. She was meant for *him*.

Tony Kelly's funeral was coming up. When that was over, surely Angie would put the boy behind her. The more Brendan thought about the funeral, the more he had an urge to see the boy up-close. To shake hands with his devastated family, knowing he was the giver and taker of life. Brendan felt God would feel similarly, if he indeed ever rode a city bus. Rubbing along, shoulder to shoulder with people, oblivious to his eminence. 'Yes' thought Brendan, it would be an enlightening experience, and quite apt.

His head swam with ideas and plans. It was thrilling imagining what lay before him, but he was nothing if not a creature of habit. Soon, the draw of his daily routine invaded his mental wanderings. As he did every day, Brendan opened his camera-system and looked for Angie's comings and goings. He had cameras mounted inside his upstairs windows, under the eaves of the roof, even in holes drilled through roof tiles. He had several cameras focused on Angie's home. One in particular was focused on her bedroom window. A programme on his computer recorded everything, using motion-detection software so he would not have to endure hours of boredom scanning the footage himself.

Brendan scrolled through the files at high speed. Today, little had happened. Brendan was about to close the folder when a movement caught his attention. A wide-angle shot captured a person leaving a house farther down the street. Brendan stopped the recording and selected a different camera, this one taking in a wider view of the street. He let the images play. He saw the skinny man who'd moved into number five a few weeks ago leaving his house. The man slinked across the driveways to ring the bell next door. The man stayed in view at the open door for a few moments before vanishing completely. Brendan let the images flash past at high speed. The door didn't open again until an hour ago. He was disgusted; he didn't need a camera to tell him what they had been up to. After all, he'd seen the blonde woman stagger drunkenly into the wrong house in the middle of the night. What galled him the most, was the fact that this moral degenerate of a woman, had the brass neck to belittle him to all the others living on the street. She was nothing but a whore.

She sickened him, she was everything he despised in females. Women were completely deviant, with no sense of loyalty. Vain, self-absorbed, untrustworthy, venal, and immoral. He knew her kind and was revolted by them. She was exactly the same type of woman who had shunned his advances in the past, opting for dullards and knuckle-draggers in his place.

Brendan isolated the image of the man in the moment he moved inside the door, saving the image on his computer. The shot was grainy and indistinct. He needed to improve the photo if it was going to be of any use to him. Brendan knew that the woman needed to be punished, and he was just the man to do it. After all, that was what he was destined to do, rain down retribution on the unjust. Brendan happened to have access to the exact place that would be able to enhance the photo. If NASA could read a newspaper from orbit, then they could improve a photo from four doors away. He had permanent access to their systems, through a programme he'd installed while upgrading their server network some months ago. Brendan logged in and accessed a programme used to enhance satellite images.

After twenty minutes, he'd a slightly fuzzy image of a man's back, around which were entwined two nude arms ending in a bare shoulder. The curve of a bare hip and a cascade of blonde hair could also be seen. What was completely clear was that the faceless man and woman were kissing. Judging by Brendan's smug look, twenty thousand dollars of supercomputer time had never been so well spent.

***

Angie hadn't left the house since the coppers had been over to interview her. She couldn't believe that someone wanted to kill Tony, or that those two thicks could believe she'd had something to do with it. Angie never thought of herself as a crier, but she had done little else since Tony died. The depth of her grief had caught her completely by surprise. Yea, she liked him and perhaps loved him. Even so, she'd never thought that anything would cause her this kind of pain. If there were any good to come out of this whole rotten mess, it was her mother.

Mary had been great since the accident, so great in fact, she was like a different woman. Growing up, Angie had blamed Mary for letting Pat bully them all the way he did. She thought that if Mary had stood up to him more, all of their lives would have been better. Angie didn't take any of Pat's guff anymore. She couldn't understand how Mary could stand even to be around him. Angie felt a little guilty now for the way she had held Mary accountable for her father's behaviour. Still, guilt or no guilt, Angie knew it had been Mary's job to protect them, and she'd let them down. Her fat moron of a father never let her down. He always was just as bad as she dreaded he'd be. The thought of his DNA running through her veins was enough to make her sick. She once joked with her friends that if any kid of hers came out looking like Pat, she'd send it straight back.

The tears seemed to come less today than they had yesterday. She even had a few moments where the thought of Tony wasn't hanging over her. Afterward, Angie felt guilty about that feeling. Was she accepting Tony's death too easily? If she were a better girlfriend, surely she'd feel much worse than she did. Her pent-up emotions found a way to vent themselves when she checked her Facebook page. Some tramp named Tina Ryan had left a shitty message about Tony. It was weirder than shitty, but fair play to her friends, they'd torn strips off her. The message still bothered Angie. She couldn't remember anyone called Tina Ryan from school. She couldn't even remember adding her as a friend. It got even stranger, when Tina Ryan completely vanished, like she'd never existed in the first place. Good riddance to bad rubbish, thought Angie. The few messages she'd read were creepy, anyway.

Angie was lying on her bed, thinking about Tony, when she heard Pat arrive home in a rage. Angie actually felt the house rattle when he slammed the door. What the hell was his problem now? Downstairs, she could hear doors slamming open and closed. Angie ignored the noise, fully expecting it to blow over like it always did. Pat's bad moods came often but were just as quickly fixed by a bottle of beer. Angie heard her mother shouting, arguing back, which wasn't normal. Mary rarely argued; instead, she stood there and took whatever Pat threw at her.

Today, Angie could hear Mary screaming at him. She sat up on her bed, listening more closely. The shouting rose in volume, and then she heard the fighting begin in earnest. Pat was roaring at the top of his voice. There were crashes coming from the kitchen. Angie opened her bedroom door, so she could hear what was going on.

"What happened to the rest of it?" she heard Pat shout.

"I used a bit to pay some bills and get the shopping. We've got to eat something, you know, or did you think the fridge filled up by magic?" Mary snapped.

"A bit! Half the money's gone. I needed that to pay for supplies, you stupid cow. How the hell am I meant to finish the job without the materials?"

"Use the housekeeping money to pay for the supplies. It's all the same thing," Mary shouted.

"There won't be any housekeeping, unless I can get the job done, you stupid cow," he roared, slamming something closed.

"We've got to eat! You're being ridiculous. What are you doing?" More doors slammed, and the sound of crashing crockery filled the house.

"You've been hiding money somewhere, you bitch!" he screamed. More crashing sounds came from the kitchen.

"Stop that, Pat! *Stop*!"

Angie heard the sounds of a struggle. It sounded like they were ripping the kitchen apart. What started as a struggle took only a moment to descend into a full-blooded fight. She heard punches land, then screaming. Then Angie heard Billy's voice in the middle of it all.

Angie threw the bedroom door wide open and ran down the stairs. Pat was yelling something about respect, but mainly, it was screams that filled her ears. Furniture crashed against the kitchen door, sending splinters of timber shooting across the hall. Glass and china flew through the air. Angie descended the stairs as fast as she could in her bare feet, running across the hall, regardless of the timber fragments.

In the kitchen, it looked like World War III had started, the way the room was torn apart. Cabinet doors hung ajar, their contents spilled across the room. The table had only three legs left, as one had been broken off when it crashed into the wall. Chairs were upturned, and the floor was littered with broken glass. Pat had Mary by the throat as he punched her in the face.

"You goddamn fucking bitch!" he snarled.

Mary lashed out at him with balled fists, but he was too strong. Billy was trying to pull Pat off his mother while Pat unloaded a savage haymaker into the side of Mary's face, sending her crashing face-first into the cooker. Her legs gave way, and she crumpled to the ground. Billy tried to get between them as Pat leaned over Mary, blind with rage.

"You're nothing but a stupid lazy bitch, and I regret the day I married you!" he spat, lashing out with his leg, aiming a kick at her head. Billy dived on Pat's foot, throwing his father off balance. The two of them landed in a heap on the floor.

"Get off me, you fool," Pat snarled, grabbing Billy by the jumper and throwing him across the room.

Mary moaned. Blood flowed from a cut just below her eye, and her face was already swelling up in several places. Angie ran across the kitchen, throwing herself on Pat before he could get to his feet. He met her with a punch to the side of the head, which sent her skidding through the debris on the kitchen floor. As Angie lay stunned, Pat got to his feet and began kicking her in the back and ribs. "You useless slut, you're as bad as her!" he roared, between kicks.

Angie thought her own father was going to kill her. She rolled across the floor away from him. Turning her head, she half expected to see a boot spinning toward her face. That was when she heard Pat scream in pain.

Pat was standing still, his two hands wrapped around his leg and blood seeping between his fingers. Billy stood a few feet away, pointing a heavy butcher's knife at his father with trembling hands.

"Leave them alone!" Billy shouted, his little-boy voice cracked with tears.

Pat didn't move. Billy continued to cry and shake. Angie dragged herself up against the wall while Mary came toward Billy, holding out a soothing hand.

"It's all right, Billy. It's over now. Give me the knife," she said. Her hand moved along Billy's arm slowly until she had a grip of the knife handle. He let it go, as if her touch had unlocked him, and crumpled against his mother, bawling.

Pat took a step forward, but Mary's arm shot out, leveling the blade with Pat's neck, his stride taking him right to the tip.

"Get back," she growled.

Fire burned in Pat's eyes. With one hand still clamped over his sliced thigh, he spat. "You don't have the guts!"

He moved forward a fraction, but the blade didn't give way. The sharp steel cut into his walrus-like neck, and a trickle of blood fell inside his shirt collar, tainting any certainty he had about his wife's will.

"Get out of this house," she said in a trembling voice, the deadly knife still extended in her quaking hand.

"It's my house!"

"Get out now, Pat, or you might never get out," she said, advancing, pushing the tip of the knife deeper into his skin. Billy tried to hold her back, his protection now favouring his father.

Pat's nerve broke. He stormed from the house, leaving droplets of blood on the floor where he had stood. The front door near came off its hinges as he left.

Mary collapsed in tears amid the tatters of her kitchen, still holding the knife. Billy hugged her, crying just as much as his mother. Angie managed to get to her feet. She took the knife from Mary's hand, and only then did she become aware of the three-inch piece of glass sticking out of her arm. She eased the glass out of her flesh, wrapping a tea towel around the cut. Thankfully, it didn't bleed too much.

"It's all right, Billy," cooed Mary, stroking his head. "He'll never hurt us again, I promise."

Mary got herself together and managed to calm Billy. She locked the front door and wedged a chair under the handle, in case Pat tried to get back in. On the hall table, Mary found the card Sims had left. She dialed the number. The cool, female voice on the other end of line was tremendously reassuring.

"Detective Sims?" Mary asked in a shaking voice.

"Yes, this is Sims. Who's this?"

"Mary Sweeney. You were at my house yesterday."

"Oh, yes. Is everything okay, Mrs. Sweeney?"

"Not really. Can you come over, please?"

"We're tied up right now, Mrs. Sweeney. Is this about Tony?"

"Not exactly, but I really need help. Please, I've no one else to call."

After a pause and a whispered conversation, Sims said, "Okay, Mary, we're on the way over."

"Thanks so much," she said, beginning to cry as the connection went dead.

The doorbell rang an hour later. Mary checked who was there, through the sitting-room window, before opening it.

"Thanks for coming," she said to the detectives. This time Sims led them into the house, Adams taking a backseat. There was concern in the detectives' eyes but little surprise. Mary led the way while they followed quietly behind her. With one sweeping glance, both detectives took in the destruction in the kitchen, as well as the injuries both women were tending.

"Do either of you need an ambulance?" asked Sims gently.

"No need for that. It's not the first time."

"Was it your husband?" asked Sims.

"Yes," said Mary, hanging her head in shame.

"Perhaps I should take the young lad away while you talk?" suggested Adams.

"There is no point. He saw everything," Mary said.

"What do you want to do about it, Mary?" asked Sims. The detective knew most domestic-violence cases fail because the partner won't testify.

"He turned on me for no reason lots of times before, but this time, the kids got it as well. I'll never let that happen again. I want him gone," Mary said with determination.

Over the next hour, both Mary and Angie made statements. Their injuries were photographed, as well as the destruction of the kitchen. While Adams issued an arrest order for Pat Sweeney, Sims photographed Mary's more-intimate bruising.

Angie took Adams to one side. "Remember you asked me to let you know if there was anything fishy happening, you know, with Tony?"

"Yes."

"There's something, most likely nothing, but you asked."

"Go on. You never know," said Adams.

"I started getting weird messages on Facebook from a girl called Tina Ryan. Then, a couple of days ago, she left a nasty message about Tony getting what he deserved. Now she's vanished. The thing is, I can't remember any Tina Ryan in my year, and neither can anyone else."

Adams didn't look blown away. "It's most likely nothing, but I can get some of the computer guys in the station to trace the computer IP address. We'll need your Facebook account and password."

Angie wrote out the details and handed them over. "Don't go chatting up my friends pretending to me, detective," she said with the glimmer of a smile.

Adams always was amazed at how resilient kids were: dead boyfriend, beaten-up by her father, and still making jokes.

"If they are anything like you, Angie, I mightn't be able to help myself," he joked right back, widening her smile and making her cheeks go the slightest bit red.

***

The drive to the airport wasn't a pleasant experience. Martha felt torn between guilt and resentment. She was a churning mass of discontent. Each time she had a handle on what she needed to do, the emotion dominating her mind flipped. The traffic was light, but she gripped the steering wheel as if she were leading a Formula One race. The harder she tried to control her emotions, the more she thought about what she'd done. The most-upsetting part was, she honestly had no idea what she wanted to do. One minute, she was blinded by the excitement with Ogie; the next, fear crept over her at the thought of losing the life she had with Tim.

Things were no clearer by the time she parked at the airport. Martha joined the waiting crowd at the arrivals gate. All around her, mothers, daughters, husbands, children, and friends waited with giddy excitement for someone they loved to come into view. Martha felt overwhelmed by dread. She shuffled from foot to foot, biting her lower lip in trembling anticipation that bordered on terror. The first person appeared in the arrivals gate. The crowd hummed with excitement as those gathered search for a familiar face.

Martha could tell which of the people arriving knew nobody would be waiting. They kept their heads down as they passed through the gauntlet of expectation, and made no eye contact. Was that what she wanted for herself? To be insular in the world, to have no one waiting? If she wasn't careful, she would end up with just that. Perhaps it is better to have no one waiting, rather than the wrong one? Nothing was straightforward anymore. The world had gone to shit.

The more she thought about it, the worse she felt. She tried to shove everything to the back of her mind and concentrate on the moment. It so happened that Tim chose that second to round the corner. Her stomach flipped, and she felt a cold sweat break out on her skin. Martha forced a smile and waved. Tim waved back and manoeuvred a slalom course of hugging couples to join her. She hugged him one-handed, reaching for the luggage trolley with the other. Tim beamed as he dived in and kissed her on her lips. She told herself to be natural, but her whole body was knotted with stress. She hoped he wouldn't notice; after all, he never took any notice of her feelings before. Martha pulled the trolley between them, turning it toward the exit.

"God, I've missed you," Tim said, genuinely happy.

"I know. Me, too, baby," she answered, aiming the trolley at the exit. She had the distinct urge to run.

"How was the conference?" she asked, because she knew she should.

"It was fine. Where's the fire?" Tim asked with a smile.

"What fire?"

"I'm practically running to keep up with you. What's the rush?"

Slowing down, she apologised. "Sorry," she said.

"Are you feeling okay? You don't seem yourself."

"I'm fine," she said, noticing that her feet were moving faster again. She forced herself into a relaxed stroll. What chance had she of keeping things under wraps, if she couldn't control her own feet?

"I hope you brought me something nice, after leaving me alone all weekend," she said, forcing a smile on her lips. Tim always brought her presents. It was another thing she'd mixed feelings about. She liked getting things—who wouldn't? It was the way he gave them that irked her. She felt he was marking his territory, like some stray dog.

"That depends. Were you a good girl?" he teased.

"I was, like always, or don't you trust me?" she asked. Her words came out harsher than she had intended.

"I was only joking, sweetheart. Of course, I brought you a present. I have it in my bag," he said, stopping to rummage in his carry-on case.

"Not here, Tim," she said, steaming toward the exit, leaving him hurrying to catch up. When they got to the car, Martha used the key to pop open the boot, leaving Tim to load his case inside. Martha walked toward the driver's door. From behind her, Tim said, "It's okay, baby. I'll drive." Martha was yet again consigned to the passenger seat, no longer trusted to forge her own way in the world.

Tim slammed the boot closed and threw himself into the driver seat. He leaned across and kissed her again. His lips felt familiar and comfortable on hers; they fit well, like a pair of worn-in trainers. As she felt Tim's tongue push inside her mouth, she thought about Ogie. His lips were strange, unpredictable, and exciting. Admittedly, in the heat of things, he'd crushed her lips more than once and their teeth had clashed, but the excitement of kissing him was magical. Tim was so predictable, even the length of his kisses were without mystery. In her mind, Martha began counting down. Right on cue, he pulled away.

"It's good to be home," he said, producing a jewelery box from behind his back. "For my good girl."

"You didn't have to," she said, taking the box.

"I wanted to."

Martha opened the box, revealing a heavy gold chain with an opal pendant. It was beautiful and looked expensive.

"Oh, Tim, it's gorgeous!" Martha took the chain out of the box and let the light hit the opal. It shimmered as if it were alive. "It must have cost a fortune. Can we afford it?"

"Gold is a good investment at the moment, and besides, any wife of mine will only get the best." There it was, Tim cocking his leg and pissing all over her, letting all the other dogs know she was his bitch.

All the way home, Tim gave her a blow-by-blow account of the conference. She was lost in a world of her own, his words bounced off her without effect. Now and again, she threw in an, "Oh, really?" or a "Yes" to keep the one-sided conversation flowing. She was delighted to see the familiar turn into Honeysuckle Lane, so she could escape his drone.

As Tim pulled into their drive, Martha stole a glance at Ogie's house. It seemed deserted, but his car was outside. He might have had a gig and went in the van with the band. Was it wrong that she felt cheated? That the band could be with him, while she had to stay at home, keeping their secret.

Martha unlocked the front door and went into the kitchen while Tim got his bag from the car. She put the kettle on to boil and got a pan out to make omelettes. She didn't hear Tim come in while she whisked eggs. She jumped with fright when he wrapped his arms around her waist.

"Don't do that! You scared me."

He laughed at her, so she hit him on the shoulder with the whisk, splattering him with egg dribble.

"I've missed you. Come up to bed."

"I'm cooking," she said, renewing her whisking with vigour.

"Leave that. I'm not hungry. Not for food, anyway," he said, pawing at her backside.

"Stop it!" she said, slapping away his hand.

"Come on, we can eat after," he said, trying to pull her toward the stairs.

Martha knew he was being playful, but the thought of him touching her, kissing her in places that Ogie had touched and kissed only hours ago was too much. He was pushing her into a corner, and the urge to run was growing.

"No!" she snapped, turning on him viciously. "I'm not some piece of meat to be pawed at whenever the mood takes you."

"I never said you were," Tim said, surprised. "I've missed you, and couldn't wait to see you. Is that a crime now?"

"That's the problem. It's all you. You missed me, you couldn't wait, you're not hungry, and you want sex. What about me? What if I don't feel like it?"

"I just thought . . ."

"You never think, Tim. You assume! The day you put this ring on my finger, you didn't take a partner. You thought you'd bought a woman, and I'm sick of it!"

Tim stood punch-drunk in the middle of the kitchen, wondering what the hell had just happened as Martha threw the whisk at him and walked away.

"Where are you going?" he called after her.

"For a walk, and don't think of following me!" she shouted, slamming the door.

In the kitchen, Tim was rooted to the spot, not understanding anything. It was as if he'd come home to a different life. Standing on their front step, Martha knew she had just made things worse, not better. She needed time to get her head straight. Martha strode away, not caring about the direction. She needed distance.

As evening was closing in, Martha found herself back at the top of Honeysuckle Lane. Her feet were sore from walking in shoes that were intended to look good, not work good. She still was no clearer in her mind about the situation, but at least she was back in control. She could see the light was on in her own sitting room. Ogie's house looked as empty as it had earlier, except now his sitting-room curtains were drawn against the encroaching gloom of evening. Ogie must have been home all along.

Martha needed to talk to someone, and Ogie was the only one with whom she could be completely honest. He already knew all the terrible parts of her story. Deep down, she needed to see him, to talk to him and see what he would say. Martha walked down the road instead of the footpath, keeping the cars between her and the houses. She slinked past her own door as quickly as possible, and slipped down the side of Ogie's house. The last thing she needed was Tim or one of the neighbours seeing her. She kept as quiet as she could, in case Tim was in the backyard.

As she was about to knock, she noticed the patio door lying open, so Martha slipped quietly inside. The kitchen was empty, but the door leading to the sitting room stood ajar, and music floated on the air. Martha walked into the sitting room, where the back of the couch was turned toward her.

"Ogie, we have to talk."

Annabelle's shocked face appeared over the couch. "You scared the hell out of me! What do you think you're doing?"

Martha stammered, "I thought you were Ogie, sorry."

"Clearly," said a snarky Annabelle. "What are you doing here? Do you make a habit of walking into people's homes unannounced?"

"What? No, of course not. Ogie said to call 'round."

"Call 'round by the front door and knock, I'm sure is how he intended it."

"You're right, I am so sorry. I'll go. Sorry."

"Hang on," Annabelle said, getting off the couch. "What did you want, anyway?"

"Nothing, I just wanted a word with Ogie."

"Nothing? You came in through the back door of your neighbour's house without knocking for nothing?"

"It wasn't nothing, I just can't remember. With the shock, it's not important."

"Hold on. Was it nothing, or not important?"

Martha knew she was tying herself up in knots. It was time to run.

"Sorry again," Martha said, walking quickly through the kitchen and out the patio door, but not so quickly that she failed to hear Annabelle say to herself, "What a flipping nutcase!"

Martha dashed into her own house and straight up the stairs, locking herself in the bathroom. Tim was up the stairs after her, like a rat up a drainpipe. She sat on the toilet in tears while Tim made heartfelt and useless apologies through the door. Why couldn't he just leave her alone? What had she done? The tears flowed down her face. Cupping her hands over her ears, she tried to shut herself off from Tim, from the whole damn world.

Chapter 22

Early on Monday morning, Brendan reread the notification from Brian Pulter. Obsessively, he returned to it, time and again. They were trying to undermine him, using any tiny excuse they could to subject him to ridicule. His work was important to him. It was the only place he felt needed; he wasn't going to give it up easily. He imagined disposing of both Potts and the imbecilic Brian Pulter, but as delightful as that thought was, the act seemed impractical. He should have been at his desk hours ago. At ten, Brendan left his house dressed like always, briefcase hanging from his hand as he sloped toward his car. Shortly before eleven, he parked the car and took the elevator up to his floor.

He crossed the open plan office, taking a route that took him close to the desk of Ms. Potts. Brendan had planned to corner the woman before the meeting and get her to withdraw this stupid complaint, but it wasn't to be. Her desk stood bare and desolate. His presence set a buzz among the cubicles. Phones rang, quickly answered, and followed by hushed conversations. Brendan dropped his briefcase on the floor beside his desk, draping his jacket over the back of his chair. He fired up his computer and found it disabled. A white-hot tidal wave of rage hovered over him, threatening to engulf everything. Brendan struggled to contain it, to control himself. It's only temporary, he silently assured himself.

Brendan thought of all the programmes he had connected back to his work station. Lots of his money was tied up in that system: all the insights he had carved into the lives of those around him, the shortcuts he had paved through the superhighway of information, which would be lost if he lost access to this system, his system. Brendan sat and waited, letting the minutes tick by. At four minutes to eleven, he stood up, bracing himself for the meeting. He knew what waited for him was going to be humiliating, and there was nothing he could do about it. Or was there? Why should he jump to their every command?

He sat back down in his chair with a satisfied smirk, watching the minutes roll by. Eleven came and went. Ten past eleven eventually arrived, and Brendan rose. He sauntered toward the lift with a satisfied smile on his face.

It was quarter past eleven when Brendan approached Brian Pulter's secretary's desk. He stood in front of her, waiting to be directed through. She looked over her spectacles at him. "Yes?"

"I am here to see Brian," Brendan mumbled.

"Your name, please?"

"Brendan."

"Brendan what?"

"For God sake," he muttered. "Brendan Roche. R-O-C-H-E."

"Thank you, Mr. Roche. Please wait," she said with a sickly smile.

Brendan saw a sharpened pencil on her desk. He wanted to grab it and ram it right up her nose, right into her brain. It was a close thing, but he managed not to do it.

Picking up the phone, she pressed a button. "Mr. Roche for you, Mr. Pulter." She pronounced *Roche* deliberately, giving the sincere impression that she was laughing at him. Brendan wouldn't forget her. She would be sorry she'd been so snotty.

"You may go in," she said with the same insincere smile.

Giving the secretary a dirty look, he entered the office, where he found two people waiting inside. One was expected. The second, not. Brian Pulter sat behind his unruly desk while a man with a confident air and expensive suit sat on the couch against the wall.

"Come in, Brendan, we've been waiting for you," said Pulter, indicating a chair on the far side of the desk. Brendan sat and said nothing, giving the unknown man in the room a steely stare.

Pulter lifted the phone on his desk and pressed a button, after a second he said "Can you hold my calls please Sarah." Once he'd hung up the phone, Pulter sat back in his chair and gave Brendan a cold look.

"As you're aware, this is a disciplinary meeting, which entitles you to have a colleague or union representative present. Do you wish to avail yourself of this?"

"No. Does it look like I brought someone?" said Brendan.

"Let's not start out being shirty, Brendan. I am required to ask these things. Are you ready to begin?"

Brendan nodded, and Pulter rummaged through a pile of papers until he found what he was looking for. "I am Brian Pulter, as you know," he said unnecessarily. "This is Max Clifford, the company's legal representative. Mr. Clifford is here to ensure that we adhere to all relevant legislation, as this is an extremely serious situation. Our main concern is the altercation between you and Ms. Janice Potts. Are you ready to proceed, Mr. Roche?" Pulter stopped and looked at Brendan.

"Where is she? I thought she'd be here," asked Brendan.

"Ms. Potts is not willing to meet with you after what happened. We've discussed the situation with her separately."

"How am I to know what she has accused me of if I am not in a position to hear what she's saying?"

"This is an investigation meeting to get your side of the story, Brendan. Ms. Potts's view of matters is nothing to concern yourself with."

"You seemed to have all the information you needed the day you suspended me. Why start investigating now?"

Pulter seemed annoyed at the interruptions to his carefully prepared presentation.

"I suspended you because it was clear at the time you were in no fit state to continue working, and we needed to have some clear air between you and Ms. Potts while we looked into things."

"I just want to go back to work," said Brendan, looking at his feet, getting bored with this charade.

"Let's continue, shall we?" Clifford said. Pulter nodded and gathered his notes in front of him.

"As I was about to say, is there anything you want to tell us before we begin?" said Pulter, still annoyed.

"Yes, I do," said Brendan.

Pulter was taken by surprise, but he sat back in his chair, pretending to be patient. He opened his hands in a gesture meaning that Brendan had the floor.

"I wish to say that I was out of line with Ms. Potts. I wish to apologise unreservedly for my actions, and will accept without question any sanction the company wishes to impose. I would like to qualify this statement by saying that I felt driven to this action by the increased demands placed on me by middle management to achieve unattainable results."

"I don't believe you were ever asked for the unattainable," Pulter countered angrily. Clifford shifted uncomfortably on the couch.

"I have felt singled out for isolation by you directly, Mr. Pulter. I felt my job was under threat if I did not achieve the greatest productivity levels in the department."

"That is completely preposterous!" Pulter stammered, slamming his hand against the desk. Brendan was about to make a further passive-aggressive attack when Clifford stood up.

"May I have a word outside, Mr. Pulter?" he said. The two men left the room, and Brendan was alone in the office. He looked around, noting the plush carpet, the slightly tinted windows, and private bathroom. Pulter didn't deny himself the luxuries of life. Brendan also noted a stack of files on the desk relating to a contract the company was chasing. It was for the NSA server bank in the US. Brendan had been involved with assessing the shortfalls in the existing systems.

Pulter and Clifford reentered the room, Pulter looking furious and red-faced.

"Thank you for that, Mr. Roche. Can you describe the events of the day in question?" Pulter asked, once he was again settled in his chair. Brendan did as he was asked and described what had happened in as bland a fashion as possible. Afterward, the men held another whispered conversation in the corner of the luxurious office. Pulter eventually sat back down in his chair to continue his meeting, even if everyone in the room now knew the real power lay with Clifford. Pulter was clearly infuriated at the interference of the legal eagle in the corner.

"After discussions with my colleague, we have decided that you understand the issues involved, and will not repeat them. We have decided to issue you a verbal warning. Any such behaviour in the future will be considered unacceptable, and may result in further, and more serious, sanctions. Do you understand?"

"I do. Can I go back to work now?"

"I don't see why not," said Clifford, without waiting for Pulter to give the go-ahead.

Brendan smiled at Pulter and stood up. He was just about to leave the office when Pulter spoke again, his words stopping Brendan in his tracks.

"One moment, please, Brendan."

"Yes, Mr. Pulter," said a smug Brendan.

"Considering your stress levels, we have decided to give you a project partner to share you workload. He will be starting with you next Monday."

"I don't need a project partner," Brendan insisted.

"On the contrary, you just said exactly that," Pulter said with a smile.

"Is that really necessary? I work much better alone," said Brendan, directing his question to Clifford rather than his direct superior. Clifford just shrugged.

"It clearly is, after what you shared with us today. Like I said, he will be joining you from Monday on," said Pulter, happy that despite having lost the battle, he was winning the war.

Brendan was raging as he walked from the room. The slimy bastard got one over on him! There was no way Brendan could have someone looking over his shoulder, It was impossible. The only way to stop the assistant was to stop Pulter. He had no choice. He had tried to handle things simply, but the rat bastard wouldn't let him be. Pulter had to go, and that was final.

Brendan walked past the snotty secretary. He hadn't forgotten about her, either. She'd get hers, too.

***

The top of the bridge was lined with faces, adults and children, crammed shoulder to shoulder, hoping to see a body being dragged from the muddy water below. The sadistic nature of people never ceased to amaze Adams. Even though it was early morning, a full complement of law services had gathered on the towpath, ready for anything the searching sub-aqua divers might recover. Technical officers sifted over a heap of items littering the side of the canal. Most were quickly discarded for the rubbish they were. The divers were working a quadrant system moving from the murder site back along the canal. The water boiled directly under the bridge as a rubber-clad diver emerged with a black hold-all suspended from one hand. It looked too clean to have spent any great time on the bottom. Jackpot, thought Adams.

The diver finned his way across the surface and plopped the dripping bag on the grass verge. Adams and Sims gazed at the bag, each instinctively feeling they'd found what they were looking for. A gloved technical assistant opened the bag. They all peered inside, but couldn't make out what lay within. It was clear that this bag warranted further investigation. A protective sheet was spread on the ground, and each item inside was carefully extracted and set on the plastic. Soon, a tyre iron, three wheel nuts, a can of spray paint, a tube of superglue, some plastic gloves, a pair of jeans, and a dark top, lay on the canal bank.

"What do you make of that?" Sims asked.

"I'm not sure. I was expecting a gun or a knife."

"Perhaps it wasn't what the man was carrying."

Adams stood up and looked at the eclectic mix of items. It seemed right, but it seemed wrong. Why would anyone kill a woman over a pile of junk like this?

"Let's keep looking and see what else they find," said Adams.

The technician catalogued and photographed the items taken from the bag before tagging them and sealing them in sterile containers for further tests. The search continued but resulted in nothing to directly connecting the tall man to a motive for murder. The black hold-all seemed to be the most-interesting item recovered, but who'd kill someone over a bag of old clothes and tools?

Adams started to doubt the theory of the woman coming across the man dumping something incriminating. Perhaps Sims was right; the killer could have been waiting for this particular woman to come along. A jilted lover perhaps. The biggest part of detecting is to keep plugging away until you get a lead. Still, Adams's thoughts drifted to the tote bag. He felt he was missing something, something right in front of his eyes.

Chapter 23

Annabelle waited for Ogie to get back from the gig, and as soon as he walked in the door, she told him about the incident with Martha. "That's weird," he said, then went upstairs to take a shower. He didn't mention it again.

Every time Annabelle tried to turn the conversation toward Martha, he just brushed it aside, telling her to forget it, that the woman was weird. One rushed bottle of beer later, Ogie said he was tired and wanted to sleep. Annabelle lay beside him in the dark, putting pieces of the puzzle together. She wasn't technically going out with Ogie, but they were getting there. Martha was stunning and bored; her husband was no George Clooney, and together, they were a dangerous combination. Annabelle didn't like it at all. She'd no right to expect Ogie to be faithful to her, but expect it, she did.

In the morning, she didn't mention Martha. She wanted to see what Ogie would say, which happened to be nothing. He talked about everything except his neighbour's strange behaviour, which told Annabelle all she needed to know. While Ogie piled crockery into the dishwasher, Annabelle went upstairs. When she came back down, she held some of her belongings in her hands.

"What's going on?" asked Ogie.

"You're banging her, aren't you?"

"Banging who, for Christ's sake? What are you talking about?" he said, his eyes taking on a wounded look. She had seen those eyes too often to believe they were real.

"Martha, from next door! You're having an affair with your neighbour's wife. Could you get any more clichéd?"

"That's preposterous," he said, throwing his hands in the air.

"You didn't say you weren't."

"I shouldn't have to say anything."

"You're right. You don't have to say anything. Not to me, anyway,"

"You're reading way too much into things. Sit down."

"I'm going. I hope you've been more honest with her than you have been with me." Anabelle walked out of the house, closing the door softly behind her. She wasn't the kind of girl that made a scene.

Ogie stood before the half-packed dishwasher. He'd known he was playing with fire by getting involved with Martha, but he hadn't expected the whole thing to come crashing through his life so quickly. What the hell did Martha think she was doing, barging into the house like that? He'd had to talk to her, sooner rather than later. Ogie hoped she wouldn't turn out to be some head-case bunny boiler, wrapped up in a knockout body. He also hoped it wasn't too late to stuff the genie back into the bottle.

***

Adams collapsed into his office chair. He'd been working long days for well over two weeks, and it was starting to catch up on him. It wasn't unusual for murders stack up on each other like this. What was unusual was the lack of a murderer.

Adams would have been able to solve all of Ireland's murders without breaking a sweat if it weren't for the interference of the law. The courts kept insisting they prove things; knowing wasn't enough, apparently. In most cases, Adams knew how a murder had been committed, and by whom, within minutes of arriving on a scene. These last two cases were completely different; it was as if they'd dropped from the sky.

Thinking about the two cases as one triggered Adams's brain into action. All of a sudden, the dots connected. He shot out of his seat, grabbing Tony Kelly's file. He removed the forensic report: four wheel-nut caps and one wheel nut. He rummaged through the file until he found a photo of the nut in question. The bag in the canal contained three identical nuts and a tube of glue. Sitting back in his chair, Adams picked up the phone and called the forensic department. He told them what he'd found, and asked them to cross check the wheel nuts from the bag with the case file on the crashed Toyota. Adams knew it would take time, but he was sure they'd make the connection. Adam's second call was to the Digital Imaging Department, asking it to source CCTV footage of the car park at Brady, McCarthy, and Doyle. His third and final call before leaving the office was to Sims, asking her and Dolan to meet him in his office in an hour.

When he returned, he was carrying a sheaf of photos. Dolan and Sims were waiting. They both had paper cups full of the office stew that everyone assumed was coffee. A cup was shoved in his direction.

"The last thing we need is another body lying around the place," Adams said, fending off the toxic liquid with a finger. He laid the photos on his desk. In the top photo, a man in a dark-hooded top was hiding his face.

"These were taken by the security camera at Tony Kelly's office, the day before his death," Adams said, tapping the photo of the man. Adams began spreading more photos around the top of the desk, but they all were blurry.

"That picture is much clearer that the other ones. Have you had it enhanced?" asked Dolan.

"No, they were all taken off the same system, but this shot is taken of the guy just before he gets to the camera. He did something to each of them, making them lose focus. I asked the building maintenance manager to check, and he called back ten minutes ago to say that the lenses are covered in tiny dots. Spray paint, he thinks."

Adams took another photo from his hand, laying it alongside the ones already resting on the desktop. This one was familiar to them all. It was the photo they had been using when canvassing the apartment block. The postures of both men were remarkably similar, as were their height and build. None of them needed reminding of the clothes they'd found in the hold-all. They were looking at a photo of a man wearing those clothes.

"It's the same guy," said Sims.

"Sure as hell looks like it," agreed Dolan.

"Forensics are on the way over to Brady, McCarthy, and Doyle to test the paint against the can found in the bag dragged from the canal, but I am willing to bet it will be a match. This could be a rock-solid link between the two murders. Apparently, the wheel nuts and glue are too commonplace, but each mix of paint is slightly different. It's nearly impossible to get the same exact combination of elements each time a batch is made. Bad news for crash repairmen; good news for us. Plus, the brand of paint in the can is an American import. Not many shops stock it," Adams said.

"By trying to hide his identity, the killer could have left the only evidence that positively links the crimes together," said Sims.

"Exactly," Adams said. "The main thing is, we have a photo to work with now. It's not perfect, but it's a start. We need to go back through the Kelly witnesses, and see if anyone knows this man. I'll take the family. Dolan, you call on Tony's friends. Sims, you take the girlfriend. If nothing else, it'll give you a chance to check on her mother, and see if Pat Sweeney came back since yesterday."

***

It was the middle of the day when Sims pulled her car to a stop outside the Sweeney house. She'd called earlier to see if Mary or Angie would be home. Mary Sweeney answered the phone, but said she was alone. Sims made the journey, anyway. She wanted to see how the woman was coping, and if she were going to stick by the statement that she had given them. There was no point in continuing to chase down Pat Sweeney if Mary was just going to recant everything she had said. Mary had made a life-changing decision the other night, and it would not be unusual to have second thoughts.

Sims knocked on the door, noticing the shiny new lock. Mary opened the door, which had a security chain now.

"Hi, Mary. It's Joan Sims," she said to the eyeball hovering above the chain. The door closed, the chain rattled, before the door opened fully.

Mary Sweeney's face looked miles worse than it had after the fight, even though she was healing. Both eyes were puffy and multicoloured. Her chin and jaw were peppered with bruises ranging in colour from yellow to dark purple.

"Not exactly the face of *Vogue*," said Mary, turning away from the detective. Sims closed the door behind her and put on the chain back on, not because she was frightened of Pat, but to reinforced the fact that Mary was doing the right thing. Mary heard the chain clink in the kitchen, and thanked God someone understood.

Sims sat on one of the three chairs that circled the breakfast bar, as the room was notably devoid of a table.

"You got some of the damage repaired already, and I noticed the new locks."

"My brother came over and did it for me last night. He wanted to go after Pat, but I told him it wasn't the way. I want him gone, not sore."

"Has Pat been back to the house?"

"This morning," said Mary, putting a mug of milky tea in front of Sims.

"What happened? Did you let him in?" Sims asked, taking a sip of her tea.

"No. I wedged the door with a chair, then talked to him through an upstairs window."

"Did he threaten you?"

"Nah, he was the same as every other time. Full of 'sorry' and 'it'll never happen again.'"

Sims stirred her tea, thinking long and hard about the question that was rattling around in her mind. Good sense told her to leave it alone, but the woman in her wanted to know the answer.

"What made you do something about him this time? It clearly wasn't the first," she said, not being able to help herself.

Sims wondered if she'd gone too far when Mary said nothing. Instead, she stared out the kitchen window onto a backyard filled with builder's trusses, lumber, and stacks of bricks. When the answer came, it surprised Sims.

"I've been thinking about that myself. It's easier to tell you why I never did it before. I was scared, not of him but of what is out there." She gestured toward the front door with her mug. "A woman like me has no place out there. At least here, I'm needed. I'm a mother, a wife. I felt that putting up with his comments, and the odd slap, was part of the job. Up to the other night, it was only ever me. He never raised a hand to the kids. When he threw Billy, that changed."

Sims smiled, resting a reassuring hand on Mary's trembling arm. "You did the right thing, Mary. I know that you see no place for yourself in the world, but that's not true. The only reason you think like that is because you've been shut off from it for so long. It's not as bad as you imagine. You've taken the first step, and that's the hardest one. It'll get easier from now on. I promise."

Mary's eyes filled with relief, joy, fear, even freedom. Emotions that she had been holding back for so very long. A tissue appeared from her sleeve, like a rabbit from a magician's hat, making Sims laugh. She pointed at the tissue and said, "Every Irish mammy has an endless supply of them tucked away, just in case."

Mary smiled and nodded while snuffling into the tissue. "True. Actually, our defence against the misery of the world."

Mary composed herself. "Anyway, enough of that. You hardly came all the way out here for a mug of tea. Is this something about Pat?"

"Not him, this time. I wanted to know if Angie recognised this man," said Sims, producing the photo.

Mary took it and had a good look. "It's not a great shot, is it?"

"No, it's taken from a security camera. Do you know him?"

"Can't say that I do, but there's something familiar about him." Taking another look, she said, "No, I don't think I do."

"I'll leave this for Angie to look at when she gets home. Tell her to keep it for me. I'll have to pick it up again in a day or two."

Mary took the photo and placed it in a drawer.

"You never finished telling me about Pat. Is he gone for good?" Sims asked.

"I told him he was never coming back inside the door of this house again. Of course, he didn't believe me, but he will. He's going to pick up his clothes tonight."

"I can arrange to have an officer here when he comes, if you like," said Sims.

Mary shook her head. "Thanks, there is no need. My brother is coming over to be in the house, but I have Pat's stuff packed already. It will be waiting in the driveway when he gets here."

"Fair enough, but remember, we are only a call away if you need us," said Sims, with a reassuring smile.

Mary unchained and opened the door. "Thanks again for coming today. I needed to talk to someone. I feel a lot better now."

"You're welcome, Mary. Don't forget about the photo."

"I won't. As soon as Angie gets in, I'll get her to call you."

Sims walked toward her car, hearing the chain rattle back into place. Words are reassuring, but steel feels better.

***

While Sims was showing Mary the blurry photo, Angie was wearing a hole in the Kellys' sitting-room carpet as she paced over and back. She wore a pair of black pants and a black blouse. The house was sombre, but far from silent. It was full of cousins, aunts, uncles, and friends. Mr. and Mrs. Kelly looked drained and detached from it all as they wandered about the place, shaking hands and accepting comforting words. A buzz ran through the house, then things grew quiet. Angie had been dreading this moment. Mr. Kelly's brother came in and said, "He's here."

The undertaker appeared in the doorway. He shook hands with Mr. and Mrs. Kelly. "I'm so very sorry for your loss. I'm here to take as much of the burden from you, as I can," he said, his voice full of remorse even though he had never met Tony.

"Thanks for that," said Mr. Kelly, choking back a sob. Seeing Tony's father so upset broke Angie's heart. She couldn't hold back her own tears and tried to keep her crying as quiet as she could. The last thing the Kellys needed was her making a show of herself.

Tears are a part of mourning, and the undertaker took them in his stride. "Where would you like Tony laid out?"

"We thought he'd like it in here," said Mrs. Kelly, indicating the sitting room where they stood. The undertaker looked around, measuring the room with an experienced eye.

"Here will be just fine," he said. "Perhaps you might wait in the kitchen, while we get the room ready."

The undertaker ushered everyone into the kitchen, then he rounded up some men to help move furniture to one side of the sitting room. The undertaker's assistant appeared with a set of folding trusses, which snapped open in his practised hands. Across them, he laid a white cloth. Angie saw the undertaker talking quietly to Tony's uncle. Shortly after that, he arranged six men as pallbearers and gave instructions on how to lift and carry the coffin.

On the pavement outside, a huge crowd had gathered to see the final homecoming of Tony Kelly. A hush fell over the crowd when Mr. and Mrs. Kelly appeared at the door of the house, being shadowed every step of the way by the undertaker. After a whispered conversation between Mr. Kelly and the undertaker, the back of the hearse was opened. As Tony's coffin appeared, Mrs. Kelly broke down, and Mr. Kelly had to support her with both hands. The coffin was raised on sturdy shoulders, and Tony was carried into the house one last time. The Kellys followed a pace behind; everyone else waited outside, including Angie. The undertaker's assistant appeared with the coffin lid, placing it in the back of the hearse, before standing guard at the door of the house.

On the street, the crowd waited as the family had a private moment with their son. With each passing minute, the mourners swelled in number. New people arrived constantly. Such was the volume of car's arriving, a uniformed Garda appeared to direct traffic, to and from the street. After a while, the undertaker came back outside. He identified cousins, aunts, and uncles, bringing them into the house. He appeared at Angie's elbow so unexpectedly and so quietly that he made her jump with fright. "Mrs. Kelly would like you to sit with the family. Is that okay?"

Angie nodded and followed the man into the house. In the sitting room, Mr. and Mrs. Kelly were hugging family members as they arrived. It was strange seeing Tony in the coffin. He looked serene, similar to himself but not the same. It was as if someone had let the air out of him. That was what Angie thought: He looked deflated.

What got her crying uncontrollably were his lips. They were exactly the same as they always had been. If she looked only at his lips, she knew it was Tony, her Tony. Angie sobbed, approaching the coffin. She laid her hand on his, which were crossed above his chest, but she couldn't drag her eyes from his lips. She felt her hand move, as if in a trance. She felt her finger trace the shape of his lips, so soft and moist in life, now cold and stiff. She had to say good-bye, and there was only one way that would do. She leaned into the coffin, and placed her lips against his. A tear fell from her lashes and landed on his cheek, rolling away on his marble-cool skin. That tear will be with you always, my love, she thought, as she ended her kiss. When she straightened, Mrs. Kelly took her in motherly arms, and Angie broke down completely.

When the time was right, the undertaker let people into the house by the front door. They passed around the coffin, shaking hands with the family that sat around the edge of the room, before leaving through the back door. The mourners kept coming, hour after hour, each offering heartfelt condolences. It was well after dark when the front door finally closed, and Angie massaged her crushed fingers.

***

Brendan sat at his desk, livid with Brian Pulter for meddling in his life. There was no way he was going to allow some spotty-faced intern look over his shoulder and report back on what he was doing. There was also no reasonable way of preventing it from happening, other than Pulter himself putting a stop to it. Now that his access to the computer system had been restored, Brendan could log onto the company server. He had many things to take care of, none of which included the work lying in his in tray.

For a long time, Brendan had been diverting money away from the company accounts into a fund of his own. It was time to liquidate that money. He also needed to redirect control of some of his programmes to remote centres. He needed to cover his tracks, but most important, he needed to get inside Pulter's computer. After searching through the manager's hard drive, Brendan found a file with his own name on it. The folder was protected by a password, but that proved no difficulty. Once he had cracked the code, the contents of the folder made for difficult reading. It was full to the brim with disparaging comments. Pulter left no doubt of the contempt he had for Brendan, or the fact that he wanted him gone from the company. The project partner was actually going to be his replacement, as soon as the area manager found a way to get rid of Brendan. It was the final straw. Brendan had to take action and take it now. If Pulter wasn't going to stop, Brendan would have to stop Pulter. It was time to take matters into his own hands

Brendan found Pulter's appointment diary in the computer. The week was completely mapped out, meeting after meeting, leaving no chance of Brendan getting the manager on his own. Then, at the very end of the tomorrow's list, Brendan found an entry labelled *Squash*. He rolled the problem of Brian Pulter around in his brain, letting his razor-sharp intellect harry at the beast, until a plan hatched. He needed to strike quick, and he needed to strike hard. He had little time to prepare so every moment would be vital. By the time Brendan started his car to drive home at the end of the day, the building security system was on a countdown, and the blocks of his revenge began falling into place. In twenty-four hours, the office, and Brian Pulter, would be at his mercy. All he had to do was figure out a way of keeping him in the building, and alone.

That night, Brendan crushed a dozen sleeping tablets and diluted them with water. He stirred the mixture until it was completely dissolved. He dabbed a drop of the liquid on his tongue. It was chalky, but nothing that couldn't be masked. Brendan sent an e-mail from his home computer, requesting a quick chat with Pulter the following evening to clear the air. In the morning, Brendan packed a roll of duct tape in his briefcase, along with the liquefied tablets.

He worked through the day, without stopping for lunch. He slipped out at about three in the afternoon, returning a short time later with a sandwich and a brace of smoothies in see-through cups with straws for drinking. One was red berry; the other, banana and mango. To the banana one, he added the sleeping potion he'd brewed. A quick taste confirmed that the chalky bite of the drug was completely masked by the sweetness of the fruit. While he waited for the allotted meeting time, Brendan ate his sandwich dry, resisting the urge to drink his own smoothie.

After four, Brendan approached Pulter's office. The hated secretary was standing guard over her domain, as usual. Brendan had his briefcase in his right hand while balancing the smoothies in his left. He forced himself to give the woman a warm smile.

"Hi, back again. Is Brian free for a minute?" he said in a cheery tone.

"Do you have an appointment?" she asked icily.

"I e-mailed him last night. He should be expecting me."

"Name?"

Surely, this stupid cow could remember him from yesterday, or was she doing it deliberately? Brendan forced himself to remain calm, and even smile. "Roche. Brendan Roche."

Picking up the phone, she spoke quickly and quietly. When she hung up the handset, she nodded toward the closed door. "You can go in."

Brendan pushed down the handle with an elbow. He poked his head inside the door and looked around. Pulter was alone, working on papers strewn across his messy desk. Brendan smiled and went in, closing the door behind him. Pulter looked up at him with a frown.

"Thanks for seeing me, I have brought a peace offering," said Brendan, nodding toward the two smoothies. The man paused to steeple his fingers under his chin. The posture was one of condescending power, and it drove Brendan's blood pressure through the roof.

"What can I do for you, Brendan?" he sneered.

Brendan forced himself into the seat across from the manager, placing his briefcase on the floor. He took the red-berry smoothie in his left hand, placing the yellow one in front of Pulter. Brendan took a sip of his drink before saying, "I feel I've behaved badly during this whole thing with Ms. Potts, and I wanted to apologise. I haven't been making things easy for you."

Brendan could see the manager soften a little. His hands dropped from his chin to the desk. "I can't disagree with you there, Brendan. I wish I could."

"Yes, indeed. I know I have a tendency to be blinkered about certain things, but the other reason I wished to talk to you today was to discuss the apprentice."

"Project partner," corrected Pulter.

"Yes, project partner. Having slept on the idea, it makes sense."

"I'm glad you think so," Pulter said, managing a smile.

"It will be very handy to have someone up to speed on things, if I had to take some time off, or go on holidays," said Brendan, taking another suck on his straw, slurping his smoothie as if it was the most-delicious thing he'd ever tasted.

"Having adequate backup for our personnel is vital. It allows them enjoy a quality, work-life balance," Pulter recited, verbatim, a section from the staff handbook.

Brendan noticed the manager's hand shift; his little finger brushed the cool condensation on the drink. Brendan felt his pulse quicken and took another drink from his own smoothie, willing the manager to pick up the bloody cup.

The silence spread out for a couple of seconds. Brendan was lost in his own world. He thought his plan was going to fail, right up to the moment that the manager's hand fastened on the drink and lifted it to his lips.

"Thanks for this," he said, taking several hefty draws on the straw. As Pulter savoured the taste, he looked at the name on the cup. "This is very good. Where did you get it?"

"At a deli down the street. The guy said the banana one is particularly good for an evening energy burst," Brendan said.

"That's handy. I have a game of squash in an hour," said Pulter, taking several more slurps of the banana mush.

"Perhaps you might give me an idea what you want me to cover with the project partner first." Knowing that the drugs needed time to work, Brendan had to spin out this meeting for as long as he could. "How about starting with the US contracts, then moving on to Europe and Asia?"

"Let's have a look at what you've pending," Pulter said, booting up his computer and taking another swig of the drink.

Brendan sat back, listening to the manager babble, watching the level of the Yellow goo sink lower by the minute. It wasn't long before Pulter was having difficulty hitting the correct letters on his keyboard.

Brendan continued to press him with questions. In the end, Pulter shook his head several times, trying to clear his thoughts before attempting to get to his feet.

"Are you okay, Mr. Pulter?" asked Brendan, his voice full of concern.

"I'm not sure," slurred the manager, his feet not quite taking his weight.

Brendan moved around the desk, placing a comforting hand on the manager's shoulder, easing him back into his swivel chair. "You look terrible. Wait there, and I'll get you a drink of water," said Brendan, going to fill a glass from the jug on the counter. By the time Brendan got back, the manager's eyes were swimming in his head.

"Here, drink this," said Brendan, leaving the glass near the manager's hand, but not putting it in his grasp.

"Air," Pulter said, trying to get to his feet again.

"I think you should stay sitting," said Brendan, easing him back down again. Brendan could see realisation filling Pulter's eyes, even through the fog of drugs.

"Sarah" he croaked, weakly trying to push his way past Brendan. This time, Brendan was far from gentle, shoving the man backward. He clamped his hand over Pulter's mouth, pinning his head against the high-backed leather chair. Weakened by the drugs coursing through his blood, Pulter was uncoordinated, and his attempts to break free ineffective. The lack of oxygen added to the potency of the sleeping pills, and Brendan was surprised by how quickly the man lapsed into unconsciousness.

Brendan removed the roll of duct tape from his briefcase, binding Pulter's hands and feet securely to the chair. He also wrapped a few twists of tape around the manager's chest and the back of the chair, repeating the procedure with the slumped man's forehead. At last, he secured several pieces of tape over Pulter's mouth. Brendan didn't want him coming 'round and calling for help before the office was empty.

Brendan felt a tremor of excitement surge through him. He rifled the man's desk to find the files he had noticed during the meeting yesterday. Then he picked up Pulter's phone and dialed the New York office.

Far across the ocean, the call was answered. Brendan said nothing, and after a few moments, the person on the other end of the line hung up. Brendan didn't. He laid the beeping handset on the desk. Gathering the files under his arm, Brendan picked up his briefcase and steadied himself for his next batch of acting.

Brendan left the office, closing the door behind him. The obnoxious secretary was hammering keys on her computer. Brendan held out the bundle of files he had in his hand, saying, "Mr. Pulter asked if you could run these up to legal. They need them to finalise the Rexon contracts."

She eyed the folders with distaste, clearly not liking that Brendan had asked her to do anything.

"Thanks," she said, taking the files and setting them on the desk, only to resume typing.

"He said it was urgent. Brian is on the line to New York right now, and somebody over there has their knickers in a serious twist, by the sound of the conversation." Brendan saw the woman's eyes flick over the line indicators on her phone. When she saw the office phone engaged, it sealed the deal. She took the folders in her hand, flicking open the top cover. Brendan walked away toward the end of the corridor, ducking into the toilet instead of going all the way to the elevator.

He waited a few minutes, and when he poked his head back into the hall, Pulter's secretary's desk was empty. Brendan hurried back along the hall and entered Pulter's office again. He was still out cold. Brendan hung up the desk phone, pushing it out of reach of the trussed man, taking the keys and mobile phone that lay next to it. Brendan left the office quickly, locking the door behind him using Pulter's key. At five on the button, Brendan packed up his belongings and left the office, making sure that every camera he passed got a good look at him leaving.

He drove home, dumping Pulter's phone out the car window in the middle of rush-hour traffic. Soon it would be nothing but dust, ground into the road. He was buzzing with excitement. There were so many fantasies running through his head. He couldn't make up his mind which one he was going to inflict on that rat, Pulter, first. Brendan wanted it to be slow. He wanted it to be painful, and he wanted his face to be the last thing that Brian Pulter saw.

The hours dragged by. Brendan had to force himself to wait. When the nine o'clock news came on the TV, he knew he had waited long enough. His hour of vengeance had come. He drove back to his office and parked in the car park, knowing all the security cameras had turned themselves off hours ago. He opened the security gate with the swipe card on Pulter's keys and continued up to Pulter's floor. The whole place was in near-complete darkness, the emergency escape light throwing an eerie green glow over things.

Brendan rounded the secretary's deserted desk and tried Brian Pulter's door, which was still locked. Brendan had been banking on the fact the office cleaners mightn't have had a key for every door. Brendan sifted through the keys on Pulter's key ring, trying two before he found one that slid all the way home. He opened the door and looked inside.

The man was still sleeping, bound and gagged in his office chair. A watery light filtered in from the street, painting Pulter in shades of death. Brendan appreciated the theatrical nature of it all as he walked to the window. He closed the blinds. At last, it was time for them to be alone.

Chapter 24

Brian Pulter tried his best to wake up. He could hear muffled sounds and a strange rustling noise. His eyes were so heavy. He tried to remember what had happened. Had he gone drinking? No, not that; he never drank on workdays. Was it still a workday? What was wrong with him? Little by little, his eyes focused, but the room was in darkness. This didn't look like his bedroom, or even his house. He tried to turn his head, but he couldn't move. Oh, God, had he been in an accident? Was this a hospital? Was he paralysed?

He tried calling out, but something was holding his skin fast, muffling his words. He blinked his eyes, straining them into focus. In the corner, something moved. All at once, the room was drenched in dazzling light. To his left, a tall figure moved away from the wall, and it took him several minutes to recognise Brendan Roche. His drug-addled brain tried to make sense of these random bits of information, failing miserably. Pulter followed the stooped figure of Roche with his eyes as he moved about the room. If he had been in an accident, why was he here? Where was his wife? Something wasn't right. Why was he sitting up, and not lying in a bed?

Brendan strolled around the room, like he was taking a walk on a beach, being creepy as always. He would feel a whole hell of a lot better if Brendan just went away, or better still, went and brought back someone to tell him what had happened. His head pounded, and his mouth was as dry as a desert. He tried to move again, but it was no use; he was stuck fast. Using his tongue, he probed at whatever was muffling his speech. He had half expected to feel a breathing tube or oxygen mask. Instead, the tip of his tongue came away with the bitter taste of glue.

As his brain woke a little bit more and his eyes adjusted to the gloom, Pulter began to recognise his own office, and panic set in. Brendan perched himself casually on the corner of the desk and smiled creepily. He was sitting far too close, invading whatever personal space anyone had. It was as if he just didn't understand the way people worked. Brendan reached out a hand, and for a horrible moment, Pulter was sure he was going to stroke his cheek lovingly. Instead, Brendan gripped whatever was covering his mouth and viciously ripped it off, taking a good lump of lip with it.

Pulter cried out in pain, but his head remained held firmly in place. His brain pounded. What was the bloody rustling noise? Brian cast his eyes downward and was shocked to see his entire body encased in a glistening cocoon. What the hell had this lunatic done to him?

Pulter screamed for help. Brendan did nothing to stop him. He just smiled, which was just about the freakiest thing he could have done.

"That's it," Brendan said. "Scream all you like. No one can hear you."

"People will be looking for me."

"No, they won't," Brendan said confidently.

"Get me out of here, right this second, or there'll be hell to pay."

"You're in no position to give orders. I'm in charge now. You're mine," said Brendan. Leaning closer, he actually began sniffing Pulter. "You're mine" was a crazy thing to say, even for Brendan Roche.

"I can smell your fear," Brendan sneered. "You stink of it."

"Of course, I'm frightened. I've just woken up tied to a chair, with you an inch from my face. Who wouldn't be frightened?" Pulter babbled. "If this about the disciplinary thing with Potts, I can make it go away."

"It's not about her," Brendan said very slowly, like some kind of dullard.

"What is it, then? The project guy? He is gone. Okay? Gone. Just let me go. Whatever you want, I can make it happen."

"It's not about that, either," said Roche, smiling his creepy smile again. At least now, he was moving away.

"What is this about, then?"

"It's about you, Brian. Everything is about you."

Pulter felt his guts knot. This guy was completely off his rocker. He could be capable of anything. Pulter searched the room with wild eyes, looking for anything that might help him escape, but there was nothing. If this were a movie, thought Brian, there would have been a handily placed knife, or a gun, but this was real. Things like this did not happen to office managers, not in this day and age, and not to him. Whatever the hell was happening didn't matter. It might be a prank, or some sick fantasy; it didn't matter. The only thing that mattered right now was getting the hell out of here, or at least getting Brendan out of here.

"If it is about me, what do you want me to do?" Pulter asked, willing to do anything to get him, or Brendan, out of this goddamn room.

"I want you to know that you have been close to God."

"You want me convert? I go to church every Sunday, as regular as clockwork," Pulter said, though he didn't.

"Religion is rubbish for fools like yourself, Brian. I said God, an all-powerful being. All this time, you've been in the presence of a creator, a giver of life. How blind you've been."

"I don't understand."

"I know you don't, Brian. That is why I'm here. To bring the light to your eyes."

Pulter could see that Brendan was far beyond crazy he was insane. His panic ratcheted up another notch when Brendan rummaged in his pockets with gloved hands, and pulled out a tube.

"What's that?"

"You'll see." Brendan laughed. "You'll see everything." Opening the tube, Brendan dribbled cold fluid above Pulter's eyes. Some of the liquid ran into the socket, stinging painfully. Brendan gripped Pulter's eyelids, pinching the skin and pinning them open as wide was they would stretch before letting go. Brian's eyes remained wide open, the stinging liquid making his vision blurry.

"Jesus, what the fuck are you doing?" He struggled against his bonds.

"Helping you to see the light," said Brendan in a normal tone of voice, screwing the cap carefully back on the tube.

There was a bottle of gold liquid on the desk. Pulter thought it looked like piss. Brendan lifted it and tipped the bottle over Pulter's head. Petrol fumes filled the room, flooding his eyes and mouth, causing him to splutter and cough. It was his eyes that took the brunt of the drenching, increasing the burning in them a hundredfold. He screamed in pain. With each panicked breath, he drew more choking fumes into his lungs. What was panic before this had morphed into complete and utter terror.

"Please, don't, don't," he blubbered.

"Shush, it is only a transition. I've seen the other side, and you'll be amazed. It won't hurt for long." Brendan didn't light the fluid; he had other plans. He began wrapping more plastic around the seated man, finishing the job of cocooning him. Wrap by wrap, Pulter was covered, until only his nose and eyes remained exposed.

"It's time we said good-bye. I wish I could say it has been a pleasure working with you," said Brendan, before circling the wrap one last time. He sat back to admire his handiwork while Pulter tried to scream through the wrap, struggling against his bonds. One tiny piece of plastic kept the air out of his lungs. One tiny film was making them burn with the need for oxygen. Pulter tried to bite at it. Then he sucked. Finally, he blew against it, trying to dislodge the obstruction. He thrashed his head from side to side, but the air wouldn't come. His heart raced, and his eyes bulged. Blackness began to creep into the edge of his vision.

Brendan leaned forward and, with one sharp fingernail, poked a hole in the film under Pulter's nostrils. A sweet trickle of air entered his lungs, forcing back the encroaching blackness. Panicking, Pulter tried to suck in as much air as he could, but breathing too hard closed the hole. With impossible force of will, he calmed himself, concentrating on taking shallow breaths. His stinging eyes were forced to watch Brendan leer at him, through a haze of petrol and cling wrap.

Brendan moved closer, using a finger to trace the shape of Brian's eyeballs through the thin plastic film. Brendan's face came steadily closer, until his lips brushed the lobe of Pulter's ear, where he whispered, "I'm the giver of all, and all can be taken away." With that, Brendan wrapped a final piece of cling film around Pulter's face, covering the tiny hole he'd made only moments ago.

Opening a box of matches, Brendan struck one. He rolled the match between his fingers, playing the flame through the air. Pulter thrashed helplessly as he asphyxiated. When Brendan was sure Pulter was on the point of blacking out, he flicked the match through air. It landed in Pulter's petrol-soaked lap. Flames whooshed into life, melting the plastic wrap, clothes, and exposed skin. The film covering his mouth melted in a ball of fire, and with one final agonising gasp, Pulter inhaled the flame, sizzling his lungs on contact.

Brendan watched the fire consume Brian Pulter. He longed to stay, but the fire alarm cut across his elation. It was time to go. Brendan left the office, carefully closing the door behind him.

***

The Black Swan, in the dead of night, was as dark as its name. A pub in the hours after closing is an eerie place. Only a few lights burned behind the bar, lending the room a cavernous feel. The thick walls released heat they had stolen from the throngs of drinkers earlier in the night. A bar is like a vampire, sucking the essence from its customers before sending them home, lessened from their time spent within. Despite this, they keep coming back for more, leaving their money in the till, and a fraction of their essence for good measure.

At night, the ghosts of patrons past fills the room, making what should feel empty somewhat otherworldly. Tonight, Harry and his son, Chris, sat alone in a corner booth, talking quietly. Only when they were finished would Greg lock up, which was only right; after all, Harry was the unofficial owner. Greg's name was over the door, but Harry's money financed the deal.

"I'm not sure we should go ahead with this job," said Harry, swirling an inch of beer in his glass.

"Christ, Pop, we put a lot of planning into this. The lads are lined up and ready to go. Stevie even nicked a van, special."

"It's not the job. It's O'Shea. I think he's gone sour on us."

"No way. He wouldn't have the balls."

"Listen, Chris, I saw a cop car on his street the other day. I don't like it."

"You're going to blow off this score just because you saw a random copper? Come on, you got to be kidding."

"I've been inside for being rash once before. I've no intention of going back there again."

"Pop, I really think you got this one wrong. That's a tasty bit of cash, and if we don't go ahead with it, we'll be out of pocket. The boys will want paying, one way or the other."

"Don't you think I know that? Look, I'm just saying we need to think this through before we decide."

"What if I stick a shadow on O'Shea? If he's setting us up, the coppers will have to meet him at some stage. Then we'd know for sure."

Harry rubbed his chin and drank the last of his beer. "That makes sense. Who have you in mind?"

"Tiny is at a loose end and needs the cash. He can smell a copper a mile away."

"All right, set it up. If O'Shea is still clean by Wednesday, we go. Which lockup are you using?"

"Lewis Road. Why?"

"I'll call 'round, before the off."

"Jesus, Pop, you know I hate that. It makes me look like the boy."

"I won't get involved, Chris. I'd feel better if I have a hand in it."

"That's not the deal, and you know it. You do the planning, I run the show. I can't have my dad turning up on a job, no matter who he is. Those fuckers would be laughing behind my back for weeks."

Harry had to smile. He found it hard to remember that Chris wasn't his little boy anymore. Chris already had a reputation, and Harry doubted that any of his crew would dare laugh at him, behind his back or not. Even so, Chris was right; Harry had to keep his distance.

"You're right. Sorry, son. I'll give you a bell at two on Wednesday. You can fill me in then. Fair enough?"

"Sounds okay. I got to split. You need a lift home?"

"Nah, thanks, Chris. I'll have one more with Greg. You can get off." Chris downed the last of his Corona with lime and slid out of the booth. Harry couldn't understand how he drank that muck. In Harry's day, if you sent back a pint for having a crack in the glass, you were a pussy, never mind wedges of flipping lime shoved down the neck of your bottle. How times had changed.

When Chris was gone, Harry waved his glass at Greg. "One for the road?"

"Why not, Harry? Why not," said Greg, filling a couple of pints.

***

Tim Murphy had been looking forward to coming home so much, but from the moment he got off the plane, Martha had been acting like a different woman. It was completely weird. Nothing felt right, but he couldn't put his finger on the reason. She'd stormed out of the house and hadn't come back for hours. When he tried to talk to her about it, she blanked him, pretending to be asleep. He had been away on work trips before, and she had never been like that. This morning was no better. She'd been sullen. Tim was worried. Yes, he'd been taking on a lot at work, perhaps leaving her alone too often; he just hadn't thought it was this bad. He knew he was going to have to spend some more time with her to make up for the London trip. He wanted to spend more time with her, all his time, in fact, but she had to realise that he was doing all this for her.

On the drive into work, he had done his best to cheer her up; she'd even smiled a few times. Tim was going to book a trip away for the both of them. She loved Cork, and that spa hotel in Maryborough. He would book it at lunchtime, spa treatments, the lot, and tell her over dinner.

That was until he opened his mail, and a plain brown envelope changed his life forever.

It sat harmlessly among countless similar envelopes. When he'd sliced it open with his silver letter opener, he may as well have driven the sharp implement into his heart rather than the paper. There was a photo and a note. Tim pulled it out he note which only said, *Tend your own garden!* He looked for something else but there was nothing. When he looked at the photo more carefully, it said all that was needed to be said. He didn't need the note to tell him he was looking at his own front door, or at his own wife in the arms of another man.

Tim was transfixed by the photo, lying innocently on his desk. A mental car crash took place inside his head, but his body barely moved. He couldn't look away. He'd always worried about losing Martha, some other man taking her from him. In his mind, he'd imagined this moment time and again. He always believed, if his nightmare ever came to fruition, he would fly into an awe-inspiring fit of rage. He had imagined driving the man away, crestfallen.

That had been what he thought he'd do. What he actually did was vomit into the trash can.

When the liquefied contents of his stomach lay pooling with yesterday's NASDAC report, he felt better. No, that was a lie. He just felt less like dying. Tim thought about going home, saying he was ill. No one would question the fact once they got a whiff of the puke-scented air in his office. What kept him at his desk was fear. If he went home, he'd have to face the fact that his wife was a cheating bitch. He could well have to face the fact that his marriage was over. Tim wasn't ready to face any of those things, so he remained where he was.

After an hour, the smell of his own vomit began to get to him. Tim left the office, getting some plastic sacks and cleaning products from the janitor's cupboard. Once his mess was cleaned up, he cried. He cried a lot. Tears of loss, tears of hurt, tears of self-pity mingled on his cheeks before falling in a puddle of worry on his desk. Lunchtime came and went. His office door remained firmly closed to the world. The e-mail backlog began to grow as his phone stayed off the hook. A receptionist came with a message but left quickly after seeing the state of the man behind the desk. When office lights began to shut off around the building, Tim was no clearer in his mind. All he knew was, he couldn't face Martha yet.

Tim fished his mobile phone out of his pocket and dialed Martha's number.

"Hi," she said. A sad, bored little *hi*.

"Hey, baby, how was work?" he asked, amazed at how normal he sounded.

"Fine. Busy, you know. Will you be much longer?"

"That's why I'm ringing. We're having a major problem here. It looks like I'll have to work late."

"Again? Can't someone else do it?"

"Not this time, babe. It's all down to me," he said sadly. The truth in the lie was a bitter pill.

"I can wait for a while."

"Better not, honey. Take a taxi home. I could be hours yet. I'm going into a meeting now, so my phone will be off, okay?"

"I suppose so. See you later."

"Sorry, babe." Tim was about to hang up, when something made him add, "I love you."

"I love you, too. Bye."

The words were cold in his ear. He killed the connection and turned off the phone. Tim locked up his office and left. As he walked blindly along the busy evening streets, he was jostled and bumped, but he didn't feel it. He need to think, but his brain was a traffic jam of emotion. All he could think of was the photo that now rested in his briefcase. He spotted a park that backed onto a church, consisting of one hard bench in a green oasis, amid a sea of concrete. Tim sat staring into space for minutes or hours; he'd no idea. He was blind to passing people, who gave his morose figure concerned glances. No one stopped; none enquired about his troubles.

The evening air grew cool, and a breeze whipped the trees into an energetic dance. Tim knew he couldn't put off going home forever. He stood. The briefcase in his right hand felt so heavy. In it, he carried the destruction of his life.

His journey to Honeysuckle Lane went far too quickly. When he pulled the car into his driveway, he looked at the door. If there had been any doubt that the photo was real, it blew away, like smoke in a hurricane, when the tangible scene stood before him. His fear solidified and dropped through his bowels, like a rock through jelly. He opened the hated door and entered his tainted home. Time to face the music, he thought to himself.

Martha had the TV on. She was sitting on the couch with her legs drawn up under her. A glass of wine balanced on her knee.

"I got fed up waiting, so I've eaten already. There are some leftovers in the fridge," she said sulkily.

"I'm not hungry."

"Why are you so late? What was so important this time?" she asked.

Tim didn't answer; he had no words. He was on the verge of forgetting the whole thing when she added her next line.

"You spend more time on work than you ever do on me."

The barb was sharp.

"I spend that time making a living for us, for you, so that we can live like this," he snapped.

"Don't shout at me."

"Don't whinge at me. At least when I'm at work, you know what I'm up to," he said.

"What is that supposed to mean?" she asked, unfolding her legs from under her.

"Nothing," he replied, shying away from the confrontation.

"Don't say, 'Nothing.' If you've got something to say, say it!"

"Have you been having an affair?"

The question was out before he had a chance to think about it.

"What? Don't be ridiculous," she stammered.

"I'm not ridiculous! Have you been having an affair?" Tim roared, and Martha went bright red.

"No, of course I haven't," she said, but wouldn't meet his eyes.

Tim ripped open the briefcase and threw the photo at her. She put her wineglass down on the coffee table and picked up the photo with shaking hands. Her eyes widened.

"That's not me," she said weakly.

"Oh, come on!"

"It could be anyone. Where did you get it, anyway? Were you spying on me?"

"So, it is you."

"I didn't say that," she backtracked.

"No, I wasn't spying on you! Someone sent it to the office. That shit was waiting on my desk this morning. How could you do this to me?"

"It's not what it looks like," Martha said, as her last avenue of escape closed on her. She got to her feet and walked around the room, dropping the photo to the table, face down.

"How could you?" Tim sobbed, her confirmation breaking the last threads of self-control he possessed.

"It just happened. Just the once."

"Who is he?"

"You don't know him."

"*Who is he?*" Tim screamed in her face, causing her to jump, drawing her arms protectively in front of her.

"Ogie. It was Ogie."

"From next door?"

"Yes," she mumbled, moving away.

Tim cradled his head in his hands. He'd known Ogie was trouble the moment he'd arrived. He remembered how Martha had dragged him over to the party, and spent the whole night making cow eyes at him. It all fell into place now.

How stupid am I? Tim said to himself. "God!" he roared, as his tears flowed again, tears of humiliation and frustration this time. His head was filled with images he didn't want in there. He had to get them out, or he'd go mad.

Martha watched Tim wander in circles, blubbering and holding his head. She was crying, too. What had she done? When Tim began to beat his head with closed fists, she went to him, trying to comfort him. He jumped from her touch as if she were acid.

"Don't touch me! Don't you dare fucking touch me!" he shouted, and stormed out of the house.

Martha lay on the couch, crying uncontrollably. She knew she'd just ripped her world apart. Nothing would ever be the same again.

Chapter 25

Adams thought he dreamed the bell. It was only when his wife elbowed him in the ribs, did he realise it was his phone, dancing across the bedside table.

"What now?" he mumbled sleepily. "Yes!" he snapped into the phone, letting whoever was on the other end know two things: The phone had woken him up, and that he wasn't happy about it.

"Sorry to wake you, Steve." Adams recognised the inspector's voice. It must be important if he were calling at this hour.

"That's all right, inspector."

"We've got another homicide on our hands. It came less than an hour ago."

"I've two live cases already." Adams sighed into the phone.

"I know. I'm not asking you to lead this one. Michael Ford is heading it up; he's on site already, but it's his first case. I thought he'd appreciate a second set of eyes to get him going."

"I'm not sure that's a good idea, chief. Too many cooks, and all that."

"I've already talked to Michael. He asked for you."

"So, he wants me. Now? No chance of a few hours' kip?"

"Sorry, Steve."

"Give me the address," Adams said, throwing back the sheets, making his wife grumble. He wrote down the address, not trusting his groggy brain. He'd give his left kidney for a full night's sleep. Adams didn't bother with a suit, just threw on a jumper and jeans. After all, he wasn't leading this team. Ford could do the meeting and greeting.

When Adams arrived at the office block, he found a mass of ambulances, fire engines, fire inspectors, coroner units, and TV reporters.

"Mother of divine grace, what a circus," Adams said to the officer keeping the reporters at bay.

"You're telling me, detective. This one will make the evening news, for sure," the officer said, lifting the crime tape for the detective to duck underneath. He had gone a few paces when he had to turn around and go back.

"Which way?" he asked, feeling foolish.

The officer smiled. "Did they get you out of bed?"

Adams smiled sadly and nodded.

"Fifth floor. Take the main elevator. It's the corner office on the back left of the building."

"Thanks," said Adams, and trudged away groggily.

As soon as the elevator doors opened on the fifth floor, the stink of charred flesh filled Adams's nostrils. At the end of the corridor, a blackened door hung lazily on one hinge. People milled around the area, most of them dressed in protective boiler suits and breathing masks. The smell was much worse here, and Adams covered his face with his hand. A suited man wearing a face mask came over and offered him a mask. Adams took it gratefully. The kind Samaritan tuned out to be Ford himself.

"Thanks, Michael. What have they landed you with?"

"One hell of a mess, that's what. Thanks for coming," Ford said, placing his hands on his hips, trying to look like he was in charge, but clearly glad to have Adams at hand.

"No worries, mate. Glad to help out where I can."

"I've never seen anything like this. I thought it was a straightforward fire until I got here. On top of that, someone tipped off the press."

"Why is everyone so excited about this? Could the fire not have been accidental?"

"The guy was tied to a chair and set alight."

"Jesus, you're kidding."

"Nope, and what's more, he seems to have something melted into him. Looks like plastic. They are taking samples and photos right now."

"Can I have a look?" Adams asked, as Ford walked with him toward the open door.

Inside the office, the photographer's flash went off about every ten seconds, making the room look like a horror-movie set. The body was lying on its side, still attached to the chair. Adams could see it in his mind how in the agony of being alight, the person must have convulsed like crazy. The mask over Adams's nose did little to control the smell in the office; it was overpowering. One of the victim's hands had come free and lay stretched away from the body, but the other hand was still bound to the melted armrest. The victim's feet also were attached to the chair. A man was peeling black, crusted layers off the body and placing them in containers.

"What is that?" asked Adams.

The technician looked up and said, "It could be plastic bags, but I think it might be cling film."

"Like, for sandwiches?"

"Yep. Lots of that kind, or some of the heavier sort, for wrapping pallets."

"Why would you wrap someone in cling film, and then set them on fire?" Adams asked.

"Because you're as crazy as bat shit," mumbled the technician to himself. Adams had to agree. This was off the end of the nuts chart, even in his experience. After a good look around, Adams walked out of the office.

"What do you think?" Ford asked.

"You have to really hate someone to do that. I'd look at the wife or girlfriend first. The only other reason to go that far is to make an example. Mafia stuff."

"That was my feeling, too," said Ford, happy to be corroborated.

"How do you tie a guy to a chair like that? He either let himself be tied up, or there was more than one perp," wondered Ford aloud.

"Could have been kinky time with the secretary, who forgot the safety word. Speaking of which, any positive ID on the victim? Whose office is it?"

"We have the name," said Ford, taking out his notebook. "Brian Pulter. No answer from his mobile; it's turned off. Officers are on the way over to his address now."

"I'd send someone to pick up his secretary, quick as you like. If she wasn't involved, she'll know something. They always do."

"Fair enough. Would the wife be number one on the hit parade for this?"

"In my experience, they're never far from the top of any list but let's not rule out something to do with work. After all, they did do this in an office."

"Right," said Ford. Adams couldn't stop a yawn escaping.

"You look bushed, Steve. I can take it from here, if you like. I just wanted to get your take on things. It's such a weird case, it knocked me for six."

"You did right, Michael. I think you should get the inspector on the horn, as soon as you can. I've a feeling this could be a major story. He might want to oversee it himself."

"You won't find me arguing about that," said the young detective.

"One important thing to get done tonight: Get someone in to work the camera system. Find out when the victim arrived. Did he stay on after work, or come in later? Who came with him? With any luck, we can watch the whole thing happen live, open and shut. If it turns out the crispy critter in there is not the owner of the office, haul him in, along with the secretary. Find out why someone would barbecue a body in his office. If the victim is Mr. Pulter, get his appointment diary for the last few weeks. There has to be a connection somewhere."

"I'm on it, Stephen. Thanks again for coming out."

"No bother. Feel free to call," Adams said, walking toward the elevator.

***

Brendan knew it was time to leave. He'd known this day would come. Brian Pulter had just speeded up the process. He spent most of the night moving money out of his accounts, into a fake company account he had opened in the Channel Islands. He deleted a lot of his files, trying to cover his tracks as best as he could. Most of his money was hidden in stocks and bonds also registered to his in-name-only company. Brendan knew he'd gone too far, dealing with Pulter in the office like that. It was all too close to home and it drew too much attention to himself.

He was almost ready to leave this life, and the name Brendan Roche, behind, but he still had one thing left to take care of: Angie. The voice in his head was on overdrive tonight. It taunted him, saying she'd never be his, that he wasn't man enough to keep a trollop like her satisfied. Brendan desperately wanted to blot out the voice with pills and sleep like he had done the night before, but with time growing so short, he had to keep moving. Hour after hour, the din in his brain got worse. He started to smell strange things; his temples felt strained to bursting. Brendan was in agony, but he wouldn't allow himself to take anything for the pain. Brendan knew that his discomfort was the result of his connection with the other side was growing stronger. *They* were trying to break through.

"Soon they'd see," he thought. They'd *all* see. He was exceptional. He was invincible, and before long, he was going to be immortal. With every hour that passed, Brendan could feel the power inside him growing, and the changes were not confined to his mind. He begun to see shadows flitting through the dark recesses of the room, nearly forming shapes, only to swim out of view when he turned his eyes fully on them. The others were taking physical form, coming into his realm in preparation for his becoming. The feeling of impending rebirth was exhilarating, but the waiting was incredibly frustrating.

Brendan logged on to Angie's e-mail account. According to her last messages, the boy's funeral was taking place in the morning, near Lucan. Brendan would have his chance to close the circle of fate, to take possession of Angie, at the funeral of the one he'd slain to win her. He didn't need a plan anymore. His future was in the hands of destiny.

***

Angie arrived home from Tony's wake to find herself locked out of the house. Mary had to let her in; the place was like Fort Knox.

"Are you all right, Mum?" Angie asked, putting on the kettle. Mary's face was in a terrible state, the worst she'd ever seen it. Despite the bruises and swelling, she was smiling.

"I am, sweetheart."

"Was Pat back?"

"Yes, but he is gone again."

"For now, you mean," Angie said, sounding sulkier than she'd intended.

"Angie, he's gone for good. He'll never do this to me again, to us."

"You keep forgiving him, Mum. Why would this time be any different?"

The kettle whistled and turned itself off. Angie piled sugar on top of instant coffee and filled the mug with water.

"I know it looks like that. All I can tell you is that things have changed for me. It's not easy to explain. I talked to that detective woman today, and realised I can manage without him."

"We've been telling you that for years. Why would you listen to her, and not us?"

"I don't think it's what she said, I think it's that I see the world differently today. I can't put it into words, but I promise you, Pat's gone for good." Mary refilled her own mug of tea. She couldn't explain how, or why, she felt stronger today, perhaps she'd never fully understand it herself. Whatever the reason for her change of heart, she was like a woman renewed.

"Enough about all that. How did you get on today?" asked Mary, turning the conversation away from herself and back on her daughter.

"It was tough, Mum, so tough. The look of poor Mr. Kelly, he's shattered. It broke my heart to see him like that. He was always so tough," Angie said. Mary nodded, and sipped her fresh tea.

"They were great to me, all the family were. They made me feel like one of their own, like I had as much right to be there as any of them, but the wake itself was exhausting. I thought the people would never stop coming. It helped somehow, all that hand-shaking stuff," Angie said.

Mary watched Angie's brow furrow, just like it had done when she was a little girl, doing the hard sums. She couldn't resist putting her tea down and giving Angie a huge hug. She expected Angie to shove her away, but she didn't. Angie moved in against her, just like she had done when she was tiny. For a few minutes, it was like it had been before the fights, when happiness filled the house, not misery and fear. It was Angie who pulled away first, rubbing tears from her cheeks with the back of her hand.

"God, Mum, see what you started?"

Mary leaned forward and kissed her on the forehead. "Thanks, Angie."

"Thanks for what?" sniffed Angie.

"For being you," Mary said, and kissed her again.

This time, Angie playfully slapped her shoulder. "Stop it, Mum, you're making me scarlet." For the first time in days, Angie smiled.

Mary said, "By the way, the detective left a photo for you to look at." She got the picture of Brendan from the drawer and handed it to Angie.

"That could be anyone. How am I supposed to recognise that?" Angie asked, after a quick glance. The photo was flipped onto the countertop, and soon forgotten. It ended up covered in coffee rings while mother and daughter really talked for the first time in years.

***

"But I need new football boots," whinged Enda O'Shea.

"The boots you have are just fine," said Barbara, peeling potatoes at the sink.

"But they're not," Enda said, as if the world were about to end.

"And what is wrong with the ones you have?" Barbara asked.

"They have studs. All the lads have blades now. Blades give you more control."

"At a hundred and twenty euro a pair, they would want to," Barbara said without missing a beat.

"Come on, Mom!"

"Enda, I said no."

"*Mom!*"

"Look, Enda," she said, turning her full attention on the sulking ten year old. "Things in this house are going to change. You think we have loads of money, which isn't true by the way. I know it's hard, but we're all going to have to make some changes."

Enda stuck out his bottom lip and looked glum, but at least he'd stopped baying "Mom" at every turn. When he made that face, he looked just like Frank. Of course Barbara wanted her kids to have the best of everything. What mother wouldn't? Long before this disaster, she'd started to worry that the kids were actually getting too much, too easily. Barbara had noticed a hint of laziness creeping into Enda's behaviour, and that whinge of his would get him nowhere in life. Kids needed to learn that hard work, not entitlement, gets you places. Perhaps Frank losing every penny they had might have one silver lining, after all. That's if she managed to keep her family together, and under one roof, any roof.

Enda trudged away, leaving her alone in the kitchen to gather herself. On the day Frank had spilled the beans about his problems, the lies, the addiction, the money, it was like a tidal wave of bad news. It had all been too much her to take in. That's why she'd stormed out of the house. She needed time to think, to come to terms with what was happening to her life. After walking for ages, she decided she wasn't going to give up on her family without a fight. She sat on a wall for ages while she tried make a plan.

Problems piled on top of problems, which had to be taken apart one step at a time. First were the lies; they had to stop, or nothing else could be fixed. Second was Frank's gambling. She'd have to help him to help himself. If he wasn't willing to change, they would end up dragging themselves out of this mess only to land in another one. Lastly, the money situation needed taking in hand. When she cut up the credit cards and managed to raise some money on the car to pay off that greasy moneylender, it was just the first step. There was still plenty more debt to tackled, but after facing down Harry McCarthy, which she had to admit was scary, dealing with a bank manager would be a doddle. She'd removed him from all their accounts, blocked all his credit cards, keeping just one in her own name. She'd spent hours going over bills. The amount they owed was huge. It wasn't insurmountable, but still huge. If the worst came to worst, they could always declare bankruptcy and start afresh.

It was Frank who most worried her at the moment. Saying the words was one thing; taking actual steps was a horse of a different colour. Now that Frank had no money, the chances of him gambling it was reduced, but it couldn't stay like that forever. He had to do something about fixing the problem, not lock himself away from it.

Tonight, he'd made a start by going to a Gamblers Anonymous meeting, admittedly, one that Barbara had found. He didn't want to go at first, but she'd insisted. She was straightening up her mental boxes, trying to keep control of the situation, of her life. It was nearly time to start working on the kids.

The front door opened, hauling her attention back to the real world. It was like waking up from a deep sleep; she felt lost for a moment. She looked at her hand holding the potato peeler and wondered for a second what it was doing there. Frank poked his head in the kitchen door, as if checking the coast was clear.

"How did it go?" she asked.

"Where are the kids?"

"Enda's in the sitting room."

Frank crossed the kitchen and closed the adjoining door before sitting at the table, folding his hands in front of him. "It was strange. In the beginning, I felt like I was in the wrong place. Did you know they say prayers?"

"No, I didn't. Was it no good at all?"

"That's the surprising thing. It actually helped. A lot."

"Go on," Barbara said.

"Like I said, at the start, I was thinking it was all bullshit. 'Hi, my name is Frank,' and crap like that. Then people started telling their stories. That was when this woman stood up. She looked like a teacher or something. Very respectable, you know?"

"Yea, I know the kind."

"Anyway, she said, 'Hi, my name is Sam, and I am a cocaine addict.' I couldn't believe it. She looked nothing like a druggie. Then she said how it all happened. It could have been me up there, the first hit, the lies, the sneaking around, trying to ignore the mounting problems. I swear, Barb, it was exactly the way it happened to me."

"So she made you realise you had a real problem?"

"I know I've a problem. She made me see that I'm not alone. She made me realise there's something I can do about it."

Barbara stood, went to him, and sat on his knee, wrapping her arms around him with delight. It seemed like years since they had held each other so close.

He whispered into her ear. "I wouldn't have been able to do it without you, Barb. I am so sorry for everything."

"I know you are," she whispered back, as she snuggled into his neck.

***

Sleep was the last thing on Martha's mind as she lay in her darkened bedroom. Tim had been gone for hours. She'd tried calling his phone, but he'd hung up on her. What else could she do? When her phone beeped, she leaped out of bed and grabbed it from the locker. Seeing the name Ogie made her feel sick to the core. *We need to chat, Annabelle is annoyed about the other day.*

Martha couldn't care less how Annabelle felt, or Ogie, for that matter. She hated him for doing this to her. If he'd not tempted her, she wouldn't be in this mess. The text she sent back was simple: *Too late. Tim knows everything.* A moment later, the phone buzzed again. *Does he know it's me?*

Ogie was only worried about himself, which wasn't all that surprising. Martha couldn't bring herself to answer that text, or the next four. Let him stew, she thought, as she deleted each message as it arrived. She could do nothing more. Right now, it all rested on Tim.

She must have drifted off at some stage, because the slamming of the front door startled her awake. Martha sat up in the bed. Tim's tread on the stairs was heavy and halting. He sounded drunk. He wasn't a good drinker; three pints, and he was under the table. Martha heard the timber on the landing creek under Tim's weight and braced herself, expecting the bedroom door to open. It didn't. Instead, she heard the spare room's door close. She wondered what she should do. Should she leave him be, or should she try to talk to him? If he was drunk, it might make things worse.

In the end, she needed to talk, and tomorrow wouldn't do. Martha got out of bed, and went out onto the landing. The door of the spare room was closed, so she knocked.

"Tim?" Martha tried the handle. The door was locked from the inside. "Please, Tim, we need to talk."

The silence was complete. No answer, no movement, nothing. After a while, she said, "I'll be waiting, when you're ready."

Martha went back to their room, leaving her door open, hoping he would come to her. His side of the bed remained empty and cold long into the night.

When morning arrived, Martha was surprised to find she'd fallen asleep again. She reached over hoping to find Tim, but his side of the bed was undisturbed. She sat up and listened; the house was silent. She threw her legs out of the bed and put on a robe. Her door still stood ajar. Looking across the landing, the spare room was now open, but the rumpled bed was empty. Martha hurried downstairs, worried Tim might have left in the middle of the night.

Thankfully, she found him sitting in the kitchen, wearing the same suit he'd been wearing yesterday, bearing all the hallmarks of a set of clothes that had been slept in. A half-full mug of coffee sat before him, as cold as the look he gave her.

Sitting down across from him, she said, "We need to talk about this."

Tim said nothing, just held her gaze with steely eyes.

"I never intended any of this."

"You didn't try too bloody hard to stop it. I was only gone a few days, or have you been carrying on with him before then?" he snapped.

"It was just once," she said, pulling the robe tighter around herself.

"Once! A thousand times! What difference does it make, anyway?" He slapped the mug in front of him, sending it flying against the wall to shatter in a spray of coffee and ceramic shards. "I don't care. I don't want to know," he said, holding his hands over his ears like a child.

"We have to talk at some stage," she pleaded. Martha never seen him angry like this; it was frightening. She'd always felt safe with Tim, but the man in front of her was broken beyond reason. This Tim was a man who might do anything.

"Do we? Do we, really?" he snapped.

"You know we do."

Tim stood up and started pacing around the room. His eyes were wild and bloodshot, either from drinking or lack of sleep, probably both. Eventually, he turned his back to her and gripped the kitchen worktop, his hands taking the full weight of his shaking body. His gaze locked onto nothing in particular in the backyard. He stayed like that for a long time, saying nothing, his shoulders rose and fell with each deep breath he took.

When he turned back toward her, he looked at Martha with dead eyes, and said. "I want you to leave."

"I've nowhere to go. This is my home," she stammered, shocked that she was being kicked out on the street.

"You should've thought about that before now," he said, his voice raw with hate.

"I wasn't happy and did something stupid. You can't throw everything we have away because of one stupid mistake," she pleaded, standing and clasping her hands in front of her, as if in prayer.

"If you don't go, I will. If I walk out that door, I'll never come back. Never!" he shouted.

"You can't mean that," she bawled.

"I don't know what I mean, or what I want. The only thing I'm sure of is that I can't stand to look at you for one more second! Why the hell should I leave? I wasn't the one whoring all over town!"

Martha's face flushed with anger and shame. "I told you, it was just once! That makes me human, not a whore! Did you ever think you might have driven me to it? Well?"

Tim pushed himself away from the sink and walked toward the door, reaching for his coat.

"Wait," said Martha.

Tim stopped in the doorway.

"You're right. It should be me to leave, if anyone must. I'll call Ann. See if she can put me up."

Tim said nothing but went upstairs instead of out the door. Martha heard the spare-room slam closed once more.

Chapter 26

Adams felt like he'd just pulled the covers back over himself when the alarm clock started screaming in his ear. "Five more minutes," he said, hitting the snooze button. An hour later, his eyes opened again. It took a moment or two for him to remember what day it was, or what he was doing awake. The cogs of his mind meshed at last, and he shot out of the bed, late. It was nearly nine when he reached the office, and his shift had been due to start at eight.

"Morning, Stephen," someone sniggered as he rushed past a desk. On the far side of the open-plan office, he spotted Ford tackling a mountain of paperwork. Ford looked like he hadn't slept at all. Adams changed direction, walking toward his bedraggled college.

"Morning, Michael."

The young officer blinked a few times, and checked his watch. "I guess it is." Ford pushed his chair away from the desk and stretched. Adams actually heard the bones crack in his back.

"Have you confirmed who the victim is?"

"Looks like it's the owner of the office, Brian Pulter. He never arrived home from work last night. His wife was in the middle of ringing his friends when the guys I sent 'round last night arrived at the house. But with the body the way it is, we thought it best not to ask her to view it yet. At least not until we are completely sure. The coroner is checking Mr. Pulter's dental records against the body as we speak."

"Where is Mrs. Pulter now?"

"Under sedation, at home. According to the officers at the house last night, she was inconsolable."

"So you haven't interviewed her yet?"

"No, the chief said it could wait a day or two in the circumstances."

Adams flipped through some of the crime-scene photos littering Ford's desk.

"What did the CCTV catch?"

"Nothing."

"You can't be serious. Nothing at all?"

"Not a thing. The whole system went down at six p.m."

"That's strange. A computer company, and their whole system failed. Was the power out, or did the fire interfere with the system?"

"Forensics are checking that, but they say it looks like scheduled shutdown. They're looking into it in more detail today with the building security manager."

"What about before the shutdown? Anything useful on the system, then?"

"Not directly. A camera in the corridor captures anyone going in or out of that general area, but we don't have a direct view of the office."

"That's something, at least. Did you find out if Pulter had left the building after work, or was he there the whole time? Perhaps he programmed the cameras to go off himself."

"I'm in the middle of making a sightings timeline right now. It seems he did leave, just before five, but we can't confirm that."

"It's a month for weird cases," said Adams, scratching his head.

"We found his PA at home, fast asleep. Her name is Sarah Quinn, married, mid-forties, no kids."

"Too much to ask. That she stank of petrol?"

"I'm afraid so. She has a rock-solid alibi. She arrived home from work just before six p.m. She and her husband spent the rest of the evening visiting his sick mother in the hospital, twenty miles across the city. No possible way she could have been at Pulter's office when the fire alarm went off."

"Was she able to throw any light on who might want her boss dead?"

"She was completely shocked when she heard what had happened. She said Mr Pulter was a lovely guy: good boss, no angry calls to the office, no threatening letters, nobody chasing him for money. She said he was 'the salt of the earth,' her exact words."

"Did you ask her how he got on with his wife?"

"Sure did. She said they were married for years and still mad about each other. He'd never look at another woman, as far as she knew."

"Any chance he was carrying on an affair with her? She seems fond of him."

"I suggested it, and she laughed."

"Did she leave before or after him yesterday?" Adams asked.

"She said he was in his office when she took some files to be processed. When she got back, his door was locked, so she assumed he had gone."

"So, the next person that should have seen him alive, was Pulter's wife."

"Nope, he was due to play a squash match at his leisure club. His wife wasn't expecting him back until eight at the earliest."

"Did he play the game?"

"He never showed up. His squash partner tried to call him, a few times apparently. He was fairly annoyed."

"The PA could be the last person to see him alive, if that's the case."

"She said Mr. Pulter's last appointment of the day had been with a work colleague, Brendan Roche. She didn't actually see Mr. Pulter after that."

"We had better call in this Brendan Roche for a chat. What's next on your to-do list?"

Ford rubbed his eyes, saying, "A few winks of sleep would be heaven, but I've got to wait on the confirmation of identity. Once I've that, I can get copies of Pulter's bank-account details and move forward on an official footing. I expect to get the ID sometime this morning, then I've a meeting with the managing director of Pulter's company in the afternoon."

Adams felt sorry for him, seeing how tired Ford was, but that was all part of the job. The bad guys insist on doing things at the most-inopportune hours.

"Give me a shout if you need a hand with anything," said Adams, heading for his own office.

"I might take you up on that," Ford called after him, starting in on his pile of paperwork once more.

Adams made his apologies to Sims and Dolan, who were waiting for him in his office. They had a quick briefing on the status of their cases before deciding on what action to take today. By the end of the meeting, they seemed to be no further along than before. No one in the apartment complex recognised the hooded guy from the photo, but the paint on the security cameras was an exact match for the tin found in the canal bag, at least that was good. The paint tin was their first concrete clue that they were looking for only one killer. The murders had to be connected somehow. It was up to them to put the pieces of the puzzle together.

They all agreed, after reviewing the profile of the jogger, her situation held no motive for murder, exactly like Tony Kelly in that respect. Was it possible that they had a serial killer on their hands, selecting victims at random? Adams prayed they hadn't.

The autopsy had proved she'd not been the victim of a sexual assault, one of the main reasons for murdering an unknown woman. All of which was interesting but left them no nearer an actual motive. Adams was still convinced the bag and the murder were connected.

Trying to link the canal suspect to Tony Kelly's murder was proving just as difficult. None of Tony Kelly's friends or relatives recognised the figure in the photo, either. The investigation was stuck in limbo. The murders had to be connected; Adams was sure of it. However, with no apparent motives, or evidence, the investigations were dead in the water.

Adams was sure they would find something, sooner or later. He had a feeling, and that feeling said whoever this guy was, he was only getting started.

***

Angie Sweeney dressed and checked herself in her bedroom mirror before leaving the house. She thought she looked mournful enough in her heavy black clothes. She walked to the bus stop at the top of Honeysuckle Lane, finding it hard to imagine that she was going to Tony's funeral. Brendan watched her leave from his bedroom window. Her head hung low as she walked, her normal strut diminished by the insipid colours she wore. Brendan thought about taking her now, but he wanted to stand before the family of the boy. He wanted that so much, it was worth leaving Angie in the dark for a few more hours.

Brendan dressed in his normal work suit; it would do fine for what lie ahead. It was far too early for him to leave for the funeral just yet. So he poured himself a glass of juice and popped some bread in the toaster. Brendan had slept fleetingly and was finding it hard to concentrate. His vision swam, and the voice in his head was screaming like an inmate of bedlam. Only an occasional word was recognisable in the deafening clamour.

To distract himself, Brendan finished packing his bag and left it in the hall. He got the stuff he needed for later: industrial-strength cable ties, already looped together, ready to act as foot and hand restraints; the remaining gaffer's tape he'd used on Brian Pulter; a heavy mag light; and a duvet cover. Brendan packed them all carefully in the boot of his car. He was ready to leave at a moment's notice. The toaster pinged when the bread was a dark brown, just the way he liked it. He buttered the hot slices of toast and added a liberal dollop of honey. After all, breakfast was the most-important meal of the day.

***

The old clunker of a car started on the fifth try for Frank O'Shea. Smoke belched out the back as it coughed into life. Barbara couldn't have picked a bigger rust bucket if she had tried. Frank found himself in the middle of a morning that should be stressful, but he was feeling as free as a bird, utterly content. He was flat broke and on the verge of losing his house, but the chain of lies that had held him captive for the last two years had been hacked from his limbs. He'd confronted his issues instead of hiding from them, and been honest with Barbara for the first time in years. She'd astounded him with the way she'd taken everything in her stride. Now, he felt he could deal with anything.

He coaxed the aging car into reverse and backed out of his driveway. As he left Honeysuckle Lane behind, the car marked his route with a trail of oily smoke. Frank didn't notice the motorbike pulling up behind him a few minutes after he joined the main road.

Tiny had been waiting near the bus stop at the top of Honeysuckle lane, his motorbike parked nearby. He'd been there for two hours. Every time a bus appeared, he'd had to walk away from the shelter so the bus wouldn't stop. Aside from that, it was a good place to watch the O'Shea house. Tiny saw the man Chris had described start an old Volvo. When the car passed, he quickly got to his bike and was comfortably behind the mark before he came to the next junction. There was no need to stay close; he could follow from a few cars back. The smoke billowing out of the back of the old pile of junk was making the job so easy, a blind man could have done it.

***

Back at the Garda Station, Ford was putting together a dossier on Brian Pulter, now that he was officially the victim of foul play. The dental records had been a perfect match, and Mrs. Pulter had positively identified the body a little earlier. The CCTV computer was being analysed by Garda experts, trying to determine who had set the system to shut off. All that could be done was being done. The autopsy report had also shown ruptured blood vessels in the eye sockets, as well as signs of oxygen starvation in the brain. The pathologist noted that these were indications of asphyxiation, but that had not been the cause of death. There was evidence of burning on the lung tissue, indicating that the victim's airway was unobstructed when he was on fire. Cause of death: coronary failure. The pathologist's opinion was that the victim was tortured prior to being burned alive. His heart just gave up before the rest of the body could.

The last two people with direct contact with Pulter were his personal assistant, Sarah Quinn, and Brendan Roche. Sarah had already given her statement and was due back for further questioning later in the day. Michael had been trying to trace Brendan Roche, but there was nothing on the PULSE database for him. Having no other information, Ford was forced to wait until the personnel staff in Pulter's company returned his call. He rang the company several times and asked for Mr. Roche's desk, but each time, the phone rang out.

After an hour, Ford got in touch with the personnel manager, who gave him Brendan Roche's home address and mobile number. Michael had rang Mr. Roche a few times and left two messages. It seemed he was on the missing list.

Ford was just about to send officers to the address when the chief inspector yelled across the office.

"Michael, you better hear this. Some bigmouth is on 'Live Line,' giving chapter and verse about your case."

"Shit!" said Ford, jogging toward the chief's office. Brendan Roche was forgotten for the moment. The press crawling all over the case was the last thing they needed.

***

Angie walked behind Tony's parents as the coffin was carried a few hundred yards from the church to the graveyard. The sun was high in the sky, making her sweat beneath her dark clothes, and she was sure her mascara was a state because she couldn't stop herself from crying during the Mass. Mr. Kelly had made a speech about Tony from the altar, but only got halfway through it before he broke down and had to be helped back to the pew by his brother. It was all so wrong, so alien. She half expected Tony to appear in the crowd, like some horrible joke, but he didn't. The number of people attending the service was huge, filling the church completely. Some even had to wait outside.

As the procession reached the grave site, a sea of people followed behind. Angie didn't take any notice; her eyes were fixed on the mound of freshly dug clay alongside the gaping mouth of the grave. All of that would soon be piled on top of her Tony. It seemed such a horrible thing to do to anyone, alive or dead.

The coffin was laid over the grave while a litany prayers were said. A decade of the rosary drifted on the summer breeze, and the pallbearers moved into place, taking the weight of the coffin on thick, white straps. They lifted Tony a few inches into the air, and the timber supports were removed. Angie cried uncontrollably as Tony was lowered slowly into the ground. The priest nodded, and Tony's dad moved forward a step to drop a single white rose on the coffin. Inch by inch, Tony sunk farther into the earth. As his coffin vanished from view, his mother moved forward and added a single red rose to her husband's white one.

Both parents looked destroyed. It only took a moment for the casket to make the journey to the bottom of the grave. Just like that, it was over.

The gathered mourners began to file past the family once more, expressing sorrow, shedding tears, shaking hands, and dispensing comfort. A tall, middle-aged man appeared in the line of mourners moving down the extended Kelly family. He regarded each of them with cold eyes, devoid of the soft shine of compassion, a look that dominated most people's expressions. He shook each person's hand without saying a word or expressing his sorrow. He was a stranger among friends but soon forgotten, as the next hand filled the uneasy void he'd left behind. When the man reached Angie, he spoke for the first time.

"It's nice to meet you," he said.

"Thanks," she said, as he held on to her hand.

"I've seen you around."

"I don't think so," she said.

"Yes, I'm certain. We live on the same street, Honeysuckle Lane."

"Oh, sorry. I've a terrible head for faces," said Angie, going red. She managed to free her hand from the longest handshake in the history of the world.

"Grief has brought us together, at last," said Brendan. It sounded poetic to Angie's ear, but Brendan intended it prophetically.

"I suppose it has," agreed Angie. "How do you know Tony?"

It was Brendan's turn to go red, as he searched for an answer that would seem reasonable. "He handled my company's accounts. I spoke with him on the phone but never actually met him. When I heard about the funeral, I had to come."

"I'm sure he would have liked that. He loved his work."

"Our lives were entwined," the tall man said weirdly as he kept looking at her, standing far too close. Several people were waiting behind him now. Eventually, a woman tapped him on the shoulder. He gave the woman a filthy look, but he moved on, walking away, ignoring the rest of the family. Angie didn't have time to comment on what a weirdo he had been, before the next hand thrust at her.

***

Somewhere in his jacket, Harry's phone buzzed. He struggled with his seatbelt, trying to find the bloody thing with one hand, steering the car with the other. When he eventually got the bulky iPhone out, *Chris* flashed on the screen.

"Hi, Chris," he said, easing the car into the slow lane.

"Hi, Pop."

"What's our friend up to?"

"Not a thing, as far as Tiny could tell. He left for work early, stayed at the office for the first two hours, and then showed a flat across from the cinema. After that, lunch. Now he's back at the office."

"I see," mumbled Harry. There were too many blind spots for Harry's liking, not to mention the fact he could have been talking to anyone on the phone. Everything was online or mobile these days. O'Shea could have been talking to the filth all day long, and Tiny would be none the wiser. "I'm still not sure, Chris. I've got a bad feeling."

"Come on, Harry. Tiny said the guy's clean. Grow a pair, will ya?"

The remark stung, and Harry felt his face harden. It shocked him, how quickly a little throwaway remark could send him over the edge. Harry had to remind himself that Chris was his lad, and not some scumbag. This wasn't a business for the meek. Around every corner lay risks. Perhaps the recklessness of youth was an advantage, after all. Harry sighed to himself as his ire faded. "You're in the driving seat. Give the order."

"We're tooling up right now. We'll be at the house in an hour."

"Give me a call when it's done."

"Right-o, Pops. Catch ya later for a pint." The phone went dead in Harry's hand, and he tossed it on the passenger seat. He was still thinking about O'Shea when he noticed that he was passing the main Fiat dealership.

"Shit," said Harry. He had missed his turn and didn't even remember seeing it. "Bloody mobile phones." He spat, looking for the next off-ramp.

***

Tim couldn't settle. Every time he tried to get his feelings under control, the thought of what Martha and Ogie had been doing in this house—his house—rose to the surface. Every time he thought of that, he was reminded that Ogie was only a few feet away. Whenever that thought penetrated his head, he felt like killing the man.

Tim waited in the spare room, listening to Martha move about the house after they spoke. Soon, he had heard Ann arrive. Martha tried to talk to him through the door, but Tim remained mute, sitting on the bed, biting back he curses he wanted to throw at her. In the end, she left with Ann, but not before saying she'd call. Once Tim was sure they were gone, he came out. The corner of his rumpled bed peeked at him across the landing. Sheets trailed over the mattress and onto the ground, a picture of wanton abandon. Tim imagined those cotton threads rubbing against Ogie's naked body as he pounded into his wife. He could see the man exploding in a fountain of cum, filling her completely until it ran between her legs, tainting everything it touched. Tim fled downstairs.

No matter what he tried, those images wouldn't leave his mind. Every time he replayed the scene, it got darker, more violent, more ecstatic, until his nightmare was a hedonistic orgy of epic proportions. Tim didn't want a trace of them in his house a moment longer. He ran upstairs and ripped the sheets from the bed, dragging them through the kitchen and out into the garden. He kicked open the shed door, not bothering to unclasp the padlock. The shattering sound of timber was balm to his anguish. He was in the mood for destruction, and nothing would stand in his way. Tim found a container of white spirits and saturated the bedding, lying on the lawn. The *whoosh* felt immensely gratifying when the flames took hold.

Tim watched the smoke spiral into the midmorning sky, but it wasn't enough. Sprinting into the house, he appeared a few minutes later, sweating wildly, as he dragged his mattress behind him. He let it flop onto the fire. Tim wanted it to explode into a fireball of retribution, but it merely singed and smoked. He doused the mattress with the remaining spirits, encouraging the flames, which refused to take hold.

"Flipping heck, I thought the house was on fire!" said a voice behind him.

Tim turned to see a shirtless Ogie standing at the side gate, peering into the garden. Tim couldn't control himself. He flew at the man, fists bunched. He wanted Ogie to crumple under his blows; he wanted to feel bones crunch and skin rip. But as Tim swung at Ogie, the man easily dodged the punches. Another haymaker whistled uselessly through the air; Ogie blocked a third and landed a short jab to Tim's tender breastbone.

The blow blasted the wind out of his lungs, even though it wasn't much of a strike. Tim staggered back, trying to take in some air. He flopped to the ground like an overgrown toddler. Ogie stood over him with his fist still balled but concern on his face.

"I didn't want to do that. You made me."

Tim struggled to breathe. The ability slowly coming back.

Ogie spoke again. "I never wanted this to happen."

"No," wheezed Tim. "You just wanted to fuck my wife."

Ogie's face whitened. The look of concern was gone in a flash. He squared his shoulders and looked down at Tim.

"It wasn't me who did the chasing. You need to look closer to home for that." Ogie turned and walked toward the gate, stopping for just a second to say, "I'm sorry," but not waiting for an answer. The damage was done.

Tim rolled onto his side, his breathing coming back to normal but his self-respect was in tatters. He looked at the smouldering mattress, resisting his best efforts to destroy it with comparative ease. The tiny flames twinkled through his tears as he wallowed in the knowledge that he wasn't man enough for anything.

Chapter 27

Brendan sat outside the graveyard in his car, waiting for Angie to leave. He'd parked close to the gate. Most of the mourners had dispersed quickly once the burial was over. The flood of people soon became a trickle, then dried up altogether. It seemed like time had stopped, he'd been waiting that long. His head thumped, and his stomach tossed with anxiety. The agony was getting to be too much. He took a packet of painkillers from his pocket, swallowing half a dozen of them dry.

Just then she appeared, like he'd known she would. Sad and alone, Angie crossed the street and walked to a nearby bus stop. How quickly the boy's family had discarded her, cast her to the pavement now that her role as dutiful partner was done. Perhaps she'd see now that she'd simply been used by the boy, by all of them. Angie reached the bus stop and perched herself on the hard metal bench, the surrounding glass magnifying the power of the sun, baking her inside her widow's garb. The heat was clearly getting to her; he noticed her opening buttons on her heavy black blouse.

Brendan started his car and pulled into the road, passing the bus stop before drawing to the kerb a few feet beyond the shelter. Angie looked at the car with curious eyes but made no effort to come closer. Brendan watched the girl in his rearview mirror and sighed. Why was she making things so difficult? He opened the driver's door and got out, smiling.

"Hi, neighbour. I saw you sitting there and thought you could do with a lift."

She didn't jump at the offer. Brendan wasn't sure if it was grief or fear that he saw in her eyes.

"It's okay. I'm getting the bus," she said, regarding Brendan wearily.

"Are you sure? I'm going straight home, and I pass right by your house."

Brendan could see the girl reconsider his offer as a bead of sweat rolled down her temple. It wasn't like they were strangers, after all. Surely, she'd take the lift. One more bit of encouragement would win the day. "It's far too hot to be waiting hours for a bus," Brendan said, using what he thought was his most-winning smile.

"All right, thanks," Angie said, gathering her bag and walking to the car.

In Brendan's mind, the voice roared, *Street-walking harlot!* then laughed vilely. Brendan got in the car, trying to hide his disgust at the foul things being screamed inside him. He leaned across to pop open the passenger door. Once they were under way, Brendan said, "It's amazing that we've been neighbours for so long, and today was the first time we've spoken."

"Yea, amazing," she agreed, not wanting to be rude but clearly not giving a damn.

"And at such a sad event," continued Brendan, oblivious to the girl's sarcasm. "It's true what they say. Every cloud has a silver lining."

"Pardon?" said Angie, not quite believing that she'd heard him right.

"I know, it's sad, but today has brought us together. That has to be a good thing."

Angie looked at him with a frown before saying, "If you say so."

The voice in his brain brayed with laughter once more, taunting him, goading him. Brendan knew his words had come out wrong. If only he could find the right words, he was sure she'd agree that today was the best of all days. It was difficult driving while trying to talk to her at the same time. Not to mention the clamour raging through his brain. It was such a racket, he was amazed the girl couldn't hear it.

Brendan decided the car wasn't the place for this conversation; he needed her undivided attention. It looked like he was going to have to use the equipment he'd stashed in the boot, after all. What he needed now was the right place to make his move.

He drove on in silence, not wanting to say the wrong thing again. The road ran alongside an industrial park, which looked semi-abandoned. It was as good a spot as any. Brendan began to wiggle the wheel in his hands, trying to make it look like the steering was shuddering.

"Holy moley! What's wrong now?" Brendan said. The car shook, making Angie sit up straighter in her seat.

"What is it?"

"I think we may have a flat tyre. I'll have to pull over and check it out."

Brendan indicated and moved out of the traffic into the industrial estate, stopping close to a high wall, out of sight of the main road. He got out and looked at the front wheel on his side, shaking his head for effect.

"Stupid flat, I'll have it changed in a minute." he said to her through the windscreen.

Brendan let the car run while he walked to the back, popping the trunk. Angie waited, wondering if she should walk back to the main road and find another bus stop.

Just as she was about to go, the man called her name. "Angie, do you think you could hold this while I get the spare out?"

Angie sighed and dropped her bag in the foot well. The tall man smiled his creepy smile at her as she walked to the rear of the car. He was holding up the floorboard of the boot, with one hand trying to retrieving a dirty spare tyre with the other.

"Sorry about this."

"No problem," she said, taking the timber cover with both hands, leaving Brendan free to take out the wheel. Brendan reached behind his back, pulling the heavy metal torch from his waistband. It all happened so fast, Angie was caught completely off-guard. He knocked her senseless with a blow over the ear. He hadn't wanted to hurt her, but she'd left him no choice. Anyway, he thought to himself, all great loves spring forth from pain.

Angie fell to the ground, stunned but not knocked out. The timber floor cover fell back into place, revealing the looped cable ties lying in the mouth of the open duvet. Brendan flipped Angie onto her belly, slipping the plastic bindings over her ankles and wrists, drawing them tight. She was helpless now. He lifted her easily and dumped her into the boot of the car. He stripped several pieces of tape from the roll, covering the girl's mouth, leaving her nose clear so she could breathe. Angie's eyes opened as her head was stuffed into the duvet cover. He slammed the boot shut.

Brendan sat into the car, leaning across to pull the passenger door closed. He smiled as he drove away. It had gone better than he could have hoped. He didn't like hurting the girl, but it had to be done; she'd soon understand. The car shook a little as Angie struggled with her bonds. He was in no rush. Better she struggle now rather than later, he thought.

***

The white van looked like a thousand others on the city streets. When it turned into the gravel drive of a large house on Davis Road, anyone watching would assume it was making a delivery. Removal would have been closer to the truth. Chris got out and walked to the front door of the house, pressing the bell several times. It was empty, as Frank O'Shea had said it would be.

From his pocket, Chris took the key and security code. He repeated the numbers several times to himself before slotting the key home. The mechanism turned smoothly, and the lock clicked open. As Chris walked inside, he heard the alarm system beeping. Flipping open the plastic lid covering the security-system keypad, he carefully pressed the numbers, finishing with the green Return button. The beeping stopped, and the house was theirs. Chris whistled to the other men in the van. They casually walked inside; there was work to do.

No expense had been spared when kitting out the home; everything was state of the art. Chris should have considered this before believing one simple code would be enough to disable the security system.

The fact was, the homeowners had opted for the most-expensive security option on the market. Dotted around the building were cameras disguised as smoke detectors. Even though the alarm was disabled, the cameras remained active. These in turn were connected to a sophisticated computer that had a facial-recognition programme, housing images of all the family members. In the minutes after the alarm was deactivated, the cameras scanned all the people moving through the house, and as long as the system recognized at least one person, the alarm remained dormant. In a case such as today, where no face matched the computer's memory, a live feed from the house cameras appeared in the remote-monitoring station of the security company. Once that happened, the security company had complete control of the system. So one minute after Chris entered the code, a security man was flicking through the cameras, watching the men removing items from the house. With a press of a button, he talked to a designated Garda hotline. He then followed up with a call to the owner of the property, who confirmed the house should have been empty.

Blissfully unaware that his every move was being watched and recorded, Chris and his crew loaded the stolen van with expensive furnishings. A short time later, the squad cars pulled into the drive silently, sirens deliberately left idle. Chris and his mates were caught red-handed, walking out the front door with a massive fifty-two-inch plasma-screen TV.

Harry saw the whole thing unfold from across the road. He had known the job was a bad idea; that's why he'd followed Chris without telling him. Harry's plan had been to tip Chris off if he spotted a tail, which he hadn't. Harry was on the verge of driving away when the Garda cars appeared. The alarm never went off; there had been no one watching the house. It must have been a tip-off. Harry started his car and drove away slowly, so as not to attract attention to himself, as even more police units appeared. He caught a glimpse of Chris being chased across the lawn by two coppers and tackled to the ground.

There was nothing he could do here, but that wasn't to say there was nothing to do. Frank fucking O'Shea had made a huge mistake, and he was going to pay for it.

***

Adams was driving back from the coroner's office after collecting a new file, cross-referencing the murder of Tony Kelly and the woman on the canal. The depressingly thin folder lay on the passenger seat. Apart from the wheel nuts and the paint tin, there was nothing to directly link the two cases. No body fluids, no blood, not even a hair common to both. Tony Kelly's death had taken place at arm's length; the woman was up close and personal. The few fibres they had lifted from the woman would be the key if only they could find the guy who had committed the crimes.

Adams had been hearing about Ford's case all over the radio, since a cleaner went on a chat show spilling his guts. He knew the young detective would need some support right about now, so he picked up his phone and dialed Ford's number. The call was answered on the third ring.

"You're a superstar, Michael," Adams joked, trying to lighten a terrible situation.

"Tell me about it. Mrs. Pulter's solicitor has already been on the phone, threatening to sue the arse off us for letting the cat out of the bag."

"I hope you told him where he could stick that?"

"The chief has taken over now. I'm just the dogsbody. He's on the way over to Mrs. Pulter's house to meet her in person."

"Anything new turn up, like a killer?"

"Ha! You're a funny man. Nothing new. I've been so busy with the media, I haven't left the office all morning. The only new info is the guy who saw the victim last hasn't shown up at work today."

"Did you send someone to check him out?"

"I had a unit on the way when it was diverted to burglary in progress. Chris McCarthy, would you believe it, caught with his hand in the till."

"That's a result. The McCarthys are a real pain in the arse. I'm at a loose end. If you like, I can check on your missing link."

"You don't mind?"

"Not at all, you've got your hands full there. What's the name?"

"Brendan Roche."

"And the address?"

"Nine Honeysuckle Lane. We—"

"You're joking!"

"No, why?"

"I've been to the same road three times in two weeks."

"That is a joke. Is it a rough area?"

"No, posh as you like. Just a coincidence. Text me the phone number. I'll be there in about an hour."

"Okay, will do. Thanks again, Stephen."

"No worries, Michael. Call you later." Adams hung up the phone and shook his head. Honeysuckle Lane again. What were the chances of that?

***

Brendan drove as if he were on his way to Sunday morning Mass. He kept up with the flow of traffic, but didn't rush. He didn't want to do anything that might attract attention to the car. In the boot, the girl's battle with her bonds was waning. Soon, no sound at all came from the back of the car. There was no turning back now; he had strayed too far from the mindless masses and showed his true self. Nothing would ever be the same again.

The voice in his mind seemed to sense this change. It diminished to the point of whispering as the miles vanished under his tyres. It took twenty minutes to reach Honeysuckle Lane, the row of houses was deathly quiet at this time of the day. Brendan turned his car around and backed up his own driveway, getting the boot as close as he could to the front door. He watched the lane for a few moments, checking there was no one about. When he was happy the coast was clear, Brendan turned off the engine but left the radio turned up; rock music floated into the air. As he opened the driver's door, Brendan heard a thump against the metal of the boot.

He opened the front door of his house, giving one final check around before he opened the boot of the car. Angie kicked and tried to scream through the tape covering her mouth. Brendan didn't think it was enough noise for anyone to hear, but he didn't take any chances. He drove his fist into what he thought was Angie's face, but made contact with her forehead instead. The bones in his hand crunched on impact, and pain shot up his arm. Brendan hopped from one foot to the other, holding his injured hand, trying to stifle the cry which rose in his throat. In the boot, the girl flopped about, stunned. When he had shaken most of the sting out of his hand, he grabbed the girl roughly and dragged her into the hall of his house, closing the door with a kick.

Once inside, he hoisted Angie over his shoulder and carried her, fireman-style, up the stairs. Brendan dumped her on the bed and quickly went back downstairs. His little finger was agony to move, and his knuckle was swelling alarmingly. Brendan went back outside and took the torch and tape out of the boot, slamming the lid home. Then he went around to the driver's door to turn off the radio which is when he spotted the girl's bag, lying in the foot well. He took that as well. Brendan checked the road one last time, but no one was in sight. He locked the car and scurried into the house. Closing the front door, he dumped the torch, tape, and bag on the hall table and cradled his injured right hand, knowing full well he had broken at least one bone. He muttered curses under his breath as he went to the kitchen to put some ice on it, trying to stem the pain before it got any worse.

***

Brendan had just closed his front door when a black BMW turned sharply into Honeysuckle Lane. It pulled into the driveway of the O'Shea house and had barely come to a stop when Harry McCarthy launched himself out the driver's door. He half ran the few steps to the house and rang the doorbell. He turned his ear to the spy hole and listened for noise. When the handle turned, Harry charged the opening door. He felt it connect into whoever was inside, throwing the person backwards. Harry stood in the hall, snorting like a bull.

The O'Shea woman was laid out in the middle of the floor. A fine gash had opened above her left eye, where the door had caught her, which was beginning to pour blood down her face. Harry slammed the front door closed and grabbed the woman by the hair. He dragged her along the floor into the kitchen. She kicked, screamed, and struggled, but she was no match for him. He hardly felt her weight as he lifted the Barbara, slamming her against the shiny American-style fridge that dominated the kitchen. Harry slapped her as hard as he could with his open hand, then clamped it over her mouth. He was shocked to feel her razor-sharp teeth bite into the meat at the base of his thumb.

"You fucking bitch," he grunted, pulling his hand free. Swinging it again, backhanded this time, the slap spun her head right around with the impact. The woman's legs slumped under her, but Harry pinned her against the fridge with his left arm, while he inspected the crescent ring of puncture wounds in the skin of his right palm.

"You bit me!" he said, sounding wounded. She turned her head and focused her eyes on his face. The blood from her nose mixed with that of her forehead and split lip, running over Harry's left hand and across the string of pearls she was wearing. When her eyes steadied in their sockets, she looked at him with naked fury, making Harry smile. This woman had some set of balls on her, he thought. At that moment, she spat a mouth full of saliva mixed with blood straight in his face. Harry wiped his face with the back of his hand, feeling his rage explode, destroying any admiration he might have just felt for the woman.

"Let me go," she said, her voice trying to be strong but trembling with anger, fear, and pain.

"Not bloody likely, missus."

"You got your money. You won't get another penny from us."

"You think you're so flipping clever, you and that spineless Muppet of a husband."

"I haven't a clue what you're talking about. Don't think you're going to get away with this."

"That's something you people never understand." Harry said, squeezing her throat hard. "I just don't care. When you decided to fuck with my family, you made the biggest mistake of your lives."

"What? You're mad," she croaked.

"First thing you've been right about since we met," he said, letting go of her throat but grabbing a fistful of hair. He dragged Barbara to the kitchen table and threw her into a chair.

Harry took out his phone and flipped it open one-handed. With a few quick swipes of his thumb, the phone was ringing. Harry was breathing hard with exertion. On the third ring, it was answered.

"Frank O'Shea."

"You stupid fucker, you just couldn't leave well enough alone. You had to play the big man."

"Harry? What the hell are you talking about?"

"You squealed on the job."

"I never said a word."

"Bullshit!"

"I swear, Harry."

"*Bullshit!*"

"Think what you like. I don't have to take any of your crap anymore."

"I reckon you should ask your missus about that." Harry held the phone close to Barbara's face and yanked her hair painfully, causing her to cry out.

Finally, she began to blubber, managing to say, "He's at the house Frank. Call the Guards."

Harry pulled the phone back from her. "I wouldn't recommend that, Frankie boy. She's a fighter, your old lady. Aside from a few scratches, she's still in one piece. If I even think the cops are on the way, I'll gut her like the pig you are. It's you I want, not her. Get your ass over here before I get fed up waiting, and do something you'll regret." Harry flipped the phone closed, cutting the connection.

"You better hope he comes alone," Harry said, yanking Barbara's hair one last time.

He threw her to the table and stalked about the room, muttering to himself. Eventually, he settled against the kitchen counter, waiting for Frank to arrive.

Across the city, Frank looked at his phone like it was a venomous spider. Harry was in his house, and he was hurting Barbara. The thought sank through his shock, causing something strange to happen. For once in his life, Frank O'Shea forgot to be frightened. Blood vanished from his veins, to be replaced with a boiling lava of hatred. Running to his car, Frank had one thing on his mind: murder.

***

Brendan's hand hurt and he needed proper medical attention, but that would have to wait. Once they were on the road, he could stop at a hospital or a clinic. The most-important thing right at this moment was to bring the girl into the light, to make her see what he'd done for her, how destiny had brought them together. He knew it wasn't going to be easy; her brain had been programmed by years of dulling banality. He'd have to break through that, to reach the white-hot centre of her soul. It was going to be painful for both of them, but the rewards would be worth it. Brendan took the roll of duct tape from the hall table and climbed the stairs.

The girl lay unmoving on the bed, shrouded in the gaily coloured bed linin. For the first time, Brendan noticed the cover had tiny red roses printed on it. Red, the colour of love, the colour of blood, the colour of life. Yet another sign that what he was doing was right. He laid the roll of tape on the bedside table and sat on the edge of the bed. When she felt his weight, she began to struggle, kicking out with both her legs like an enormous salmon in a net.

"Take it easy. I'm not going to hurt you."

In response, the girl kicked once more in the direction of his voice, but then lay still.

"I'm going to take the cover off," Brendan said, kneeling on the bed to reach around the girl's body. He freed her feet and could see the cable ties were biting deeply into her skin; it looked extremely painful. He worked the material under the back of her calves and up her legs. As the cover came away, it gathered her long black skirt with it, revealing firm, youthful legs encased in sheer black tights. Brendan ran his hands against the back of her legs, lifting her, working the rose-covered bedspread higher. Brendan felt his fingertips slip between her warm thighs, and delighted in the feel of her young skin surrounding his. Her body accepted his touch, without flinching. The feeling was electric. He let his hand dwell there for a moment. Heat began to gather in his crotch and he couldn't help but move his hand a fraction deeper, forcing the girl's legs apart.

Angie launched a vicious double-legged kick, catching Brendan under the jaw. He felt a flush of embarrassment wash over him, like a naughty schoolboy caught peeking into the girls' bathroom. He didn't like the feeling one bit and lashed out at the girl for causing it. He landed on her, pinning her swinging legs under his body, driving an elbow in the general direction of her neck. He let his full weight pin her to the bed until she stopped struggling.

"It is up to you how this goes. All I want is for you to listen. If you struggle, it'll only make things worse. Understand?"

The girl's body was rigid under him.

"Do you understand?" He repeated the words deliberately. Brendan felt the resistance go out of her, and he took his elbow off her neck. He stripped away the duvet cover, quickly this time, careful to touch her as little as he could. He balled up the material and threw it in the corner of the room.

The girl's eyes were wide and frightened. A dribble of dried blood traced its way from her hair to her neck. A fresher streak of blood crossed the tape on her lips, originating from her nose. Brendan noticed her ankles again. The plastic ties were even tighter now, after she'd tried to kick him.

"They look sore," he said, nodding at her feet. Angie's eyes flicked down for a second. Remembering the pain, her fear was dulling. She looked at him and nodded.

"If you promise not to kick, I can do something about that."

Angie nodded her head a few times. Brendan took the roll of duct tape in his hand and sat on the end of the bed, causing Angie to flinch away from him.

"I'm not going to touch you. Lift your feet off the bed."

Angie didn't move.

"If you don't do as I ask, how am I supposed to help you?"

She did nothing for quite a long time. Brendan didn't mind waiting. She had to come to the decision herself, or what good would it be to either of them? Angie regarded him with equal parts fear and loathing, but eventually, she raised her legs a few inches off the bed.

"That wasn't so hard now, was it?" said Brendan, as if he were talking to a child. He pushed Angie's skirt up; she flinched, pressing her thighs tightly together but keeping her feet raised.

"I'm not interested in that, unlike all your other men," Brendan said in a hoity tone. He wound the tape around her legs several times. When he was satisfied, Brendan produced a penknife from his pocket. The sight of the blade caused Angie's eyes to grow wide, even though it was only small. The fear the weapon caused wasn't lost on Brendan, who gloried in the power he held over Angie. He ran the tip of the knife across the nylon of Angie's tights, moving it closer to the dangling roll of tape.

"I don't have to help, you know. I do it because I care. All of this is because I care," he said.

Angie didn't move, frozen to the spot by the madness wafting off the creep, as well as his blade. Brendan sliced through the tape, and then cut away the plastic cable ties, which left deep red groves in her legs.

"Roll over, and I'll do your hands."

Angie did reluctantly, only because the plastic bindings were agony. Brendan repeated the procedure, and when he was finished, Angie rolled on her back as quickly as she could, not wanting to take her eyes off this madman for a second longer than necessary. The blood flooded back into her hands and feet, causing painful pins and needles, but the tape was much more comfortable than those vicious plastic straps.

"I'm going to take the tape off your mouth soon, but if you start yelling, it's going straight back on."

Angie held his gaze but made no effort to agree.

"Do you understand?" he asked.

Angie nodded enthusiastically this time. Brendan reached for the corner of the tape, but his hand stopped in midair.

"You must think I'm a monster. It isn't true. I've watched you, loved you, for so very long. No one could ever love you like I do. Our destiny is preordained by forces you can't begin to understand, not yet, anyway. That's why it had to be this way. It's too much for any ordinary person to take in. It is going to take time, but you'll see in the end. I know you'll see."

Brendan took the corner of the tape and peeled it carefully from her lips, the lips he longed to taste. She barely moved, even when her skin snagged on the glue. When the tape was off, she didn't scream. Instead she said in a shaky voice, "Please, just let me go."

"I can't do that. I've things to tell you."

"Let me go. I want to go home."

"You are home. I'm your home now."

At this, Angie began to cry.

"Shush, I'm not going to hurt you. I love you."

"You are hurting me," she said, raising her voice.

"Only because I have to. A change is coming. I'm changing, and with me, the world. A new dawn is coming. Angie, you were chosen to be by my side as I rise to a higher plane of existence. It's a great gift I'm giving you."

"I don't know what you're talking about, and I don't care. Can't you see that? *I don't care!*" She shouted the last words into Brendan's face, carrying with them spit and tears. He clamped his hand over her mouth. Angie struggled, and every time she got her mouth free, she screamed as loud as she could. Brendan knelt on the bed trying to hold the girl, but he was losing the struggle. He slapped her hard across the face, sending blinding pain up his injured little finger. The blow stunned Angie enough to let him get a strip of tape over her mouth again, soon followed by several more. When he was finished, Brendan was sweating from exertion and discomfort. He stood at the end of the bed and looked in Angie's eyes.

"You're disappointing me, Angie, but I won't give up on you. Nothing is going to stand in the way of us. Not that fool of an accountant you were whoring yourself to. Not your pig of a father. Nothing. You're mine. Not even you can change that." Brendan's mad rhetoric was flowing from his mouth when the doorbell rang, slicing through his words like a scythe.

***

It didn't take Adams long to cross the city. Most people were at work. Honeysuckle Lane and the roads around it were as close to deserted as you could get these days. How had such an ordinary little road used up so much of his time lately? Adams was more at home in the high-rise slums of the inner city. Shoebox-size flats, piled one on top of the other, reaching for the sky. The people living there were easier to understand. They did what they had to do to survive. The nastier ones fed off the nicer ones; the nicer ones did their best to hide. The rules of engagement were clearly defined for all, including Adams.

These middle-class places annoyed him. Nobody here ever thought they were in the wrong. They had a sense of entitlement that they believed gave them licence to walk all over anyone they liked. It was this attitude that was ruining the world, in Adams's opinion.

As he took the sweeping turn into Honeysuckle Lane, he spotted something very out of place, a true turd of humanity, or at least, his car. Harry McCarthy again. What's going on around here? he wondered. The shiny BMW stood in the drive way of the second house. Mrs. Sweeney had mentioned the name of the owner, but for the life of him, Adams couldn't remember it. The car was empty, which could only mean that McCarthy was inside the house. Wherever Harry McCarthy went, he was up to no good.

More confusing still was the fact that his evil little minion had been bagged on a breaking and entering, so why wasn't Daddy rounding up the best lawyers in town? It could be a coincidence, that he'd been here the last two times Adams had reason to visit. But Adams didn't believe in coincidences.

He drove on, looking for number nine. It was the last house on the row. A dull-brown Mondeo was in the driveway, so someone must be at home. Adams parked his car on the road and picked up his two-way radio.

"Detective Stephen Adams to dispatch."

"Go ahead, detective."

"Can you pass on a message to the officer in charge of Chris McCarthy's case? Harry McCarthy's car is currently parked outside Two Honeysuckle Lane. This is the second sighting of him in this area this week. It's worth checking out, as those two are as thick as thieves, literally."

"I'll pass that on detective. Anything else?"

"Can you show attending a witness interview at Nine Honeysuckle Lane for the next hour?"

"No problem. That's logged for you, detective."

Adams hooked up the mic and got out of the car. It was too hot to bother with his jacket, so he left it on the passenger seat. If he hadn't stopped to call in the sighting of Harry McCarthy's car, he would've heard Angie screaming. Life's funny like that. Instead, he walked to the door of Nine Honeysuckle Lane with his notebook in his hand and not a concern in the world, beyond Harry McCarthy. He pushed the doorbell on the dishevelled looking house.

***

After the news report aired giving details of the murder on the canal, dozens of people contacted the Garda station with sightings of unusual activity in and around the block of flats on the night in question. Most were time-wasters looking for their fifteen minutes of fame. Regardless, Sims had to call them all back and conduct a phone interview to assess if they had anything worthwhile to add to the investigation. Even the fruitcakes had to have a record logged in the crime file, just in case. It bugged Sims that so much of her time was spent arse-covering.

Sometimes, however, the slog paid off, as was the case with Margaret Shannon. Sims had just talked by phone with Mrs. Shannon, who had been visiting a friend in the flats on the night of the murder. She happened to be returning to her car when she saw a tall, well-dressed man coming from the direction of the canal gate. She also saw him drive away in a dark-coloured car which she was able to identify it as a Ford. The time of the sighting fit perfectly with the time on the video footage, and the woman's description of the man was close to what she had seen on the CCTV image. Sims arranged to call 'round with a still photo of the suspect for her to look at later in the day.

She finished off some of the reports and called back a few more dead ends before grabbing her car keys. She leafed through the ever-thickening murder file for a photo of the canal suspect. Twice, she searched the file, both times coming up empty. Surely, Dolan hadn't taken the last copy of the photo. She was fuming after checking the third time. No photo, and the only one that sloppy was Dolan. He was such a lazy git.

Sims stomped up the stairs toward the tiny video room. She knocked at the door and was greeted with a cheery, "Come in."

"Sorry for bothering you. Do you happen to have a still shot of the suspect from the underground car park CCTV at Brady, McCarthy, and Doyle? And one of the tall man seen exiting the towpath on the canal case?"

The shirt-sleeved technician smiled, but shook his head.

"Out of luck there, but we can run the footage again and print one off for you, as soon as I finish with this. Ten minutes, and I'll be done."

Sims pulled up a chair and waited as people sped through a bright office on the main display screen. Every now and again, the technician would stop the footage and print an image of whoever was in the frame.

The footage moved on, and a figure walked down the bright hall, double quick and out of sight. Something about the man was familiar to Sims. The technician spooled back the footage, looking for the best shot. The man in the picture was tall, with a slight hunch to his back.

"What are you working on?" she asked.

"This is the office footage from the arson murder Michael Ford is investigating."

"Ah, I see," said Sims. She sat back in her chair as the video technician selected the best frame and pressed Print. Once that was done, he let the footage play forward at double speed again. The printer beside Sims rattled and spat out a photo of the man on the screen.

Bored, Sims picked it up and studied the shot. She was *sure* she knew him.

"Can you rewind that part, and play it at normal speed?" Sims asked.

The video technician did, and both watched the tall man stride down the hall with his head swinging, shoulders hunched in what could only be described as a shifty manner.

"Can you play it again?" said Sims, sitting all the way forward in her chair, her eyes glued to the screen now.

When the man walked past the camera, she said, "It's the same guy."

"Same guy?"

"Same guy as the canal murder, and the Kelly murder. Can you do a side-by-side?"

"Sure thing."

With a clatter of keys, the screen divided. One side showed the office, with the tall man frozen midstride. The second screen sprang to life, and the dark fuzzy image of the apartment's car park appeared. The operator consulted his notes, fast-forwarding to when the man arrived into the shot. He let both sets of footage play simultaneously. The figures were of similar build and had the same gait, but it was impossible to be certain it was the same man.

"Could be him," said the video operator.

"I better get Adams to have a look," said Sims, flipping open her mobile. When Adams's phone rang out, Sims left a message. She tried a few more times but received no answer.

"That's not like him," said Sims, after a third missed call

Chapter 28

Adams pressed the doorbell a third time, but the house remained mute. Being ignored on a doorstep wasn't a new experience; the trick was to get louder. In the end, he always got in. Adams pounded his balled fist against the door and called, "Hello, I know you're in there!"

Upstairs, Brendan was scurrying around the bedroom, getting Angie's hands bound to the headboard and her feet attached to one leg of the bed. It was a rushed job, done with even more duct tape, but it was the best he could do. With a warning glance over his shoulder, he left the room, closing the door behind him.

Whoever was outside was practically hammering the place down. Brendan hesitated halfway down the stairs, trying to will away this unwanted intrusion. A longer, harder rap on the door put paid to any hope of that. Brendan had no choice but to get rid of the caller. He descended the last few steps and opened the door, but only after securing the chain.

"What is it?" he snapped through the gap. Brendan glared at the well-built man on the doorstep dressed in suit pants but no jacket. The light shirt looked as if it had seen a full day's wear already.

He held out a Garda identity card. "I'm Detective Stephen Adams. Can I have a word with you, Mr. Roche?"

"What about?"

"It'd be better to speak in private," said the detective, pocketing his ID.

"It's not convenient right now. Can't you come back some other time?"

"It's a matter of some urgency, Mr. Roche. Can you at least open the door?" The detective saw the sliver of face frown in annoyance before the door closed sharply. He heard the security chain rattle as it was disengaged.

When the door reopened, a tall man filled its frame, making no effort to invite Adams inside.

"Yes, what do you want?" the man asked, holding the door in one hand, as if he may well slam it shut at any moment.

"Sorry to disturb you, Mr. Roche, but there has been an incident at your workplace, and I need to ask you some questions. You are Mr. Roche?"

"Yes, I am. Ask them, detective. I'm rather busy."

Adams knew a nut job when he saw one, and this guy was almonds and pecans to the core. He got out his notebook, ready to record the man's answers. "Do you know a Mr. Brian Pulter?"

"Yes."

"When did you last see him?"

"Yesterday."

Adams wrote the man's curt answers into his notebook. He didn't like this guy and was liking him less by the answer. Perhaps it was the snappy tone, or the way he wouldn't look him in the eye that made Adam's hackles rise. He also noted that the man hadn't asked what had happened to Brian Pulter, or why he was being asked about him. These would be normal questions—unless you already knew the answers, of course.

"Are you and Mr. Pulter friends?"

"No, he's my boss."

"But you get on?"

"Sure, we do."

"Weren't there some issues lately between the two of you?"

"A minor difference of opinion, nothing more."

"Do you live alone, Mr. Roche?"

"Yes."

"Where were you yesterday evening, about nine p.m.?"

"Look, what's all this about?"

"Like I said, Mr. Roche, there's been an incident. It's best if you answer my questions as fully as you can," said the detective, beginning to lose his patience.

"And as I said, detective, this really isn't very convenient," Brendan countered in a superior tone.

"I don't particularly care if this is convenient or not, Mr. Roche. You can answer my questions here, or I'll arrest you, and you can answer them at the station. Your choice." The detective left no doubt that he wasn't to be dissuaded or pushed around. Brendan didn't crumble as quickly as Adams would have thought he would. He stood for a solid five seconds of saying nothing.

Adams was beginning to believe he might just have to arrest the fruitcake when Brendan sighed theatrically and said, "Ask your questions if you must, and get it over with."

"Again, where you at nine last night?" asked Adams, not trying to hide his annoyance.

"I was at home all evening."

"Can anyone confirm this?"

"I was alone."

The detective scribbled this into his notebook, seeming to make a lot of notations for a very precise answer. It was an old detective's trick. If it seemed like someone were lying, draw out the time and see if they offer more information. Most people do, but Brendan Roche wasn't most people. After what seemed like an age, the detective looked up and asked, "Why were you not at work today?"

"I had a funeral to go to."

"A relative?"

"No, a friend. A friend of a friend, to be exact."

"Why didn't you return to the office afterward?"

"I didn't feel like it," said Brendan huffily, causing even more scribbling in the little notebook.

"How would you describe Mr. Pulter's demeanour when you saw him last?"

"He was fine. Very chatty."

"Was there anyone else there?"

"No, except his secretary. She was at her desk. He asked me to give her some files."

"Mr. Pulter?"

"Yes, who else?"

The detective flipped his notebook closed and crossed his arms across his chest. "You haven't asked me what happened, or why I am asking about Brian Pulter, Mr. Roche. Why is that?"

Brendan stammered and reddened. "I assumed you would tell me in your own time, detective. You come here, harassing me on my doorstep, asking loads of random questions, and I'm the strange one for not being nosy?"

"Do you know what happened to Mr. Pulter?"

"No, how could I? You haven't told me yet."

"There has been some coverage in the media. Perhaps you've heard it?"

"No, I don't watch TV."

"It was radio, actually."

"Or radio."

Just then, a crash came from someplace upstairs. It sounded like a glass dropping to the floor. The detective tried to see past Brendan, but the man didn't move or even turn toward the noise. He was acting extremely strangely.

"I thought you said you live alone, Mr. Roche?"

"I do, but that is not to say I am alone now, detective."

"Who else is in the house?"

"My partner is here. Thus the inconvenience."

"I'll need to talk to him or her as well. I think I'd better come in."

"This is too much, I must insist."

"No, Mr. Roche, I insist. Are you trying to impede a Garda investigation?"

"Of course not."

"Then perhaps you will be good enough to let me inside?"

With reluctance, Brendan stood back, holding the door open to allow the detective to pass.

"Please wait in the parlour," Brendan said, as the detective entered. Parlour? Who said parlour anymore? As Brendan closed the door, he snatched the heavy torch from the hall table, where he had left it earlier.

A bigger crash came from upstairs. The detective stopped and looked up. Brendan took aim at the back of the detective's neck, just like he'd done with Angie. The blow landed solidly, and the detective staggered a little but managed to keep his feet, reaching instinctively to where he'd been hit. Brendan lashed out twice more, but Adams still had the power to turn on him, dazed but still strong. He grappled with Brendan, trying to wrestle the torch out of his hand. The men locked together in a wild, thrashing knot. Brendan was driven into the wall, sending a mirror smashing to the ground. Ornaments flew into the air, and coats were ripped from their hooks. Eventually, the detective crushed Brendan's injured hand into the newel post of the stairs, sending the torch flying out of his grasp. Adams tried to get his arm around Brendan's neck, but he stepped on some shattered mirror that littered the floor, and his foot slipped from under him. Brendan spun to his left, and the detective's grip was lost.

Brendan dashed up the stairs before the groggy detective regained his feet. This was nothing like dealing with Angie, or the woman on the towpath. This man was far too capable. Brendan had nearly made it to the top step when his ankle was taken from under him by a swipe of the Adam's hand. Brendan sprawled headfirst across the landing, and was still sliding when he flipped on his back to face the enraged man flying through the air.

Somehow, Brendan got his foot on the detective's chest and shoved with all his might. Adams was thrown backward into the open stairwell, landing with a sickening thud at the bottom. Brendan ran down and retrieved the torch. He straddled the Garda and pummeled him with a flurry of blows, oblivious to his injured hand, or anything else for that matter. When his rage was spent, Brendan's face was covered in blood spatters; the detective was a mass of cuts, and his nose was a bloody mess. Bubbles of air slowly formed and died on his crusted lips, then formed no more.

Brendan threw the torch away and got to his feet. The voices were back, this time in praise; saying the pig deserved to die. He had it coming for interfering with the transformation. Brendan knew the detective would be missed, and soon. It was time to get out of here. He took the stairs two steps at a time. Things would have to jump forward a few stages, whether he was ready or not. Brendan stuffed his laptop and important documents into a bag, zipping it closed. He ran down the stairs, stepping over the body of the detective and grabbing the small suitcase he'd packed earlier from under the stairs.

He cracked the front door and scanned the road. It was still empty. Brendan threw the cases into the backseat of his car before opening the boot. Whatever semblance of a plan he had been working toward was well and truly out the window now.

He hurried back inside the house and grabbed the detective by the ankles. He dragged the body away from the bottom of the stairs, but got blood on his hands. He tried to wipe them clean on his trousers, but the strange thing was, when he began wiping, he couldn't stop. Harder and faster, he rubbed, until panic bubbled through his brain in great, suffocating waves. It was all going wrong. *Wrong, wrong, wrong!* He felt like screaming. None of this should have happened. It had all gotten out of control. A cold sweat coated his body, and in his head, whispered words floated, half thoughts full of disappointment and spite.

From the clutter, one word became clearer than all the rest: *Run.*

That's exactly what he did. He ran to the kitchen, snatching a wicked-looking knife from the drawer. In a few swift bounds, he climbed the stairs and burst into the bedroom where he'd left Angie. She lay half off the bed at a painful-looking angle. The bedside table had been knocked over, and the lamp lay smashed on the floor.

"You shouldn't have done that," Brendan said, his voice ice cold. Angie's eyes grew terrified as she spotted the twelve-inch blade in his hand.

She cried through her gag. Brendan looked at the knife, and then the girl.

"You don't deserve another chance," he said, in a deathly cold tone. She struggled against the tape as he rounded the bed, but she was trapped by her own weight. He leaned across her, gripping her face painfully. The tip of the knife hovered just above her eye.

"You're lucky I'm so forgiving," he said, reaching behind Angie to slice through the tape binding her elbows to the headboard. She fell to the floor, but her legs were still attached to bed. With another slash of the knife, her feet fell also. Brendan dragged her roughly upright by her taped hands until she stood. As he pulled her toward the door, she hopped after him in a ridiculous rabbit fashion. This would never work. Brendan didn't want to take a chance on her running, but spending half the day herding a hopping, gagged, and tied girl toward the car would be even worse.

He pulled Angie roughly until she was facing him. "I'm going to cut your legs free, so you can walk down the stairs." He held the kitchen knife to her throat, pushing it higher, until she was standing on her toes. "This will be one inch from your heart, so don't make me use it."

Brendan knelt, slicing through the tape securing Angie's feet. He took her left elbow from behind, holding her close, his right hand pressing the sharp edge of the knife between her shoulder blades.

One careful step at a time, they descended the stairs. When the detective's body came into view, Brendan felt the girl tense in his grip. He shoved the blade firmly into her skin. "Take it easy, or you'll end up like him."

Retrieving his coat from the ground, Brendan put it around the girl's shoulders, throwing the hood up over her head. His knife still pressed into her back, his hand under the hem of the coat, he controlled the girl like a grotesque living puppet.

Adams moved slightly, a weak groan escaping his ruined lips. *He's alive, after all,* Brendan thought. *Amazing.*

He pushed Angie toward the door, taking a second to check that the road was still deserted. He bundled her over the threshold, and into the gaping maw of the open boot of the car. The lid slammed shut like a coffin, trapping her in total darkness.

Brendan rushed back inside and stood over the detective, massaging his injured hand. The adrenaline was wearing off, allowing the pain to return with a vengeance.

"Damn you to hell," said Brendan, kicking Adams in the head. Brendan paced the floor. Even in his madness, he knew he couldn't take the chance that the detective would survive. Leaving any witnesses wasn't good. Searching the kitchen, he found nothing that would fill his needs, but in the sitting room, a half-full bottle of whisky was just the thing. Brendan soaked the curtains and the couch with it, then set light to both. The flame took hold and began to grow, slower that Pulter's pyre, but growing nonetheless. Brendan walked out without a second glance at the detective, slamming the front door closed behind him.

***

Frank had the accelerator pressed right to the floor of the rickety old Volvo. The engine whined in agony as it tried its best to shove a tonne of rusting steel a little bit faster. Frank felt the outer wheels lose contact with the ground as he took the sweeping turn into Honeysuckle Lane. It was a miracle he didn't plough into the dirty-brown Mondeo coming out against him. Frank passed so close to it, he could see the fear in his creepy neighbour's eyes.

Frank lifted his foot off the accelerator, only to slam it straight onto the brake without even changing down the gears. The old car's engine stalled as it shuddered to a stop, half off his own driveway.

Frank threw open the driver's door, sprinting for the house. He had no plan, no idea what he was going to encounter, and not an ounce of fear in his body. The only thing coursing through his veins was hatred for the man that was hurting his wife. As the door loomed, Frank realised he'd left his keys in the ignition of the car, but instead of stopping, he sped up. Frank hit the door with his shoulder, like a linebacker. His momentum disintegrated the lock as if it were made of tinfoil.

Harry had heard tires sequel on the road outside, and had moved toward the hall to confront Frank. When the door exploded inward, he was shocked. Frank staggered for a microsecond as the door gave beneath his weight, but seeing Harry put wings on his heels. Harry hadn't time to react before the estate agent rugby-tackled him, driving him backward through the hall and across the kitchen. Harry's ribs collided painfully with the sink. Barbara sprang from her place at the kitchen table, joining her husband in the attempted destruction of Harry McCarthy. Frank landed a number of good punches before grabbing Barbara and shoving her toward the door.

"Come on!" he shouted, as she tried to attack Harry once more. Frank wanted to kill the man, but he had a chance to get Barbara away from all this, and that was all that mattered. Revenge always comes back at you in the end. It was time to do what he normally did best— get the hell away from trouble. Frank held his wife by the hand and ran through the hall, and out the wrecked front door. He knew Harry wasn't beaten by a long shot; he'd gotten lucky, and that was all. When Lady Luck smiled, grab it with both hands and don't let go.

Frank had no idea how right he was. If he'd looked over his shoulder, he would have seen Harry climb to his feet and charge after them. While running, Harry produced a silver butterfly knife from his jacket pocket and expertly flicked it open. Frank hauled Barbara past the BMW and his own stalled Volvo as fast as their feet would carry them. He careered into the road without a glance either way, never seeing the car coming.

Sims's heart nearly stopped when the couple dived out in front of her. The man made it past the bonnet of the car, but the bumper caught the woman square on the hip, and sent her sprawling down the road. Sims hadn't been going fast, thank the Lord. She jumped out of the car, just in time to see Harry McCarthy emerge from the house, brandishing a knife. It didn't take a mastermind to figure out why they'd run blindly into the road. Sims put herself between the couple and McCarthy.

"Put the knife down!" she barked, fishing in her pocket for her Garda badge.

"Fuck off, bitch," Harry snarled, advancing on her and the people behind her.

Sims finally got her badge out and shoved it at Harry. "I said, put down the knife, McCarthy. Now!"

He stopped moving forward, but the knife remained raised and poised.

"This is none of your business."

"Of course, it is. I'm a bloody Garda. Put the knife down, and kneel on the ground."

"It was those fuckers that attacked me. I haven't touched them. You're the one that knocked the stupid cow down."

"You're the one holding a knife, as far as I can see."

"What's the difference? I didn't use it."

"The difference is ten to fifteen years, depending on the judge you get."

That seemed to sink in. Harry shrugged and threw the silver knife across the driveway, dropping slowly to his knees, stapling his hands behind his head. He did all this with a huge smile on his face, which never quite reached his reptilian eyes. He clearly didn't give a damn for the law, but he knew when to quit.

Sims walked forward, keeping out of McCarthy's reach until she was behind him. She took his left hand and pulled it behind his back. The handcuffs made a clacking noise as they closed over his wrist.

"Book 'em, Danno," Harry said, laughing, as Sims expertly snapped the cuffs over his other wrist. With nothing but hatred, Harry stared at Frank O'Shea, trying to help his wife to her feet.

"Don't think this is over, you bastard," Harry roared at the cowering couple.

"That's enough out of you," growled Sims, as she forced the gangster toward the back of her car with twists of the manacles. Once he was safely locked inside, Sims retrieved the knife, using a little plastic evidence bag and zipping it into her jacket pocket, along with her Garda badge.

She hadn't even had a chance to ask the woman on the ground if she was all right before a *boom* echoed through the air. The window of the end house shattered outward; smoke and flame rose into the sky.

On the street outside of the house was Adams's car.

"Call a fire brigade!" Sims yelled at Frank as she ran toward the house.

Chapter 29

Angie bounced around like a rubber ball inside the boot. Her hands were bound, her mouth gagged, but at least her feet were free. Angie was so terrified, she thought she was going to throw up. Ever since waking with a massive lump on the back of her head, she had been angry and scared, but also fairly sure that she was going to walk away from this whole ordeal. Seeing the guy at the bottom of the stairs changed all that. Angie knew that she'd no chance of being let go now. If she was going to survive all this, she'd have to make it happen herself.

Angie was no fool. Once this guy got her somewhere quiet, she knew she was as good as dead. Probably raped, then dead, but dead in any case. She'd seen enough TV crime shows to know witnesses never live to tell the tale. She tried her best to calm herself, which wasn't easy in a fume-filled metal coffin. She used her legs to try and force the lid of the boot open, but it wouldn't budge. When that failed, she searched the inside of the compartment for a latch. After ages of searching blindly in the dark, all her fingertips encountered was smooth plastic. Having her hands behind her back was making her search all the more difficult, being forced to work backward and in the pitch black.

Her head collided with the side of the car again and again, as it twisted and turned on its journey. In the end, terror overcame good sense. Angie began to kick at the inside of the boot for all she was worth. The lid stayed closed; the backseat didn't budge. The only thing that happened was a plastic cover popped loose from someplace.

"Stop that banging, or I'll make you stop!" shouted Brendan from the driver seat. His words were muffled through the thick back seat, but the meaning was clear. Angie stopped kicking. If he tied her legs again, she'd never get away.

She kept feeling around with her hands and found the opening where the lid had popped from, it was some kind of compartment in the corner of the boot. She rolled her body around and explored the cavity with her fingertips. She could feel wires, metal edges, and what she guessed must be the taillight of the car. Angie got her taped wrists as close to the metal edge as she could, and rubbed for all she was worth. It was useless; she couldn't get the tape to stay in contact with the edge. She wiggled her hands under her bum and tried to get them down behind her legs. She pulled her knees up as far as they would go, and soon, they were pressed hard against the boot lid. She could feel the tape brushing against her ankle, but that was as far as she could get it. Her shoulders burned with the strain as she contorted herself into backbreaking positions. Each time, she came a fraction closer to being free but increased the agony on her joints a hundredfold.

Eventually, she felt the tape slide over her right ankle, and one leg was through. By comparison, getting the second leg through was child's play. Angie began to saw frantically at the tape with the sharp metal edge of the light housing. Now that her hands were in front of her, it was way easier. The metal scored her skin, but it also made an indent on the tape. The car took yet another corner, throwing Angie forward, jamming her hands into the opening. She felt something pop loose. A crack of light filled the dark interior. There was more room to get her hands into the opening now, and Angie renewed her sawing with vigour.

As she worked, the taillight got pushed more out of place. In the end, it was swinging to and fro with the movement of the car. At last, the tape gave way. She stripped the black sticky mess from her wrists and massaged them for a second or two, she got the blood flowing again; then she pulled the tape away from her lips. She knew if she started screaming, he would know that she'd gotten free. Instead, she scooted as close as she could to the damaged light, pressing her eye to the opening.

Behind her, she could see several rows of fast-moving traffic. Angie knew that there was no way anyone would hear her calling for help in the middle of all that. She had to find some other way of attracting the attention of the cars. She poked her fingers through the hole and pushed the dangling lamp to one side. She managed to get three fingers through the opening, and felt the cool air stream over her skin. Only the thickness of a piece of metal stood between her and freedom. That few millimetres was the difference between life and death.

In such fast-flowing traffic, three fingers weren't a lot to notice. Angie withdrew her hand and lay as flat as she could on the floor. Hitching up her skirt, she worked her tights down. When they were off, she found the toe of one leg and fed it out through the hole, until a couple of feet of nylon dangled out of the back of the car. She pushed her fingers through the hole and grasped the end of the pantyhose, waving them as much as she could. There was nothing else she could do except pray that someone would see her cry for help in time.

Chapter 30

The smoke billowed in great dark clouds from the shattered window, blackening the wall above it. Occasionally, a red tongue of flame licked through the hot, noxious gas. Sims tried the front door, but it was locked, so she flipped open the letter box. Inside, the hall was quickly filling with smoke; the heat was already intense, making her eyes water. There had clearly been a fight, as the hall was strewn with broken glass. Near the foot of the stairs lay a body roughly the size of Adams.

"Stephen! Stephen!" she shouted through the letter box. She gave the door a charge with her shoulder, but it was far too sturdy for her to force open. She ran around the back of the house, shielding herself from the flames. She found that the kitchen door was made of glass, but it also was locked. Sims could see the key hanging from the lock on the inside. She needed something to break the tough double-glazed window!

In the corner of the garden, she spotted a ceramic flowerpot with the corpse of a shrub still in it. Picking up the heavy pot, she ran at the door, letting go at the last minute. When the glass shattered, the roar of the fire became intense. Heat and smoke billowed out of the hole as Sims reached carefully over the jagged glass to turn the key.

When the door swung open, Sims barged into the smoke-filled kitchen. She hadn't gone four steps when her eyes began to sting, and the acidic vapours caught in her throat, making her cough, taking in even more of the poisonous fumes. Her vision swam with every breath she took. All around her, the smoke thickened; she had difficulty finding her way into the hall. Sims felt her knees go weak, as she staggered blindly a few more steps. Tentacles of fire laced through the red-hot gas gathering along the ceiling. Some tidbit of knowledge crept back from basic training, causing her to get down onto the floor. With her face against the sticky lino, she sucked in refreshing gasps of nearly clean air. Her vision cleared a little, and she saw the open doorway into the hall.

Crawling on her belly, she inched along. The heat was building all around her. Sims could feel her skin prickling, and she imagined she could smell the downy hairs on her arms singeing. In front of her, she began to make out the shape of Adams, laid out on the floor. Sims hurried over on hands and knees, seeing for the first time his ruined face. It was a huge shock. Sims got behind Adams and gripped him under the shoulders; she dragged him a few inches, then a few more. The kitchen now was completely full of smoke, and flames had engulfed the room, fed by the air sucked through the smashed back door. In the hall, the smoke was only inches off the ground. A huge flash of flame shot over Sims's head, rolling like a deadly wave along the ceiling.

There was no escape through that inferno. She felt the skin on her arm blister as she fended off the surge of heat. Her only chance was through the front door, which was only feet away, but it felt like miles. She pulled the dead weight of Adams along the blood-soaked floor. She finally felt her feet touch the timber of the door. She tried to pull the door open, but it wouldn't give. The ever-thickening layer of fumes completely blinded her. Sims had no choice but to reach into the boiling cloud to find the handle. It felt like dipping her hand into a bath of scalding water.

Searching the door for a latch, she prayed it wasn't secured with a mortise lock. If it was, they were both dead, even if Adams wasn't already. Her fingers searched but only encountered smooth timber. When she was about to give up hope, she found the familiar shape of a Yale lock. The most-delicious sensation of her life was feeling the latch click, and the door move.

As Sims dragged Adams onto the driveway, and the couple that Harry McCarthy had been trying to stab only minutes before rushed to help her. Once she had a few breaths of air in her lungs, her head started to clear. She was racked by coughs as her lungs tried to expel the poison she had been breathing. As quickly as she could, Sims felt for a pulse on Adams's neck. His face was a mess, both eye sockets reservoirs of pooling blood; there wasn't an inch of skin that had not been ripped or gashed. Adams's nose lay at a strange angle, slightly off-centre and crooked. The skin under her touch was lifeless. She moved her fingers slightly closer to his jawbone, and thought she felt something but wasn't sure. Pressing harder, she felt the weak but steady flow of blood through a vein. Sims held her ear to Adams's split lips. The slightest flutter of air brushed her cheek. He was alive!

As best she could, she staggered up the road to call for backup. She'd just about got the address out of her mouth when a wave of nausea overcame her. She threw herself out of the car before vomiting into the O'Sheas' flower bed.

***

A crowd soon gathered around the burning house, not knowing which was more entertaining, the man beaten to a pulp, or the building being consumed by flames. When the fire brigade arrived, all their attention shifted to the house. Adams's struggle for life was old news. One of the firefighters had fitted an oxygen mask over Adams's face, setting the gas flowing freely. Whatever little was getting into his lungs would help. The same man insisted Sims get oxygen, too.

Within minutes, an ambulance arrived, and the crew began working on Adams immediately. The amount of equipment they carried with them was breathtaking. Sims sat on the rear step of a second ambulance, watching the house burn to the ground while the firefighters played jets of water over the flames with little hope of saving anything. Several

Garda units arrived in a near convoy, and a few minutes later, the chief inspector and Dolan turned up.

"What happened?" asked the inspector, as he arrived at Sims's side. She removed the oxygen mask, feeling like a fraud, getting treatment for a bit of a cough while Adams lay at death's door only a few feet away.

"I'd a lead connecting the Tony Kelly murder to the fire death at the office block," wheezed Sims, her throat still raw from the smoke. "I tried contacting Adams to bring him up to speed, but he wasn't answering his phone, so I checked his call log at the station. His last check-in was here, doing a witness interview. When I still couldn't get through to him on the radio or the phone, I decided to follow him over here. When I arrived, the house was already on fire. I found Adams beaten close to death in the hallway. He's lucky to be alive."

The inspector peered into the back of the ambulance where Adams was laid out on a stretcher, but the paramedic waved him out of the way, closing the door.

The chief inspector looked a little embarrassed at being dismissed so bluntly. He looked around and noticed Harry McCarthy glaring at them from the back of Sims's car. He pointed and asked, "How come you've that piece of shit in the back of your car?"

"That is a whole other story. When I arrived on the road, I found him chasing a pair of local residents around the place with a flick knife. I don't think the two incidents are connected. If McCarthy had been the one who attacked Adams and set the fire, why would he waste time hanging around to pick fights? It has to be the person Adams came here to interview. It's the only thing that makes sense," said Sims, her voice coming slowly back to normal.

"I'm inclined to agree, but let's not jump to conclusions. Let's follow all the leads back, no matter how faint, until they have proved themselves useless. You did a great thing by getting Detective Adams out of there alive. That's more than a good day's work, it's a great day's work. It might be better to let us take it from here, you have been through a hell of a lot," said the inspector.

Sims nodded and looked abashed, she should have known better to jump to conclusions, and voicing them to the chief inspector was plain stupid. He was always preaching about the importance of dotting all the i's and crossing all the t's before making any decisions.

"Dolan, follow up with Michael Ford. See who Adams was due to interview here," said the Inspector. "Get a description of whoever it was out on the wire. Find out how many people lived in that house. We need to know if there is one on the run, or a couple, or a whole family. Find out what they drive. They can't just vanish into thin air. Make sure you get the make, model, and number of that car to every toll bridge, airport, and ferry terminal, ASAP. I don't want them getting off this island, north or south."

"Right away, chief," said Dolan, waddling toward his car.

"And Dolan!" called the inspector, making him turn back after a few steps.

"Yes, chief?"

"Don't get lazy on this one, or you'll be retiring a lot sooner than you think."

Dolan's face reddened, and he looked at his shoes. "Yes, chief," he replied in a whisper, hurrying away double-time.

The chief inspector turned to Sims. "You had better get yourself to hospital and get checked out. I'll get McCarthy taken in for charging."

"I'm fine, chief. I can do it," said Sims, taking off the oxygen mask fully and standing up.

"Don't be silly, Sims. You're in no fit state to continue working."

Sims hated being fobbed off as some helpless woman, and it must have shown in her face. "I said I am *fine.* "

Sims didn't know what had come over her, talking to a senior officer like that, and as soon as the words had escaped her lips, she regretted them.

The chief inspector merely held up his hands in surrender. "Okay, okay. You run him in," he said with a wry smile.

"I didn't mean any disrespect, sir. I just want to see this through," she stammered.

"No apology necessary, Sims, but after McCarthy is booked, I want you to go straight to the hospital. Deal?"

"Yes, sir. Of course, sir."

***

The crowd outside Nine Honeysuckle Lane was growing by the minute. Tim had heard all the commotion, but because he had no interest in anything, he ignored it. The curtains of his house had remained firmly closed to the world, since the morning Martha had left. Still, when the wailing siren cut through the hubbub, even he couldn't resist taking a look. A few houses down the lane, flames were shooting toward the sky, and a huge crowd had gathered in the street. Tim slipped on his shoes and walked out to the foot path in front of his house to get a better view. He watched while a man was loaded into the back of an ambulance, and another man in handcuffs was driven away in the back of a silver car.

When Ogie's door opened, Tim felt his stomach drop. Even the thought of seeing that man made him want to hurl. Thankfully, it wasn't Ogie but Annabelle. She had a hold-all in her hand, her face as pale as a sheet. She saw Tim, and her face went even whiter, if that were possible. Her step faltered, not knowing what to do. After a moment's indecision, she walked toward him.

Inside, Tim's guts knotted again. He didn't want this; he wished he'd never set eyes on any of them. She got close and stopped, clasping her hands in front of her nervously.

"I'm sorry this happened," she said.

"You know so?"

"Yea, I found out, but only the other day. I'm so sorry."

"You didn't do anything, did you? It was them," Tim snapped.

"Well, yes, I guess. I just wanted to say good-bye," she said, holding out her hand.

"You're leaving him?"

"Yes, I was stupid to think I'd change him," she said, dropping her hand when Tim made no move to take it.

"This wasn't the first time then?" Tim asked.

Annabelle looked ashamed and didn't answer the question. Instead, she asked one.

"And what about you and Martha? Will you be okay?"

"I can't think about that yet. It's too soon, and she's gone as well, as it happens."

"Don't let Ogie ruin your marriage. He's not worth it," Annabelle said.

"That is easier said than done. How can you glue a marriage back together? What do you do when you can't ignore the cracks anymore? Sometimes it's better to face things straightaway," said Tim, turning his attention back to the burning house.

"I really hope you can work things out," she said, turning and walking away. Tim watched her out of the corner of his eye. She stopped a few yards up the road, as if she'd forgotten something. She stood there in a quandary, torn between going back and continuing on her way. When she turned back toward Tim, her face was different, less drawn, less pale, more determined.

She walked to him with purpose. "I think you deserve to know everything," she said.

"Jesus, what more can there be?" said Tim, throwing his eyes to Heaven.

"Lots. Can we talk inside? It's important."

"I don't know if I want to know anything more."

"It's important, Tim, really. It could change everything."

Tim thought for a second or two. He wanted to hide from it all, but at the same time, his need to know what happened was greater. Nodding, he walked back into his house, holding the door for Annabelle to follow. In doing so, he was opening Pandora's box one more time.

Far across town, Martha was curled up on Ann's sofa, half watching some rubbish on TV. She hadn't slept properly since Tim had thrown her out. She'd nearly called him several times, but Ann convinced her to wait and give him the time he needed to sort his head out. Martha hadn't heard from Ogie, either, not that she wanted to, but she thought he might have at least tried to see what was happening. When her phone buzzed on the coffee table, Martha nearly didn't check it, assuming that it was Ann checking on her for the tenth time that day.

When she did check the message, it wasn't Ann. It was Tim. The message was short but hopeful: *Can you come over? I have to talk to you.*

Martha's fingers were a blur as she punched in the text: *Of course, when?*

She hadn't even put the phone down when it buzzed again: *As soon as you can. Tim.*

Martha sent one more message before dashing off to shower and change: *On my way, right now.*

Chapter 31

Sims drove away from Honeysuckle Lane with a moody Harry McCarthy in the backseat. The worst of her coughing had subsided, but every now and then she had to hack deeply into her hand. A description of Brendan Roche was being broadcast over the Garda radio, set in the dash of the car: "The suspect's last-known vehicle is a late-model Ford Mondeo, brown in colour."

"He sounds like a wimp to me," sneered Harry. Sims ignored him as she drove, taking the on-ramp for the motorway.

"What's happening to cops these days? Even the nerds are beating the crap out of you!" He laughed.

Sims knew responding would only egg him on, so she bit her tongue. But ignoring scum like him was like trying to ignore a fart in a crowed lift. Behind her, the aging criminal relaxed in his seat and watched the passing countryside.

"It's nice to be driven for once. You miss so much when you have to drive yourself." He was making it sound like she was his chauffeur, and in the process, making her hate him all the more.

"You better make the best of it," said Sims, her voice still rough from the smoke she inhaled. "Your next room will have a view of barbed wire and bars."

"Shows how much you know, slut. I'll be out on the streets before dinner. Mark my words," said Harry.

"Whatever about you, I don't think your idiot son will be so lucky. I heard he practically ran into the squad, still carrying the evidence. What a fool." Sims chided, watching Harry in the rearview mirror, and she could see the comment had stung.

Just then, the radio screeched out an all-points bulletin: "All units. Vehicle traveling on the M50 southbound, between Junctions six and five. Brown Mondeo, license plate 99 D 15874. Motorists trailing the car report some sort of dark materiel and someone's fingers sticking out of the rear lighting unit. Repeat: There appears to be someone in the boot. Approach with caution."

Sims wasn't far behind that point on the motorway. It had to be the same guy who had attacked Adams. It was far too much of a coincidence to be anyone else. Sims flicked on her blue flashers and floored the accelerator. In the backseat, Harry was thrown from side to side as the car weaved through the traffic. Smiling, she gave the car an extra aggressive jerk of the wheel, slamming Harry into the door.

"For fuck's sake, take it easy!" he cried.

Sims pushed the engine all the way into the red in an effort to catch up. She was doing close to one hundred twenty-five mph when the next call came on the radio.

"Suspect car has just passed through the express lane on the toll bridge. CCTV pictures confirm one male occupant, matching the description of man wanted for questioning in relation to the assault on Detective Stephen Adams. This man is considered armed and dangerous. Approach with caution."

The toll bridge was only five miles ahead. Sims kept her foot down on the gas, eating up the distance between the cars. The guy in the Mondeo must have no idea he'd been spotted. Sims picked up the radio and pressed the transmit trigger.

"Detective Sims to control."

She waited until an operator responded.

"I am on the M50, five miles behind the suspect Mondeo, and closing fast. Have you units standing by on exits four and three?"

"Roger that, Sims. Stop teams are in place on four and three. The stop team from exit five is currently shadowing the vehicle."

Sims clicked the button. "I'm driving an unmarked silver Audi A4. Inform the shadow team I'll take point from them as soon as I catch up."

"Have you forgotten about me?" asked Harry.

"I didn't think you'd be in a rush to get to jail. Anyway, I thought you said you were enjoying the ride," said Sims, dodging around another slow-moving car.

"The sooner I'm in, the sooner I'm out. Anyway, women can't drive for shit. You'll kill the two of us!"

Sims threw the car into the fast lane, overtaking a truck. She heard Harry grunt behind her as he crashed into the door again. Served the pig right, she thought. Time to rub it in.

Sims laughed at him. "I thought you were supposed to be a hard man, Harry."

Harry straightened himself. As Sims looked in the rearview mirror, she could see his face was boiling red with rage.

"When I get out, you'd better watch your back, you bitch. I promise you one thing: When I'm finished with you, you'll never feel safe again. Ever!"

"Are you threatening me, Mr. McCarthy?" Sims asked, her tone completely official.

"I'd say it was more like making a date. A nice romantic meeting, in the dark of night. I'm going to enjoy it so much, I might bring some friends along to watch."

"You think that I haven't heard shit like that from scum much worse than you? You've got to try harder than that if you want to rattle my cage, Harry.

The thing was, he *had* rattled her. As if her body was betraying her lie, she had to stifle a long hacking cough, which made her eyes water. Something told her he was sick enough to follow through on his threat, but she couldn't let him see he'd gotten to her. Up ahead, the toll bridge loomed. Like Brendan Roche, she went through the express lane. Unlike Brendan, she was doing nearly eighty, with her lights flashing and sirens blaring.

When she cleared the traffic on the far side of the bridge, she killed the siren and lights. The car couldn't be far ahead, so she lifted her foot slightly off the accelerator. Up ahead, she spotted the two marked Garda units in the middle lane.

Sims picked up her mic and called Control. "Can you patch me through to one of the shadow cars?" she asked.

A few seconds later, a man's voice said, "Go ahead, detective."

"I have you in sight. I'm moving up on your outside," Sims said, as she drew level with the lead car. "How far ahead is the suspect?"

"Middle lane, just over the horizon. Doing about sixty. We didn't move any closer, in case we spooked him."

"Good work. I'll move up behind him, and keep you posted. Be ready to move up at speed if I need you."

"Roger that, detective."

Sims stayed in the outer lane, pushing her car back up to seventy-eight. She passed the traffic using the fast lane, but not going so fast that she would draw attention to herself. Within minutes, she spotted the brown car ambling along in the middle lane. Sims passed an articulated lorry and slowed to keep pace with the moving traffic. She indicated and moved across the lanes, one at a time until she was in the slow lane. Drivers on the motorway tend to watch the overtaking side of the road, and ignore what's happening on the slow side. She moved stealthily past a minivan and a blue estate with a dozen dogs in the back until the brown car was only a few car-lengths ahead.

Sims could see the man hunched over the steering wheel, repeatedly rubbing his head and shaking it from side to side. He looked like he was having a conversation with someone, but there was no one else visible in the car. The taillight on the passenger side was hanging off at an angle. A black tongue of material flapped in the wind, and just visible holding on to it were three slender fingers, wiggling like mad. Sims activated her mic, keeping it well below the level of the windscreen while she talked.

"I'm in position now, Control. One male is visible in the car, but there may be others out of sight. He seems to be talking to someone. There's definitely someone in the boot of the car. There are fingers waving through a damaged tail section. The fingers are small, so it could be a woman, or a child. I'm moving back a few car-lengths. I think our best option is wait and attempt to make a stop when he exits the motorway. The driver seems unaware of our presence for the moment."

"Roger, detective. We have cars standing by on the next two off-ramps. Let's hope he takes one of them."

Sims lifted her foot off the gas, letting the brown car move ahead a bit, before she eased back into the middle lane. Signs for exit four began appearing. Sims willed the suspect's car to move toward the off-ramp, but it remained steadfastly in the middle lane.

"He didn't take the turn," Sims relayed to Central Control, using the microphone resting on her lap.

"Roger that, detective. The stop team from exit four are joining you as backup."

Sims didn't have a chance to say anything else, because a marked unit screamed down the ramp to her left, lights and siren going full blast.

Sims stared out the window stupefied at what was happening. "Pull back you idiot, pull back! You're far too close. *Pull back!*" she roared uselessly.

It was too late. Up ahead, the brown car swerved as the driver saw the Squad car appear to his left and jumped into the fast lane, picking up speed.

Harry cackled. "Whoo-hoo! Look at that rabbit run."

***

What Brendan imagined to be a casual drive into the sunset wasn't going quite as he had planned. Things seemed to go wrong from the moment he'd started the car. Before he'd even left his own street, that maniac O'Shea nearly crashed into him. It was insignificant when viewed against all that he'd been through over the last few days, but the near miss got his nerves jingling. As he drove away cursing the fool, his hands began to shake. The more he tried to still his limbs, the worse the shake became. This tiny loss of control became an avalanche of emotions, drenching his nervous system. Soon, his shake was accompanied by sweats and shivering.

He'd nearly jumped out of his skin when Angie began pounding on the boot. If he were anywhere but on the motorway, he'd have pulled over and done something about her. He crushed the wheel with temper, and his injured hand throbbed. Brendan was for all intents a walking wreck of a man, or in this case, a driving wreck of a man.

In the end, it took a simple threat to quiet the girl; he knew no one would hear her, anyway. Brendan steadied the car in the middle lane, ambling along at just under sixty mph. The hum of pavement passing under his wheels was soothing. With every minute, he put another mile between himself and his last problem.

A whispering voice entered his world. *Where to run? Where? Where?* it questioned.

"I don't know. I haven't thought that far," Brendan said, to nobody in particular, running his fingers through his sweat-soaked hair.

Think. Think now! the voice commanded.

"Not Ireland, anyway. What about up north? No—that's no good. Not far enough. England. I have to get to England."

England, yes. England, good, agreed the voice.

Brendan drove on. At least now, he had a destination; the ferry terminal seemed to be the only sensible place to go. As it transpired, he was already heading in that direction, yet another demonstration of his connection with destiny.

A car drew level with him in the fast lane before he had gone too far. It seemed to keep pace with him rather than continuing on past. From the corner of his eye, Brendan could see a woman in the passenger seat; she had a phone to her ear and was talking animatedly. In a dark recess of his mind, a warning bell tinkled. Did that woman just look at him? Why would she look at him?

Brendan took his eyes off the road and stared directly at the woman. She looked away, like she had been caught doing something she shouldn't be doing. The man driving the car was annoyed; he was waving his hand in the air and saying something. Brendan saw the woman shush him with a wave of her hand, but the man seemed to have enough and accelerated away into the distance. In the backseat of the car, Brendan saw a baby in a car seat, smiling out the window.

Why had that woman looked at him like that? Had she looked at him? Brendan wasn't sure. It could just be his mind playing tricks on him, making him see things that weren't there. They certainly weren't fitting police cars with infants. Brendan concluded the only rational explanation was he'd imagined it.

The toll bridge was coming up, and Brendan flipped open his coin holder, fumbling for change. After a second, the absurdity of what he was doing sank in. He'd just left a near-dead policeman in a burning house; he had a girl tied up in the boot of his car, as well as two murders to his name, and he was worried about paying a toll. Chuckling, he dumped the coins back into the plastic tray and slammed it shut. This little act of disobedience seemed to calm his frayed nerves, and his shakes subsided.

As the toll booths approached, Brendan moved into the express lane, where tagged cars drove right through. No barriers, no waiting, no chance of Angie drawing attention to herself. It went flawlessly. By the time the fine letter landed on his doorstep, he'd be elsewhere. Brendan laughed at the thought.

"I'm a real criminal now." He sniggered at his latest act of civil disobedience.

The whispering voice, as dry as autumn leaves, appeared to miss the joke. In a grave tone, it repeated, the word *trapped*, again and again.

"No, no, rubbish!" Brendan said, rubbing his damp hair in frustration. Why were the voices so determined to inject fear into him? How could there be a trap? No one knew where he was.

She knows. Behind, the voice cackled, as if responding to his statement.

"Of course, she knows. She's in the boot," he rallied.

This time the voice laughed, but said no more.

Brendan drove on. His sense of calm was destroyed, and the shakes started to return with a vengeance. He argued aloud with himself about the stupidity of jumping at shadows, but the voice remained mute.

He had himself nearly convinced everything was fine when a Garda car swooped in behind him, ablaze with flashing lights. Brendan swerved into the fast lane, using every ounce of speed he could coax from car.

The voice chuckled. *Trapped, you fool.*

***

The Garda car on the ramp seemed to hang back, as if unsure whether to follow. All that changed when a silver car behind Brendan leaped forward in a surge of speed. From inside the windscreen, blue lights flashed. The marked Garda car then dived onto the motorway, falling in behind the silver unmarked car, both of them gaining on him quickly. They must have been following all along, choosing now to make their move. Brendan had no intention of giving up, or being caught, for that matter. He pushed the Mondeo into the thickening tide of traffic with reckless abandon, weaving wildly around slower-moving motorists. His pursuers remained a steady distance behind, having no difficulty keeping pace with his less-powerful Ford.

They made no attempt to cut him off, seemingly content to follow directly behind him. Brendan knew he couldn't afford get caught now; there was far too much at stake for him to fall at the last hurdle. He had to get off the motorway, and it was vital he lose the police before then. In the narrow streets of the city, they would have no trouble boxing him in, and if they did that, all would be lost.

Further back on the motorway, Brendan could see more marked units racing up the fast lane to join ones already hot on his heels. Up ahead, the traffic began to bunch and thicken even more. He was going to run out of space very soon unless he did something drastic. Brendan flashed his lights and leaned on his horn. A small blue car remained steadfastly in the outer lane. Brendan had to break hard and in doing so he nudged the blue car's bumper, sending it careening across the carriageway. It was only pure luck that the car didn't roll or crash into something. Brendan saw the Garda cars behind him ease off as the blue car vanished far behind the chasing pack.

Brendan clipped another car as he jumped lanes. The wheel shuddered in his hand, but the Mondeo was solid and took the impact well. The other driver wasn't expecting the contact and skidded into a van in the slow lane. Both of them ended up as a knot of twisted metal on the hard shoulder. Two of the pursuing police cars stopped to help the crash victims.

Brendan didn't give the people in the cars around him a second thought. The only thing that mattered was being free to finish what he had to do. Brendan began deliberately nudging and rubbing cars as he caught up with them. The motorway became utter chaos, with shocked drivers cascading around the blacktop like kids in bumper cars. Soon, all but two of the chasing Garda cars had stopped to aid the innocent motorists caught up in the melee.

Brendan knew he had to do more to stop the ones who doggedly persisted in perusing him. Up ahead, a VW Beetle tried to make way for the fast-approaching Mondeo. Brendan drove straight for it. He caught the little car on the corner of the back bumper, keeping his foot down hard on the accelerator. The car went into a spin, pirouetting around the Mondeo directly into the path of the following Garda cars. The driver of the VW locked up his brakes, causing the tyres to send clouds of stinking rubber into the air, forming a near-solid blockade across two lanes of the motorway. The silver Garda car dived toward the barrier dividing the lanes of the motorway, scraping along it, sending a fountain of sparks into the sky. The marked unit had no such luck; it struck the stranded VW straight on, bending the tiny German car in a ninety-degree angle. The impact was huge.

Now only the silver car remained to give chase. The driver's side wing was damaged, but it still refused to be shaken off. Brenden frantically racked his brain for an idea, any idea.

An off-ramp appeared on Brendan's left, and at the last moment, he dived across three lines of traffic, causing even more braking and folding metal. Brendan raced up the narrow ramp with the sliver car still glued to his tail. Rounding the bend, he was amazed to see a Garda car pulled across the road ahead. There was no point in stopping now. Brendan gripped the wheel, bracing himself for the impact. He became aware of screaming, not in his head this time, but coming from behind him. He had been so engrossed in the chase, he'd not noticed it before. If Angie were screaming, she must be alive, but Brendan knew that in seconds both of them may be dead. That was just fine with him. His life and Angie's were forever entwined now; they'd never be apart again, either in this life or the next. He had done so much for her up to this; there was no possibility he would let her go now. As he hurtled toward the Garda car, time seemed to slow down. For once, his mind was blissfully quiet.

***

"Stop chasing him, you crazy bitch. You're going to get us killed!" screamed Harry from the backseat of Sims's car. Since the chase began, he'd been sliding around uncontrollably on the leather upholstery, his handcuffed wrists providing no assistance whatsoever.

As it happened, the Control Commander's voice on the car's two-way radio was saying more or less the same thing. "All units, end pursuit immediately! Repeat, immediately!" The fleeing car was crashing into everything in sight, and there was only Sims and the Garda car from exit four that had spooked the suspect, left in pursuit. Sims knew if she dropped back now, the guy was as good as gone; she couldn't let that happen. Her mind told her to pull over, to do what she was told, but her heart kept her foot planted all the way down on the accelerator. She knew she would have to answer for her actions later, but Adams had given her a chance on his team. She wasn't going to let him down. Anyway, this guy had someone locked in the boot, for Christ's sake. That's kidnapping, at the very least. What's wrong with Control?

Right about then, a VW Beetle spun directly in front of her, sideways across the whole bloody road. There was no time for braking, even if Sims had thought of it. She turned the wheel away from the VW, an act of pure instinct, and kept her food down hard. In the back, Harry McCarthy was screaming for all he was worth—no words, just sounds of terror. The VW hit the passenger side of her car, sending it crashing into the barrier dividing the opposing lanes of the motorway. Sims fought for control of the car, and managed to keep all four tyres on the ground. She just squeezed past the wrecked car when a thunderous impact echoed from behind her. Sims could see the smoking ruin of the VW, now impaled on the Garda car that had been directly behind her. The crash looked horrific. The man up ahead may now have added murder to his list of crimes. Sims had to keep going.

From the dash, the Control Commander was now calling her directly. "Detective Sims, stop immediately. That is a direct order. Stop immediately!"

Sims grabbed the mic. "If I pull back now, whoever is in the boot of that car is as good as dead. We may never get a chance like this again to catch this guy."

"The risks to the public are too great. Stop, detective, that's an order. Air Support is on the route. He won't get away."

Her foot came off the accelerator, reluctantly. Despite everything, she knew she had to think of the danger to the public. Behind her, God knows how many people were injured, or even dead. Control was right; the risks were too great to take for just one person. Up ahead, exit ramp three loomed. She clicked the mic. "Detective Sims. I'm dropping back. Exit ramp three is in sight. Is there a stop team in position?"

"Confirmed, detective. Stop teams on all exits. He's nowhere to run."

She watched the Mondeo scream up the fast lane, looking like he wasn't going to take the exit, anyway. Sims had lifted the mic to her lips, ready to relay the information, when the brown car slammed on its brakes and cut across all traffic at the last second. Sims pressed the mic button and the gas pedal at the same time. "He's taking it! Tell the stop team to stand by."

Sims tore up the ramp after the vanishing Mondeo, the steering wheel heavy in her hand after the impact with the barrier; something must be damaged. A single Garda car was pulled across the middle of the road ahead, its lights flashing, and the two officers standing on the road were waving down the oncoming driver. The Mondeo made no attempt to stop; it actually picked up speed. Sims realised he was going to ram them. This guy was on a suicide mission! The officers stood in the road, trapped like rabbits in the headlights, unsure whether to dive right or left. In the end, both went right, and the Mondeo chose the other direction, thank God. The passenger side of the brown car grated along the crash barrier, making a sound like a thousand chalks on a blackboard. A wrong-way sign was sliced in half as the car mowed through it. The yellow diamond came down on the roof like an axe, piercing it, before the sign clattered to the ground behind the fleeing car.

The driver's side of the bonnet made crushing contact with the Garda car, just behind the rear wheels. Both cars were tossed into the air. Amazingly, the Mondeo landed on its wheels while the Garda unit was left on its side, with half its boot missing. There was no way Sims was going to get through the gap left between the upturned Garda car and the safety rail. Sims stood on the brakes as hard as she could; her car shuddered to a halt, ten feet from the dirty undercarriage of the stricken patrol car.

She pounded the wheel, saying, "Fuck!" a lot before picking up her radio.

"The suspect has crashed through the blockade on exit three. His car has sustained substantial damage, including damage to the roof. Tell Air Support about that. It may help identify him."

She threw the mic into the foot well before anyone had the chance to respond. From behind her, she heard Harry let out a breath he had been clearly holding for a while. His breathing was fast and full of panic.

"I'm going to sue the arse off you. Do you hear that? I'm going to sue the fucking lot of you!" he snarled, his fear turning into rage.

"Did you know you scream like a girl?" said Sims, before getting out of the car to see if her colleagues needed help.

***

Honeysuckle Lane was a hive of activity when Martha's taxi pulled up outside her house. Tim was standing on the doorstep with his arms crossed, watching the firefighters extinguish the last of the flames coming from what was left of the house at the end of the lane. It was very confusing, like falling into another dimension. Everything had changed so much in such a short space of time. Martha half walked, half jogged up to Tim, resting her hands on his crossed arms, and asked, "What's happened?"

"I don't know. There was a fire. People are hurt, and one guy was arrested. That's all I know."

"Are you all right? You weren't hurt?"

"No, I'm fine. What makes you think I'd anything to do with it?" he said, moving away from her touch.

"It's just that I wasn't expecting your call, and when I saw all this, I didn't know what to think."

"Come inside, we need to talk," Tim said, holding the door open for her.

Martha felt like a stranger in her own house. How had that happened? She'd only been gone a couple of days, and it was like she didn't belong anymore. She opened the door to the sitting room and was shocked to see Annabelle perched on the couch, a hold-all by her feet and a cup of coffee on the table in front of her.

"Hi," Annabelle said, not in a nasty way but not friendly, either.

"What are you doing here?" Martha stammered.

"Tim asked me to be here. I can go, if you like," she said coldly, standing and lifting her bag to her shoulder.

"No, stay. Please," said Tim, walking into the room and closing the door.

"If this is about making me feel worse, you're wasting your time. You can't. I hate myself for what happened. I want to go back in time and change everything, but that's not possible. I'm so sorry about all of it. You'll never know how sorry," said Martha, her pent-up guilt flooding from her lips without either Annabelle or Tim asking as much as a question. Tears gushed from her eyes. Her words were like a cork in a bottle of champagne; once her grief was released, it couldn't be stemmed.

After a few seconds, Tim placed a hand on her shoulder. She'd never felt such a wonderful thing in all of her life. Sadly, it only made her grief deeper, but he didn't know that.

"It's not about that. Well, it is, but it's not about blaming you," said Tim. He was being too nice, which wasn't right, after what had happened. None of this was right.

"Sit, sit," said Tim, ushering her toward a chair. Martha got her tears under control, wiping them away with the back of her hand. Tim stood by the door, and Annabelle sat back down on the couch, both looking more concerned than angry.

"Is someone going to tell me what this is about?" asked Martha.

Annabelle looked at Tim, and Tim's chin dropped to his chest. At last, he began to speak.

"Annabelle told me some things, things you should know."

"What kind of things?"

This time, Annabelle answered. "Ogie's always been a flake. I'm the first to admit that, but one thing he's never been short of is attention from women."

"I want nothing to do with him, ever again. If this is about me staying away from him, you don't have to worry. I hate him!" Martha jumped in.

"I'm finished with Ogie. Whatever he does has nothing to do with me. He has used up his last chance with me," Annabelle said, looking both deflated and determined. When she continued, there were tears hanging in her eyes. "I'm just saying that he's not always responsible when he should be. He's charming but selfish, and sometimes careless with both his own life and others."

Martha was as confused as ever. She looked from Annabelle to Tim, and back to Annabelle, waiting for someone to explain whatever it was they were talking about.

When Tim spoke, his words were more cutting than earlier, and he got straight to the point. "When you had sex, did you use precautions?"

"I don't think going into that is going to help."

Tim got mad, his face pulled taut with disgust. "You think I want to talk about it? Do you think I even want that shit in my brain? It disgusts me. You disgust me." Tim looked away, unable to go on.

Annabelle broke the silence. "Did he wear a condom, Martha? We—no, you need to know."

"He didn't," she said quietly.

"Did he tell you about his problem?"

"No. What problem?" Martha asked, the worry beginning to show in her voice.

"Ogie has hepatitis," Annabelle said, her tone stoic.

"Is that all? You scared the life out of me. I thought you were going to say HIV or something."

"Hepatitis is serious, Martha. It can cause all kinds of problems: liver failure, cancer, even death."

"I was only with him once. No way I got anything. I feel fine. Just look at me," Martha said, standing up and walking around the room. Her body betrayed her bravado; her arms crossed tightly across her chest showed her inner turmoil.

"It's very contagious. You need to get yourself checked out," Annabelle said.

Martha turned on Annabelle, her fear transforming into anger, "And what about you? Are you infected?"

"I was lucky. He didn't tell me, either, but I happened to see his medication in the bathroom. I nearly left him after that. Perhaps I should have. Since then, we had to be more careful. There is a good chance you'll be lucky, too, but you had to know everything, no matter how hard it is to hear."

Annabelle stood, lifting her bag on her shoulder. "I'll leave you two talk." As she walked toward the door, Tim held out his hand, which Annabelle shook.

"Thank you for this," he said.

She smiled a sad smile and walked away, not giving Martha another glance.

After Annabelle had left, Martha strode around the room, muttering to herself. "There's nothing wrong with me. I'd know if there was. I'd feel it."

"I hope you're right," said Tim, flopping exhaustedly onto the couch.

"Do you really mean that?"

"Of course," he said, sitting forward, holding his head in his hands. "I might hate you right now, but that's not to say I don't love you. That's why this is all so bloody hard."

"Do you think I deserve to catch it after what I did?"

"I won't lie. That thought had crossed my mind for a fraction of a second, but the main thing I felt was fear."

"It might not be as serious as Annabelle said. She is bound to want to punish me for what I did."

"I looked it up. There's no cure, and it has mortality figures of twenty percent. That sounds serious to me."

"Jesus," Martha said, going white and sitting down.

"Look, we'll get you checked out first. Then see what's what after that," said Tim, looking at her with wounded eyes.

"We?"

He didn't say anything for a long time, but when he spoke again, he said, "Yes, we."

Martha began to cry and rushed to him, throwing her arms around his neck. Tim was stiff, but the fear and vulnerability he saw in his wife softened him. He held her loosely in his arms.

After what seemed like hours, she whispered in his ear, "Can I come home?"

Tim knew it was too much, too soon. "One step at a time. I'll pick you up at Ann's tomorrow morning. Let's go from there."

"Okay." She sniffled, keeping her head tucked into his neck like a frightened little girl.

***

Brendan couldn't believe he'd gotten past the roadblock and was still able to drive. The Mondeo was nearly as jittery as he was. The engine was making a terrible knocking, and the whole car shook like crazy every time he went over forty mph. At sixty, it was like riding inside a washing machine on spin cycle. There was nobody behind him now, but Brendan was determined not to repeat his earlier mistake of being too complacent. He made several turns in near-random sequence, so many that he ended up lost.

About the same time he realised he was lost, he also realised there had been no noise from Angie since he crashed the roadblock.

"Are you all right, Angie?" he called.

The silence that greeted him was worrying.

"Angie? Angie! Can you hear me?"

Still nothing. Brendan searched for a quiet spot to pull in. Up ahead, he saw an empty sports field with an equally deserted car park. Brendan indicated and pulled off the road, stopping behind a row of low bushes. Brendan let the car idle, as he didn't want to take the chance it may not restart for him.

He had to push his door hard to get it to open, and metal squealed in protest. At first glance, he was amazed how little damage had been done to the car, but that soon changed as he took a closer look. The nose of the car was crumpled, but the driver's side was more or less intact. Lines had been gouged down the length of the car, but it was better than he had feared. As he walked around the front, he winced at what he saw: The car was a complete wreck. One light was missing, the grill caved in, and the bonnet was buckled. The passenger side of the car was an array of deep abrasions and flattened metal. Brendan shook his head. There was no way he was going to get this thing onto a ferry without attracting a whole load of looks, attention he could not afford right now. There was nothing for it but to board the ferry on foot, which meant Angie would have to willingly do the same.

Walking around the back of the car, he saw one taillight hanging askew, with a few feet of black nylon stocking trailing from it. That was how they'd found him, she had betrayed him with a Judas kiss.

"Angie, are you okay in there?"

Still not a peep out of her. Brendan pushed the release button, but the boot lid remained stuck in place. It took several hard yanks to get it open.

Angie was lying on her back and her head was gashed in a number of places where she'd been thrown against the side of the car. She was breathing, but unconscious. The gag was gone from her mouth, and the tape binding her wrists had been hacked off in lumps. She was making life very hard for him, but the important thing was that Angie was alive. It was a miracle she hadn't broken her neck.

Brendan wanted to tell her about the voices, about what she meant to him, about how they were destined to be together, how he'd wanted to take her away from her life of squalor and tedium. He needed time to do all that, and time was a luxury he didn't have. Brendan had to remind himself that the girl didn't understand, yet. It was a natural thing, that she should try and escape, until she had all the facts. The only thing he could do was to keep moving and explain as best he could between here and the ferry. Leaving her free wasn't going to be possible; look at what she'd done already. Brendan walked to the front of the car and found cable ties in the glove box. He re-secured the girl's hands, in front of her this time, as well as her legs, while she was still groggy. Unfortunately, he had no more tape, so he had to trust she wouldn't be heard if she began yelling. Brendan could see the girl was starting to come around as he finished securing her.

He slammed the boot lid home, several times, before it clicked. As he got into the driver's seat, two solid kicks to the inside of the metal told him trunk was properly closed, and that she was well and truly awake. It was time to get the hell out of here.

***

It didn't take Sims long to assure herself that the two officers were nothing more than shaken. Before she could do anything else, she needed to give the car a quick inspection, to see if she could push the wounded machine a little further. To her eye, it didn't appear mortally wounded; nothing a few weeks in a panel beater's wouldn't fix. As she walked around the vehicle, she tried to ignore the constant stream of vile abuse and threats issuing from Harry McCarthy, squirming around in the backseat.

Something had happened to her in the heat of the chase. She felt much calmer than she thought she would, nearly at peace. Perhaps everyone has their own way of dealing with danger. For Harry, anger was the order of the day; for her, the aftermath of the chase was calm, even pleasant. She got back into the driver's seat, leaving her door open. A nice breeze rustled her hair as she leaned her arm across the back of the passenger seat, turning to look at Harry.

She give the shouting man in the back her full attention. His face was dark red; veins pulsed all over it, from his forehead to his neck. His lips were a blur of motion, flecked with spit. The words were lost on her, as if someone had pressed his mute button. She watched this dangerous man's face and found a horrific beauty in his savagery. It could have been seconds or minutes; she didn't know. It was then that some unseen hand turned up the volume on this unfolding scene.

"What the fuck are you smiling at?" he roared.

"Pardon?"

"What are you smiling at, you fool!"

"Am I smiling? I didn't realise. It must be you, Harry. I'm smiling at you."

"You're mad."

"Up to a few moments ago, I might have argued that. But right now, I'm feeling a little crazy. Slightly unhinged. Do you ever feel that way, Harry? Like you could do anything, anything at all, and not give a flying shit?" Sims face was crusted with grime from the house fire, her eyes were bloodshot from the smoke and coughing fits, and her hair was tossed. But Harry was right, she wore a half smile. She looked like a woman who had just escaped from a mental institution.

"What crap are you talking now?" he asked.

Sims's words were soft, spookily so. "Oh, I don't know. I feel like walking off down the road and never going back to work again, for example. Or . . ." She smiled wider, wiggling her finger in the air. "What about finishing what we've started?"

"What? What the hell are you on about?"

"Car chases are dangerous, Harry. You could have been injured back there, especially as you're not wearing your seat belt. How about I back down the ramp as far as we can go, and try again?"

"Try what again? You stupid bint!"

"Try and get between that Garda can and the crash barrier, of course. Looking at it now, I think I might just make it, if I was going fast enough, that is."

"You'll never fit through there, you mad bitch!"

"Maybe, maybe not, but this time I mightn't hit the breaks. This time, you might go through the windscreen like a bowling ball, splattering your filth-filled head against the bottom of that nice state-owned car. What you think of that?"

Sims slammed her door closed and started the engine. She rammed the car into reverse and let the clutch pop without care. The car jumped back, and Sims floored the accelerator. The tyres screamed in protest as another layer of rubber was ripped from them. The car fishtailed backwards, down the curved ramp, with Sims casually steering one-handed. They'd reached the motorway when she slammed on the breaks, throwing Harry back hard against his seat. A car, preparing to take the turnoff, had to veer wildly back onto the main carriageway, blaring its horn as it passed.

"You won't do it."

"Most days you're right, Harry, but this isn't most days, is it? I have been under a lot of stress today. And, like you keep telling me, I am a mad bitch."

"You'd never get away with it."

"Of course, I would. The only witnesses are friends of mine. Friends just like the ones you promised would come visit me some night. In the end, I'd get a caution, but you'd be dead."

Harry sat back, watching the woman slit-eyed. Sims smiled at him, and let the car surge forward. She'd not even got into second gear before Harry was shouting for her to stop. She braked severely, and turned to face the criminal in her back seat.

"I'll make you a deal, Harry. You're going to shut the hell up, and let me get on with what I have to do. I'm going to drop you at the station, safe and sound, when I'm good and ready. That'll be you and me, finished. You get a slap on the wrist, and go about your nasty business, until someone else makes good on the thoughts I have running through my mind right now."

Harry didn't say anything, which was a pleasant change.

"Good. Now that's sorted, let's get going," she said.

She drove back up the ramp at a normal speed, and eased the front of her car against the tipped up Garda unit. She pressed down on the gas slowly, pushing the stricken police cruiser, until she could fit through the gap. Then she backed away a few feet and stopped the car. She picked up the two-way radio. "Detective Sims to Control, over."

"Go ahead, Sims," came the Commander's voice, as level as it had been before the chase.

"Has Air Support spotted the suspect car yet?"

"Negative, detective. They are scanning all main routes from exit three. It won't be long. Keep station, and manage the crash site."

"Negative, Control, I can't do that. I have a civilian in custody."

"You have a civilian? In the car?" The Commander's cool cracked for a second, before regaining composure. The air was silent for a minute before his voice returned, measured once more. "Return to base ASAP, and report to the chief inspector as soon as your civilian has been processed."

"Roger, Command," said Sims, hanging up the mic.

Harry sat forward. "Sounds like your ass is on the grill. You'll never catch the guy now."

Sims laughed. "Don't be so sure."

"You're out of the loop. When the chopper finds the car, there is no way they are going to tell you where it is."

"That doesn't matter. I know where he's going."

"How do you know? When nobody else has a clue?"

"I'm a detective, remember? I detect," she said, as the ferry-terminal sign passed overhead.

***

Brendan pulled out of the football field to the sound of screams coming from the boot.

"Angie, let me explain," he said loudly over his shoulder.

"Let me go! I want to go home! *Let me go!*" was Angie's response, punctuating each part of the sentence with bangs of flesh on metal.

Brendan drove on, trying his best to explain his actions, letting her see into his world, opening himself up to her like he'd never opened up to anyone. He took random twists and turns, moving through the edges of the city as much by instinct as design. He tried to keep as far from prying eyes as he could. Brendan knew the car stood out like a sore thumb. He thought of stopping somewhere to hire another one, but that wouldn't work; it would take too long, too much paperwork. The only other option was to try and take a car. Brendan kept having to remind himself he was already on the wrong side of the law. What was another breach, more or less? Soon, he came across a large builders' merchant. The place was littered with vans and cars, not an owner to be seen. Surely, someone would be careless enough to leave their keys in the ignition. It was worth a try.

Brendan parked behind a furniture warehouse that seemed to have been closed for years. He walked the short distance back to the builder's yard, making a show of inspecting the lumber stacked on pallets. He tried three vehicles. Amazingly, two of them were open, but the keys were nowhere to be seen. He may be a criminal, but hot-wiring a car was beyond his abilities. Brendan had his hand on the door of a white van when a voice behind him made him jump.

"What do ye think you're at there, bud?"

Brendan spun around and was faced with a man the size of a jockey dressed in a white T-shirt and track-suit bottoms. He carried a roll of pink foam under his arm.

"Nothing," he stammered.

"It doesn't look like nothing to me."

Brendan went to walk away, but the guy shoved him back, his dark eyes hard, and his small body as taut as a bowstring. "You were trying to break into my van, ye shit. Weren't ye?" said the little man, shoving Brendan once more.

"No, I wasn't. Leave me alone," said Brendan, his words sounding childish to him.

"Leave you alone? You're lucky I don't knock your bleedin' block off, scumbag," the man said, shooting his foot forward in a boxer's stance and cocking his fist.

Brendan stumbled backward, nearly falling. He ran from the van and the yard, not daring to look back, his ears burning with humiliation. Nothing had changed since those days on the school bus; there were always bullies waiting in the wings. Just when you overcome one, another rises up to take his place.

As he fled, a cloud of despair settled over him. It felt like an unbreakable wall of blackness. He skirted the edge of the derelict warehouse where he'd hidden his car, then was greeted by Angie's constant banging and shouting. Everywhere he turned, people were trying to thwart him—even her! How had he gotten everything so *wrong*?

Brendan stood in the middle of the cracked, weed-strewn concrete, wishing it was all over. He was so very tired, and there seemed to be no end in sight. He missed being invisible, the ability to vanish from the eyes of the world. The girl's yelling got inside his head, like a splinter working its way deeper into his skin. Hadn't he told her how much he had sacrificed to be with her? Didn't he tell her what he'd done to save her? Why was she fighting against him at every turn? It was too much. If only she'd stop screaming! He already had enough screaming in his mind, in his life.

Brendan ran at the car, slamming his arms onto the boot lid.

"Stop it, stop it, *stop it!*" he yelled, beating his fists in time with his words.

The sounds inside the car stopped.

"Why? *Why* did you make me do all this? Why did you make it so *hard!*" Brendan felt like crying, big heavy sobs, but instead he sat on the ground, putting his lips near the broken light.

"There are other worlds, you know, other dimensions. I've seen them, heard them. Some imagine they may exist, but I know. That's the difference. I *know*. Death is only a beginning; it's a doorway. Some go through sooner than others, but we will all face it at some stage. It's just a doorway. Remember that. It's just a doorway."

Brendan placed his hand over the hole, knowing there was no hope left. He'd tried everything; there was only one thing to do. He had to send her on ahead. Perhaps it was always meant to be this way, building the foundations of an epic love in this reality to be finally realised in the next. Perhaps all of this had been inevitable. Brendan searched for something that would fill his needs. He didn't want to bludgeon her, to have to watch the light go from her eyes as she passed over with her blood soaking into his hands. He wanted her to transition, intact. He searched the area, and in the end, a rusting washing machine supplied the solution. From the back, he ripped a grey hose and trailed it along the ground behind him as he returned to the car. It wasn't a very long hose, but it didn't have to be.

He started the engine, then walked to the rear of the car. Brendan stuffed one end of the pipe into the heavily smoking exhaust, and the other end, he threaded into the very same hole Angie had hoped would save her life. Neither seal was perfect, but they didn't have to be. In such a confined space, it only took a few seconds for the poison gas to build. He could hear her struggling inside, and his heart grew heavy. This wasn't like any of the others; he didn't want this to happen. He had to be resolute and follow through, or else the voices would've been right. He wouldn't have been worthy of greatness at all.

"It's only a doorway. It will be over soon," Brendan said when Angie began to cough. Then he heard something more. At first, he thought it was a voice from the other side, but soon, he realised she was calling to him.

"I'll go with you. Stop this. Please. I'll do what you want," she said through her fits of choking.

"You don't mean it. This another of your tricks," he said, keeping the pipe shoved in the hole as she tried to force it back out from the inside.

"I swear, I'll do anything you ask. I promise. It's what I want."

Brendan wanted to believe her, more than anything. It gave him hope, and a way out. If Angie were telling the truth, he could have everything he wanted, after all. No matter what way he looked at it, Brendan had nothing to lose. He pulled the hose out of the hole in the boot, but it was a struggle to get the lid open. Once he did, it took a few seconds for the fumes to clear, and the girl to get some air in her scorched lungs.

"Do you mean what you said?" he asked.

"Yes, yes, I do. After all you've done, how could I lie to you?"

"I know that you don't believe that."

"I swear, I do. You made me see the world for what it is. You made me see what my life could be like. I was scared, that's all."

Brendan wanted her, more than anything, so he chose to trust her.

"I want to believe you."

"It's true, I promise. I'm yours, and will be forever."

"We'll have to get away from here, away from Ireland."

"Anything. I'll do anything."

"You will have to stay in here until we get to the ferry."

"I will. I promise. Just don't kill me."

"No more noise."

"Not a word."

Brendan knew he was taking a chance by trusting the girl, but if she was telling the truth, he had everything to gain.

"This will be all over soon," he said, closing the boot lid on the girl. He had to get to the ferry terminal quickly, if they were going to make it.

Chapter 32

Trapped in the boot and bound fast, Angie couldn't escape the ravings of her lunatic neighbour. It was hard to imagine he could believe the nonsense he was spouting, which made him all the more sinister. Clearly, he believed every word, totally, completely. He was sick, which was far scarier than plain bad. Even evil would be better than sick with a capital *S*. To a nutter like him, the whole world must seem crazy.

She *had* to believe there was some way of getting through to him. If there wasn't, she had no hope left. She didn't understand how he could say he loved her. He didn't even know her. She was only part of his twisted fantasy. The way he was talking about her, it sounded like she was some kind of princess. God knows, she had pushed the boundaries of good taste more than once. The innocent image he had of her would be shattered, good and proper, if only he knew. That might be a way to get him to see her for what she was, but it could also backfire on her, big time.

Maybe she should use his delusions against him. If he believed he loved her, how hard would it be for him to believe she felt the same? As he drove, she tried pleading with him, begging him, reasoning with him, threatening him, but she may as well have stayed mute. Nothing she said was getting through. It was as if he'd erected a mental barricade, only letting in what fit his picture of the world.

When the car had stopped, her mouth went dry, and her heart raced. She heard him walking around outside. Fearing whatever was coming next, she began shaking. The boot remained closed, and she heard his footsteps recede into the distance. Angie prayed he'd abandoned her, to make a run for it himself. It didn't take long to realise that praying wasn't going to get her free, so she kicked and yelled for Ireland, hoping someone passing the car would rescue her. Nothing happened for ages, but when the metal above her head exploded under a hail of blows, her heart nearly burst with fright.

He'd never left at all! The sick bastard was playing with her, making her think there was hope where there was none. She'd thought nothing could be worse, but she was so very wrong. His insanity cracked and fell to another level of Hell, sweeping her along with him. His lifeless voice seeped through the damaged tail section, oozing with madness, babbling about other worlds and death. That word, on this guy's lips, was terrifying. "Death was but a doorway," he said. What the hell was all that about?

When the car started again, she was relieved—up to the point the hose was rammed through the hole where the taillight should be, and fumes filled the tiny space. She tried to block the hose with her hands, but the gas came, regardless. She choked on the fumes, and her head swam. He was killing her, and there was nothing she could do—or was there?

Her only chance of living was to lie. She would say anything, do anything, to stay alive another minute. That was what all she had left, a minute, which was running out fast.

Between coughing fits, Angie promised the guy everything he had wanted from her. Angie couldn't believe he bought even one line of the rubbish that came out of her mouth, but he must have. When the boot opened, the thin slice of blue sky was the most-beautiful thing she had ever seen in her whole life. She hacked up the toxic vapours in her lungs, and took in huge breaths of delicious air. As the fumes cleared, the creep beamed at her, making her feel even sicker than the carbon dioxide. She held her revulsion in check; her life depended on it. The look on his face was like a kid's at Christmas. She lied like a champion, and he ate it all up.

When the car drove away once more, she was still in the boot, but by some miracle, she was alive. Now, she had the slightest chance of staying that way. She could so easily have been a lump of lifeless meat. A couple more minutes with that hose filling the space with poison, and she was a goner. Angie knew her only hope was to play along until she was somewhere public, then make her break for freedom. Nobody was coming to save her. It was all up to her.

***

Sims had made good use of her siren, slicing through the evening traffic. In her experience, when a criminal runs, he wants to go as far as he can, or he ends up going where he feels safest—home. Going on the run on a small island like Ireland wasn't easy. Most times, if they head west, they are staying in the country, but this guy was going east. On that side, there was only Dublin city and the ocean.

He might have someplace to hide, but Sims doubted it. Roche clearly hadn't intended to leave the house on Honeysuckle Lane; his dash had been prompted by the appearance of Adams on his doorstep. Even in the dodgiest parts of Dublin, dragging a person out of the boot of a car is bound to get everyone paying attention. A hotel or guest house was no good. What would he do with his captive? If he intended to kill or rape whoever he had, he would need some-place out of the way, someplace private. She prayed that wasn't what Roche had planned, or it might already be too late for whoever was in the boot.

All her instincts told her this guy would try to leave the country. If he was caught, he was facing a long time behind bars. That's real motivation to get over the border as quickly as possible, before all the gates get slammed shut. The airport is to the north of the city, and this guy was driving away from it. The only other way off an island is by boat, and the ferry terminal Dun Laoghaire was his best bet. There was a chance of driving on board and never being searched, assuming, that is, he still had a body in his trunk. It was a guess but an educated one that drove her in the direction of the port.

Surprisingly, Harry had been as quiet as a mouse since their words on the on-ramp. She could sense the barely controlled rage, wafting off him in waves, but as long as he was being quiet, she didn't care. Soon, the ferry terminal appeared. Sims parked close to a lorry, from where she could watch the ticket booths and the cars pulling up to them. Hopefully, she wouldn't be spotted before Roche tried to board the ship. Dun Laogharie was a busy place, with lots of traffic moving about, but if the suspect drove inside the ferry loading area, he'd have no place to run.

"What's the master plan, detective? Sit and wait?" Harry needled.

"Have you a problem with that?"

Sims worried he may have a point; it wasn't much of a plan. She kept an ear trained on the radio. So far, nobody had found the battered Mondeo, but least the helicopter was involved in the search, which would speed things up. Once the chopper latched onto someone, he nearly never got away.

The controller called her directly once or twice, but she ignored him, even though every ounce of her being demanded she respond. Sims knew this was a moment of her life that would define her. She should do as the operator said, but in her heart, she knew the right thing to do was to catch this guy. They clearly wanted her back at base for a dressing-down. It was going to happen now or later. What was the difference? She had already made her bed; the length she lay in it was immaterial.

On the horizon, the massive bulk of the car ferry rounded the mouth of the harbour. It wouldn't be long now. If the perp was going to show, it would be soon or not at all. Sims buzzed down her window, so she could hear as well as see, what was going on around her. The air was full of gulls, riding the breeze coming from the ocean, scanning the ground for a dropped ice-cream or a discarded chip. Cars were already queuing at the booths, presenting their tickets to the tellers, before moving to the holding area. There was no sign of the brown Mondeo. Sims began to doubt herself.

Across the road, the long-term parking lot was separated from the pier by a wire fence. One or two people were unloading luggage and walking toward the ferry terminal. Sims was sure that Roche would try to drive on, so she concentrated her attention on the arrival booths.

Across the water, the ship's horn boomed as it took a sweeping turn to line itself up with the embarking ramp. Sims could feel her heart quicken as the minutes passed. It was now or never—or was this whole thing a total waste of time? The ship's horn sounded once more, and Sims watched its bow bear down on the harbour wall. Had she looked over her shoulder at that moment, she'd have seen the battered brown Mondeo pull into the long-term car park, but the approaching boat held her full attention.

***

Brendan manoeuvred his car into the farthest corner of the car park, throwing the barrier ticket into the passenger foot well. He was never coming back to collect this thing again. Where he was going, there was no chance of a return journey, at least, not without chains on his wrists. He turned off the engine, leaving the keys dangling from the steering column, and got out to unload his bag from the backseat. What if she let him down again, he wondered, as his fingers hovered over the handle to open the boot. He felt a moment of dread, and with doubt filling his mind, he pressed the shiny button home. He wrestled open the damaged lid and looked at the beautiful creature within. He'd no choice but to trust what she'd said. She was worth the risk.

Still, he was nervous. He made sure nobody could see inside the trunk before he opened it all the way. The girl didn't scream or cause a scene, which was good, because she could have. It seemed trusting Angie had been the right thing to do.

"We're here," he said.

She looked at him through tear-streaked makeup. Her eyes were terrified and puffy.

"Look at you, that won't do at all," he said, pulling the tail of his shirt out of his waistband. He rubbed her face vigorously until it was free of makeup and glowing red from the friction. Her skin felt warm and soft under his fingers. This time she didn't pull away from his touch, as she had done before.

"I never wanted to hurt you," he said softly.

"I know. I made you do it," she said, her voice calm and resigned. "I don't blame you. You did what you had to do to save me."

"That was all I wanted all this time. To rescue you."

"You have. I can see that now."

In his mind Brendan heard the voices constantly. They were so clear, it was disorientating. He kept looking around to see if they had materialised while he hadn't been watching. They were calling to him, saying it was time for him to cross over, time for him to become one of them. His moment had arrived, and he was to be transformed.

Now he had Angie by his side, Brendan felt like a conquering warlord, enjoying the well-deserved spoils of war. He needed to cut her hands and legs free, so Angie could board the ferry with him. Brendan searched the boot for something to use, but there was nothing that would cut the plastic bindings. He was about to search the front of the car for his penknife when he became aware of the thump of rotor blades far above his head.

He searched the sky, and among the wheeling seabirds he spotted the helicopter, moving in this direction. It grew large and passed overhead before banking sharply over open water and falling back on its original course. As Brendan watched, the helicopter began to loosely circle the harbour. Brendan knew they were searching for him, and it would seem that the bloodhounds had found their prey. He looked into the trunk of the car. The girl was so close, so very close, but always out of reach. Why would they not let him be? It was time to run once more.

The voices howled with rapture, and one phrase rose above all else: *Death is only the beginning!* He slammed the boot lid closed, knowing he could not be caged, no matter what the cost.

Inside, the girl screamed, "No!"

Brendan knew that no matter what the authorities did, no matter how hard they tried to chain him, they'd never break the bond between him and Angie. He wouldn't allow it. They were going to be together forever, no matter what it took. It was destiny.

Chapter 33

Sims's ears pricked up when she heard the voice of the helicopter pilot on the radio.

"Suspect vehicle has been located. It is currently at the Dun Laoghaire ferry terminal. One male visible. Repeat, one male has exited the vehicle."

"Roger that, captain. Ground units are on route to your position. Maintain surveillance, as this suspect is reported to have at least one captive in the car," said the Control Commander.

"Roger, Control. Switching to infrared camera." There was a pause before the pilot's voice sounded again. "I am registering a faint heat signal in the boot of the car, but the suspect has become aware of our presence. He's closed the boot and is entering the vehicle."

"Control to all units in the vicinity of East Bank ferry terminal: Male suspect considered armed and dangerous, driving a damaged brown Mondeo fleeing the area. This is a STOP, STOP, STOP command. Possible hostages. Repeat STOP, STOP, STOP."

Sims craned her neck and spotted the car through the wire fence. How the hell had she missed him? She gunned her engine and performed a tyre-screaming U-turn from a standing start. The Mondeo weaved through the lanes of parked cars, trying to get to one of the main exits. This time, Sims was determined not to let him get away. Just as the barrier arm lifted, Sims slid her car sideways across the exit, feet from Brendan's bonnet, getting her first good look at him. He was hunched over the steering wheel, all of his teeth showing in a manic snarl. His eyes behind his oversized glasses were wide and crazy.

"He's going to ram us!" shouted Harry from the backseat. "Move the bloody car! Jesus, move it!"

Sims didn't move an inch. She held her ground as the brown car revved his engine wildly, making the car rock on its axle. Instead of shooting forward, the brown car shot backward in a stinking cloud of burning rubber. The barrier arm dropped back into place. Sims rammed her car into gear and took off after him, following his every turn as he looked for another way out. Brendan was trapped on the inside of the wire, with her guarding the perimeter like a Border Collie herding sheep.

Sims picked up the mic. "Control, this is Detective Sims. I have the suspect contained in the ferry terminal car park. Send all available units."

"Roger that, detective," the Control Commander said, but she could hear the annoyance in his voice upon hearing her name. Sims knew she had the guy trapped, but no matter how much she wanted to, she wouldn't be able to snap the cuffs on him without a lot more help. All she could to do was wait and make sure he didn't get away.

Brendan had other ideas. Every time he drove toward an exit, the faster silver car blocked his way. Brendan tried one last time, but again, the blasted woman cut him off. He was trapped and running out of time fast. He could hear sirens approaching in the distance. Brendan spun the car until he faced the approaching ferry. Just a few strands of wire stood between him and freedom. The people who were queuing to board the ship had decamped their cars and were crowding the fence, watching the automotive rodeo in progress. Brendan sent the revs of the engine into the red and drove straight at the gawping crowd. They scattered in all directions, as the already damaged car ploughed into the wire fence, tearing a whole section off.

"Shit!" said Sims. She rammed through a car-park barrier, snapping it in half, as she chased the escaping Mondeo, but it seemed that Brendan had jumped from the frying pan into the fire. Cars were blocking the ticket booths, and a sturdy concrete barrier separated the departing traffic from the incoming cars. There was no way he was going to breach that. All that lay ahead of him was the long curling arm of the harbour wall. The crowd Brendan had just scattered dispersed even further when Sims screeched through the hole he had made in the fence.

The ocean side of the pier was protected by a twelve-foot-high wall, but the harbour side was a sheer drop into the water far below. Sims chased after the brown car as Brendan raced along the cliff of white steel, which was the side of the docking ferry. A section of wire was trapped under Brendan's car, sending a rooster tail of sparks flying out behind it. Brendan slammed the car into third gear and was doing close to forty mph as he reached the open end of the pier.

Sims stood on her brakes, but the Mondeo never hesitated. It sailed through the air like something from the "Dukes of Hazzard." The water lay a good twenty-five feet below the edge of the pier, and when the car struck, the impact was devastating.

Hitting water at speed is like hitting a wall. A huge plume of spray was thrown into the air as the Mondeo went in nose-first. Sims vaulted from her car before it had even fully stopped. She ran to the edge of the pier and was amazed to see the brown car half floating, but the heavy engine was starting to pull the nose under. Only the air trapped inside the car was keeping it up. At least the boot was high and dry, sticking out of the ocean like a mini brown iceberg. Sims knew she had to do something to help whoever was inside, or they were as good as dead. She was confident the helicopter hovering overhead had already relayed what had just happened to Control, but by the time the emergency services arrived, the Mondeo would be sitting on the ocean bed. Whatever happened now was up to her.

Sims dove off the edge of the pier, knowing she had to get that boot open before the car went under. She was a strong swimmer, but the shock of entering the frigid water made her gasp. Flipping hell, it was cold! She swam after the car, which was bobbing farther and farther away from the pier. The water was dirty brown, filled with fine silt stirred up by the passing of the ferry. Her throat was still raw from coughing and the salt water stung her burnt hands. It took her thirty strokes to reach the car. She tried to pop open the boot lid with one hand, but it was stuck. Sims dragged herself up on the back bumper and tried again, with both her hands this time.

She could hear a girl screaming inside. Through the back window, she could see the tall man struggling to get his seat belt off, which must have jammed when the car hit the water. The airbag had exploded from the steering wheel, which was getting in his way. The water was already up to his waist inside the car and covering half the windscreen on the outside.

Sims tried the boot lid one more time, but it wouldn't budge. The car was sinking fast. Through the window, she noticed the release knobs on the back of the rear seats. If she got inside, she would be able to get the woman out through there. Sims slammed the glass with her fist five or six times, as hard as she could, but got nowhere. By now, the water was halfway up the driver's chest and beginning to spill over the back of his seat. She needed something to break the window. As if to remind her, the pocket of her jacket clanked against the metal of the car. Harry's knife!

She unzipped her pocket and pulled out the bagged knife. She stripped away the bag frantically and held the closed knife in her fist, with the butt protruding a half an inch. Summoning all her strength, she drove it into the middle of the back window. The glass frosted with cracks but didn't give way. Her second blow caused the window to explode into a million tiny pieces. The car lurched beneath her as the air escaped.

Sims lost her balance. She put her hands out to steady herself and dropped the knife into the car in the process. The car was diving for the bottom, and taking her with it.

Sims climbed through the back window and released the latches holding the seats in place. It took a fraction of a second for the water to completely cover the man, struggling in the front seat. The water raced up Sims body as she reached inside the dark maw of the boot, trying to control the violently thrashing woman. Taking a deep breath, she ducked her head under the water and pushed her shoulders fully into the boot to get a good grip on the woman inside. With every ounce of her strength, she dragged the woman into the back of the car and pushed her out the shattered back window. The car was completely underwater now, and racing for the bottom. The panicking woman kicked for the surface frantically, using her tied limbs like a mermaid.

Sims hooked her fingers around the shattered window and was about to follow the escaping girl when she felt fingers encircle her ankle. Turning, Sims saw the trapped man's face, distorted by the muddy water, glaring at her. She struggled, but his grip was viselike. As the pressure increased, she felt her ears pop. The light dimmed more with each foot the car sank.

***

As Angie's head broke the surface coughing and spluttering, after which she sucked in great whoops of air. She pumped her legs and tried to use her bound hands as best she could to keep her head above the water, but the waves slapped into her, threatening to send her back under the surface. She heard a siren close by, and a helicopter hovered overhead. From nowhere, a uniformed man dove off the end of the pier and into the water. Two red-and-white life rings were thrown from the pier, but both landed out of reach to her left. The swimming man reached Angie before she even had a chance to try and grab one. He wrapped his arm around her middle and held her head clear of the water.

"Where's Detective Sims?" he demanded.

Angie was confused. She couldn't think straight.

The man asked again, "Where is the woman who got you out of the car?"

Angie still had no idea what was going on. One moment she was in the boot; the next, she was swimming for the surface of the ocean. How that happened, she really couldn't say.

Before the man could ask again, a woman exploded out of the sea, windmilling her arms, coughing out water, and trying to take in some air. The man swam toward the struggling woman, hauling Angie along with him. Another flotation ring landed within arm's reach. This time the man managed to grab it and he shoved it into the struggling woman's arms, while continuing to support Angie in his own.

Bubbles appeared from the depths, but nothing else. As the three of them waited to be rescued from the water, Angie had a chance to get her thoughts together. She had gotten away, after all, after everything that bastard had done to her, to Tony. It was over now. Angie looked at the filthy swirling depths below her.

"There's your doorway, freak. See how you like it."

Chapter 34

Sims stood on the edge of the pier, wrapped in a blanket, watching the divers fin out into the distance, dragging a rope behind them. Where her car had been parked now stood a large red crane, playing out cable. The chief inspector stood by her side, and the pier was a hive of activity. Sims was amazed to find, the woman she'd rescued from the sunken car was actually, Angie Sweeney. The girl was far too traumatised to be interviewed at the scene; those questions would have to wait till later. Mary Sweeney had been contacted, and Angie was taken to the hospital, under Garda escort.

As for Harry McCarthy, he was more than likely sitting in a cell somewhere, feeling rather chuffed with himself, as he was likely to make a hell of a lot of money from the department in a future court case. For that reason, Sims was sure he would be released without charge, as long as he forgot all about what happened today. That was just the way the world worked. You scratch my back; I'll scratch yours.

Sims herself was in an unusual position. She was simultaneously the hero of the department while also being in serious bother with the chief inspector. He had told her to go in the ambulance with Angie, but she'd refused for the second time today. She needed to see the car being lifted out of the water, to make sure it was all over.

The divers emerged from the water, giving the crane operator a thumbs up. The powerful winch turned slowly, like a giant fishing rod, hauling the sunken car back into the light. It took a good five minutes, until the cable hung directly down in the water. The pitch of the motor changed as the crane took a heavier load, lifting the sunken car off the bottom of the ocean. Inch by inch, it rose, until the roof broke the surface. Water poured from every joint as the car was hoisted from the filthy ocean floor. It was difficult to see anything more from her vantage point.

The car eventually was swung over the pier, to be lowered behind a cordon, stopping rubberneckers and paparazzi from getting too close. Sims and the chief inspector approached the car to look inside. Sims knew that Brendan's eyes would be wide open in death, his swollen tongue protruding from his mouth in search of that last breath, never to be taken. She steeled herself for that image, but the car was empty.

"It's not possible. He was belted into that seat. There was no way he could have got out!" said Sims.

The inspector leaned into the car and picked up the end of the seat belt, which had been cut through. He leaned further into the car retrieved the silver knife from the driver's side of the floor.

"Is this the knife you told me about?"

"Yes, that's Harry's knife, but I felt it go into Roche's shoulder. I felt it hit the bone!"

Sims looked at the knife, remembering the agony in her lungs, and the unbearable urge to take a breath, even though there was no air to satisfy that need. The man was trying to drag her down with him. That was when she saw a glimmer of silver in the darkness. Sims snatched at it, and the knife fell open in her hand. It was as if the guiding hand of providence had reached down to help her. She turned and drove the blade, as hard as she could, into the guy shoulder; his fingers opened, and she was free. Even now, she knew with every fibre of her body that he would have killed her. She felt no remorse at all. She knew that Roche was dead—he had to be dead—but Sims wouldn't rest easy until she was face-to-face with his body.

"It was him or me," said Sims to the chief inspector.

The chief nodded. "There is nothing more we can do here. The divers will have to recover the body. It must have fallen out of the car when it was being winched to the surface."

Sims picked up the sliced end of the seat belt. Could Roche have gotten out of the car? He would have had to come to the surface to breathe. There was nowhere he could have hidden.

The inspector looked at Sims and said, "Will you go to the hospital and get checked out now?"

This time, Sims nodded. She felt tired and weak as she was led away to the waiting ambulance by a paramedic, feeling like an old woman who needed nothing more than a warm bed, and a long time to lie in it.

Epilogue

Hospitals all over the world have the same smell. Sims hated that smell, it reminded her how vulnerable life was, how vulnerable she was. Every day she came face-to-face with the worst society had to offer, and all she had to fend them off, was a confident stance and a belief that things will be okay. She roamed the maze of interconnecting halls, her shoes squeaking on the worn lino flooring. If this were a TV show, there would have been a dozen patients and two dozen doctors zooming about the place. The reality of Ireland's public health care is starkly different. Room after room of robe-wearing people passed the time between meals, drifting in and out of drugged sleep. On each floor, a couple of nurses tended their patients as quickly and efficiently as possible. The hospital was old and looked more like a boarding school than a seat of high science. The setting may look shabby; the effort invested by the staff was world-class.

Sims spotted the sign for St. Bridget's Ward and turned down the olive-green corridor, identical to all the others she had walked to get here. Adams had been in an induced coma since she'd pulled him the burning house on Honeysuckle Lane three weeks ago. The doctors said he'd the heart of a rhino, but his brain was as delicate as anyone's. They kept him asleep to let the swelling on his brain subside. His nervous-system had responded well to the treatment, so they were hopeful he'd make a full recovery. They'd performed a few minor surgeries to fix his broken cheekbone and reset his nose, but what he had needed most was time. Time to allow his body to pick up the shattered pieces and reassemble them as nature intended.

They'd begun weaning him off his medication earlier in the week, and he'd first opened his eyes yesterday. Sims asked at a nurse's station for Adams, and she was directed to a room at the end of the corridor, a room with six patients in it. Adams was in the bed closest to the window. She wouldn't have recognised him, except for the name stencilled on his medical charts, as his head was swaddled in bandages.

She approached the bed and Adams opened his eyes, he gave a wave of his fingers.

"Sims," he said, in a dry voice.

"Jesus, you look worse now than when you came in here," she said with a smile.

"Don't make me laugh, I'll pull a stitch," he said, suppressing a grin.

"How do you feel?"

"Fuzzy and sore. I've been trying to remember what happened, but I'm only getting bits and pieces. I believe I've you to thank, for being here."

"It's nothing. It was your turn to get lunch, and I wasn't about to let you welch on the bill," Sims said, pulling up a chair. "So, what do you remember so far?"

"I remember driving over to Honeysuckle Lane. I remember a tall, weird-looking guy. Then I remember fighting," said Adams. "Oh, I remember Harry McCarthy. He was there. Did he do this to me?"

"No. For once, he had nothing to do with it," said Sims.

She began to fill in the blanks for Adams. Each bit of information seemed to nudge another forgotten moment to the surface of his recovering brain. When she mentioned the name Brendan Roche, Adams said, "The tall guy."

"Yes, you were going to interview him, and reported seeing Harry McCarthy's car when you arrived in the area. When I got there, the house you were in was on fire, and I saw you in the hall. You're bloody heavy, by the way," Sims said with a smile.

"There was a woman," said Adams, rolling his head slightly as he tried to remember the events of that day.

"It was Angie Sweeney. Roche had kidnapped her. After he left you to cook, he went on the run with Angie locked in the boot of his car. She managed to kick out the taillight and attract the attention of a passing motorist. We got her back in one piece, but Roche wrecked a dozen cars during the chase."

"Smart girl, I wouldn't have thought of that. Is she okay?"

"She's alive, but a long way from okay. Roche drove off the end of Dun Laoghaire pier with her still locked in the boot. I managed to get her out of there, in the nick of time."

"You were there?" asked Adams, not fully understanding how Sims came to be involved in the chase.

"Yea, I played a hunch and waited at the ferry terminal. I guessed he might try to skip the country. It was just a lucky guess."

"Rubbish, Sims, you make your own luck," said Adams, smiling under his bandages. "What about Roche?"

"We don't know yet. The body hasn't been recovered, but I'm sure he is dead. He went down with the car and was trapped by his seat belt. He had a hold of my leg and was trying to take me down with him. I had to stab him in the shoulder to get him to let go of me. It looks like he might have pulled the knife out and used it to slice through the seatbelt. But he never surfaced. There was no way he could have survived; he was down there for ages. I nearly didn't make it back to the surface myself. The currents are strong around the harbour, the coast guard said we may never find the body."

"Did this Roche guy murder his boss, what's his name?"

"Brian Pulter, yes. Forensics have positively linked Brendan Roche to the drugs and propellant used in that murder. Angie Sweeney also said he confessed to the murder of Tony Kelly, and the woman found on the canal, while he held her captive."

"Why'd he do it all? What was his motive?"

"Roche has a history of mental illness, stretching as far back as his school days. Once we started digging through his work history, it soon transpired that he had an increasing problem with authority, as well as irrational fits of rage. Once, he'd been sent to a psychologist by a former employer, who noted possible schizophrenic tendencies, accompanied with megalomania."

"How come that wasn't acted on? Surely, they didn't want a loose cannon and schizophrenic running around their company?"

"He left the job, nearly as soon as he'd been assessed. After that, he kept moving, not staying in any one position for more than a few years. Every employer we have talked to so far has reported problems with Roche, just before he left."

"If he'd so many issues, how did he keep getting new jobs?"

"None of the companies ever gave proper references. They were too scared of being sued for defamation to tell the truth about Roche. They just passed him onto the next unlucky person."

"What about McCarthy? Where does he fit into all this?"

"It was a pure accident Harry was in the area at all. He'd been shaking down Frank O'Shea on the same street for a gambling debt. It turned nasty, and he was turning the thumbscrews on the O'Sheas when all this went down. The real estate company O'Shea works for was selling the house that Chris McCarthy broke into. Everyone knows Frank O'Shea gave him the security code, but nobody is talking. The company doesn't want to make a big fuss about it, in case it damages their reputation, and O'Shea has resigned and is moving away from the area."

"You've left me nothing to do when I get out of this place, it seems."

"It's about time you took a day off. Is there anything you need before I get going?" asked Sims.

"The food in here is awful. Any chance of a burger?"

"I can't get you junk food while you're in the hospital!"

"Sure, you can. This rabbit food will be the death of me, go-on."

"Okay, one burger, but that's it." Sims got up and walked for the door.

"Sims," Adams called after her.

"Yes?"

"Burger King, okay? McDonald's is shit."

"Okay."

"And Sims?"

"Yes," she said, turning one last time.

"Thanks."

She smiled and shook her head. "I can't believe you caught me for lunch again."

Sims walked down the green corridor, feeling like the world was coming back in line at last.

The End.

A note from Squid.

There are so many people I'd like to thank, the list is endless. I feel like one of those gushing movie folk on Oscar night, clutching a golden statue, while baying for world peace. Regardless, I am going to take this opportunity to recognise those people who deserve it.

The first, and most important person I want to thank, is you. The day you flicked open 'Honeysuckle Lane', was the final stop on a dream journey for me. Now that you have reached the end of my story, I hope you are still happy with your decision to place your trust in my hands.

I never set out to write a book. In the beginning, 'Honeysuckle Lane', was a short story idea for my blog. As the themes bubbled to the surface, and the characters began to evolve, it became clear this story was never going to fit into in ten thousand words. I challenged myself to write each chapter within a set time. I had planned to share the chapters like a mini-series with my friends on G+. The reality was, I couldn't write half as quickly as my buddies could read. For them, keeping the story alive in their minds between posts, was a major challenge. Thankfully they stuck with me, giving advice and feedback, all the way through the process. Which leads me nicely to my second big shout-out.

Without my friends on G+, Twitter, and Facebook, this story would not have been completed, it never would have been selected by Kindle Scout, nor would I be finding my name on the cover of an actual book. I have been blessed to find some of the most amazing people on the planet, through the art of writing. When I opened myself up to the world I was rewarded with epic friendship in return. There are hundreds that I want to mention, and thousands that I should. To them all, I want to say that I am honoured to count you among my friends. You have made my life richer than I ever expected it to be.

When it came time to put all the parts of this book together, only one man's opinion would do. My Dad. He is a lifelong lover of books, and I knew he had to get the very first draft. I also knew he wouldn't sugar coat the verdict, my Dad calls it like it is, at all times. I was on tenterhooks waiting for him to finish reading. He came back with a mixed review, pointing out character shortcomings, plot questions, as well as a list of things he liked. Overall, he gave it a thumbs up. With his comments in mind, I gave 'Honeysuckle Lane' a rewrite. When Dad read the next draft, he handed it back with a smile and said, 'Better'.

So, like any good Oscar speech, I get to thank my parents for getting me where I am today!

There is one lady who deserves a medal for bravery, and her name is Kathleen Rothenberger. She took on this jungle of miss-spellings, grammatical errors, and wandering sentences, and whipped it into shape, armed with nothing but a big red highlighter. As far as editors go, I can honestly say I was blessed to find her. She came back with thousands of corrections, but at all times she kept the feel of the story unchanged. She helped develop my own voice so it could be heard more clearly. She was patient, kind, and understanding, from start to finish. Thanks Kathy, you're the best.

Finally, I wish to say a huge thanks to the Kindle Scout team, particularly Caroline and Valerie who were amazing. I believe Kindle Scout represents the way forward for E-publishing. They are creating a platform where quality is prized above all, where a reader knows they will get a book that has passed more than one stringent test before making it to the point of publishing. Most importantly, the main criteria they have set, is the opinion of their reader. Yes, this makes getting published much more difficult, but a rising tide floats all boats. The Kindle Scout concept can only be a good thing for the writing community as a whole, and I am honoured that they have allowed me be counted among their number.

That's it. I'm all out of people to thank. I hope you enjoyed 'Honeysuckle Lane' and will take another journey with me sometime in the future.

Best wishes and warmest thanks,
Squid McFinnigan.

Copy and Proof Editor - Kathleen Rothenberger
www.KathleenRothenberger.com

Cover art and Design - Travis Miles
probookcovers@gmail.com

Made in the USA
Charleston, SC
08 October 2015